Matthew Hart

THE LAST ITERATION OF
DEXTER MAXWELL

BOOK 1 OF THE SERIES
THE LAST ITERATION

CAPSCOVIL

A CAPSCOVIL BOOK | GLONN | GERMANY

International English Edition published by CAPSCOVIL,
Glonn, Germany, December 2012
ISBN Perfect Paperback 978-3-942358-30-9
Copyright © CAPSCOVIL, 2012

Editor: Helen Veitch
Typesetting: Beth Flemington
Art work and design: Tom Jester

CAPSCOVIL® is an imprint and registered trademark of Britta Muzyk

Electronic editions are available for various reading devices and platforms.

Capscovil and their authors support several non-profit organisations.
For further information please visit:
www.capscovil.com

Attention: Organizations and Corporations
For information on exclusive editions or special offers for sales promotions, premiums or fund-raising, please write to:
projects@capscovil.com

About the Author

Matthew Hart is the author of six technology books and has been working in the middle of different corporations for fifteen years. He lives in Kansas City with his family.

This is his first novel.

Matthew will be supporting dedicated non-profit organizations through the sale of this book.

Connect with Matthew through http://about.me/hartmatthew and follow his blog on http://www.matthew-hart.com where he shares his view on all kinds of technological topics.

Acknowledgements

Thanks to Daniel Nguyen, for making the connection. Thanks to Britta Muzyk, for listening to Daniel, meeting with me in NY, and subsequently reading, believing in, and publishing Dexter's story.

Thanks to the creative team: Helen Veitch, for working through the slang and overall horrendous language; Tom Jester, for the cover and great advice; John Hart, for invaluable creative and technical input; Eric Fleischmann for the sweet website.

My deepest debt of gratitude goes to Beth Flemington, who not only did the typesetting as a member of the creative team, but who also performed critical early (and late) readings, cared for offspring in my absence, and always made herself available for intense-conversations-about-the-looming-death-of-a-favorite-character. Beth: I am, as always, yours.

Mostly I want to thank you for reading this tale. Without readers, an author is just another monkey at a typewriter.

FOR ERIC, WHO BELIEVED EARLY AND OFTEN

PART 1

GREATER METROPOLITAN FRONT RANGE (GMFR), SEPTEMBER 27, 2113.

One.

Tick, Tick, Crackle.

It was Thelo, coding him on the com. Dex ignored the hail long enough to pass the roll of cash out the window of the truck, give a smile to the attendant taking the bribe, and wait for the tollgate to rise. Then he pulled the collar back on his heavy worker's coat and engaged the small chip on his throat with a *tap tap rub*, and breathed, "Thelo, whachya need?"

"Bored. Checking in. Hadn't heard from you in a while."

Dex tried to picture Thelo's location. Thelo had pulled the short straw for the cross-70 turnpike, straight through downtown Grenver, past the DMV helipads. Past Central Dispatch. Past Fed Park.

"One more toll station," Dex said, "then I'm down to outer bur-bring, no problem."

"Crackpipe, Dex, you're way behind."

"I know."

"Everyone is minutes away from zero go. And you are, what, twenty minutes from go?"

"I know. Don't worry."

"I'm not worried. I'm mostly pissed."

"Don't stress it. Everything's fives."

"I doubt that."

"Stop shrinkin' your peener. A few minutes ain't no deal."

Thelo spoke up, ever so slightly, but it was as good as a yell in Dex's earpiece. "Now you listen to me, you orphan-rot. We've been planning this exact moment for months, and I am not about to let your druggy hangover screw everything up. Do what it takes to get there on time. Understand?"

"Crackpipe, Thelo, who crapped up your coffee? I told you–"

But Thelo had coded out. Dex slammed his fist into the dash. What had gotten into him? First Mal was acting dripped, and now Thelo seemed straight uphill-bunged. What was happening to his friends?

11

Thelo had had him there for a second, Dex realized, but he got it now. Thelo was just firing up his crapper. Getting him into the moment. Well, if Thelo wanted a fire, he'd give him one. His mind took off, unleashed. The hangover vanished.

Dex downshifted as he approached the final toll booth, and his truck gave an angry groan against the autumn cold. Today he was driving a Halliburton 260, one of the oldest garbage carriers around; the kind with the large compacting space in the back behind the cab so it could hold as much garbage as possible. It was a good six feet higher than the cab where he sat. Dex figured his truck must be twice as old as he was. It still had an old-fashioned transmission, and the central brain controller had been an after-market add-on by Old Man Newbury himself.

He pulled up to the booth, rolled down his window, and slid his repurposed work permit through the small slit in the bulletproof glass. The overweight attendee looked up at Dex, then hit her mic button.

"Newbury Trash don't have a listing for Tuesdays," her voice crackled. "Can't let you pass." Then she smiled.

Dex smiled politely back, and reached for the rubber-banded roll with the name ROSEANNE inked on the outside. "Newbury Trash never dumps on Tuesdays. Of course, how could I be so dumb? Here, I just need you to swipe my work order, explain things to Newbury." Dex put his hand out toward the toll attendee. She took the wad of cash he offered, and started counting it. Then she wacked a large button with her thumb and the gate rose. "Have a good morning, Charlie. Try and remember your permit days next time."

"Thanks, Roseanne," Dex said, and put the truck into gear. He pulled his glove off to code up Mal to let her know where he was at.

"Wait, there, Charlie, you almost forgot your permit," the woman said, handing Dex his pass card. Without thinking, he reached for it with his left hand.

"Jeez, Charlie, what happened to you?" She asked, grimacing at his hand, which was missing the pinkie and top digit of his ring finger.

Dex smiled at her. "Lost a bet," he said with wink.

Roseanne chuckled. "Helluva bet, Charlie."

"You shoulda seen the other guy," Dex said.

As he pulled the truck away from the booth, he scratched at his throat com again, and put his glove back on. But Mal didn't answer, so Dex re-focused in on the task at hand.

The truck groaned as it picked up speed, the transmission of the hybrid issuing a loud hydraulic hiss as Dex threw it into overdrive. His foot had already started to ache from holding the gas pedal down all the way, but he didn't release it. He was starting to pass the few small 'muter cars that dotted the freeway in front of him. They laid on their horns, the angry little bleats of the sheep, barely heard against the chugging of the huge truck's engine.

A disjunctive, pre-recorded male voice came through the overhead mic: "Warning, driver, Newbury Trash, permit... six, three, five, six, nine... your... two or more axle vehicle is close to maximum allowable speed. Please be careful."

Dex reached across to the passenger-side floor and picked up his ratty old backpack. He threw it onto the seat next to him. As he sat up he saw a small, red car right in front of him, going a good twenty miles per hour slower than he was. Dex pulled the horn lever next to him, and the car swerved back into the right lane, narrowly avoiding being bumped from behind.

His heart raced. A reported accident this early would bring the DMV sooner than he wanted. Before he was anywhere near his checkpoint. He pictured the place in his mind: the first exit into outer burbring, the cars already lining up for the race into the central commerce districts. It was sixteen miles out, and he only had three or four minutes. The freeway veered south and east soon, away from the Peak, and downhill to his destination. Downhill was good; it would help a little.

He unsnapped his backpack with one hand, weaving the huge truck through the traffic with the other. He pulled out his only valuable material possession—a worn old portable—from inside and placed it on the expansive dash. He'd glued some Velcro down on the surface to mesh with the strip on the back of his portable. Two red wires hung down from the portable's face. Dex reached for them.

Another zoned out 'muter strayed into the left lane. Before Dex could swerve, he grazed the side of the car, sending it spinning off into the shoulder.

"Shit!" Dex said out loud.

The voice came back from the overhead com immediately. "Warning, driver, Newbury Disposal Service, permit... six, three, five, six, nine. You have been involved in an automobile accident. This incident is currently being reported to Section 7 of the Department of Motor Vehicles. Please pull over to the shoulder slowly and wait for further instruction."

But Dex didn't pull over. His leg shaking visibly under the pressure, he stood on the pedal, using his weight instead of his muscles to hold it down. Finally he managed to get his hands around the data jack cables and reached them back under the steering column.

Two.

Dex inserted an I/O jack into the truck's central controller; it was so easy on those aftermarket jobbers. Then he dropped a cable into the jack and taped it under the steering column somewhere... there! He found the cable ends, pushed them into place on his portable, and the power indicator of his portable went live. He threw open the clamshell display.

The portable blinked, and a terminal appeared. Without looking, Dex reached over and typed in the commands to run Money's hack. The terminal showed his keystrokes in an oversized font. He touched the big green GO button, barely readable and worn down from use, and lines of executing code scrolled quickly past. Then the screen cleared and a simple, one-word question remained, blinking lazily:

ENGAGE?

Dex had to time it just right. Engage too soon, and the program was useless. Too late, and the program suffered the same fate. He would only have a fraction of a second to engage.

The voice came back over the speaker. "Warning, driver, Newbury Disposal Service, permit... six, three, five, six, nine. You are exceeding the posted allowable speed for freeway... 625... southbound...

at mile marker ...thirty...four. Your driving permit is being penalized now. You have thirty seconds to disengage your throttle."

Before the warning had even finished, he heard the com go live, and a real voice came over the speaker. "Permit, uh, permit six three five six nine, you've been reported as the primary in a traffic incident at mark 30. Immediately desist your speeding and pull to the shoulder." Dex could hear the heli blades beating in the background. They'd already sent a chopper his way.

It was six more miles to his destination. His current speed was ninety-three miles per hour.

Now this is fun. There was no trace of his hangover left. He felt the moment; it was upon him, starting to take. He let it take him.

Three.

Mallory Aquinas coded Thelo fast, *tap rub tap rub.* He came on, sounding distracted.

"Yes? What do you need?" Thelo asked.

"Did Salvador code you with the patched broadcast?" Mal asked quickly.

"Yes. I heard."

"They've got two helis dispatched. He started *speeding,* for Chrissake."

Thelo paused, then said, "He also hit a 'muter."

"No. No, he did NOT."

"Yeah. I can't get through to him. He's coded me out."

"Crackpipe. Okay. I'll give him a try. Are we going to abort?"

"No!" Thelo was breathing heavy, irregularly. "The dominos fall without him."

"I don't know, Thelo. We could reschedule. It's not too late."

"Are you losing it, Mal? Getting cold feet?"

"Whoa, there, Thelo, where did that come from?"

"Call your damn boyfriend. Now." Then he coded out.

What is his problem, Mal wondered. She looked at her watch. Two minutes. She could see her target ahead, on the horizon, just a few moments away. She took a bite of the stale bread that was lying in the seat next to her. Keeping food in her belly seemed to be the only thing that stood between constant nausea and outright puking. She coded Dex quickly.

His voice came back fast, distracted. "I'm a little busy here, Mal."

Mal barely waited for him to finish. "What the hell are you doing? Get that rig pulled over and hoof it outta there! They've got two helis on your tail; they're gonna take control of your truck any second now!"

"Got it under control, Mal. Just make sure you're on time."

"We're thinking of aborting, Dex. You're jeopardizing the entire mission right now."

"No. Don't abort. I'm fine."

Mal could almost hear his smile through the radio. *He's enjoying this. The lunatic is enjoying this. He's probably doing that thing, the thing he does under pressure.*

"Are you doing that thing, Dex?" she asked.

A pause. "Yes."

She let her breath out, like a sigh. "Well, how's it going for you?"

"Better than average."

Mal almost laughed. "Look, Dex, you have to be careful. This is not just another little–"

She was cut off by an electric screech, and then radio fuzz.

"Dex. Dexter Maxwell. Dex." She coded him again, but only heard the fuzz. He hadn't coded her out. He'd been cut off. She tried coding him again.

Tap rub rub tap.

Tap rub rub tap.

And then she only had a split second between giving up on trying to reach him and realizing her target was upon her. In that split second, she thought of just driving, of just going on, parking the truck, and walking away from everything, from everyone, from Dex. She saw herself checking into a center and getting put on the Charts. Hiring a lawyer. Calling her parents. *Sorry Mom, I'm not actually dead. Sorry about the anguish and despair.*

She didn't keep driving. Without decelerating, she cranked her steering wheel counterclockwise, as hard as she could. The truck screeched, teetered, and jack-knifed across all three lanes of traffic.

Four

Dex had been able to do it since he was a little kid. If he got his adrenaline rushing, a good concentration on, and the chaos level was going up, up, up, things around him just seemed to sort of slow down.

He could compartmentalize all the different variables around him, separate them into their distinct parts, and extrapolate the possibilities they presented. Then he'd make the best decision based on all the factors, and execute. All inside the space of a fleeting moment. When Thelo first saw him do it, back when they had sprung out the orph, he'd said, "you can take a moment and really own it. I mean, you had that moment in high jack." The phrase had stuck. *The moment in high jack.* It felt like the right way to describe the feeling.

He'd seen the pop-up message on his portable display, heard the screechy beep. It was an old autoboot prog he'd found years ago, one he always left running. He hated to leave Mal hanging like that, but the beep coming from his portable indicated a low level snoop had been initiated on his truck cab. As soon as the little electronic beep had started, he had immediately torn his throat piece off its adhesive base on his neck, and rolled the delicate little microphone between his finger and thumb until it was nothing but metal dust. Whoever had initiated that snoop would have captured the conversation, maybe even traced the source.

Someone suspected something. He put that data aside in his mind and began analyzing the meaning, even as he pulled the ear bud from his ear and put it between his teeth and bit down.

He looked at the mile marker as it flew past him. Thirty-nine. Five more miles. Everyone else should have done their work already. The news would start to get out to the regional traffic controllers, and then to the heli pilots. *Time to play.*

He glanced at his portable's display. The single word ENGAGE was still flashing on the screen, but the rate was steadily increasing. The technician in the heli had engaged the root triangulation prog for his truck's central brain controller. They were tuning the satellite receiver to the truck's frequency in order to take control and apply the brakes. They were getting close.

But they didn't have him yet.

He was flying along at nearly 100 miles per hour now, and the traffic controllers had engaged the emergency road safety broadcast system, asking all 'muters to pull over to the shoulder. Anyone who didn't comply got a fine, so the road was completely empty, except for his truck and the steady shadows of two helicopters pacing him, to the left. As he watched, the shadows where joined by a third, and then a fourth.

Four helicopters. Dex sorted the information with the electronic snoop he'd discovered. How could they respond so fast?

A live voice came back on the overhead com. "Driver, please identify yourself."

Dex smiled. They'd tried to engage his chip, get his registration number, maybe give him a drip of serotonin, but found out he didn't have any mech in his brain. Now the technician had to do it the old fashioned way, and just ask him who the hell he was. The voice had changed, too; this was the senior tech, probably in a different heli. *My threat level has been upgraded in just two minutes. File that away next to four helis.*

"I repeat: identify yourself immediately. You are illegally operating a class C four-axle hybrid that has been involved in a traffic accident."

Four minutes.

ENGAGE was blinking faster. They were getting closer. He had to wait. Wait until the exact moment they initiated the override to the manual truck controls; until the signal had already arrived and was being processed for completion. If the signal had not been sent, his little hack would be worthless. But if he waited until the control signal had been fully processed, his override loop would be lost. The window of opportunity, he figured, would be about point-three seconds.

So he kept part of his mind glued to the display.

The speedometer of the old truck maxed out at 120, burying the needle. The steering wheel shook violently in Dex's hands, which he had firmly gripped at 10 and 2 o'clock. His leg was shaking like a sewing machine from the downward pressure he applied to the pedal.

He glanced in the side-mirror, and saw three, no four, no *five* trooper vehicles rounding a curve, and gaining on him. New models, and fast. They must have been going 140 to close in on him like that.

How could they be grouped together already? And already so far south from the metro?

Ninety seconds.

"Driver, you are under arrest for reckless driving and motor vehicle endangerment. By the power vested in me by the Department of Motor Vehicles I am taking control of your vehicle. A ground trooper has been sent out to accompany you to central dispatch for sentencing."

Seventy-one seconds.

And then he saw it. ENGAGE was flashing at a rate of twelve times per second. Dex wrenched his right hand from the steering wheel and reached for the portable's keyboard. ENGAGE stopped flashing and went solid. Right as it made the transition, Dex slammed the GO button with his open palm. The truck gave a kick to the left, and for a fraction of a second Dex thought he'd missed it, missed the moment. But it was just the steering column shaking free of his grip as he'd reached for the portable. Once he had both hands back on the wheel, he knew he had control. Still.

"What the–?"

Dex smiled at the voice on the com. In his surprise, the tech had forgotten he was broadcasting live. It was this illusion of control that made this entire mission work, Money had always said.

Dex was looking for the break in the median between his southbound lane and the oncoming northbound lane. Right before the first outer burbring entrance, there was a thirty foot break in the concrete median. He knew it was there. It should be just ahead–

There it was.

Twenty-six seconds.

Northbound traffic had not been halted with the emergency road safety broadcast, as the maniac was only on the southbound freeway. Which was part of the plan. But this was a new thing. A new part. The plan hadn't called for a truck going 120 miles per hour. Should have been a safe sixty-five. And not so many 'muters already on the freeway.

He finally let go of the accelerator. The troopers were now directly behind him, and they must have thought that control had been usurped; when the truck's speed broke, they slowed as well, planning to escort the latest head-case to the shoulder.

19

Dex did the math. Thirty feet wide: he would have to be going no faster than seventy when he hit the hole if he was going to make it. Thirteen seconds.

But he wasn't going to make it.

Time had slowed down for Dex, and now it pulled up to a crawl. He noted his speed was a quickly slowing eighty-eight miles per hour. He calculated the amount of torque he would need to put on the steering wheel to at least put the cab through the median break, based on his understanding of the amount of play in the steering column and adjusting for possible skid from the old tires. He then calculated the impact point at the back of the truck and the physical repercussion for what would be an eighty-two-mile-an-hour concrete-on-steel kinetic energy transference.

Then he yanked the wheel counterclockwise as hard as he could.

This put the six-ton garbage truck up on two wheels as its inertia and top-heavy hybrid design pulled it forward instead of the direction the front wheels now pointed. Dex leaned into the turn (like it mattered) as the truck righted itself, but it lurched too far forward. Dex recalculated the impact point. He still had the truck aimed at the median break, but at a little too obtuse of an angle. Too late to adjust. Behind him, the troopers were slamming on their brakes and attempting to follow, their abject surprise reflected in the jerking and screeching of the cars. Overhead, the copters were pulling up, heading directly into the faint blue morning sky, in an effort to slow themselves.

Dex yanked the feeds of his portable out of the truck jack. The truck immediately locked up with the automatic freeze command the idiot in the copter had provided, and which Money's hack had looped in a permanent wait. The steering wheel snapped into position, and the hydraulic brakes began their tired exhale. Dex tore his portable loose from its perch and braced himself for impact.

The cab made it through the concrete median hole, but the front of the median caught the back of the truck, just behind the rear axle.

The metal-on-concrete tearing sound cemented itself in Dex's ears. The impact sent the back end of the truck swinging pendulum-like out into the northbound lanes, into the oncoming traffic. The fishtail motion forced a lateral momentum of the truck's speed on the driver-side tires. The truck tipped with enough forward force to keep

20

it rolling onto its top, and then slid to a stop, tottering, balanced awkwardly upside-down on the rounded hump of the trash compartment.

Northbound traffic began to rave into the shoulders, into each other. The first 'muter to hit the upended truck smashed into its back end, sending the entire truck spinning and rocking on its central hump again. The small car did a full 360, leaving the driver side facing forward again. When the next car caught the truck dead-center, it pushed it a few feet, and was then hit from behind by another car. And then another; each one in turn softening the impact on the truck, but jamming all the cars into a single, tangled mass of aluminum and fiberglass. Soft, life-saving foam dripped out the broken windows of the 'muters' cars.

Five.

And it had been such a gorgeous morning. Time was speeding up again, gaining its normal tempo. Dex was hanging from the five-point harness around his chest. He could hear distant screeches, and the sound of metal hitting metal. It seemed to have worked.

I need to get out of here. Now. The escape route is too far away. Plan B. There was a plan B.

He thought of Mal, and his heart skipped a beat. Hopefully it had gone smoothly on her route. He felt sick thinking of her stuck upside down in a garbage truck, the sound of helis overhead. Mal being Mal, she'd probably laugh at this display of typical male nonsense, but that didn't stop him from feeling it, it just made him feel a weird kind of guilt like–

Get out. Now. He shook his head, trying to clear the cobwebs, and a big glob of blood dripped down onto his portable, lying on the roof below him. He clicked the release device, but it was jammed. *The traffic tech's override included the safety harness. It won't release.* He reached up, and could just get his hand on his backpack to pull out the fold-away knife and start sawing at the straps. He could hear voices shouting, and, not too far away, sirens. Everything was moving way too slow.

And then he was scared. He felt caught. *Time for your chip,* he heard the orphanage doctor say with that sick smile of his. With that corn-chip breath against the nape of his neck. *Time for your drip, you little psycho bastard. You won't mind, then. You won't mind anything at all.*

Thinking of Dr. Johansson kicked his adrenaline back up, and Dex cut through the straps. He fell to the roof, rolled over, grabbed his portable and shoved it in his pack. He carefully crawled out the broken driver-side window.

The cutting wind and dull roar of helis flying too low to the ground was all around him. Without standing up, he instead rolled underneath the first 'muter that had collided with the truck, and began to crawl military-style toward the bottom of the next car. He had made it about three vehicles back before he ran into one on its side, preventing him from crawling any further.

But he wasn't going to get away from this mess by inching from car to car. He started going through the highway maps in his head. Where was he? This was all new concrete, completely overhauled in '09 or so. They had had to rebuild it after the, after the... *floods. Plan B.*

He jumped straight up and felt the wind of the heli blades cut into his face, squinting through the wind. He looked desperately around, until he saw what he needed. Forty feet south, on the right. A brand-new, up-to-code, built-for-the-new-millennium, gov-installed storm drain. He looked up at the heli just overhead, and saw three men conferring. Suddenly one pointed at him ferociously and pulled something from behind. In the wind and noise, he couldn't quite make it out, but it sure looked like–

He has a gun! And so Dex ran. He ran as fast as he could, his right leg still shaky from holding down the pedal. Still, he practically leaped a small blue 'muter in his path, planting one foot on its hood and jumping to the other side. Then he heard a ping and saw a hole appear just next to his foot as he launched off the car. He pitched himself onto the ground sideways, at full speed, and rolled into the ditch, and against the storm drain door.

He landed against it with all of his momentum, and the safety latch snapped and broke. Dex tumbled through the hole and fell into the darkness of the sewer.

Six

Thelo wished for rain.

Not that it would come. It hadn't rained in a year; probably wouldn't rain for another. You could just tell by the, well, by the smell. How the afternoon air smelled. The stale dryness had an edge that promised to be there for a while. But Thelo still longed to feel the cool drops against his massive, tattooed shoulders, bare except for the light t-shirt. He closed his eyes and lifted his face upward, imagining the cold pelts against his eyelids, his lips, his cheeks.

There was a time, when he was still living in the orph with Dex and crazy ol' Jones, when it had rained for thirty-six straight days, big globby drops of rain that slammed into your head. That kind of rain, they say, hadn't surfaced in the West for thirty or forty years, not since the days before the township federation. It took down a bunch of cozy bungs that had sprung up on the face of Pikes Peak, and brought down a bunch of mud and debris where they'd cleared the last set of trees.

They'd called it the Great Flood of '06. The streets flooded, and the entire Greater Metropolitan Front Range slowed, and then came to a stop. There was nowhere for all the water to go. In response, they'd built all those storm tunnels under everything. The tunnels that now housed a large part of the unaccepted populations. The tunnels that had been dry since construction had finished.

During that epic rainstorm, Dex and Thelo would sneak out of the orphanage window with Jones and they would just sit on the roof, quiet, not saying a word, and let the rain pour down on them. They didn't go run and play in it, because the grassless yard had turned into two feet of mud underneath six inches of flowing water. But they still went out, every night, for thirty-six nights, and let the rain soak them until they were too tired to stay out any longer. Jones would fall asleep, and Thelo would shake him awake to go in. Dex would usually stay out all night.

Thelo pretended that rain was falling now, washing him clean, pouring over his face, down his neck, over his shoulders. The rain would make little rivers down his oversized biceps, find a path around his elbow and down his forearms. Then it would rinse over his hands, turn all the blood into a diluted orange, and then, as if from a faucet, pour off his clenched fists. It would fall onto the cold cement floor and make a puddle, then a river, and the body that lay at his feet would slowly drift away, and out of his mind.

Thelo opened his eyes. The blue sky burned bright, the late afternoon wind already whipping in from the mountains. There was no rain. Just blood everywhere and a dead man at his feet.

You didn't need to check for a pulse when you saw that much blood. There just wasn't enough left inside to run any of the moving parts. Thelo couldn't recognize the person, but it looked to be someone important. Rich people clothes. Rich people shoes.

When the blackout wore off, and Thelo regained consciousness, it wasn't like a switch turning on and off. It was always a blurry reentry, and he'd found it best to stand still until he could get his bearings. He looked around. He was on the roof of a low-rise; it was probably apartments. He had a view of the downtown skyline to the east, but he was at a lower level than most buildings to the west. Downtown Grenver, probably the Mid District. For a moment he listened for traffic. He couldn't place somewhere this close to the metro center that had no traffic. Maybe he was more north than he expected.

Still, there should be some traffic noise. And indeed, there were a few blares, but it was far from the dull rush he would expect.

He realized that his fists were still clenched, and aching, so he loosened the grip, and heard a clatter. He looked down at the cement. His fold-away knife had been in his left hand, and now it lay there unfolded, the blade covered in blood and clots of skin, the sharpened tip pointing directly back at him.

I'm not left-handed. And it never rains when you need it to.

Seven.

Mal looked at the clock on her portable. The sun would just about be dipping below the Peak. She looked at her 'cast snooping prog again. Still no signal. She pulled a new list down and sent the review snoop across a new band, but there was nothing. Nobody this low was broadcasting for a signal, so she'd just have to wait. Sooner or later, someone would want to get hold of the day's events, pull it down to their viewer, check in. Folks that lived in the storm sewers were not that different from anyone else. They knew when things happened. They talked to each other, had communities, opinions. And they were connected. More than anyone on the surface suspected.

And they still liked to catch the occasional broadcast, especially with events such as today's. But no one was putting up a signal right now. *Damn it.* Mal changed her band spectrum again and sent out a snoop.

Should have scripted this process a long time ago, she thought. But she hadn't. She would always start, but then look at the blank screen and not really be able to think where to begin. Besides, she had to admit that she liked keeping it all inside her head. *When you write something down, you give yourself an excuse to forget it.* Those were Jones' words, and she liked them. She told herself it was a safety precaution, but she knew that if her portable was ever taken into custody they wouldn't be worried about a few illegal snoop programs. They'd take one look at all the illegal data she had stored and know enough to put her on ice forever.

She pulled a new list and expanded the frequency range. This time, she got feedback, on a really low band. *Someone is trying to hide their signal,* she thought. And they were doing a good job of it. Typing madly, she wrote her usual Trojan horse prog and attached it to the signal. Then, because of the frequency range, she added an independent default recast, in case her carrier dropped before she was done. Then she waited. In just a few seconds, her prog had done the work and she was being asked if she would accept a loop transfer. She said yes, hardwired the link to her location, and began typing.

She always rewrote the application on the spot. It meant that there was never a way to track her interference based on an application footprint—another reason to avoid scripts. The 'bots that roamed the database thrived on patterns. It was how they operated; they were hardwired into their little triggered brains. Once the application was written, she scrolled the directories until she found the entrance she was looking for. Then she used the same back-door procedure she'd been using for years, ever since she'd fled Academy. With a few more keystrokes, she was in. A flashing cursor was all it was, but to her it looked like an open door, beckoning.

The Charts. She knew the real name of the singular database format used by the ruling American elite to track the medical and personal data of each citizen: The International Citizen Safety and Welfare Information Tracker, or ICSWIT. It had become known as "the Charts" back when it was primarily a unified database for medical tracking. The name had stuck, even though its use had been expanded to incorporate nearly every piece of data that was generated by almost anyone or any connected thing within the United States, or by anyone outside the United States deemed worthwhile of tracking.

And it only took twelve minutes to crack in, if you knew what you were doing. And happened to have a root-level, permanent security key, Mal thought uneasily. No reason to be that proud of her programming skills.

She immediately navigated to new criminal record activity and pulled up the base table for any new ice that had been created since early that morning. She selected Unaccepted Citizens to narrow the list down to a manageable amount of data, but still the list scrolled off her display. She ran the query again, and then watched the list of names.

No Dexter Maxwell.

She changed her selection to Unnamed Unaccepted, but none of them matched his description or whereabouts either.

As of seven-thirty, Dex was still running free. A readout on her display told her that the original connection she'd piggy-backed had dropped, so she was now running an independent line. There was a risk, but she was too anxious to keep her eyes off the Charts. She ran through the list again.

No Thelonius Hollywood. Still free, as of 19:30 hours.

Habitually, she moved to the med records and started digging. Back when she'd first met Dex, she'd started looking for a record, any record, of his existence prior to when they'd met. It had turned into a routine to get warmed up to the Charts and its organizational systems. She'd looked through meds, births, arrests, obits. She'd cross-referenced the orphanage that he'd spent all those years in, and found a loose thread or two of data. These were mostly records of trouble, violence, or mischief, always cross-referenced with one Thelonius Hol-

26

lywood. Then there were the records of the chemicals they had put into Dex. She pulled up the list of drugs again; it had always amazed her that he was still standing, let alone a coherent and intelligent young man, considering the types of compounds and the dosage levels they were pumping through his body at the age of thirteen. But it did explain the destruction of most of his early childhood memories.

When she tried to dig any deeper, any farther back, the Charts were a dead end. So she'd cross reference with Thelo's name, because they'd been attached at the hip as long as either of them could remember. Now Thelo, she'd been able to track his path from the first orphanage, as a small child, all the way to them being bunk-mates when Dex had arrived at age thirteen.

But no Dex. Where he came from, what his life had been prior to the orph—the Charts didn't know anything about it. And so neither did she. Dex never talked about it, and when asked, he always just said his parents had raised him in the old hills and then they'd gotten in an accident and been killed.

So she'd cross-referenced accidental deaths in the days leading up to Dex's incarceration at the orph, but every surviving child of every dead parent could be accounted for on the Charts. There was no line that connected Dex to anything, anywhere.

As she looked through the same old records, she heard someone approaching her room, the echo of footsteps on concrete. She dropped the hard link and cleared the display in a mad tapping of keys. A knock came to at her door.

"Yeah, who is it?" she asked.

"Money."

"Come on in."

Money walked in, looking exhausted, like everyone else. "Hey, I used a low frequency band to order up some broadcast loops of the day's news reels. We're gonna watch them on Pedro's display. See if we can catch anything on Dex or Thelo."

Mal closed her eyes. "Low frequency bands, eh? No chance of a trace?"

"Not a chance," Money said. "No one hits the bands that low except for dirt-bags like me."

Mal gave an exhausted smirk. "I'll be right there."

27

GREATER METROPOLITAN FRONT RANGE (GMFR), SEPTEMBER 28, 2113.

Eight.

The blackness began to peel away, leaving the hint of red behind it, like sunlight through closed eyes. Dex tried to scrunch his eyes closed against the surfacing heat, but he knew what was coming. He'd been here before. He knew this dream well: its texture, its shape, its outcome. As always, he gave in, scared of what he might see, but more scared of what would happen if he did not look.

He opened his eyes to the burning surface, extending in all directions. He knew it fell away in an odd, semi-spherical shape, with rough edges and inconsistencies, but he was too close to be able to make that out now. He was moving toward the heat, toward the energy that already burned at this skin: the gravity behind him weakening, the gravity on the other side growing stronger.

He fell faster and faster, approaching the hot white plane. If he fell any further, he would die, eliminated at the broiling surface. The moment slowed almost to a halt. And so he began to pull apart the pieces—pieces of himself——until he was just tiny parts. He had done this so many times now and he knew the routine. He just had to make sure he could remember how to put it all back together. The concentration occupied his entire mind. And he knew that if he didn't put it all back together immediately, some parts would be lost.

But the heat of the burning surface would start to eat away at his skin again. He would pull every little piece apart, and then tear each one apart again, until he was a billion indivisible pieces. Only then would the burning go away. But then he would have to put it all back together again straight away or else the pieces would float away and he would be nothing. Over and over again. The fear of the burning surface was so great that he couldn't stop the constant reorganization. But it was exhausting. He was starting to fall apart and couldn't find all the pieces. Panic took over and the heat became blinding–

Nine.

Dex woke to the sensation of someone tearing at his sneakers violently. He tried to open his eyes, but only his right eye complied. His left eye was swollen shut. The hammering in his head nearly matched the pain of the dream, and he could still feel the panic at the back of his throat. But he put it all out of his mind and jumped at the dark figure trying to steal his shoes. He lunged at the neck with one hand and started squeezing.

The woman must have been in her fifties, or at least had the look of someone that age. She was incredibly fat, but that could have been all the old clothes she had wrapped herself up in. Her eyes bulged and she tried to scream, but her air supply was cut off by the pressure of Dex's hand. She clawed at his arm and face, and he let her go. She wasn't a threat.

She fell and scooted away quickly. "Kiddy kid, not dead! I thought you was dead."

Suddenly dizzy, Dex fell back hard on his behind, and steadied himself with his hands. "No. Not dead. Not yet."

"You look set to kick," She said, still backing away. She pointed at her own forehead with her thumb, and drew a line down the side of her face, past her left eye, down the check, to her neck. "You got it bad, like this. Bloody blood everywhere."

"It can't look half as bad as it feels." He reached up and touched his head gently, and winced, closing his eyes against the dizziness. The slightest pressure pushed the roaring pain to a whole new level. He waited for the pain to drop a few decibels, and then he opened his one good eye again. The old lady was gone, and, he realized ruefully, she'd made off with his shoes.

He looked around in the dim light. Half-buried in refuse, he was leaning against the rounded side of a large storm drain. He couldn't place where, exactly. He looked up. The top of the pipe must have been only ten feet above him. Judging by the size, he was still pretty far south. There was mild reflective light coming from the left, and only darkness to his right. *Where am I and what happened to my head?* Gradually the memories began to return in flashes. The truck over- turning. Crawling underneath the 'muters. The gun. Falling down

29

the drainage hole.

They had come after him, he remembered that. But they were so dependent on the tech, on the chips, they had no idea how to actually track someone down on the run. So he had run, and run, and taken a few detours through connected sewer holes, circling back, and ultimately deciding–

South. I went south.

But how far had he gotten? As he traced his way back to the present, the memories became less distinct. He could only remember staggering, step after step, for the longest time–*but how long?* It was impossible to know. The drains were still ten-footers, so he can't have strayed too far from the main line.

Just as he decided to attempt to stand up, he heard voices coming from the left, where the light was. He thought he could make out three or four distinct voices, but with the echo he couldn't tell for sure. He lay back down in the refuse and tried to pile up the slick paper and trash around him, but it was no use. He rolled onto his side and closed his eyes.

The voices became clearer. It sounded like young boys yelling at each other, throwing invectives back and forth. *Sewer rats.* His heart raced. He was a sitting duck. *Crack, if they found me, in this state, I'm wet for sure.*

In addition to the yelling, Dex could detect a strange metallic sound that would clang, scrape, then pause, then clang, scrape, pause, over and over again. Based on what these street kids typically carried with them, he could only imagine what was making that sound.

Suddenly the voices were upon him, right at his feet, and whatever was making the scraping noise clanged down. He felt the scrape reverberate through the concrete pipe. They were not big kids, just the usual half-starved silhouettes that roamed the pipes looking for a new way to die. They made quite the racket passing, and were so deeply involved in some joke that they didn't even look down as they passed him. They just continued on south with their clang, scrape, pause. As they rounded the bend of the pipe, their echoes quickly began to fade.

Dex finally took a deep breath, and sat up again. He wouldn't be that lucky again. He needed to get out of here. In this condition, he didn't stand a chance down at this end of the pipes. Even as he started to imagine the possibilities, he heard a voice interrupt the jabbering sewer boys, and he froze. It sounded like the old lady that had taken his shoes, and she was talking with the boys. There was some muffled back and forth he couldn't make out. Then, loud and clear, he heard one of them say: 'Just right back around that corner? And you just took his shoes right off him?"

Dex pulled himself up, leaning as best he could against the curvature of the wall, and headed north. His head pounded, and his entire body felt like a car wreck. He stumbled a few yards, hearing the sound of someone running behind him and approaching fast . He looked around with his one good eye, looking for any alternate routes. But there were none. Whatever was putting off that light, it was too far away.

And then he tripped, and landed hard. The footsteps were right behind him, but instead of trying to run, he rolled onto his right side and just lay there. The rats closed the gap in no time. They slowed to a walk as they approached, and he could make out four of them. One of them carried a long object. As they got closer, Dex could see it was a makeshift sword, about two feet long. He had heard of this new trend among the street fighters, but hadn't seen one of these blades for himself yet. They were fashioned from auto bumpers, grates, and whatever other steel could be found, and then sharpened by being dragged along the concrete floors of the storm drain.

I have to get that off him, or I'm dead.

"Oi, here's the bandejo, right here," he heard one say and noted that they had split into two sets of two, to circle either side of him. Very good form.

"Man, this licker is wet already. Look at his face."

"Damn. Juice, look at that jacket. Trucker jacket, almost brand new." The one with the blade used it to poke at his side, pull the jacket up a bit from his chest.

"It's mine. You can have whatever else he has. The jacket is mine."

"All yours. Look at the blood all over it–that's never comin' out."

"Nah, you can get it out. You just have to soak it down below the old factories..."

Dex knew his moment had come. The one with the blade had turned to argue, so Dex swung his left arm and hit him at the back of

31

his knee. The boy went down with a cry. Dex caught his sword arm as he went down, and gave it a violent twist. He felt–and heard–the tendons pop. The kid screamed, and the blade fell from his hand and clanged to the ground. Dex released his grip on the boy's arm and grabbed the blade.

In a second he was up on his feet, a little dizzy, but clutching the sword's long hilt in both hands. At his feet, the boy had curled into fetal position, and holding was his arm, gasping. Dex gave him a kick, more for effect than anything else. The other three boys had distanced themselves immediately into a circular arrangement around Dex, and were now inching slowly around him, clockwise, at a uniform speed. *This isn't the first time they've taken on a man with a sword. These kids are going to kill me.*

Dex swung the blade awkwardly around him. "I suggest you take your friend here and move on," he said calmly. His heavy breathing betrayed his pain, though, and the boy directly in front of him smiled meanly. He must have only been fourteen, maybe fifteen.

"You know what to do with that blade, bandejo?" he asked.

"Of course," Dex said. "I stick you through the nuts with it."

The boys all laughed, and came in closer. Dex swung the blade menacingly. But the boy across from him didn't even flinch. Instead, he reached over his shoulder and slowly pulled another sword from a hidden sheath on his back.

"Let's see what you got, Northender," he said.

Dex blinked his one good eye. He had lost a lot of blood, was most likely concussed, and now he found himself facing off against a fearless sewer rat, brandishing a weapon he had never used before. Swords, he couldn't believe it.

But then, this was a fitting end. He'd pulled a lot of good stunts, had his fun, and raised plenty of hell. Now he was about to die stuck on the end of this kid's sword. So instead of letting panic set in, he felt his fate descend on him like the answer to a question.

Time to play. He pretended to have a coughing attack, stumbled a little, and then lunged at the boy, sword swinging.

The kid wasn't fazed by Dex's little routine. Seeing the blade coming at a high angle, the kid blocked with his sword just enough to deflect the blade past his body but without taking any of the weight from Dex's attack. He turned his body sideways. As Dex went flying by unstabilized, the kid adeptly swung his other hand around and caught Dex on the wrist. Dex cried out. The blade flew from his hands and fell to the ground. Juice stood over him.

"Shit, Northender, you suck at this," he said. Then he kicked Dex hard in the ribs, more for effect than anything else.

"Hey, don't mess up the jacket," one of the other boys said. "It's almost new."

"Right, I'll just take out that ugly-ass face."

Dex rolled onto his side, and saw the kid holding his sword high above his head with both hands. It was aimed directly at his good eye. Dex smiled through his swollen, bloody face. The moment had not slowed down. There was no high jack. He didn't own it. It owned him; and he felt a weight lifting from him. He thanked the moment, for taking him this one time. The relief was unbelievable. All Dex could see was Mal, smiling like she did when he made her laugh. And then with a grunt the kid brought the blade down with all his weight.

Ten.

As the blade traveled downward, a huge body hit the rat named Juice hard from the side. The blade changed its downward trajectory just enough to miss Dex's head and clang against the concrete. With both Juice's and his attacker's weight on the sword, it bent in half and they fell on top of it. There was a muffled grunt, and the two other boys lunged for the two rolling bodies.

Dex squinted with his good eye.

Thelo. It was his friend.

Thelo rolled up from the tackle he'd laid on Juice, who just lay there, unmoving. Then he met the other two boys with the crouching stance of a seasoned wrestler. Dex saw his eyes flash in the low light. Without hesitation Thelo jumped at the first boy, hitting him in the lower jaw with the top of his head. Immediately he kid went slack and fell to the ground, unconscious. The final boy took one look at Thelo's huge frame, and took off running. Thelo stood to his full height and looked over at the crumpled frame of his friend. .

33

"What the hell took you so long?" Dex tried to smile.

"You're welcome my friend, but really, no need for thanks," Thelo said. He reached down to help Dex up. "Crackpipe, look at this mess. Y'okay?"

"No, I'm all cranked," Dex returned, thankful to be able to put his weight on someone else. "But I'll live."

Thelo pulled Dex's arm over his large shoulder, and shot his friend a wide grin that could not go unnoticed even in the dim light of the tunnel. "I wasn't so sure there, for a minute. You looked like a goddamn sewer noob." He looked over at the kid with the broken arm, who had pulled himself even tighter into fetal position. "You do that?"

"Yeah."

"So I at least taught you *something* over the years."

"They carry swords, now. *Swords.*"

Thelo helped Dex northward along the tunnel. "I noticed. It's a different world, these days. It's not like when we used to roam these pipes."

"I'm tellin' you, this is no place for aging street kids like us," Dex said, jokingly. But it didn't come out funny. It came out true.

Thelo said nothing for a while. "Mal is worried sick. I've got a 'muter at the next maintenance entrance, about three hundred yards yonder."

"How'd you find me?"

"You forget that I know exactly how you think. Besides, I've been looking for a long time."

"How long have I been down here?"

"About twenty-eight hours, give or take."

"Huh. How did everything go? I mean, with the thing?"

Thelo laughed, truly laughed, and the sound echoed up and down the tunnel. "How did it go? I ain't tellin'. Money saved the 'cast. See for yourself when we get back to the shanty. What the hell happened to your shoes?"

Eleven.

Dex winced as the needle entered the thin skin at his temple. With all the cleanup and the straight alcohol that had been dumped into his gaping head wound, he would have thought that the pain would die down. But it didn't. He groaned audibly.

"Just relax there, ya ninny," Thelo said, pulling the fiber through carefully. "This is gonna scar no matter what, but hopefully we can make it so you're not *too* much uglier than when you started."

Dex was lying on his back on a cold plastic bench in the great room of their little organization's makeshift headquarters. Everyone had come by to say something snide about his injury and then give him a pat on the foot, on the leg, on the shoulder. They didn't like to look at him too much at first, but the swelling was starting to subside. Money was the most amazed. He hadn't been around that long, Dex supposed, and hadn't known Dex to pull something like that. He wanted to hear all the little details, wanted everything explained. How had he stopped the truck control override system? How had he known that the auto troopers would slow down along with the truck?

"That's enough questions for now, Money," Mal had said. Dex could still see the look on her face. How could someone have a look that said relief and anger at the same time? But she had, and it didn't really matter. Dex was so glad to see her that he'd almost fallen flat on his face trying to get to her. Then he'd just held her, and she'd held him back, and everyone else had just seemed to melt into the background.

"Thank god you're okay," she whispered.

"You too," was all he could whisper in her ear. She had almost cried. He could feel her swallow it down, and he had to do the same thing.

Then she'd left him with Thelo to get fixed up, and he'd passed out again. When he woke, it was to the sting of alcohol on the cut on his face. He'd begged a few swigs of the bottle before the cleaning continued, and had been lying flat ever since, getting his face sewn shut.

Money came back in the room. Dex recognized the heavy foot-steps. The footsteps of someone not accustomed to walking inside a concrete box all the time. Then he heard his voice.

"You ready to watch the news 'cast yet?" Money asked excitedly.

"You know, I'm dying to, but Thelo's not done torturing me yet."

Thelo gave a tug at the stitching fiber. "Put it on. He can't watch, but he can listen."

Money hurriedly queued up the saved broadcast on his display. Dex could hear the news analyst speaking in that sing-song voice that all news analysts use.

"Turn that up, Money; I can't hear it."

The voice came in shaky, fuzzed from the reception at 100 feet below the surface. Dex recognized the voice from the 'Full Story, one of the popular nightly news magazines

"...as we are receiving more and more data, the entire picture of this despicable act of terrorism is just starting to come into focus. Deborah Jessing has been covering this story from in Southern GMFR, just north of outer burbring and the most turbulent location of the striking points today. Together with our team of story specialists, Deborah has as-sembled a timeline of all of today's events so that we can bring you... the full story. How do things look down there, Deborah?

"Thanks, Doug. I have to be honest with you; the cleanup is going very slowly. The traffic specialist for the DMV, Jerry Davis, told me earlier that he expected regular traffic flow to be restored sometime later this evening, but he encouraged all travelers to continue to honor the traffic moratorium im-posed by the governor-general. As you can see behind me, forensic experts still have the primary attack vehicle corded off, and are undergoing a full spectrum of criminal tests. Most of the other commuter vehicles have been pulled away from the scene at this time, except for a few involved in the primary accident.

"Questions abound. How did this act of terrorism start?

What did the terrorists hope to accomplish? And how did they pull off the largest traffic stoppages in the history of the country?"

At this last statement, the room erupted in a cheer. Dex's eyes popped open and he tried to look around, but only saw Thelo's face smiling down at him as he pulled the fiber tight again. "Looks like everyone wants to see it one more time," Thelo said. Dex closed his eyes again. The broadcast had queued to commercial.

"Largest of all time, eh?" Dex asked.

"Of all time," he heard Money confirm from across the room. "The governor started ordering arrest warrants for people just for leaving their vehicles on the highway. I mean, they had just left them there. Walked away. Most amazing thing I've ever seen."

"They had riots in Old Boulder City," Donna said enthusiastically. "Riots like no one has seen in years. Because of traffic, man, *traffic*."

"Everyone, hush up, I'm trying to act like a crackin' doctor over here," Thelo said, overly loud. But he meant it, and everyone quieted down. The Full Story returned with its urban drum beat intro.

"We are back. Thanks again for joining us. Deborah Jessing is with us from outer burbring, where she has put together a timeline of today's events for the Full Story.

"Today started like any other in the Greater Metropolitan Front Range. The sun brought a little warmth to the chilly September air, and our great city-region was just beginning to shake off the night's sleep and prepare for another day of honest work. Just another Wednesday.

"But today would be different. Today, terrorists had different plans."

There was general exclamations of enthusiasm from the team around the display.

"The groundwork for the devious act lay in the waste management complex of Newbury Trash, a small subsidiary unit of Guy-Col International Waste Disposal. Martin Newbury, the proprietor of the contract disposal service, often hired drivers from the huge masses of unnaturalized citizens that hang on at the edges of society, taking what handouts they can beg and working what small menial jobs they can find. Hiring 'uns,' as they are commonly referred to, is neither a practice uncommon among small-time contractors around the city, nor is it currently illegal, although democratic Senator Mathers from the Western Coalition introduced legislation to this effect just last week.

"But simply hiring uns was not the mistake that Mr. Newbury made. Mr. Newbury had more waste business than he could handle. Again, not an unlikely tale—with the remarkable growth of GMFR since the township consolidation, there is simply not enough space on our roads to transport the garbage fast enough. Newbury, however, did not find enough satisfaction in the honest dollar he was earning. Instead of garnering the proper rights to move more waste, and pay the appropriate taxes, he took advantage of his uns and what has turned out to be a vast network of grift and bribery throughout the toll station system of the entire GMFR.

"It was unclear this morning how exactly the trucks used in the attack were allowed past the toll checkpoints. Full Story has learned that all eleven waste disposal trucks used today passed through checkpoints illegally. If you are not familiar with the minutiae of current waste management law, let me summarize it for you: you pay a set fee per truck-load based on the number of tolls you will be passing through, and then you are assigned a specific day each week to move the trucks. If you want to move your trucks on more than one day each week, you have to up your per-truck fee for the second day. Now, if you only have a certain number of trucks, it is beneficial to run your trucks on more than a single day. But Mr. Newbury clearly didn't feel that the increased cost per truck was fair. Or perhaps he simply didn't want to do the paperwork. Mr. Newbury will have his day in court to answer these questions."

"They already arrested him?" Dex asked.

Thelo sighed. "Yeah, they already put him on ice. His arraignment's in three months."

"I really liked old Newbury."

"Me too."

"... he used a system that has been described to us by anonymous drivers as the 'low-toll booths.' The low-toll booth system consists of a network of toll station operators that work together to fix a black market price for allowing illegal trucks to pass through all the stations. Every individual operator gets a payout as the truck passes, but the price is fixed for each of them so that the payer is guaranteed a price and a route in or out of the metro. It wouldn't do to get through five booths, only to get stuck on the sixth, would it? The operators work together, and anyone looking to move something illegally on our already-busy roads simply has to get a list of which exact booths to hit, and how much to pay each operator.

"So on September 17, at roughly six AM, Mr. Newbury dispatched his usual fleet of twenty-six waste disposal vehicles, each of them equipped with enough cash to make it to the outer waste deposits using the low-toll booths. Fifteen of those went about their business, collecting the trash from your curbside disposal systems. But the rest of those trucks headed out onto the eight major highways leading in and out of GMFR. Those eleven trucks had a different destiny.

"When we return, we will track the eleven trucks as they make their way onto each freeway. Meanwhile, morning commuter traffic is building along the freeway entrances. Disaster waits just around the corner."

Money snorted. "I love it: 'disaster waits around the corner.' Who writes that kind of stuff?"

Mal spoke loudly, in her lecture voice, so that everyone could hear. "They are portraying our actions as akin to a natural disaster, such as a flood or big snowstorm, and as a life-endangering act of treason. That way, they can make it out to be something that was an act of god, or an act of a crazy bunch of violent lunatics. Either way, it will deflect attention from the DMV's inability to either stop us from doing it, or to cope intelligently with the after-effects. The media works on their behalf. Never forget that."

"...Newbury Trash has dispatched its fleet of illegal garbage trucks. Eleven of them skipped the trash route and headed out immediately for the eight primary freeways that serve the GMFR area. The following map shows each of the freeways out as far as the burbring. It was clear that they targeted the hardworking folks of the burbring in this attack. Had the trucks gone any further out, nearly eighty percent of all traffic would have been unable to get to their destinations.

"The Full Story has been able to extrapolate the start time of each terrorist's truck from the known time that each truck reached its target. The first thing to notice is that the terrorists had been studying the traffic flow for some time, and accounted for the growing business sectors in the minor business district on the east side of the burbring, and also the northern military industries. Therefore, those were the only highways that the terrorists decided to shut down in both an incoming and outgoing fashion, as seen by these two trucks here... and here.

"The second item of interest is the delayed start of the southbound truck on Interstate Loop 625. Officials have been at a loss to explain this delay, except to guess that perhaps there were technical difficulties, or a tie-up at an early toll station. But that delay was crucial to the spectacular chase that ensued.

"Back to our timeline. As you can see, most of the vehicles got into position very early. Officials have denied that there was any form of communication between the different trucks..."

Everyone laughed heartily at this, and Money's face lit up with a smile as everyone slapped him on the back.

"...would have either been recorded by the mandatory cab-recorders in each truck, or by the radio interception bubble that exists for the entire GMFR, as governed by federal law. Without communication, the terrorists most certainly had to have practiced these exact routes numerous times to get the timing just right."

"Or, just capture the slight motion of the vocal cords when whispering," Money was saying, "and translate that into a digital signal. That's the easy part. The hard part is disguising the signal and encrypting it."

Everyone turned to look at Money. He kept going, pushing his long mop of hair off his face and adjusting his glasses. "I did a little historical digging for something old enough that current systems might not be prepared for. Found some IP crypto packages that were commercially available mid-century. NanoCrypto and NanoVOIP. High-quality vintage code. But this stuff is powerful, and it's small, and it's focused on 'thing-to-thing' security, not hub and spoke nonsense. So, it's small and I can fit the crypto right onto the stickies on our necks. It's custom-built for voice encryption, so I barely had to write any code to get it to work."

Money was on a roll. But everyone was listening to the 'casts except for Dex and Thelo.

"Now I've got a nearly-silent, encrypted digital signal," he went on. "Just need to get it from car to car. And you can't make it look like the data is encrypted. That would stand out like a sore thumb. So, what is the most common form of information going from car to car? Music. So, first, mask the encryption as music packets, then move them over the low-frequency radio broadcasts they use for car-to-X communication. There's a slight delay, but you can get to the other cars and decrypt the stream at the earpiece. Decent in-device crypto with no break-points between the peers ensures the traffic is gibberish if intercepted. The packet headers describe the traffic as music sharing, with just enough crypto for interceptors to smile knowingly and assume someone's trying to disguise their illegal music sharing. Illegal, but petty."

By this point, Money was mostly talking to himself. Dex smiled. He'd be proud of himself if he'd been able to make it work, too. But Dex also knew that someone had cracked it. They had compromised the system, even if the 'casts weren't saying so. He turned his attention back to the female voice.

"At 7:26, the first truck overturned twenty-eight miles east of midtown, heading east on the I-225 extension. Without warning, the truck swerved wildly, and with the top-heavy construction of the trucks, fell on its side, across all three lanes of traffic."

That had been Mal. Dex opened his eyes again and wondered if she was watching now. It was as though Thelo was reading his thoughts.

"She watched this once," he said, still working on the stitching, "and it drove her to distraction. She kept standing up, then sitting back down. She refused to watch it again. She's probably reading through the–" his voice dropped to a whisper. "You know; through the Charts. I think she finds it soothing to be surrounded by all that data. "

"... and at 7:30, the entrances opened for the morning, and the freeway was flooded with commuters. The backup was immediate, and had extended all the way down to the eastern edge of the burbring by 7:45.

"Minutes before, at seven twenty-seven, there were three simultaneous attacks, all at the north end. The Boulder turnpike was hit, as was the north and south-bound two-five. It took only minutes for traffic to come to a complete standstill as far north as New Fort Collins. Likewise, all city traffic jammed all the way to the capital building as city dwellers tried to get out to the minor business centers.

"The Calhan bypass was hit at seven twenty-nine, as were the 825 and 925 loops. That left just two more targets: The Cross-70 turnpike at midtown, and the northbound 625 below Pikes Peak.

"Perhaps the most audacious of the terrorist targets was the midtown turnpike that runs past nearly every major law enforcement agency in the GMFR. Even more significantly, the only reason to force a traffic accident at the turnpike would be to stop the flow of traffic directly to these agencies–the DMV, Central Dispatching; you name it. The concentration of these agencies means that the turnpike is used almost entirely by agency traffic–support staff, administrators, troopers reporting to duty. So it was a daring target, but a necessary one. In order to be able to escape from certain capture, the terrorists needed to be battling against only the bare-bones night staff of these agencies–or whoever reported in early on this fateful day.

"We'll be right back."

Mal had been avoiding Dex since his return. Was she angry at his actions on the freeway? The thought baffled him. This kind of bravado had always made her laugh before. *What is different?* The broadcast had come back from a break.

"...The midtown turnpike. On an average day, it loads an estimated 13,000 federal, state, and local authorities into the midtown government buildings, which have over time consolidated into the area known by most as 'Fed Park.' But Fed Park would sit almost completely empty today.

"At seven thirty-eight, a garbage truck was heading west on the turnpike, and had just entered the two-lane exit that merges with 38th Street and heads toward Fed Park. As most people know, this exit heads up to the 38th Street overpass bridge, and is quite steep. Eye witness reports tell us that the truck, taking up both lanes, slowed to a stop just as it reached the top of the steep entrance to the bridge. All traffic came to a stop behind it.

"This is where our information becomes more reliant on eye witnesses, who differ over the details. Most reports say that without any warning, the back of the garbage truck opened, and quick-dry cement began pouring out and down the steep exit ramp. The two cars directly behind the garbage truck were covered entirely, and the men inside barely able to escape. Behind those two vehicles, the cement crept down past three or more commuter vehicles before it dried into an immovable mass.

"As you can see in this video from our traffic heli, an emergency road crew has finally been mobilized at this late hour, and the huge earth-movers you see here are already shoving the cement aside. The first two cars are still trapped in the cement. Experts believe it will take about sixteen more hours to fully clean up the mess and allow access again."

"You are a violent maniac," Dex said, smiling up at his doctor. Thelo gave an extra hard pull on the stitch, which made Dex wince, and said: "There's a cliché somewhere about a pot, kettle and the color black, but I'm not going near it."

"...It was first believed that this was a freak accident, and early reports on almost all frequencies cited city sources as saying that there had been a contained spill of concrete, and that all Fed Park-bound traffic should reroute onto the 25 freeway to get to work. This, unfortunately, exacerbated problems on I-25, and led to more agency workers being stuck than would have been the case otherwise.

"Required employees spent the next six hours navigating the crammed city streets, looking for a path into work. Ultimately, helis from the DMV were used to evacuate certain troopers, staff, and administrators that were required to sort through the mess and get the city back on its feet.

"But such actions would come too late.

"Before we get too far into the fallout from today's attack, let's finish describing the terrorists' work. They still had one more target: the northbound 625. Because of the timing, the Full Story was fortunate enough to have a traffic copter near the action. And we weren't the only ones. Due to a training exercise at Fort Carson, the DMV had three traffic-control units at the south end of GMFR, rather than the usual single flyer."

"Crackpipe, one of those copters was the damn media?" Dex asked.

"Did no one tell you?" Thelo was genuinely surprised.

"They caught me on tape?"

"Uh, yes."

"Pull me up! I gotta see this!"

"We're not done yet, I still gotta—"

"Later!"

Thelo moved out of Dex's way, and helped him to a sitting position.

"...We spoke to DMV officials, who told us that they had pieced together the event rapidly, and were able to relay the gravity of the situation to the local flyers, who put immediate chase to the final garbage truck. Its exact destination was unknown, but counter-measures began at once. Note in this footage that there are also four trooper vehicles on the ground. According to the DMV, they were involved in the training exercise as well.

"It may not be clear from the footage, but that truck is traveling at speeds in excess of one-hundred miles an hour. We caught about six minutes of the chase, but skipping forward now, to seconds before one of the most gut-wrenching scenes ever witnessed by this reporter. No doubt you've already seen this footage a hundred times today, but we feel it's worth reviewing one last time.

"As you can see, the truck begins to slow, and the troopers slow with it, expecting the override commands from the flyer to bring it to the shoulder safely. But instead, it takes a hard left... and almost makes it through a maintenance gap in the concrete median between the southbound and northbound lanes. But the impact here... sends the truck careening wildly into the oncoming traffic, where it topples over and is immediately hit by two–then three–commuter vehicles. The pile-up totaled nearly fifty commuters, as the automatic buffering chip in the first vehicle didn't process the information of a vehicle breaking through the sideways opening on the freeway. The truck also failed to send any collision warning data. Therefore, no information on the collision could be passed on. This case couldn't possibly have been accounted for in the V2V coms systems of the commuter vehicles."

Dex suddenly realized that the room had gone quiet, and everyone was looking at him. *They want to know how I did it. They think I'm a magician or something.* He began to lie back down.

"It ain't over yet, Dex," Thelo said, nodding toward the display. You're about to be a star."

Dex turned back to the display.

"...and as the accident unfolded, our camera operator was focusing on the long line of vehicles slowing down into the southern distance. But in the bottom right-hand corner, watch carefully. We've digitally enhanced this out-of-focus area.

"That is a person, jumping off the hood of a wrecked commuter, diving to the ground, and then... he disappears."

"After returning to the scene, the Full Story was able to determine that the terrorist rolled directly into a storm drain. This was confirmed by DMV officials on site. Those same officials are currently concentrating their search for the terrorists in the shanty towns of the underground storm drains.

"That's too grainy to gather any data from," Dex said, squinting at the TV.

"Let's hope," Thelo said.

"...at seven forty-one. By eight o'clock, every major entrance into the city was blocked by an unmoving traffic jam. As the news spread, commuters began trying every conceivable alternate route, only to find that everyone else was doing the same. Within an hour, accidents due to the concentration of commuters on non-regulated roads began to multiply. The buffer signals from the mag-lev don't exist outside the primary freeways, and most drivers have become accustomed to using the signals to regulate their speed and proximity to other vehicles. So the damage of the impossible amount of traffic on the non-federal roadways rose steadily throughout the day. The number of incidental accidents overwhelmed an understaffed DMV, and they could not respond to even a fraction of incidents.

"By nine o'clock, the entire city of the Greater Metropolitan Front Range had come to a standstill. Businesses shut down for the day–if they ever made it in to open them up, that is. At nine-thirty, the governor-general put out the order for anyone still at home to stay there. He pleaded with the good folks of this city to stay off the streets. By ten, the order had been upgraded to an official moratorium, and anyone found driving would be cited for illegal traffic. The Old Grenver Exchange froze trading for the first time since the Great Floods of '06. The Exchange expects to remain closed through tomorrow. Of course all school districts have cancelled classes for today, and tomorrow as well.

"Reports came in of entire groups of citizens leaving their vehicles on the freeways, most of them still running. This proved catastrophic on southbound I-25, where the first garbage truck was removed. By that time, however, the highway could not be cleared unless these individuals came back for their abandoned vehicles, or they were towed away. But access to tow-trucks was limited to availability. As of this report, most major highways are still obstructed by abandoned vehicles.

"Cleanup concentrated on clearing drivable routes through the highways to get required workers in and out of the city to facilitate further cleanup and investigation. That cleanup is still slow going, but city officials assured me that there was the possibility that the driving moratorium would be lifted for most freeways by the weekend.

"Back to you, Doug.

"Thanks, Deborah. Have you been able to find out anything about the mounting investigation into the attack?

"Doug, the DMV is spearheading that investigation, along with the FBI, and right now they are staying pretty tight-lipped. They do believe that an organization known as the Urban Rebel League, or the URL, is behind the attack."

Everyone cheered at this, including Dex and Thelo.

"The URL, sources claim, has been behind similar acts of metro mayhem, but they noted that, until today, URL incidents have amounted to no more than large acts of vandalism, or political protests, but nothing this wide-spread. In fact, one of our sources inside the DMV felt that such an organized, large-scale assault could not have been planned by a small group such as the URL, and claimed, I quote, 'The URL amounts to little more than just another street gang, reminiscent of those that roamed the cities at the turn of the millennium. With something like this, well, you have to assume someone else is pulling the strings.' End of quote."

Everyone shouted protests and groans at the display.

"Okay. Thanks again, Deborah. That is all for tonight's Full Story. Be sure to catch our morning edition, available for purchase every weekday morning at six, when we will provide the latest on this horrific act of terrorism, and the manhunt for the culprits behind it. I'm Doug McDonough; good night."

Dex lay back down and Thelo went back to work on the stitches. Everyone slowly cleared the room, heading for their beds. Dex closed his eyes, trying to relax, but his heart was racing. They had done it. Brought the whole town down to its knees.

He reached up to touch the cut running down his face. A small price to pay for that kind of mayhem, he decided. And he had to give kudos to Money for helping out with that code on his little portable. As he closed his eyes he remembered their conversation a few days back.

"There's a race condition," Money had said.

"I don't know what that means," Dex had said. The two of them were sitting comfortably on the ratty old couch in the makeshift headquarters. The overhead light was dim, but they both had their portables on and the light from the screens lit up their faces. Dex was leaning over and staring at Money's screen.

Money sighed, pushed his spectacles up to his forehead, and rubbed his eyes. "Dex, I think it's great that you're serious about coding, but I really need to concentrate on this."

"Bollocks," Dex said. "Tell me what a race condition is."

"It's when one software routine is reliant on another routine to occur at a certain time, but it doesn't wait. So it keeps racing, looking for the other routine, but never waiting for the information to be returned."

"Like, I ask you a question, but before you answer I just ask you again. And before you answer I just ask you again." Dex tried.

"Well said."

"See, I'm not slowing you down. So the race condition is a good exploit?"

"I thought so. That's why we built that loop code."

"The stuff yesterday?"

"Right."

"I didn't catch all of that."

"Doesn't matter, Dex. I want to catch the race condition and give it a count to infinity. But there's a problem. The race condition was fixed."

"Crack, Money. How do you know about it then?"

"Because it's sloppy code, that's why. They didn't track down the underlying race; they just created another routine to watch for the race condition. When it's discovered, the new routine gets the right answer and inserts it into the asking routine at the correct interval." Money turned to his portable and slammed his hands into action.

Dex loved it. He wanted to make his hands work magic across the keyboard like that. Have tricks, like Money. Better yet, like Mal.

Money was done. "Watch," he said. "I've generated code to make this light flash as my simulation of the triangulation beacon heats up. Watch as it reaches its mark. Then it will download the override, which inserts the race condition into the brain's nav module.... right there." The blinking circle stopped at Money's breakpoint. "So, I just caught the race condition. And, theoretically, I could do just what the bug fix does–look for the race condition and then insert the answer, faster than the bug fix itself."

"Sounds great!" Dex said. He was actually starting to understand this stuff.

"Not so fast," Money said, typing. "Let me show you the window we have between the download of the overload protocol and the race condition fix." Money clicked his GO button and the circle flashed again, faster and faster. Finally it went solid, and then in a blink went from green to red.

"That was it?" Dex asked.

"That was it," Money said. He rubbed his neck. "We have to be able to kick off our software after the download protocol hits the brain, but before the race condition is fixed. It's a manual step. No way to engage the software that fast."

"Can I have that code?" Dex asked. "I'd like to look at it."

"Of course. It's worthless now though, Dex. We'll have to go in a different direction."

Twelve.

Thelo lay awake in his bedroll, staring up at the complete darkness of his small sleeping compartment. He'd retired early, after the broadcast had been turned off and he'd finished sewing Dex's destroyed face back together. There'd been something at the end of the broadcast that had caught his attention–after the story on the URL had come to an end. He'd finished dressing Dex's wound, and then made off to his room to think. Now he waited for everyone to finally get to sleep.

His memory of the day before had finally come back to him, as it always did after one of his episodes, and he was replaying yesterday's events. He had pulled his modified cement mixer truck up the exit. He'd thrown the back open, and then high-tailed it over the exit edge and down into the smelly underbelly of downtown Grenver. But instead of following his rehearsed path back to the URL headquarters, he had made his way deeper into the city, running the whole time.

He kept looking at his watch, and muttering about how big and cumbersome he was. Thelo did not recognize that part of town, but in his memory, he knew exactly where to go. He headed west for about twelve blocks, then three north, before ducking into an alley. He came to a fire escape, and pulled the ladder down.

After running up all the steps to the top floor, he climbed onto the roof. There, standing in the middle of the roof, was a man. The dead man off the news. Only he was not dead then, standing in his rich man clothes and his rich man shoes, all but untouched by blood.

And then the conversation. He still couldn't make any sense of it. But he had spoken to the man like he knew him, even though the man had asked 'Who the hell are you?" when Thelo had clamored over the roof's edge.

"I'm Moses," is what Thelo had said.

The man paused, and then nodded. "I hear that a lot, these days," he said. "But not everyone is the Moses I'm interested in talking to."

Thelo grinned. "You should have agreed to my terms. All of this could have been avoided."

The man shrugged. "No use dwelling in the past."

"Dwelling in the past," Thelo said, "is all I seem to do these days."

"That's funny. I get that."

"Did you intercept the package?" Thelo asked.

"No. Your message was... too cryptic; a little too late. We couldn't mobilize in time. Then someone from the copter shot at him.

50

With a gun. I thought maybe the legendary Moses could explain *that*."

"It's not exactly a hive mind type of thing."

"Still, you and yours are… unruly."

"No matter. You understand now that I can bring him to you."

The man shook his head. "I've called off the hunt. We don't need him."

Thelo felt his face reddening. "What do you mean, you don't need him? Of course you need him. The ghoster is lost to us. Only Dexter can help us now. After all of this time, he's the only one who can replicate the shift."

"No, Moses. I… I have hunted for this since I was a child. But I am an old man now. I am tired of chasing a far-off future. I have sacrificed so much of the present for the search."

"What about our deal? We've come too far!" Thelo roared.

"You spread like a disease. You threaten what we are trying to accomplish for the human race. You infect those around me so I cannot trust their intentions."

"The human race will be fine. Believe me. But you won't be there to see it. I can change that. Dexter is the secret."

"It's over. All of it. I'm shutting it down. Goodbye, Moses."

Thelo felt something snap inside his head: a last line being crossed, the anger in his head overwhelming his senses. He pulled out his fold-away knife and flicked it open.

Thelo looked down, expecting to see his small knife. But instead of a six-inch blade, he was holding a grey-white sword in his hand, with strange symbols running up and down the blade. It already had blood on it. He looked back up at the man, but it wasn't the nameless old stranger he saw, it was Dex, and he was on his knees, bleeding from his abdomen and face, his curly black hair too long and hanging in his face. They were no longer on top of a building, but surrounded by corrugated metal and hospital equipment, on all sides, and it was hot. Too hot.

Thelo heard himself say "I win, clone-boy," and then swung the blade at Dex's exposed neck, cutting through flesh and bone with ease.

Thirteen.

Thelo woke with a start, his heart racing, his bedroll drenched in sweat. He threw off his threadbare blanket and sat up. He closed his eyes, hoping it had all been a dream. But it wasn't. He had stabbed that man to death. The part about Dex, though—that must have been a dream. But even that had felt real, as real as all his blackout memories. But Dex was alive, sleeping soundly next door, a massive cut healing down his face.

He clicked the small light on. It was three AM, and the entire facility was quiet. Thelo stepped into his shoes and tip-toed into the main meeting room. The display was still set up. He sat down at the terminal and pulled the recorded broadcast up. He queued past all the URL footage, until right at the end.

"...the manhunt for the culprits behind it. I'm Doug Mc-Donough; good night.

"Up next, we've got today's other headlines, including the murder of one of the true pillars of the GMFR business community. Also, an update on the so-called Millionaire's Disease followed by a recap of today's sports scores, and a special report on the latest addition to the Broncos' offensive arsenal. Stay tuned."

Thelo queued through the advertisements until the headlines banner came up. He chose "Top Stories" and then "CEO MURDERED." A click and whir, and the broadcast came up.

"In a disturbing turn of events, Jonathan Luckey, President and Founder of the GMFR-based medical cloning company MedBed, was found murdered today. With most investigators tied up in the traffic attacks, the murder was not discovered until late this afternoon. The forensic report claimed the body had been stabbed over thirty-two times throughout the upper torso and face. Officials state there are currently no leads, and no motive. Family members, dealing with the shock, said he had no known enemies, but could not explain what he was doing on the rooftop of a downtown tenement structure either. At this time, officials are treating it a botched kidnapping attempt, most likely to secure some kind of ransom.

"Business associates all claimed shock and horror at the attack, saying that Luckey had personally been involved in a new research project that was going to 'revolutionize the life-extending business.' Luckey is best known as the son of early twenty-first century technology magnate Mitchell Luckey. Jonathan went on to revolutionize what he called the 'hyper-aging business' –going into any line of product that prolonged life. When Luckey celebrated his 100th birthday in 2101, he claimed to have the body of a fifty-year-old, running a marathon to prove it.

"Luckey was 112 years old. He has no family, raising questions about where his vast fortune will go."

The screen went back to the headlines banner. Thelo breathed deeply. Jonathan Luckey. He did not recognize the name any more than he had the face. Thelo pulled down 'Top Stories' again, and chose "New Funding to look into bizarre mental disorder."

"The Center for Disease Control announced today a new initiative to track down the cause of a new mental disorder that has been flaring up among the country's richest families. Known in the vernacular as Millionaire's Disease because of the pattern of those affected, the bizarre disorder has yet to be fully classified and still remains something of a mystery. CDC officials stated that the disease manifests itself as a type of bipolar disorder, or multiple personality syndrome. Although those kinds of problems were thought to have been eliminated in 2075 when Praximol was approved by the FDA, this is different, CDC officials insist.

"Officials also dismissed rumors that the disease 'spreads' like a virus. 'There is simply no way a mental disorder of this nature could spread as an infectious disease,' one spokesperson said. 'It appears simply in the patterns in which it has been reported. But the CDC reiterates that there is no possible microbe that could affect a human's mental capacity in this way.'

"The first case of Millionaire's Disease was diagnosed over fifteen years ago, in 2097. It was thought to be a kind of dementia caused by exposure to certain experimental metals used in pilot programs conducted by the now-defunct medical company StemFirst. The early warning signs include blackouts, unusual behavior and voice patterns, and referring to oneself as a different person. Ultimately, the victim will turn violent and, if not properly treated, will experience increased epileptic attacks, followed by death.

"The CDC is urging anyone who feels they might be suffering from this disease to call this number, or to check themselves into a hospital immediately. If you know someone in the late stages of the disorder, please use the same phone number."

"Thelo? What are you doing?"

Thelo jumped and turned to see Mal standing behind him, watching the broadcast over his shoulder. He switched it off, and they were bathed in darkness. The only light came from Thelo's ajar door, silhouetting the figure of Mal. "Crack, Mal, you scared me."

"Sorry," she put her hand on his shoulder. "You can't sleep either, eh?"

"Killing time with the broadcasts Money left on this display."

"Yeah. I watched them earlier."

Thelo turned to her. "You know anything more about this Millionaire's Disease?"

Mal shrugged. "I've pored over the data. There's very little that's been put together. They do know that it's related to the chip implants naturalized citizens get. And only a certain type of chip: high-end ones—that's why they call it Millionaire's Disease. Anyway, so all the uns down here are safe."

Mal gave Thelo's shoulder a squeeze. "You're okay? You're all tensed up there."

"No, I'm fine. I mean, I'm worried—about the URL. We really stirred up the pot."

Mal gave a low whistle like an incoming mortar shell. "Yes.

Stirred it up good. I'm worried, too."

"They'll have everyone back on tomorrow at Fed Park. Then they'll start sweeping the tunnels, rounding everyone up. Like last time, only worse."

Mal sat down next to Thelo and sighed. "They've already ordered the sweep. Checked it out a few minutes ago. We really punched the DMV in the nuts."

"That we did, girl. That we did."

"We've made it through these sweeps before," Mal said, trying to muster her confidence. "I mean, there's no way they can find this bunker."

Thelo's mind was racing. He kept going over his conversation with Jonathan Luckey. Then he realized that Mal was waiting for him to say something. "Of course, girl," he said, throwing his huge arm around her shoulders. "This place is untrackable, unfindable, and, let's face it, unbearable."

Mal gave a little laugh, and hugged Thelo.

"I'm not so sure we're safe here." A voice came out of the darkness. Mal and Thelo turned to see Dex, the left side of his face buried in gauze and tape, walking toward them.

Thelo spoke. "Even with a concussion, the man cannot sleep."

"Too many dreams," Dex said.

Mal shuffled over, and pulled Dex down onto the bench next to her.

"Can I put my head on your lap, Mal? I thought I wanted to stand, but I think horizontal is better."

"Sure thing," Mal said. She played absent-mindedly with his curly black hair spread across her lap.

"So we're not safe?" prompted Thelo.

"Nope," Dex said. "What we got here is a snitch."

Fourteen.

Mal and Thelo sat speechless. Finally, Thelo said, "Impossible. Jones knows how to pick our kids. No way we got a rat."

"I agree," Mal said. "Why haven't they stormed in here yet? Why

55

did the traffic stunt go so well?"

"I can't explain everything," Dex said. "But I know what I know. And those troopers were expecting me down on 625."

Dex told them about all the clues he'd picked up when he had the moment on high jack: the four copters, the four brand new DMV cars, the low-level electronic snoop.

Mal was dubious. "That can all be explained, Dex. It doesn't mean they knew you were coming."

"Each one of those facts in isolation—maybe. But when they happen all together, it starts to look suspicious, right?"

"Sure," Thelo said.

"Mal, you did all the recon for the traffic stunt. When you looked through the DMV records, do you remember what the standard-issue traffic heli has for Wednesdays on the six-two-five?"

"Sort of," she said, thinking. "One pilot, one traffic trooper, an on-board 'puter with long-range frequency broadcasters. One hard-link to the Charts for instant record updates. Two safety-foam dispensers for disabling a fleeing offender. A taser, I think... that's about it."

Dex said, "Right. That's what you briefed us on. But when I came out from the truck, before I hit the storm drain, I looked up at the helis. They all had three people in them. And as I looked up, one saw me and pulled out a gun. Started shooting at me."

Thelo scoffed. "Your head is rattled. Troopers haven't had guns since '99, when they banned them from law enforcement agencies. They don't train with them or anything. Mal's data searches prove that."

"My head is definitely rattled, Thelo, but I know what I saw."

They were quiet for some time.

"A gun?" Thelo asked.

"A gun," Dex said.

"Not a taser?"

"A gun."

"A netter?"

"Nope. Fired bullets at me."

Mal said, "That changes everything, doesn't it?"

"Yes," Dex said.

56

"Who you think it is?" asked Thelo. "The snitch, I mean."

"Turnstyle," Mal said. "Has to be."

"That scared little ant won't shit unless I tell him he can," said Thelo.

"Only the three of us knew enough details to get an alert out," said Dex. "Except for..."

"Money," Mal finished for him.

Dex nodded. "Yeah, but... I just don't think it was him. I mean, everything adds up to him. He's got the contacts up the hill. He's got the cash to make it happen. But... I don't know. It seems like he has the most to lose."

"But who else?" asked Mal.

Thelo was thinking it all through. He was never that good at putting all the pieces together, not like Dex or Mal. But they didn't know everything. They didn't know about his blackouts. Or about Jonathan Luckey's fate. *And they don't need to.* He stood up.

"We don't have to know exactly who it is to know that we're all in harm's way right now," Thelo said. "But I know what to do about it."

"And what's that, big guy?" Dex asked, closing his one eye.

"Disband the League."

Fifteen.

"Crackpipe," Dex said, sitting up. "Don't you think you're over-reacting a little?"

"No. It's the only safe thing to do."

"Mal, help me out here," Dex said. She just sat there, and in the dark he couldn't see her face. "Come on, Mal, you don't think he's right?"

"I... I don't know," Mal put her head in her hands.

"Listen, Dex," Thelo said. "I don't mean for good; not forever. But under the circumstances, I think we need to get everyone out of here; disband. We'll set a signal for everyone to reconvene after things have settled down a little."

"But we'll never know who ratted us out."

"Maybe, maybe not. It'll give us all some time to figure out a good way to smoke out the cheese-eater. In the meantime, everyone is safe."

"Where would we go? Where would anyone go?" Dex was pacing back and forth now. "We recruited these kids off the streets, remember. It's not like they have anyone to go stay with. Any resources to live on. Except for Money, of course."

"I don't know, Dex. I'm not the brains of this group. I just know we have to get everyone away from here for a while." *And away from me*, Thelo thought.

"Go wake up Money," Mal said all of a sudden.

"What?" Dex and Thelo asked at the same time.

"Go wake up Money. He's got an account, a personal one. Untrackable credits. We'll cash it out, distribute it. Like severance or something."

"Yeah, that's good," Thelo said, standing up.

"Crack, Mal," Dex said, shaking his head. "I can't believe you want to do this."

"Thelo's right," she said. "This place won't be safe. All of us together like this, it's a bad idea. The Charts are lit up, and I mean on *fire*. This thing we did, it rolled downhill fast. Other cities felt the slowdown in commerce. People lost millions of dollars. The Federal Bureau has got to either find us, or find someone they can blame this on. And fast. The amount of people they already put on ice is unbelievable. All the booth station operators. Newbury's entire organization. Everyone."

Dex saw the fat woman in her booth, sweating even on a cold September morning. *Roseanne*. He didn't want to feel bad for her. But he did.

"I'm doing this, Dex, whether you agree with it or not," Thelo said.

"We worked so hard for this place; for this team," Dex said, but he knew he wasn't changing any minds. "And we're gonna let a witch hunt tear it all apart?"

"We'll rebuild it," Thelo said.

"I don't want to rebuild it!" Dex said. He staggered to his feet, still dizzy. "There's a war here, Thelo. Right? Isn't that what we do this for? The struggle? They're reprogramming people up there, one at a time, inserting a tech chip and a chem drip in each and every person so they can regulate them. Then they wire them into those slogan-spewing broadcasts so that they've got 'em coming and going. They don't know it, but we're all that stands between tyranny and freedom. Right? Isn't that what we always say? And you, you wanna take a year off. Catch some rays on a beach somewhere in South America maybe, top up your tan? Why don't you use that really useful mess of grey matter up there to think about who ratted us out. Good plan, Thelo. Good cracking plan."

"Dex, settle down," Mal said, reaching for him.

"And you! You're the one that convinced us all that this is a fight worth fighting. You with your mysterious free pass to the Charts. You with your righteous war. What happened to your fight, Mal? Where'd all the fire go?"

"Fuck you, Dex," Mal said, standing up. "You know what we have done lately for The Cause? Nothing but a bunch of Money-inspired pranks. He's got us convinced that stopping traffic for the day will set the world free. But did it? Or did it just piss everyone off enough to finally come exterminate us for good? You ever 'high-jack' the moment enough to think of that?"

"Fuck you back." Dex stormed away, out the front bunker door and out of the headquarters.

Thelo put his hand on Mal's shoulder. "I'll go get Money."

She didn't say anything, but he could feel her shaking with tears. He let go, trying to pretend he saw nothing, heard no sobs. *Next time I see that little prick, I'm gonna smack him in the ear for hurting her like that.*

Sixteen.

Dex had a place to go that he had never told anyone else about. It was a place he went to in those few moments he desired loneliness. He'd found it when he was younger, maybe fifteen, when he and Thelo had been separated after a mugging above ground. A trooper had been close by, and chased Dex down into the storm pipes, barking into his com the whole time. Dex had been so scared, back then, fresh out of the orphanage and new to scrapping along for a living, he hadn't known the tunnels that well and had just kept running.

He had taken a few wrong turns, and ended up near the western edge of the storm drain complex, near where they went uphill and connected with the inter-mountain drainage system. This was where they would have collected the rain overflow that came down from the mountain houses and the construction sites. They had built a series of collector pits, Dex had discovered, where they intended to run the water into so as to capture it for use. But after all the drainage systems had been built and no rain had come, they had been forgotten.

But Dex had found them. He'd gotten lost, and scared, and he'd seen the entrance tunnels above him, so he'd climbed up into them. He had found a series of concrete rooms, about ten feet by ten feet each. They were all attached by a three-foot hole at the top, where water could flow from box to box, like an ice-cube tray. There had been all kinds of water purification equipment, charcoal filters, and the like.

That first time, he hadn't believed they would remain empty for long. Fresh air purified by the water filters flowed in through the aeration pipes, and Dex just assumed there would be squatters in them any day. But nobody ever seemed to find them. He had retraced his steps a hundred times to the location, always by himself, and had never found a trace that anyone else had been there. So he moved most of the equipment out, built make-shift ladders, and started to use the space for collecting little things. Little things to try to remind him of himself. Here was where he tried to remember. Remember where he came from. Who he was.

He could have told Thelo. But he didn't. When Mal joined their little band, he'd thought about showing her, but then life had gotten complicated, fast. With Mal around, he hadn't needed the collection rooms. Hadn't needed all his little things to convince him he was real. With her, he knew that he existed.

But tonight, he'd come back here. With the URL falling apart, he needed to run. He didn't even know he was coming back to the collectors until he was already here, climbing up to the shaft, and squeezing through the entrance. He closed his eyes, inhaling the cool, fresh air that was wafting down through the collection pipes. The water filters hyper-distilled the air, even as it came directly off the mountains. The place was pitch dark, the kind of dark that you only find in a cave. He reached to his right and found the small candle. The lighter was still there, too.

By the flicker of the candlelight, he looked around his claustrophobic retreat. It must have been two years since he'd last set foot in here. Very little dust found its way in, so everything stood as he had left it. The dirty little stuffed elephant. The old car license plate. The drawing pad of real paper, with his childish sketches. Always pictures of the dream. The burning surface, the reorganization. His collection was a random assortment of things. They were all well-worn; they meant something.

In the far corner there was a low table he'd assembled from bricks he had brought up, one at a time. On the table was a single plastic jar, about the size of a child's hand. He picked it up, and gave it a shake. The contents clinked around inside, and Dex smiled. He popped the top of the jar off, and turned it upside down.

He caught four little bones in his right hand. Three from his left pinky, one from his left ring finger. He rolled them around in his palm, feeling the rounded edges, the sharp corners. They felt almost polished from being handled so often.

He'd screamed the first time the orph doctor had strapped him down and slowly, surgically removed the top bone of his pinky. He'd screamed and screamed, pleaded with him to stop; pledging: he'd do it, whatever the doctor wanted.

But he didn't stop. He didn't say anything until he was done, dropping the finger in the jar of formaldehyde. Dex had been sobbing, barely able to breathe, and Dr. Johansson had come back and leaned over his face, real close so that Dex could smell that corn-chip breath. He'd said calmly, "Every time you say no, I take a piece of your hand. No exceptions. Do you understand?"

Dex understood. He understood everything after that. He understood why everyone was missing the top of their left pinky finger. He understood now why Jones had no fingers, no toes, no eyes. And he understood why no one talked about it. They were prisoners. No one was coming to save them.

Who were they to save, anyway? And Johansson, leaning over him that first time, had made it very clear. "You are nobody, Dexter. You are not a real person. You're a mistake of this society, nothing more. They throw you away because you serve no real purpose, and you could expose their darkest secrets. However, you have a purpose to me, Dexter. Now you serve *my* purpose. But I do not tolerate dissent."

He didn't fight for some time after that, while his finger healed to an ugly stub. But then Johansson would call him into his office, and Dex's blood would go cold, his vision red. And he'd go in, and pretend to comply, then bite, or hit, or curse the doctor to the depths of hell. He'd fight. And whop, there'd go another digit.

And whenever Dex lost a digit, Thelo would see it. He'd get called in next, and sure as hell he'd come out missing a digit, too.

The doctor didn't call Jones in anymore. There was nothing left of him to take.

One day, Johansson came back from somewhere, happy. You could tell he was happy because he immediately began calling the boys into his office for appointments. He called Dex in first, and talked the whole time about a new implant experiment, and how all his boys would get drips finally so he could control them with a push of a button.

It was that night they finally did it. Thelo and Jones and he finally found a way to bust out. Before they left, Dex had snuck into Johansson's examination room and turned the water on in the sink, plugged the drain, and left the water running. Then he had cut the cable on the broadcast display and left the live wire on the floor. He'd grabbed his jar, and Thelo's jar, and left. Jones didn't want his jars. There were too many to carry, he'd said. At the time, his empty eye sockets still drove Dex mad with anger; he still saw Jones' blindness as a sign of weakness.

Dex opened his eyes and pushed the memories back. He put the bones back in the jar.

The part that always made Dex the maddest was that the doctor had been right. He had been right then, and if the sick ol' doctor said the same thing now, he'd still be right. Dex was nobody. Discarded by his parents, left for dead after a car accident that had wrecked his memory, he wasn't even a real person. A sewer kid who had outlived his sewer-kid existence. What do you do when there are new sewer kids to replace you: younger, meaner kids still willing to fight for survival?

At least with the URL, he had people to live with. Somewhere to focus the hate. He never really bought into the ideology, into the politics. But it gave him something to do. Gave him an excuse to dance with the devil. Without it, well, what did he have? Dex felt a sensation not unlike vertigo, staring straight down from the top of a skyscraper, and he wondered to himself, *how to get down?*

Seventeen.

The concrete walls echoed even worse when the place was empty. Dex tried to step into the URL shanty quietly, but there was no disguising his footsteps. Not that it mattered. All the furniture that could be removed had been; the maps on the walls, the electrical wiring taped everywhere, the broadcast receivers, everything had been taken down, folded away, and packed out.

Dex walked through the main room and back to his compartment. All his stuff was there, for what it mattered. The bed roll. His banged up portable, with all his adapters and mini-receivers. His second pair of shoes. The blood-soaked driver's clothes. He shoved the portable and all the attachments into his backpack. He grabbed the single lantern that hung from the ceiling, too. Then he turned to leave.

Mal was standing there, looking relieved and scared at the same time.

"I wasn't sure you'd come back," she said.

Dex gave her a resigned smile. "Had to get my stuff," he said, walking out past her. But at the last minute he noticed her shoulders start to sag, and grabbed her hand and gave it a pull that ended in a hug. They held onto each other for a long time.

"Where's Thelo?" Dex asked.

"Still here," Mal said, her face buried in his shirt. She sniffed and looked up. "He's waiting for you, too."

She led him back down the long hallway to the second set of rooms. All the doorways were open, empty, and dark. A single lantern still hung in the hallway, but the candle had virtually burned down to the wick and flickered weakly. Dex thought of the sunlight that comes through the trees when you are driving.

Thelo was in the second common room, sitting in the middle of the open space, rolling cable methodically into rings. He looked up, gave a smile. "I promised myself the next time I saw you, I'd hit you," he said.

Dex put up his hands, offering acceptance. "Here I am. Let me have it."

Thelo jumped to his feet, and lurched at him. But it was a hug. "I break my promises all the time, you know that," he said. "Help me with all this. It's hard to find these days, and we'll need it for later."

The three of them sat down in a circle, and began rolling the cable into manageable lengths, before cutting and taping it. Thelo had found a number of large canvas bags, which they stuffed the wiring into.

"So," Mal said.

"So," Thelo said.

"So, where are we headed?" Dex asked.

Thelo sighed. "I'm going my own way this time."

Dex stopped rolling, but didn't look up. He started rolling again. He said nothing.

Thelo studied his friend, and continued. "It's for safety–everyone's safety."

Mal was looking back and forth between her two favorite men. Finally, she spoke up. "That's crazy talk, Thelo. We're always better off together, us three."

"Not this time," Thelo said softly. "Not this time."

All had been taped and put in the bags. There was nothing left to do.

Thelo stood up and grabbed the bags. "I love you, Dex," he said. "And I love you, Mal. Know that." Then he walked out the door.

Dex didn't move until the ache in his had jaw subsided and there was no chance he would shed a tear. Then he grabbed Mal by the hand and got to his feet, pulling her up with him.

"You got all your stuff?" he asked her.

"Yes," she said.

"Then let's get outta here. There's someplace I want to show you."

Eighteen.

They cashed out their combined allotment of Money's credit above ground, and picked up as much food as their packs would hold. Dex led Mal to the collector basins, and helped her through the bottom valve opening first, before pulling himself up.

Mal said nothing. She just walked around the small concrete cube, looking at all of Dex's strange possessions, touching some of them.

And they made love, in the dark. It felt like old times, when they were just two sewer kids looking for a way to remind themselves they were still alive. And maybe also keep warm into the bargain. When they had exhausted themselves, they would sleep, or eat something.

Dex started to talk. He told Mal everything. About finding the basins, and hiding out up there for weeks at a time. About the orphanage, and Dr. Johansson. About Jones, and Thelo, and getting free. He showed her the contents of his jar.

And then he told her about everything before that, what he remembered. Strange snapshots of adults that didn't seem to love him, nor he them. They were the faces he called parents, but could never really be sure. His memories were so muddled before the orphanage. He remembered hospital settings, and being surrounded by equipment. There were memories of running, laughing with a person he thought of as his dad. He told her about the car accident, or at least the part he remembered, which was being dragged out of the mess of steel and protection foam by a DMV officer. How his memory skipped forward, to the orphanage, and how he hadn't been able to remember his own name, or anything about his parents or who he was.

Mal just listened. She knew he needed to tell her these things. And she wanted to know. But deep down, she knew that there were things she needed to say, too.

Two weeks went by, and they barely left the basins. Being this close to the surface, Mal found easy signals to jack into, and she monitored the Charts for activity. The DMV troopers had found the URL headquarters, and it had made the news. There was a lot of video footage of the torn down headquarters making the rounds. Other than that, they had made no progress in the investigation, and life started to go on again above ground, much as it had before the traffic stunt.

Mal and Dex would lie in bed and make up stories about Dex's childhood. That his parents were anti-government spies working to bring the corporations down. Another time they were tragic lovers from warring families who had a love-child that was left to his own devices after the families killed the lovers. After one such story, after they had stopped laughing, and Mal was lying across Dex's chest, he kissed her forehead and said, "Let's not change a thing. Let's just the two of us do this. I don't want anyone else in the world to know me but you."

"Nobody else?" Mal asked.

"Nobody. Just you and me, here in the basins. We can pretend that this is all that matters."

Mal closed her eyes. "Yes. Let's pretend."

Nineteen.

Under the pretext that they needed to restock their food supplies, Mal headed for the surface. She had never felt nausea like this before, and she wanted to see if she could walk it off.

And she needed to talk to Jones.

She stayed hidden underground as long as she could, and even once she was up, she stayed away from the bustle of civilization. Her eyes would be showing now; she would be no good to anyone if an iris scanner tried to get a read on her. Besides, it wasn't like Jones was out someplace with a lot of detection tech lying around.

Without looking up, she walked quickly past the old strip malls. There was a lot of commerce still taking place here. But she wasn't buying; or selling, for that matter. The sun had gone down quickly, like it always does when there are mountains to the west, and the late autumn air bit at her ears and nose. She'd forgotten about the sun, having been under for so long, and it had felt good to get a little sunlight while she could.

After the old strip malls, there was the old burbring. Barely erect houses, crammed too close together, with depressing weed growth across the broken concrete roads that spun wildly in nonsensical arcs and unexplainable dead-ends. What did they call them? *Cul-de-sacs.* She pondered over the kind of sick sense of humor that invented cul-de-sacs. *How could you live in a dead-end?*

There was a sense of quiet in the old burbring that was unnatural. It was the silence of people living where they weren't allowed. Her very presence after sundown was an affront to the squatters hiding behind every closed door—if a heli saw her, they would be forced to grab her and it would lead to awkward media questions about the possibility that there were actually large numbers of people living in these condemned areas of the city.

It was like that old saying, "Don't ask, don't tell." That was how everyone thought about the old burbring. One step up the economic ladder from the sewer dwellers, the old burbring squatters typically tried to make it back into regular society. They'd live out here, scrape up enough cash for a chip implant so that they could qualify for government-approved employment, legal tender, credit, you name it. You put a chip in your head, and your life got better. It wasn't just a slogan, it was real life. Mal had seen it.

She found the house she was looking for. There was a well-worn old couch out on the front porch, sunken in the middle from the daily weight of a single person. Hanging above the couch was a set of small metal pipes of different lengths. They were strung up in a circular arrangement around a wooden circle that the wind would blow about, creating a peaceful tune. *Chimes*, Jones would say. *They used to call them wind chimes.* This was Jones' perch; all day, every day. She knocked gently on the door.

"Come on in, it ain't locked," came a voice from inside.

Mal opened the door and stepped inside. The smell of rotting carpet and old wood that lingered behind the smell of disinfectant surprised her. She hadn't been in a house in long, long time. She reached out and touched the plaster, just to see what it felt like. It was so much smoother than concrete.

She was standing in a huge, imposing room, the kind that was popular a hundred years ago. There was nothing actually in it, but it was very clean. Jones had a lot of fans, and they did plenty for him.

"I'm in the kitchen," the gravelly voice said. "Making some damned toast. You want some damned toast?"

"Yeah, I'll have some damned toast," Mal said with a smile.

"Mal!" Jones was genuinely surprised. He emerged from the kitchen, hobbling as usual. He had taken his shoes off, and Mal could see his toeless feet. He had taken his dark glasses off, too, and his empty eye sockets stared out into the great room like holes in the universe. He wore the same dirty baseball cap with a Broncos horse on it. The old logo–back before they'd changed it again. Underneath, his smile was wide, genuine, and had that touch of the mischievous. He held out his hands, his greeting to everyone. All fingers were missing.

Mal lifted his outstretched palms to her face. He felt his way around her face, gently, and she closed her eyes. She loved Jones' hello. She wished for it every day.

"Somethin's different," Jones said. "You've put on some weight."

"Hey, is that any way to talk to a girl?" Mal said.

Jones turned back toward the kitchen, waving his arm dismissively. "It's about time. You sewer folks are always a stone's throw from dead, the way you eat."

He attached a prosthetic device to his forearm that had a rudimentary set of pinchers at the end. He used it to turn on the gas stove, and then put a piece of bread directly on the burner.

"These days, it seems all I can do is eat."

"The will to live strikes at the oddest times."

Mal smiled. "And not-so-odd times, too."

Jones nodded. "It's pretty much non-stop."

Mal looked around. "Someone left all your lights on."

"Really? Must've been li'l Tony, from next door. He comes over and cleans up the place. He runs untaxed tobacco up from the south. The farmers are really getting hammered down there."

"I've heard."

"Here's your toast. You know, that little stunt of yours cost li'l Tony a lot of money. They rounded up all the low-costers from the toll stations. They still haven't worked out a new network yet."

"I'm sorry."

Jones sniffed. "You should be. If that little organization of yours was worth anything, you'd stop playing with traffic and head out of town; get to work in the farmland. That's where help is really needed."

"We're not a welfare group, Jones."

Jones flipped his toast. He was good at it, just the right amount of brown on both sides. "Maybe you should be, Mal."

Mal sighed. "You're right, Jones. The highway trick was a gimmick. A pointless, dangerous gimmick. Sound and fury, signifying nothing."

Jones took a bite of his toast, and shrugged. "Dangerous, yes. But pointless? Well, the law of unintended consequences is at hand. You cannot know the future. And events like the one you and Thelo and Dex were behind just kind of roll downhill. You never know where a rock will roll when you push it off the top of a mountain."

"But *you* know the future, Jones."

Jones smile widened. "I see the present very clearly. There's a difference."

Mal sat down on one of the two chairs in the kitchen. Jones shuffled into the other. *How many years had they been doing this? How many times had they sat and ate plain toast in this kitchen?*

"Dex told me about the orphanage a few days ago. Told me about his hand. About your hands. Your feet. Your eyes."

"So my past is unraveling around me. There goes my mystique. Don't tell anyone, or all my company will dry up."

Mal smiled as she finished the toast. "Your secret is safe with me."

"You know, Dex holds onto those details about himself so tightly because he has so few of them. If you couldn't remember much about the first eight years of your life, you'd do the same. Don't fault him for his secrets."

"I don't."

"To let them go like that, he must really be in love with you. Not like that's a surprise."

"We've been getting closer, lately. After the highway trick."

"Without the URL, Dex has very little in his life."

"How did you know?"

"Thelo comes to visit, too, you know."

"Right. Thelo. How is he?"

Jones' face darkened for a brief moment, and then came back to life. But Mal saw it, and it scared her. "Thelo is struggling with demons right now," Jones said. "He was right to get away from those he loves."

Mal was quiet for some time. Then she said, "I have a secret that I am keeping from Dex."

"Is it the one I felt in your face?"

"Yes."

Jones sat quietly, rubbing the nubs of his lost fingers against the stubble on his chin. "That changes everything, I suspect."

"Everything?"

"Love is a gamble, isn't it? The problem with gambling is knowing when to put all your money on the table. All or nothing, to get the big payoff."

"I want the payoff. More than anything."

"Then I suspect you're gonna have to put everything on the table. Dex, he's a good kid, but he's had a tough go of it, like most people we know. That's not a judgment, see, it just means he's unpredictable. But I'll tell you what I know. First of all, Dex never really believed in the URL. It was just a way to keep his nightmares away. Second, Dex doesn't really believe in anything right now."

"Not even me?" Mal asked. Her heart was in her throat.

Jones reached out and found Mal's hand, easily. He stroked her long fingers with his palm. "Rich people in the world, Mal, they got it easy. All they have to believe in is the thing that made 'em rich and happy. It's not even believing really; they just know that what they got is pretty good and that they can live with it.

"Now, the desolate of this world, they're the ones that've gotta actually believe in something. They don't have nothin' else to go on. If they don't believe in something, well, they curl up with a pipe full of something, or a needle full of bliss, or they just curl up and die. Now, Dex, he ain't got nothin' less than anyone in the whole world. But he don't know what to believe in yet. He's lookin', though. He's looking desperately." He pulled his hand away from Mal's. "And that's all I got to say about *that*," he concluded. "More toast?"

"Please, I'll take another piece. For the walk back."

Twenty.

Thelo made his way to the penny shop quickly. The shop was a little hut at the end of the mainline drain tunnel. It sold the few essentials that the sewer people needed; mostly it gave them away.

Salomon Salazar ran the thing, a wrinkled old mass of sun-leathered skin and graying hair. Before the shop, he'd worked the migrant farm routes his whole life, always making just enough to get by on. When they started requiring chips for all work contractors, he had just walked away from the farms. "No cheep in thees noodle," he liked to say in his thick Spanish accent, slamming his worn old finger against his forehead.

Salomon also coordinated communication for the URL, and it was through him that Thelo had gotten the message. It had been a newspaper article, cut out of a Grenver paper, and delivered with the single word MONEY written on the back, along with URGENT: PENNY SHOP AT TEN TONIGHT. Thelo had been tempted to ignore it, but then he had read the headline.

MURDERED MEDBED CEO DEEP IN DEBT, LITIGA-TION UNDERWAY TO SETTLE.

The name of the CEO, Jonathan Luckey, had been underlined by Money with two hand-drawn exclamation points.

So here he was, at the penny shop. *What did Money know? And how did he know it?* Thelo walked behind the shop's sturdy frame, and found the metal plate that covered a jack-hammered hole in the tunnel's construction. There was a lock on the plate. Thelo fished in his pocket for the key, threw open the plate and stepped inside.

The storeroom was kept remarkably tidy, Thelo noted. It reminded him of Jones' house in the old burbring. As he absentmindedly starting going through the dry goods, looking for nothing in particular, he heard the metal hinge squeak behind him.

"'Ello, Thelo," Money said.

"Money," Thelo returned. He was trying to disguise how tensed up he felt. "Got your message, not sure what it means."

"It means," Money said with a smirk, "That you need to put the League back together—tonight."

And Thelo blacked out.

Twenty-one.

Mal was surprisingly calm when she made her way back to the collector basins. Jones had a way of doing that—making you feel at peace with things, no matter what they were. No matter what the gamble was. She pulled herself up through the bottom entrance.

"Dex?" she called. The place was completely dark. She touched the microlight that they had installed next to the entrance, and it slowly radiated a dull yellow through the small room. He wasn't there. "Dex?" Her calm was fading now that she was approaching the moment of truth. She wanted to get it out while she still had her Jones-buzz on.

She saw her portable power indicator blinking, and reached for it. There was a message. She tapped her passwords in, quickly. It was from Dex.

URL BACK TOGETHER FOR SINGLE NIGHT ENGAGE-MENT. THELO MADE CONTACT. MEET US AT THE PEN-NY SHOP ASAP!!

Then the message deleted itself. The calm was gone. The buzz was gone. Just like that. In its place stepped pure dread, bordering on panic. Mal threw the portable into her pack and headed back into the tunnels.

Twenty-two.

Mal carefully opened the heavy metal door to the storeroom, and heard their voices talking in an excited whisper. *Don't gamble your money on this hand. But what if it's the last hand?* Dex saw her first. His face showed unadulterated glee.

"Mal! Come here! You gotta see this!" Dex said, beckoning to her. He was hunkered down over what appeared to be a building blueprint with Thelo and Money. She walked over and sat down, throwing her pack off behind her.

"What's this about the URL?" Mal wanted to know. "What is this print?"

"It's the cloning facility up near the old orph," Dex explained. He didn't look at her, just straight down at the plans, as though trying to absorb the entire picture at once. "Up where they held us. Me and Thelo used to watch the trucks roll in and out the back of that place all day, right?"

Thelo looked up from the plan. "What? Yeah, all day. Seems like yesterday."

Mal's eyes burned into Thelo. *What were the demons Jones had spoken of?*

74

Dex nudged Money, who had a portable on his lap and was typing madly. "You tell her. It's your brainchild."

Money looked at Dex eagerly, then turned to Mal. "It was something I missed in all the noise surrounding the highway trick," he said, handing Mal a clipped article. "On the same day we shut down the city, MedBed CEO Jonathan Luckey was murdered. No big deal by itself, except it caught my eye. I worked for MedBed for three years, before I had my chip nixed. It was my experiences there that convinced me to drop my former life.

"Anyway, so I kind of kept my eyes open for follow up stories, you know, just out of curiosity. I've had a lot of time on my hands the last few weeks. Then I saw that story you're looking at now. Everyone thought this guy was rolling in it, but he'd sold the farm for some speculative project that he kept secret from everyone else. The project was lost when the guy bit it. With that much debt, the banks started lining up at the estate lawyer's door, wanting access to any material goods they could make off with. Houses, cars, boats, you name it. It's a feeding frenzy.

"The problem is, in order to hide the debt Luckey had gone to so many banks, through so many false organizations, third parties, that no one knows who's got first rights on all the goods. On his property. So the lawyers get involved, and the first thing they do is freeze all of Luckey's assets, so that no one can touch them 'til everything gets settled."

Money paused to catch his breath. Mal just looked at him, waiting. She wasn't sure where this was going yet, but she was starting to get an idea. And she didn't like it.

"I pulled the legal filing. It's some of the most comprehensive asset motions I've ever read; the banks really know how to make use of a good lawyer. No matter what, under any circumstances, nothing is to be done with the assets. Acts of God included, even burglary." His eyes were wide open now. "Well, like I said, I used to work at MedBed, at their primary cloner up at the north end. An interesting side note is that most orphanages exist near cloning facilities. Those facilities have a lot of extra space that they buy up around their buildings, so that they can install huge freezers underground, beyond the officially displayed boundaries. Then they sell off the land above ground, with clauses letting them keep anything below about twenty feet."

"Stay focused, Money," Dex said, winking at Mal.

"Right. When I worked up there, I actually had plenty of access. Really had my fingers in a lot of operations as a primary graft engineer–that meant I designed the process of putting a new hand on someone, or a new liver, or what have you, I made the process faster, cleaner, whatever–and so I roamed the halls a lot. Therefore I happen to know that one of Jonathan Luckey's primary assets is his body part collection."

"His what?" Mal asked.

"His body part collection. He was always getting new parts: a new pair of eyes, a new heart, and the like. If it was engineered to be better, he wanted it. You could say, he really believed in his own product. He'd get blood work done, they'd grow a new liver–only one that processed toxins more effectively–and then he'd go under the knife to have it put it in. Anyway, he's got this entire room up at the cloner that's just his body parts. Entire freezers of eyes, hearts, lungs, hands; whatever you can think of. They even tried a few brains, but they're decades away from getting that kind of tech done right."

Mal had caught up already. "But even if we steal his parts, what can we do with them? The guy's dead, Money."

The three men gave a laugh. "That's where we all have to tip our hat at the legal profession. When they froze Luckey's assets, they froze *everything*. His passwords, his access rights, everything. Frozen. Not disabled." Money said.

"And you know this for certain?" Mal asked.

"It's golden. I swear. We get a pair of eyes, some hands, and we can go anywhere we want in this town. Get anything we want. Or until the Feds figure out what's happening, anyway."

"I don't know, Money, it seems pretty–" Mal started, but Thelo interrupted her.

"We should come in from the north entrance, here," he said, pointing at the map. "That's where the cleaning service comes in, right?"

"Good guess, Thelo, that's where the night-help enters," Money said, staring at the map. "It's all old-school tech as far down as the third sub-level. Card entry, voice recognition."

"And you've already got us a card and a voice?" Dex asked.

"Yeah," Money said.

"What about eye scanners?" Mal asked. "They're gonna take one look at your eyes, and if you don't match the chip records, the alarms will go off and you're busted."

"MedBed uses only uns for its help. They claim it's a cost thing, but it's really a security thing. With the amount of illegal business we did up there, you couldn't have a bunch of wired janitors running around. You needed ignorant folk, ones too scared to take a piss. The turnover is so quick that they don't register anyone. When the eye scanners don't find a chip match, they treat you like a ghost. They rely entirely on cards and voice password recognition."

Thelo flipped the top print over, and another. "That gets us as far as sub-level three, here. But how do we get past these security checkpoints?" He was pointing at three different places in the blueprint.

Money looked at Thelo. "Again, an astute read on the floor plan. That level, it's basically just one big refrigerator once you get past the main entrance lobby. And all three of the security checkpoints require a nat's chip to code us through."

Mal looked expectantly at Money. "And?"

He was smiling. "And I called in a favor from the rent-a-cop that lets the night crew in to clean the coolers. He owes me from back when. He just codes his chip up at the three doors, and lets the janitors in. Happens every night, like clockwork."

"Crack, Money, they guy will get iced," Mal said.

"Naw, we're gonna pop his chip after we're done and put him on a train to the tobacco fields. Just another burn-out city man looking to make an honest wage in the country."

"What did you do for this guy?" asked Dex quietly.

"Stole a pair of eyes for his son," Money said. "The kid lost 'em in the digital burns of the late nineties. Don't worry about this guy. He's glad to be helping–there's no love lost between him and Luckey's organization."

"Why tonight?" asked Mal. "We really should think this through a little better, let it settle in. Work on some exit strategies."

"Has to be tonight," Money said. "Too many variables already lined up. Either we're a go, or we're a no-go."

"Then it's a no-go," said Mal, standing up. "The risk is too high."

Dex laughed, without looking up from the prints. Then he made eye contact, and his smile faded. "Crack, you're serious Mal. What's got into you?"

"Nothing. But we dismantled the team for a reason. There are safety concerns now."

Dex stood up. "We're not passing up this opportunity. It's fool-proof. There's hardly any risk, and the upside is beyond anything we've ever seen before. We can get into any building, through any security gate. Shit, if one of us did the surgery, we could even get on an *airplane*."

"I agree," Thelo said. "We're going. Money, make the call. Let's set it for 2 AM, that should give us enough time to prepare, and get there."

Money started typing frantically at his portable. Thelo rolled up the blueprints and snapped a rubber band around them. Dex was still staring at Mal, his eyes burning into hers. "Mal, can I talk to you alone for a second?" he asked.

They came out of the storeroom into the main storm drain. Street activity was picking up as the night crowds came out of their holes and began to creep up above ground to look through the trash and maybe mug the occasional nat caught alone in the wrong place. Salomon had unlocked his shop and had started to open up for the night. He nodded silently at the two of them as they emerged, then turned back to haggle with his first customer of the day.

"Mal, what's going on?" Dex asked. "You've been acting strange, getting all freaked out. Skittish, Thelo called it. Tell me what this is about."

"I don't feel good about this trick, Dex. I don't think we should do it. I mean, you said it yourself, there's a rat, it might be Money. He could be setting us up."

"That's not what I'm talking about, and you know it."

"Please, don't do this. Just listen to me this one time, and let's just go back to the basins."

"Goddamn it girl! Why you gotta ruin this? Doin' tricks for the URL is all I got! It's who I am. Sure, we might get caught, but what else am I going to do the rest of my life? If I don't get caught tonight, then it will be next week, or next year. It all ends the same, Mal, it's just a matter of when. Why should I be scared of it and run and hide–"

"I'm pregnant."

She said it so quietly it was barely audible. But he heard it. Dex looked at her, drilling into her eyes, trying to look past them into her head. Then he looked away.

"You're kidding, right? This is a joke." Dex asked, but he knew it wasn't. Mal just stood there, trying to catch his eyes again.

"No joke, Dex. This is the real thing. Two months in. It's a go."

"I can't believe this," he was pacing now. "I cannot believe this." Mal couldn't catch his eyes.

"Look at me," she said.

"I-I just can't *believe* this, I mean, right now? Right now? I mean... crackpipe, Mal."

"Look at me Dex! Look at me!" She grabbed him by the face and made him meet her gaze.

"I'm putting everything on the table here," she said. "I want this baby. I don't want them to take it from me."

Dex gave a cynical snort. "But how is that going to work? It's illegal, Mal, you know that. You won't be able to go anywhere near a hospital. And I've seen the women down here, trying to give birth. The babies don't live, Mal. At least they don't live for very long."

She was crying now. "I know, but we can think of something, I know we can."

"We? What's this 'we' shit?" Dex said, shaking free of her grip and backing away. "You drop this on me right now, and you're talking like I'm gonna be a part of it? Think again, Mal. I never signed up for the family package."

Mal could barely see through her rage. "What, do you think I did this on purpose? You think I made a decision about this? Fuck you, you self-absorbed little bastard! We both made this! I didn't do it to myself!"

The metal door to the storeroom flipped open, and Thelo and Money emerged, laughing. Mal turned away to hide her tears, but the two clearly sensed something was up.

"What's the matter, Dex?" Money asked.

"Just a little something between Mal and me," he said.

"So are you up for this or not?" Thelo asked, handing Dex his pack. "Because we have to go now."

"Yeah," Dex said, taking the offered pack, but never moving his eyes from Mal's back. "Yeah, let's do this thing."

"What about you, Mal?" Money asked carefully. "I've got a car lined up to get us there. We need a driver."

Mal turned, her face wiped clean of everything. Tears, emotions, everything. "Yeah, I'll drive, but I'm not going in."

Twenty-three.

It was that brutal cold of the high mountain desert, where there's no cloud in the sky. The wind had been whipping down all week and had cleared the smog.

It had left behind a sense of calm and a sharp cold that stung at Dex's face. He covered his ears with his hands. He spent so much time underground that he often forgot how cold the nights could be with all that open space above you. They parked in the 'muter lot outside the old orphanage, and had to walk through the carbon processing park that separated the lot from the cloner.

The nearly-full moon stared down at them, the dull grey light making the trees look taller and more foreboding than usual. The artificial trees all ran the same height of fifty feet–massive pillars that must have been ten feet in diameter at the base. The pillars narrowed and then branched out into groupings of massive, flat panels attached by flexible armed branches and looking very much like uniform, rectangular leaves. Below the canopy of leaves, a complex web of pipes and feeds reached from tree to tree, connecting them to each other in ways the eyes could not track in the low light. The effect was a stretch of land interspersed with cobwebbed giants that obscured both the sky and the way ahead.

Money caught Dex looking up at the trees. "It's called an Atrice Park," he said. "You often see 'em next to large private industry."

He pointed up. "The leaves at the top are bioreactors with solar panels. And see the tangle of pipes below the leaves that look like creeper vines? They connect all the trees over to Luckey's cloner fac. Half of 'em bring waste from the cloner to the trees. Like, carbon dioxide produced by generators and residual water. Then the trees use solar energy and a cocktail of micro-organisms to convert the waste into ethanol. The other half of the pipes carries the new fuel back to the cloner where it gets used to run the whole place. They even power their cars with it."

"Seems like a hassle," Dex said, looking at the trees as though for the first time. He'd stared at them for so long from the orph, he'd always just taken them for the usual artificial trees like they have out in the burbrings. "Why not just get electricity like everyone else? Seems like Luckey could afford it."

"Energy tracking raises big questions about what you are up to," Money said. "Trust me; tracking who uses electricity, when they use it, and how much—that's the future of surveillance and control. Life is a lot simpler if you are self-sustaining, and this park produces enough. Hell, enough gallons of fuel in a year to power one of your stunt trucks for a journey 'round the world. If they need more, they just plant another tree."

Dex looked down. "What do you suppose a real forest looks like?" he asked.

Money gave Dex a sad smile. "Everything is messy. More dangerous."

They walked on in silence. Their badges wouldn't work until they got to the back door of the facility, so they were left to good old-fashioned sneaking in the meantime. When they had parked at the orphanage, Dex had wanted to go break in and take a look around. See if ol' Johansson still stuck it to the kids. See if his secret route to the roof was still there.

But he hadn't. They left Mal to shiver in the parked car, waiting quietly in the dark for her friends to come back. She hadn't said a word to Dex, and his stomach was still digesting how loud the silence had been on the drive up. He could still hear himself yelling at her. Hear her crying. He'd never heard Mallory Aquinas cry before.

He looked over his shoulder, and from the hill, through the artificial trees, he could see her shape in the darkness, sitting unmoving in the empty parking lot of the orph. What a joke, installing parking at that place—like anyone with cars ever came, other than the DMV bus with the latest enrollees.

Money and Thelo walked next to him, briskly, their breath visible in the moonlight. Thelo was carrying his usual battered pack. But tonight it wasn't slung low over a single shoulder; it was squared in the middle of his back. In his left hand, he carried his fold-away blade. Dex thought it strange to see it brandished that way. Especially in his left hand.

Dex had left his pack in the car. There was nothing in it but his portable, which he'd left for Mal to use if she needed it. He'd offered it, but she had said nothing.

Money was kind of skipping to keep up with the two of them, his short legs incapable of the clip Dex and Thelo kept. He had a new pack on, one that seemed too large for his small body, with a waist-belt added for stability. It was the kind of pack rich kids always seemed to wear. He was glancing around at the trees warily, wondering what might jump out at him. Dex had to smile. The guy had probably never been out at night, on foot, in this part of town. He must be freaked, down to his core. By all accounts, he was doing great. Dex was really starting to like him, he realized. Liked having him around, his funny nasal voice, the intellectual confidence, the weird way he always went off on these tangents when he talked. Like he could barely keep his own brain on track.

The memorial was not that big, just a few acres. As they approached the low, two-story cloner, the artificial trees slowly began to thin, in that way peculiar to fake things. As they reached the last ring of trees, all three stopped without even realizing it. They stared across the hundred-yard clearing toward the driveway that connected the front gate with the basement door, sunken one story from the main level. The moon seemed very bright. Money glanced at his wristwatch.

"Outside security walks the perim every three minutes," he whispered. "There are cams at the driveway, but by then we'll just look like the cleaning crew. If anything goes wrong, use your throat piece, code out to Mal, and start running. We can make it back across the memorial in just two minutes if we're quick. Look over there." He pointed northeast with his whole hand, military style. "Just over that rise, it's straight downhill to the 'muter. You'll see the orph parking lot as soon as you step over the hill. We'll leave our packs here, in the trees."

They all stared hard, as if trying to see over the ridge. Then Thelo said, "But nothing's going to go wrong, right, Money?" His tone was a little too ironic for Dex. *What was his problem?* Money stared at him queerly, then took it as a joke and laughed. "Not a chance. This is tight, top to bottom. See, there's the security dispatch. Right on time."

They watched as two men, amusingly overweight, shuffled

around the building, laughing at each other's jokes. They walked so slowly that Dex thought they might never clear the eastern side. But they did. And Money said, "It's a go. Remember, we run down to the west side, where that dumpster is, and then walk slowly toward the basement entrance."

As they were running, fast, down through the soft light of the moon, their footsteps crunched loudly against the bioteched ground cover. They hit the back wall, next to the dumpster. Just as Money had promised, they looked inside and found the one-piece "MedBed" jumpsuits, standard issue for the cleaners. Inside the breast pocket of each was the ID card that would identify them. They put the suits on, quickly. Out of his pack, Money pulled three sticks the size of chewing gum and handed one to each of them. They proceeded calmly toward the basement door.

Money had told them not to make eye contact with any of the cams, but they burned into Dex's skull, as if they were detecting his heart-rate, ready to sound the alarm. It took all his strength to keep his eyes fixed on the path. The cameras buzzed and followed the three of them as they walked. They reached the back door, and Money instructed them to look into the eye-scanner, one at a time. The read-out declared:

NO IDENTIFICATION FOUND. PLEASE SWIPE WORK PERMIT HERE –>

They each did, and were greeted by a reassuring green light. The door clicked open, and they went in, one at a time.

Dex exhaled as he stepped into the cloning facility.

They stood in a low, dimly lit and surgically clean waiting room, with no furniture, and cold white tiling covering the floor and walls. Dex could not imagine a use for the room, other than to freak out any would-be burglars. Suddenly there was a hiss, and light steam descended from the ceiling. Dex looked up in alarm, but Money engaged his throat piece and mouthed, "Relax, you're getting cleaned. Remember?"

Right. Money had explained all this. Dex mentally checked himself. He felt too fractured, all over the place, and probably not a good partner for anything illegal right now. He just kept thinking of Mal, sitting alone in that 'muter. Perhaps crying.

Then a vacuum sound was heard, and the air cleared. The acidic smell faded, and a green light came on in front of them. They looked into the scanner again, and one by one they were allowed in.

When they reached the next grey steel door, a man in a security outfit stood, hands behind his back, in front of it.

"Gentlemen," he said loudly. "Where are the usuals? Where's Manuel?"

"They took off, back south," Money said clearly, but he was holding the small metal bar in front of his mouth, and the voice that came out was not his. It had a Spanish accent, and was too low to be Money's. "We're the new cleaners."

The guard sighed. "New cleaners? Again? Alright, let me see your permits."

They pulled out their cards, and the guard looked at them, one after the other. "Okay, speak into this box right here with your name and work passwords for the night. Then I wait for auth from central, after that I let you in. You understand?"

"Si," Money said. Thelo said, "Si," and Dex put the metal stick to his mouth and said, "Si," but it came out, "Yah, sure."

Money was first. "Garcia Garcias, password six-two-five-yellow-nine." There was a pause, and a green light flashed.

Thelo said, "Jesus Morianda, password six-two-six, nine-red-sun." A pause, a green light.

Dex stepped up next to the guard, and looked him in the eye. He was sweating all down his face, and was clearly scared. But he gave Dex a wink; it was barely noticeable, but a wink nonetheless. Dex leaned over and said, "Tommy Doogan, password six-two-seven, clear-day-three." Pause, green light.

"Okay," the guard said, turning to the door. "Thanks, guys. You know the drill. Three to a room, one room at a time, no shortcuts. I'll be in the hallway the entire time, watching each step. Understand?"

They all nodded, and the guard held his face to the scanner. There was a blip and a click, and then he pushed the huge latch down, and pulled on the door. It opened slowly, with the heavy scrape of a door that was meant to hold all things either in or out. Or both.

They stepped inside–the security guard, too. Once they were in, the guard took a deep breath, and said, "Crackpipe, that was harder than I thought." He wiped his face with his sleeve.

Money dropped the metal stick from his mouth. "It's okay, guys," he said to Dex and Thelo. "No mics inside. No one wants to be recorded in this place." He turned to the guard, and they gave each other a hug. "How's Joey?" Money asked.

"Doing great. Excited about seeing the country," the guard said. "How's your dad?"

"Still an asshole," Money said, and they laughed like it was an old joke.

"It's been a long time," the guard said.

"Too long," Money said. Then he turned. "This is Dex and Thelo."

The guard offered his hand, and they shook it. "The pleasure is mine. Nice work with that traffic trick. I've been a fan of yours for a long time."

"Thanks," Dex said. "So where we going, here? The sooner I'm outta this place, the better I'll feel about having come."

"Right," The guard said. "This way. It's the first full room, here on the first floor of coolers. Luckey didn't like to have to walk past everyone else's meat to get to his." The guard walked down the long narrow hallway to the first doorway on the right. He coded something into a keypad, and stuck his face into the eye scanner. Pause, bleep, green light. The guard threw the door open.

"Enjoy," he said with a dramatic inviting gesture. "If you don't mind, I'm gonna go down the hall to the first available outtake fan and have myself a smoke."

They walked into the cooler. The guard propped the door open with a small wooden wedge he had pulled from his pocket. "Don't let the door close. It requires a chip ID match to get out, just like to get in." And then he was gone.

Inside the room, the temperature was not that different from the cold air outside. The lights had come on automatically, but only directly over where they walked. As soon as they passed, the lights behind them would go out. The room itself was about twenty feet by eighty feet, as big a space as Dex had ever seen. But it was low-

86

ceilinged, making it feel that it sloped away from you. Along with the buzzy blue fluorescent light, it made Dex even more uncomfortable.

"Check this out," Money said, turning to a large machine. "First step for regenerating any tissue is to get a vascular system set up."

Dex looked at what resembled an empty box frame surrounded by metal struts with a metal plate base. Two bars ran across the top of the empty space, and there was a device suspended from them. As Dex watched, the device on the two bars began moving back and forth rapidly across the struts, pushing a fluid out in a controlled fashion across the base.

"It's a blood vessel printer," Money said, watching carefully. "Squirts sugar in lines, lets it harden. Pours living vessel tissue around the sugar. Dissolves the sugar. Then…" Money turned to another machine, "You have what you need to keep larger organs and tissue alive. So you take those blood vessels and you begin to grow something around it. Such as that muscle there."

A rhythmic metal thumping came from the machine next to the vessel printer. The machine consisted of two metal arms that jutted out parallel to the ground; one was stationary, while the other spun in a lazy ellipse. A blue-purple slick material had been attached to the ends of the arms, and grappling hooks stuck out. When the one arm slowly made its circle, the material was being stretched and contracted. As Dex watched, a third robotic arm dropped from above and attached a hair-thin strand of the purple material first to the stationary arm and then onto the end of the second arm, before retracting back into the stainless steel body of the machine. The new strand was immediately lost in the thick purple material being stretched and contracted. Dex looked more closely, and he could see that the material was made up of thousands of thin threads.

"It's muscle," Money said. Dex jumped at his voice, then recoiled in horror.

"They call it the taffy puller," Money went on, even as Dex's stomach tried to settle back into its original location. "Old-fashioned tool for creating candy. Pulls it out, folds it over. I guess it sort of looks like that muscle-printer," Money shrugged, and moved his eyes further down the room. "The eyes and stuff, they put them in those huge stand-up coolers back near the end of the room," Money said. "I'm gonna go get a few pairs. You guys look for the hands up here." And then he was jogging back toward the far end of the room.

Dex tore his gaze from the muscle generator and began looking around at the chest-high glass cases that lined the two sides of the room. It reminded him of the way jewelry was displayed in the old malls he used to go steal from. But here, you could get a new hand, a new heart, or maybe a liver or a kidney.

"It would just be so *easy*," Thelo said from behind. The ice in his voice made Dex stop and turn around. Thelo was right behind him, a wild hatred in his eyes.

"Crack, Thelo, are you dripped?" Dex backed up.

"So simple, just to end it here," Thelo said, but his gaze wasn't exactly on him. Through him, was what it felt like. "Maybe they'll put me on ice anyway, maybe not. But I could just end it right here. You're so small, so weak. So *broken*."

"What the hell are you talking about, Thelo?" Dex said. He was backed all the way up against a glass case full of organs. The look in Thelo's eyes, it was one that Dex knew. Pure hatred. And it was aimed at him.

"Thelo, look, I don't know what Mal told you—" he started, but Thelo grabbed him by the neck and lifted him off the ground.

"My name," Thelo said, "is Moses." And then he started squeezing.

Twenty-four.

Dex clawed madly at Thelo's arm, but he could not reach the man himself, and his eight fingernails could not convince that muscled arm to stop squeezing. Sparks exploded before his eyes, and his legs kicked about uncontrollably. In the back of his mind, he could feel the dream coming on. The burning plane began to approach, and he started categorizing the pieces, getting ready. But he couldn't breathe! He opened his eyes, and then he heard the crack.

The hand went slack and Dex fell backward, crashing into the glass container of Luckey organs. The safety glass broke into a thousand pieces. He could feel the cold ice and slick muscle underneath his hands. Thelo, with a shocked look on his face, fell to his knees. Behind him stood Money, a long metal tube in his hands. Thelo reached behind his head with his right hand, the one with all five fingers, and then looked at the blood. He looked up at Dex, perched on top of the jewelry case of organs.

"Where am I?" he asked. The cold hatred was gone, replaced by a desperate, scared look. "Dex, where are we? What happened to my head?"

"Run, Dex," Money said, his voice breaking. "He's infected. I don't know how, but he's infected. Run!"

And then Money was around Thelo, who was rubbing his blood between his thumb and forefinger, squinting in pain. Money grabbed Dex by the hand and pulled him toward the front door.

Dex was breathing heavily, too dazed to do anything but allow himself to be dragged toward the front door. "Thelo, what's up? What's going on?" He asked.

Thelo, still down on his knees, turned. "I, I don't know... I have blackouts..."

The guard was at the front door. "Damn, guys, what's all the commotion?" he asked, looking inside. But Money was at the door now, and he pulled Dex out and kicked the wedge out. The door slammed shut.

"Money, Thelo can't get out," Dex said numbly. "Did he just try to kill me?"

"It's not him," Money said, breathless. "He's infected."

"With what?" the guard asked, going white.

"Millionaire's Disease." Money took off his spectacles and wiped his face. "I don't know how, but he's got it."

"That's impossible, Money," Dex said, but he had a hard time believing himself. Thelo had most certainly turned into someone else. "You gotta have a chip and drip to get that."

"I know! I can't explain it, Dex, but it's true. It's the name he called himself: Moses. It's a dead giveaway."

"What? The disease gives you multiple personalities, right?"

"Personality, Dex. Just one. It gives you one particular personality. A violent, angry one that goes by the name of Moses."

"I'm not following you."

"What you can't know about Millionaire's Disease, not even with your secret access to the Charts, is that it's a nanotech infection."

"What's nanotech?" Dex asked, rubbing his sore neck.

"Crackpipe, Dex, you really are a street rat," Money said. He was pacing now, but he stopped. "What it means is that it ain't like a virus, or a bacterial infection. It's an infection of a technological agent, little microscopic computers that invade your head and try to take it over."

"Mother Mary," said the guard.

"Yeah. And no one's talking but it's probably from government labs. They did a bunch of studies back in the seventies, but they were shut down because of an information leak that spoke to the huge dangers involved. Anyway, that doesn't matter. The bottom line is that among the elite in this country, they don't call it 'Millionaire's Disease.' They call it the 'Moses Disease.' That's because everyone–everyone who gets the disease–starts calling themselves Moses."

"But, but I've heard enough to know it's spread because of the chips they implant. Thelo doesn't have a chip." Dex was racing through everything he knew about Thelo, trying to put the pieces back together. The world was falling apart around him. *Who was Thelo?*

"I know, I can't explain it, but I've seen the Moses Disease before. Seen it first-hand," Money took his glasses off, wiped his face again, and pointed at the cooler door. "And now you have, too."

The guard was running for the doorway. "Let's get out of here! I can't be getting any disease! I got a son to take care of!" He had already coded in and was getting his eyes scanned.

"No!" Dex yelled. "Disease or not, we are not leaving without Thelo." He looked at Money, daring him to challenge. But he didn't. Without even looking at Dex, he nodded and turned to the guard.

Tick, scratch, tick, scratch.

It was Mal, and she spoke quickly. "Code red guys. Repeat, code red. Get the hell out of there. There are two helis, repeat, *two* helis overhead. Trooper cars coming in all over the place. They know you're in there. And Dex, your portable is beeping like crazy. I'm not sure what progs you got up, but it's going nuts."

Dex coded her back as fast as he could, "Mal! Get the hell outta there! It's a snoop! They can hear this conversation! Start the car! Move!"

He thought he heard her start to say something, then he heard electrostatic snow. The fuzz of being cut off.

"Mal! Mal!" He coded her on his throat piece. *Tap, rub, tap-tap. Tap, rub, tap-tap.*

Twenty-five.

"We have to get out of here now!" Money was dragging Dex toward the door. Dex looked toward the door, and saw that the guard had managed to get the door open, but was now lying face down, jamming the door open, unconscious.

"They sent a shutdown routine to his chip," Money said. "Lucky for us he got that door open first."

"What about Thelo?" Dex said. He was in full panic. "What about Mal? Shit, what about Mal?"

"One step at a time, Dex." Money was pushing the heavy door open and pulling something out of his pack at the same time. It was a small, hand-sized portable CPU. One of those portables the rich kids always seemed to have on them. He flipped the lid and coded a mad string, as fast as Dex had ever seen anyone type.

"What are you doing?" he asked. They were back in the main room where they'd met the guard.

"They've disabled the code access for our badges. We need a security override, and I've got one. They'll know exactly who I am in about five seconds, but at least we'll get out."

He pushed one last button, and the green light went on. They burst through the first door, into the tiled room, and out the back door.

Dex looked at Money. "Who are you?"

"Don't ask," Money replied, and then they were running.

The sound of the heli blades greeted them rudely. They didn't stop or break their speed. They both kept running, up the hill toward the trees. Halfway across the clearing, they were bathed in the blinding white glare of the floodlight. The obtuse angle cast their frantic shadows long in front of them. They heard shouting behind them, and then they were in the trees.

Barely slowing, Dex grabbed his and Thelo's packs, and made for the ridge. Money couldn't keep up, but Dex didn't stop. Over the top of the ridge, he would be able to see the 'muter. He would see Mal. She would be waiting impatiently for them. His lungs hurt from the cold air and the sound of the helis was getting closer, again, as they flew in over the trees. He could see the spotlight combing the fake trees, looking for him. He kept running, up onto the ridge, and looked down toward the orphanage and its pointless parking lot.

But the lot wasn't empty. There were six trooper cars, all surrounding the small blue 'muter they had arrived in. Mal was bent in half over the hood, a trooper's hands holding her head down and her arms behind her. Eight men dressed in black had guns pointed at her head.

Dex stopped, staring. *They'll take her baby. No, no, they're going to take her baby.*

He heard heavy breathing behind him, and turned to see Money come up over the ridge, dragging his huge pack. He ran up to Dex and stopped, surveying the scene below.

"Shit," Money said between breaths.

Dex's head swam. Everything was crashing down around him, and he couldn't get the moment to jack. This was the moment, this was it, but it wouldn't take him. He couldn't feel it. Instead, he just stood there, his heavy breathing pushing little steam clouds out into the wide open air.

Money was fiddling with his pack. "Here," he said, offering the pack to Dex. "Take this."

Dex looked at him. "Why?"

"Look," he said, holding up his portable. "I still have access to the security info generated by that building. I pulled it up while we were running. The alarm was tripped by you."

Dex just stared at him. "That's impossible."

"Yeah, there's been a lot of that tonight. But when you held those eyes of yours to that scanner, it found you."

"I'm not on the Charts, Money! There's no way it found me!"

"There's more than one database out there, Dex," Money said. "The Charts aren't the only place to put data. Now, I don't know who you are, but you're more important than any dead CEO's eyes. So, take this pack. It's a military escape unit. You push here, and it's got a jet here," he pointed. "Use this to steer. It has a range of about two miles. It should get you to a sewer hole somewhere."

The helis were right overhead. They could hear humans shouting, very close to them.

Dex looked at Money, trying to figure out who this short little kid was, with his military-grade escape gear. Who did he say his dad was again? But it didn't matter, not anymore. Money had the pack ready and was pushing it into Dex's hands.

And the moment finally came. Dex felt it all slow down, way down, and he pictured Thelo, confused with blood on his hands, kneeling among the frozen livers and kidneys and hearts. He saw Mal being held down roughly over the hood of a 'muter, fat troopers aiming guns at her head. And he looked at the young, smooth, undamaged face of Money, staring up at him in the moonlight that speckled through the fake leaves of the fake trees. The decision was easy.

"No, Money," he said, giving the pack back to him. "No, I'm going with my friends. Wherever they go."

Money looked relieved. He was scared out of his mind, Dex realized, but trying to be brave. He wanted to get out. He didn't see a future on ice. It hadn't been the inevitable outcome of his entire life, as it had been for Dex, and for Thelo, and even to some extent for Mal. They knew they would all be dead or iced by twenty, and so the moment had come; it had surely come.

"Thank you," Money said as Dex handed it back with a nod. He had the pack strapped on in no time. The jets were hissing and he was flying through the air, up through the roof of the artificial trees, over their cone tops, and away to freedom, whatever that meant.

But Money didn't make it far. As Dex watched, there was a screeching sound, and a string of bright light lit up the canopy of trees, arching low and fast across the night sky. The streaking light hit Money in the back, right in his military escape unit. The backpack exploded into a hundred pieces, and Money plummeted toward earth. With the moment in high jack, Dex could see exactly where Money would land, and just how many broken bones he would have. Not that he could have survived the explosion. But Dex was running to him anyway. He ran to where the body lay.

His body smelled of burnt hair and flesh, and Dex fell to his knees. He picked up Money's head, and pulled it onto his lap. He was still alive. His arms were both broken, but he used them to grab at Dex.

"I can't feel my legs," he rasped.

"Your back is broken," Dex said, holding him. His glasses were nowhere to be seen, and his face was a matted mess of blood and bio-degradable ground cover.

"There are so many of them," Money said.

"So many of who?"

"The troopers, Dex. They're everywhere. Coming from all directions."

Dex looked around, expecting to see them all at once.

"Who are you, Dex?" Money asked, coughing.

"I don't know, Money." Dex looked around. He could see shadows creeping in toward him from all directions.

"So many...they coded your threat level for *snipers*... When they saw your eyes in that scanner." Money was shaking all over. "Who are you?"

"I don't know," Dex whispered.

"Who are you? Who are you?" Money kept asking. He was shaking so bad that his arms and legs were twitching.

"I don't know! I don't know!" Dex was yelling at Money, tears streaming down his face. "I don't know who I am," he said, wiping the blood off Money's face. But Money was dead.

Dex looked up and around, and now he saw them, a circle of maybe thirty troopers at twenty yards, crouched over with their rifles aimed at him. A heli settled in overhead, high, at about two hundred feet, and aimed a light directly down on him.

Dex stood, and Money's limp body slumped the ground. *So this was it. This is how it would end.* And he closed his eyes. The moment gone. All moments were gone. Money lay dead at his feet. Mal would get her baby surgically removed, delivered to someone up the mountain too old to conceive. Thelo would get thrown into an institute for crazies. And they would execute him, right here, for being whoever he was.

But no one fired.

Dex waited, and finally he opened his eyes again. No one had moved. They were still crouched down low and aiming up at his head, but no one fired. Dex rotated slowly, his arms outstretched.

"Well?" he asked. "What are you waiting for? Here I am! Take your shot!"

But they didn't. No one moved but Dex. He hit himself in the chest. "Shoot! Come on! Shoot me!" The tears ran down his face, blinding him. "Shoot! Shoot me!"

Then the helis were gone, as was the spotlight. But the snipers didn't move. A single flashlight was shining in Dex's eyes, blinding him. He held up his hand, but he couldn't see past the light. Then he heard the voice, and it sounded like a memory.

"Yeah, that's him alright. Even with that scar, that's him. Bag 'em and tag 'em. I want him off-planet pronto. No bullshit, okay? I gotta call it in."

Without thinking, Dex launched himself at the light, at the voice. There was a rage in him he had never felt before, and he screamed at the taste of it.

Before he had even made it three steps, he felt a hundred pin-pricks as the tranq darts hit. And then there was blackness.

PART 2

MIDDLE DRAGGISH TOWNSHIP, DAY ONE.

Twenty-six.

The dream overwhelmed, coming up into consciousness so fast. The burning surface stretched like the surface of the sun in all directions, burning his eyes dry.

The vertigo came, the sense of acceleration, and Dex felt the uneven plane churning and exploding, rising up to meet him, or himself falling down to meet it. There was a gravity to it; it made sense, but there was no explaining it. It was like describing blue without naming blue things. His skin sizzled. The panic rolled up from his gut, through his chest, and detonated in his head. The light fell away in every direction, a single convexity. He would hit the surface in a moment, less than a moment, burning into nothing, exterminated by the hot glow.

He felt the hot touch, and he could feel the moment go into jack. The pain slowed down, the burn, down to a hotness so acute he could feel each micrometer of the tips of his fingers on his outstretched hands. The panic turned into a thousand systematic decisions translated into actions, into a triage so instinctive he could not begin to grasp at it, or even remember it, when waking up.

He broke down all the pieces of his flesh, all the layers of cells in his bones, his muscles, his organs, everything. He broke the cells down into molecules, the molecules into atoms, the atoms into the smaller pieces that he didn't even know the name of. He remembered where everything went; he stored, catalogued, checked it all into the recesses of his mind's reach. He broke it down into nothing, into the nanosecond itself, into the exact moment he touched the burning surface. And right then, the smallest pieces, the little dead-ends of the universe, they did their inevitable dance across the surface, bubbling, fizzing, popping, looking for little holes only they could fit through. Looking for their partners on the other side, looking to trade places.

Then the smallest particles were across the plane, out of the fire, and he was reorganizing them, putting them all back together into the next level, all billions of them. Then the smaller pieces into the less small pieces, and then the molecules. Then they were cells, the cells, his body parts, and it all happened faster than life itself. It happened so fast it felt like it didn't happen at all.

And he was holding it all in his mind, categorized, filed away, jacked into place, until all the billions of pieces were apart, and passing through the pure burning heat of it.

But he started to slip, started to forget where all the pieces went. He was disintegrating.

The tiniest pieces of him began bubbling, dancing, colliding away from each other and finding their own logic, their own place, their own gravity. He couldn't keep it all organized, memorized, jacked, so he brought everything back together. But it was a panic not a plan, because it was too soon, and the pain was acute, it was all over him, it was eating into his skin, his body, and he was going to scream, and he would wake up. *Please, wake up.*

But the waking up, this time, didn't feel so much like relief.

Twenty-seven.

He felt the hand on his neck first before he tried to move and felt the restraints around his arms, his torso, his legs, his head. Someone checking his pulse. He couldn't move more than a few centimeters, and he felt groggy, like he had a hangover, like coming down off some chemical compound. *Where am I? Why am I tied down? What's going on?*

And after a few moments, the question finally began rolling through his mind: *Who am I?*

He tried to open his eyes, but they were open, he just couldn't see anything. He instinctively tried to look around, but his head was immobilized. He tried to yell out, but his voice was muffled by something soft and firm over his mouth.

"Relax, young man," a deep, hoarse voice said. "You'll remember it all, very soon, and the panic will subside."

Then he did remember, and the panic was going nowhere fast. Dexter Maxwell found his name, his memories. Everything came back, like a flood, and he felt dizzy, spinning, like woofies did. He could feel his head fill up with all the memories, all the space of his life, glaring at him, rushing around madly. Like a flashlight shone right in your eyes.

Mallory pushed face-first into the hood of a car.

Thelo looking at his own blood on his fingers, surrounded by ice and frozen human hearts.

Money, burnt, bleeding, a frightened look on his charred face, falling lifeless from the sky.

He tried to open his eyes again, and felt the need to break free. Straining every muscle, he screamed through the hot covering over his mouth.

"After the dizziness," the deep voice said calmly, "And the anger, you will feel cold, yet sweaty." The warm hand checked his neck again for a pulse. "Unfortunately, I do not have time to allow you to lie here and safely go through the stages of re-entry. Instead, I am going to unbind you. Do you understand? Snap once for yes, twice for no."

With his right hand shaking, he snapped once. He was already starting to feel the chills, and his palms were perspiring.

"Good," the voice said, and whatever had been covering his mouth was removed. "Now, for everyone's safety, I suggest you do not scream."

Dex tried talking before he actually had a breath, and he coughed. His lungs burned with the short fast breaths he pulled in. *Hyperventilating, that's what they call it.*

"Where am I? Why can't I see anything?" He finally got out. His voice was hoarse, his mouth gummy. There was something wrong with his mouth, but he couldn't figure it out. His teeth felt wrong, his gums too sensitive. He felt raw, cold, exposed.

"You are a resident of the Planetside Medical facilities of Governor Goldman, although I doubt that really helps you much. Even the people from here don't know what this place really is. And you cannot see anything because you are wearing a blinder."

"Take it off," Dex said.

"Demanding. Right from the start, I see."

"Well, if you're breakin' me outta here, I gotta see, right?" He could feel the restraints on his legs loosening.

"Mmm. And observational. What a treasure trove I have unearthed. If only there were time to really dig into that neural pattern, to get at some of the nuances of you at this stage in your development..."

"You talk funny," Dex said. He could feel the restraints loosening on his chest.

"I'm afraid it is you, Dexter Maxwell, who is talking funny."

"You seem to know my name," Dex said. "What's yours?"

"My name is Logos."

"Sounds like a kid's toy. Well, *Logos*, take this mask off," Dex said again. The restraints on his arms were slackening.

"I cannot do that," the voice said. Dex could tell the man was close, right over him.

Dex reached with both hands to grab the man. Instead of grabbing the shirt and flesh of a person, both of his hands slammed into a cold, hard, surface. The pain reverberated through his arms, and he yelled with the raw newness of the hurt.

"Crackpipe!"

"A fighter. I suppose I knew that. Well, I can't let you out of that shell just yet, Dexter Maxwell. You are not ready."

Dex rubbed his sore knuckles. Then he reached up to his face, feeling for the mask. It was there. But as he touched the warm, smooth plastic, he could feel the contours of his forehead, his cheeks, his eyes. He instinctively blinked, but the mask covering his eyes stayed bubbled out, over the top of the blinder. He kept feeling down, past his eyes, until he felt the edge of the plastic below his cheekbone. He tried to get his fingernail underneath the mask, but could not.

"The mask will not come off, I assure you," Logos said, but more distantly now, as if he were looking away.

Dex picked at the edge, but his skin came up with it, as though strong adhesive had been laid down inside the mask. He let go, and instead felt out toward whatever shell he was lying in. It was just a few hands above his head, and domed away from him in both directions. He trailed along the slick surface until he felt it reach the pad he was laying on.

"The shell is uni-directional, young Dexter Maxwell," Logos said, and touched his neck again. "I can reach through the eighteen inches separating us, but you cannot reach back. A marvel of modern technology."

Dex tried to touch the hand on his neck, and felt only the cold, hard plastic. Then the man removed his hand, and the plastic moved away with the hand until it reached its uniform position.

"Are you ready to listen to what I have to tell you?"

"Doesn't seem like I have a choice, man." Dex made fists. What was wrong with his left hand?

"I'll interpret that as a yes." Logos cleared his throat. "The mask is attached to your face because you are currently blind. You are blind because your optic nerves are coming out of deep stasis. Do you understand what I'm telling you?"

"Yeah, I understand," Dex said with disgust. "The bungers put me on ice. How long have I been down? A few months? A few years?"

"Yes, yes, a few years," Logos said, and chuckled. "But no, that is not why you cannot see. You are blind because you are a clone."

Twenty-eight.

"I don't think I'm following you, Logos."

"You are not *you*. You are a clone. An iteration, to be more exact. And the last, let's hope. A physiological and neurological reproduction of another human being."

"Are you dripped?" Dex asked. "Look, the feds caught me in that park, they juiced me and dropped me on ice. That's how this works, right?"

"Yes, yes, Dexter, all those things happened. But not to you. They happened to the *original* Dexter Maxwell."

"But how can I remember everything then? If I was a clone, there's no way I could remember stuff that happened to someone else." Dex shivered. He was freezing and he could feel the sweat all over his body. Why was it so cold?

"A marvel," Logos said, "of modern technology."

"You really are dripped," Dex said.

Logos sighed impatiently. "This is harder than I expected. Okay, let's try this: the 'feds,' as you call them, will discover my treachery very soon. They will come in here and find you and me having this

103

inane conversation about the intricacies of comprehensible reality, and they will summarily kill me and perform painful experiments on you. Do you understand that?"

"I get that, but–"

"I'm not finished. I am going to deactivate the shell now, and then you and I are going to walk calmly and precisely to the nearest exit. Do you understand?"

"What do I look like, a–"

"Answer the question."

"Yes. I understand." He heard a series of twangs and tones, then a muffled shoosh, and suddenly the air was much colder. Logos spoke again. "You may sit up now."

Dex reached up, and felt nothing above him. He sat up hesitantly, and swung his legs over the side of the bed. His feet didn't touch ground. He reached out hesitantly, trying to feel something, anything. Logos' fingers felt rough and shaky as they grabbed Dex's hand. "Here, young man, let me help you down," Logos said gently.

"Why are you doing this?" Dex asked.

"Because you, of all people, deserve a chance," Logos said. "Here, turn around. I have something for you." He flipped his blind patient around and began strapping something heavy to his back.

"A chance for what?" Dex asked. He was rubbing his arms, trying to stay warm.

"Who knows? A chance to undo all of this, perhaps. Listen carefully. What I have just strapped to your back is a weapon known as the Judas Sword. It is a telescoping two-foot straight-blade made from the silk of the Earth-side Arachnars. It can pass through metal sensors undetected, conducts no electricity, and is invisible to the miles of weapons-detection systems which now surround you."

"What the hell am I supposed to do with a sword?" Dex asked. "I'm tellin' you, and this comes from recent memories *of mine*, I really don't know what to do with a sword. No matter how special you make it sound."

"You know what to do with it," Logos said grimly. "You just don't know that you know."

"Is riddle your native language?"

Logos laughed. "I get that. I do. You can be humorous, Dexter Maxwell. I had forgotten." He pulled extra tight, and the weight shifted slightly on his back. Just like that, the weight of the sword on Dex's back felt... familiar. "It is hidden from view beneath your travel pack. I recommend keeping it a secret if you can. I've adjusted it, with a slight lean to the left shoulder, to your preference for using your right hand to unsheathe it."

"I guess I'll just have to take your word for it, Logos."

"That's a good idea. Take my *word* for it. These," the doctor said, putting something around his neck, "are your docs. The card provides a one-way to Morgish on the train. You show it to anyone who asks, and you don't say a word, okay? It identifies you as a blind-mute. I suggest you play the part."

"Blind-mute, got it. Take the bus to Morgish. Never heard of it, but sure. Morgish. Sounds as good as anywhere. Anything else?" Dex felt himself calming down, remembering the information. But the calm was in his head; his heart was racing, and his stomach was a knot.

"When you arrive in Morgish, take a hired transport to this location," Logos put a piece of paper in his hand, "and hire a room. There's money on your card for everything you need. Once you are inside, lock the door and wait. A contact will come for you. 'The future bakes in the sun like new adobe' will be what you are told."

"That is the dumbest passphrase I have ever heard."

"Get used to it, young Dexter Maxwell."

"I'll try."

"I suppose that is all I can ask. So far, I have given you a lot to remember. But there is one more thing. In the outside world, there are followers of a man who is known as Fuel. If you find yourself alone and in danger, try to find the followers of Fuel. But never ask for him by name."

Dex shook his head. "How can I find him if I can't say his name?"

"You are not looking for Fuel; you are looking for his followers. Sword, travel docs around the neck, head to Morgish, hire a room. The future bakes in the sun like new adobe. Find the followers of Fuel."

There was a pause, then, with Dex just standing there, Logos was off somewhere doing things a blind man cannot know. Dex could hear the strange twangs and sounds, like a string instrument being played. The cold spell was passing, slightly, and it all started to sink in.

Jailbreak.

This guy was springing him from the icer. Giving him a passport, some cash on a card, a place to go. "Logos, listen," he said, "Sorry that I freaked. I don't feel right. I appreciate gettin' sprung like this. I don't know if we'll ever meet again, but when I'm back in the sewers under Grenver and you should ever need a place to hide out, you know, like if you're in trouble just come to Salomon's Penny Shop and ask for Dex. I'll hook you up good."

Logos was back at his side. "You are a long way from Grenver, Dexter Maxwell. But I appreciate your gratitude. If you knew what I am getting you into, though, I doubt you would do anything but cut me down with that sword on your back."

"Okay, you dripped old man. Whatever you say. Just trying to be nice."

"Come. This conversation is over."

With that, Logos grabbed Dex's arm and dragged him away from the bed.

Twenty-nine.

Walking, putting one foot in front of the next, there was danger in every step when you couldn't see. Dex thought of Jones, walking confidently around that huge old house in the burbring, having memorized every square foot of the place and committed it to memory. *Everyone does the same thing with their space, it's just easier for me cuz I don't look at nothin',* he'd say. *And so I'm free of mankind's real crutch.* Jones, crazy ol' Jones. And here was Dex, trying to step confidently forward but afraid of every sound, every hustled shoulder that pressed against his.

There were plenty of people, now, and more space. The echo of containment was still there, but the din was farther out, the space larger. When Logos had first led him out, they had taken a series of turns, and he had tried to remember them, like it was important. But he got turned around, didn't know how far he was walking, and stumbled over something hard that bruised his shin good. The chills, they came and went, and pretty soon he just fell into the mindless rhythm of walking, awkwardly, with Logos leading him by his right shoulder. Logos gave a squeeze and Dex slowed down; Logos gave a tug, and they turned right; a push, they turned left. Automatically, Dex just let his mind roll out, trying to get everything sunk in good.

But it isn't capable of being processed, now is it? Wherever he was right now, he'd never been here before, and he'd never heard of any place called Morgish. And there was this crazy old man, crazy like Jones, talking in riddles, pushing him around by his shoulder, strapping swords to his back, and telling him, what? That he's a clone?

But it was there. The resolute honesty in the voice. The matter-of-factness of it all. Like Logos didn't have time to lie or make up some other story. Just tell the scared kid the truth, and then let's go, out the door, out to freedom. *Freedom.* He wanted it, certainly, but he wasn't sure what it meant. He didn't remember being shackled, jailed, imprisoned, anything. From the minute he went under out there in that fake tree park, until right now, it was just a blip, a night out, one big darkness. One dream, just one single burning nightmare.

But he had been iced. He knew that. He'd been caught, out there in the fake forest, just like Thelo, just like–

"Mal. Where's Mal?" He asked out loud, without even thinking, and the hand on his shoulder tightened painfully.

"Blind *and* mute," Logos hissed into his ear.

Logos was scared, Dex realized, and he wondered if the fear was for what had been done already, or for what lay ahead.

And then a tug, a right turn, a long squeeze, and they came to a halt. Logos spoke to somebody, coolly, calmly, clearly.

"Lieutenant Xaveer," he said.

"Doctor," the voice came back. Dex could hear something in the voice, through the formality. Mockery? Glee? He couldn't place it. "The usual screen and clean?"

"Yes, sir, make sure I'm not exposing us all to a deadly virus," Logos said. And this time, Dex got it; got the sarcasm. This was a transaction. A grift. Like the low-toll highways.

The lieutenant laughed, and Logos' hand left Dex's shoulder. Dex felt his heart race, feeling unbound, unleashed, afraid. That hand was his guide, and he liked it better on his shoulder.

There was a pause, a mechanical blip, the strange twanging sounds he had heard earlier with Logos, and then the lieutenant spoke again. "Where's this one off to?"

"Where do you think?" Logos asked. "You think asteroids mine themselves?"

The lieutenant laughed. "I got this brother, works up one of them rocks. Says these old-timers, they work with a fire he never seen before."

"The working class, it just isn't what it used to be," Logos said.

"Got that right, doctor." There was the sound of the man standing, walking to a door, and there was some kind of electronic transaction. "You know the drill, doc. Two minutes. That's all I can give you."

"My gratitude, as always, Lieutenant. You'll note the fee has increased, I hope you spend it well. Say hello to Lana for me."

"Oh, and she says to give you a kiss. Pardon me if I don't, doc."

Logos had his hand back on Dex's shoulder, and was pushing him forward, leading him through a door while saying back over his shoulder, "I appreciate that, Lieutenant. I do." The man laughed and then the door closed. There was no sound. Logos let go of his shoulder.

"I get it, doc, I get it," Dex said turning in a circle, trying to discern where Logos was. "I'm destined for some rock mining? Good old-fashioned slave labor, eh?"

"Shut up, Dexter Maxwell," Logos said quickly, from far away. "And stand still."

"Why, so you can brand me? Give me my brand-name? Get me ready for the mines?"

"No, so that the nice man outside, the one staring through the window at my *blind-mute*, can operate his medical devices and give you a cleaning."

"Why, am I dirty?"

"You are not. You are as clean as any human could ever be. You have been created and have lived your entire life in a medical facility. The good lieutenant, however, thinks you are an age-old criminal put on ice, a carrier of ancient diseases, and a legitimate threat."

Then came a dull roar, and Dex felt a warm wind blowing directly up from underneath him. He reached out, and his hand felt the cold plastic of another shell, surrounding him on all sides. He slowly turned in a circle, breathing in the acrid smell of medicine.

"But I'm not a criminal, am I? I'm a *clone*, right, doc?" Dex was yelling over the rush of the air at his feet. Then it was over, and suddenly Logos was right up next to him, so close that Dex could feel his breath on his chin.

"Your sarcasm burns the very air around you, like a weapon," Logos whispered harshly. "So I shall take the bait. Do you know why your hand feels different? Why you keep stretching it?"

Dex said nothing, but he stopped flexing his hand. He hadn't realized that he had been doing it.

"Your hand feels weird because it is whole."

Dex looked down at his hand, even though he could see nothing.

"Reach your hands out in front of you and grasp them together."

"Why would I do–"

"Just do it."

Dex interlaced his fingers. He pulled his hands apart, and then put them back together again.

His left pinky. His left ring finger. All there. Complete. Uncut.

Thirty.

"Self-discovery time is over; we have to move." Logos had him by the shoulder. Dex kept touching his fingers, running his hands together.

"I'm going to get you on the train, but then I have to leave you. So remember this: in eighteen hours, the mask will begin to pull away from your skin. Do not take the mask off immediately. It will stay fixed in place indefinitely, but will pull away from the skin cleanly. You have an med bracelet on your left wrist. An alarm will go off when your eyes are ready for light and the act of focusing."

"Okay," Dex said. "Bracelet. Check. Eighteen hours. Check."

"And another thing–" Logos started, then his hand tightened painfully, too tight. Dex was going to say something, but he heard it, too: The door behind them had opened, with people filing in, more than one. A whole group. In loud boots.

"Someone close that observation window," a voice said.

"Dexter, back up against that wall," Logos was turning him around, pushing him to a wall. "Stay there."

There was a laugh, too loud for the confines of the room, and it echoed quickly around, tinny with the treble of metal walls. "Dexter," a man said, casually. "Dexter. Now that is a name I haven't heard for a really, really long time."

"Hello, Ashion," Logos said. There was venom in the greeting. No, not venom, Dex decided: a vengeance. A mad hatred. Dex knew that kind of contained rage. Knew it well.

"Logos, my friend, my colleague, my *doctor*," Ashion said. He was walking around; Dex could hear the footsteps. "You know, Logos, I've tolerated your little flesh trade for years now. Ever since you opened vault 286 back in '05. But this? You had to know I would personally get alerted to *this*."

Logos said nothing. His hand was still tight on Dex's shoulder. Dex's heart was racing fast, his head pounding. They had been busted. Completely busted. It was over, back on ice.

"I can only assume you thought you'd have time to escape, at least at first, because of the location. But lucky for me, Logos, I'm down here in Draggish on Family business, cleaning up the Guvnor's little messes, and then I loop the recon thread. Look what he did, it tells me. Poor old dying Logos."

Silence. Logos did not respond. Dex was going crazy, trying to keep up. And that voice, it sounded so familiar; Dex swore he knew it from somewhere.

"So who was it, Logos? Who wants the iter? Don't tell me it's Morgan—not her style. One of the Gregors? That dook of a man that Lewiston calls a son? Some miner over in Transish? You can tell me. It's for the best."

Logos still said nothing.

"Come now. Your silence nets you nothing. But," Ashion paused, "I'd wager a space-class tug that you've thrown your lot in with this folk-hero clown they call Fuel."

Dex felt Logos hand tighten.

"What, you think I don't listen? Don't hear the stories? This Fuel character threads more often than that Earth-side godder religion everyone whispers when they think no one is watching. But of course, someone is always watching."

Logos' silence extended for a few awkward moments. Then Ashion spoke again.

"You know, Logos, I've been trying to get a bead on Fuel. Listening to the dogma and all of its nonsense. Fuel for the fire already burning inside everyone. Fuel for everyone to light the long nights. On and on and on... But you know what I think, Logos? You're not working with Fuel. I think you *are* Fuel."

Dex's heart had slowly started to settle down again, but he wasn't following the conversation. He was beginning to realize that this felt like the moment in the southern pipes with the sewer rats. There was no escape.

"No witty response, Logos? I just accused you of being a secret folk hero who magically brings electricity to the people." A sigh. "We used to talk so much, Logos. No matter. I'm through with you. Through with this meat shop. I don't need any of your iters anymore. Done with it all. What do you think of that?"

Logos burst, like a dam. "I think the minute your body turns a day over twenty-two, you'll be back here begging. *Begging.* You'll get a nick or scrape, and you'll want to be all pretty and new again. *Pretty please, Logos.*"

Ashion was suddenly very close, right up next to them. "Not this time, old man. Not this time. I don't need you, not anymore. And I certainly don't need this Fuel nonsense. And you know what that means?"

There was a sound of metal scraping, and then something hit Logos, hard, throwing him back against the wall. Logos let out a gasp, and the hand on Dex's shoulder fell.

"It means I get to put a sword through your heart," Ashion whispered.

Dex panicked. His heart rate sky-rocketed. He put his hand out toward Logos, felt him there. But he was limp, unmoving, even though he was still standing. "Logos!" he cried out. "Logos!"

"My god, I've wanted to do that for so long," Ashion said, walking away. Dex heard a short blip, and then: "Ashion here. Hello, Morgan."

111

Dex was grabbing at Logos, feeling his body, trying to figure it out with his hands. There was something warm and wet on Logos' clothes, and as Dex felt upward from his belt, he ran into something hard, sticking directly out from his chest. His left hand came to rest on it. It was a hilt. Of a sword. He could feel it bending slightly under Logos' weight, but it was firmly stuck in the wall behind him.

"No, listen, Morgan, I'm over at the med box," Ashion was saying, pacing back and forth. "Personal business, personal. No, *personal*. Actually, it's funny, see, there's this place down here where–" there was a pause, and Dex could make out the small squeaky sound of a person yelling over a phone. "Just cut the juice, Morgan… Right. Of course. No reason to yell. I'll be there in minutes. Yes. Of course."

Ashion let out an exasperated sigh. "Boys, let's go; the local terrors actually took control of the sewage box over in Morgish. No time to lose, and all that." There was a pause. "I wish I had time to unload and decode that iter, see what Logos was after. But no matter. Taj, Borl, Alix, destroy that thing, and then get rid of them both. I want them burned. Annihilated. No record, okay? Bio-cleaned. There's no overhead in these decontamination rooms, so have a little fun if you like."

There was a chorus of Yes, sir's, and then the sound of boots walking out of the room. "Oh, and Taj," Ashion said from the door, "Don't forget to bring me that sword stuck in the doctor. It's one of my favorites."

Then the door closed. Dex was facing the dead body of Logos, stuck to the wall, and he could hear heavy footsteps approaching, the metallic sound of swords unsheathing.

The panic, the anger, the fear; it was right at the surface, and it was different this time. Dex couldn't put his finger on it. He knew the sensation, the desperation, the finality of the threat. *Destroy that thing.*

But now, there was a power to it. A strength, where he expected futility. Confidence, where he would usually find panic. Time began to slow down to a crawl, the moment rising up within him. His mind expanded to fill the space of the moment. Without even thinking, he reached over his left shoulder and snapped open the backpack. He grasped the sword that Logos had given him, pulling it out slowly in an arc over his head, and held it out in front of him. The moment was moving slowly, slowing down, standing still. He knew this sword very well.

Very well indeed.

Thirty-one.

The weight of the sword, the way it felt in his hand, the balance; he could see the pale white hue of it, dulled grey with age and use. He could see the black glyphs carved along the blade. Dex gave it a shake and a twist. The slightest of movements and it telescoped from sixteen inches to twenty-four inches with a satisfying *shunk*.

He hadn't turned yet. Only heard the murmurs of surprise and the boots coming to a halt. He stayed facing the wall, feeling the moment. There were three of them, in common attack style, arched around him, not more than eight or nine feet away. He could hear them breathing, slowly shuffling, checking their weight, their balance. Preparing for an unexpected defense. They were unsure now what to do, how to start, what the plan was. *Not a leader among them.* Just three troopers, facing down a blind man with a sword.

The moment made its way into the next. And then from his left, he heard the sound of a decision, as a trooper's weight shifted and made a heavy step forward.

The step had been in an outward direction, toward the left perimeter of the invisible circle they had created around Dex. *The trooper is left-handed, and bringing his blade around from the outside, the fastest way to end the fight.*

Dex spun around clockwise, his arm pulling the weight of the sword up and around. The sword hit the arcing downward drive of the trooper's blade, pushing it out and away from Dex until the momentum of both men brought them together at the hilt of their swords. For a fraction of second, Dex could smell the unwashed body of his attacker, could inhale the grunt of surprise. Then he was pushing off the momentum, swinging his light blade around quickly and catching the attacker at the neck. The blade sunk deep, the body going immediately limp. Dex pushed his foot into the midsection of the trooper and pulled his blade free of the man's vertebrae even as he felt a rush of air to his side, as the second attacker was bringing his sword in low at Dex's knees.

Just as the sword left the flesh of the dead trooper, Dex brought it underneath his left arm, catching his attacker's blade and deflecting it down. But the weight of the thrust pushed his right arm down toward the heel of his left foot, throwing him off-balance. In that instant, Dex felt the third attacker bringing his sword around fast, at his chest, attacking him from the front. Dex reached his left arm out and caught the shoulder of the attacker behind him. He pulled, falling backward over his bent knees, over his own sword that was now stuck into the ground.

The third trooper's brash swing took the second trooper in the head, and for a moment the power of the strike countered the downward pull of Dex, before the second trooper's skull shattered and Dex fell to the ground.

He rolled into his fall, into the feet of the dead trooper as he collapsed over the top of him. Just as the final trooper took a new swing at his legs, Dex sprung up. He jumped forward, over the swinging blade, the Judas Sword held straight in front of him. It hit the trooper in the jaw, and Dex's weight pushed it all the way through the back of his mouth, into his brain stem, through the back of his skull.

Dex landed on his feet, before he realized that he'd jumped a clean nine feet over the man. He was gasping hard, waiting for another attack, but none came. The room was quiet, except for his labored breathing. His arm rung from the impact of the blade, and it felt good. It felt familiar. It felt found.

The moment started to speed up, and then turned into a rush of vertigo, a dizziness so profound that Dex fell to the floor. He vomited air, dry heaving the nothingness in his stomach.

Thirty-two.

Dex didn't remember rising, but he was up, and it hadn't been too long, because his heart was still racing. His head still spun. *How did I learn to do that?* But as he tried to search his own mind for the answers, the only thing he found was the spinning, the nausea, the vertigo. He found his way to Logos, who was still warm. Dex felt the panic as an itch in the back of his brain: the only person he knew was standing skewered against a concrete wall. But there was panic in all places and all spaces—in the three troopers he'd just murdered, in the blindness that held him hostage, in the familiarity of the sword in his hand. He gave the blade a twist, pressing the release underneath the hilt to push it back to its compact form, and put it back behind his shoulder in one motion. Another trick he knew, but did not know.

He groped for a dead trooper and tried to wipe the blood from his hands. Then he stepped back into the cleaning unit and found something that he hoped was water and scraped blindly at his hands for as long as he thought he could. He felt his way along the wall, looking for the door. He found it near Logos' pinned body, and opened it.

Because of Jones, Dex had heard all the folklore about blind people, about how all their other senses rose up to meet the challenge of their missing sight, compensating, enhancing. Maybe it was that, but he couldn't tell.

The heat came billowing in from the open door, a pressurized, humid, thick heat that drowned his lungs, made him gulp at the air. By itself, an overwhelming sensation, but he couldn't really separate the blast of heat from the smell.

The stench in the air was thick enough to nearly make him gag. Human sweat, human waste, and something that was maybe sulfur mixed with the heat; it all made the act of breathing feel less like an instinct and more like something he had to work hard for.

And the noise. Wrapped up in all the thick, hot stench was a dull roar of what sounded like fans, maybe, but also perhaps a train.

The train. He finally managed to push himself out the door, into the brash, insane pile of sensation, and tried to figure out what to do. *Shouldn't a blind man have a walking stick in public?* People walked past him, avoiding him with their hurried steps.

He had to find the train, get to Morgish. Show someone his docs, get to a hotel. *And then—what? To the mines? Home to Grenver?*

He didn't realize he was just standing there until someone ran into him and said, "Heah, blindy, gets a fire burnin. Transit waits for no man."

Blind and mute. Dex held his tongue and tried to show the voice his papers, still hanging around his neck. But then a rush of people were pushing him, like a surge, and he had no choice but to move with the masses. There were rude remarks thrown his way, people shoving past him. He stumbled, lost his balance and fell, swinging his arms wildly in front of him.

A strong hand grabbed him by the shoulder and pulled him firmly to his feet. Even once he was standing, the hand did not let go.

"Blindy, you's catch this transit?" said the surly voice holding his arm. "Wants Morgish, eh?"

Morgish. Yes. Dex nodded vigorously, and held his docs out desperately.

"Lessee, eh, yasure, Morgish. This transit, it's take you. Slides ya pass."

A hand took his and turned it around until he felt a card-reading device. The hand helped him line up his card and slide it across.

"Sits, blindy," the voice said, more mildly this time. 'You's blind and wit no voice, th' pass says. Tough goin, eh."

Dex just sat there, remaining silent, trying to work through the heavy accent and slang. It wasn't anything he'd ever heard before, and it took him a bit to understand it. He heard a loud twang, the rush of closing doors, and then a jerk as the train pulled away. He was so lost, there were barely words for it.

"Fresh off th' bed, blindy?" the man asked.

Dex just nodded. It seemed to describe his predicament.

"Ya, I's sees it in ya skin. Still got some of the bloods on ya hands."

Dex instinctively tried to wipe his hands on his trousers.

"My's Booker," the man said. "Lessee th' card again, so I's can gets ya name, blindy."

Dex showed him the card.

"Miles Goldman. Mmm. Owned, I's see."

Dex said nothing.

"Ya, th' Families, they's get lotsa crims off da beds, these days. They's gots a storm brewin but they's don't say nothin bout it. But I's sees it. Lotsa iters, fresh off da beds, doin all kindsa new dirty work. I's sees it."

116

Dex worked through the thick accent, trying to place it. Where was he? It wasn't America, that's for sure, but it was English they spoke. With the heat–maybe Australia? He'd heard they speak a lot of English in India. He'd never met anyone from India, maybe they talked like this.

"Ya, da Families, they's don't think any 'siders can sees it, but we's sees it. We's knows it somethin comin." There was a pause. "Where you's headed? 'Roid mining?"

Dex worked through it. Yeah, asteroid mining, that's what Logos had said. Dex nodded.

"I's sees it, eh? Sees it all, I's do. Every 'sider wit a head does. Heah, fresh meat for th' hole."

The voice paused, as though deciding something. Then, the man who called himself Booker was right next to Dex's ear, close enough to feel the wind of his breath. Then Booker spoke again, in an urgent whisper.

"Th' Families, they's gots a wind brewin, heah. Tall storm. But down here, blindy, there's new winds blow, oh ya. New wind. Flamin da fire. God sees all, and he's brought us fuel for da fire. Da 'siders, we's start makin our own future."

Dex tried to make sense of this, but it sounded like gibberish. Booker continued. "Lord says, asks and you's get what you's need. We's asked, and he's brought us Fuel. 'Member that name, blindy. Fuel is da new 'sider prophet, comes to right da boats of history. Freedom after the burn."

The train lurched to a halt, and Dex perked up, trying to make out if he should get up. He tried to stand, but he felt the hand on his shoulder again. When Booker spoke, his voice was loud, but farther away again. "No, blindy. Not to Morgish. You's stay sittin, I's gets ya to ya hire."

There were no more words, and Dex leaned back against the cold metal seat. He breathed deep, trying to quiet the knot in his stomach, the buzzing in his brain, the shaking in his hands. He hoped for any one of the three, but there was no solace anywhere.

Thirty-three

A hand on his shoulder, shaking him awake. When had he fallen asleep? How, exactly, was a different question altogether, because the minute he found consciousness, there was the knot in his stomach again, the shaking hands, the brain running circles around this reality, and he was back on the verge of dizziness immediately.

"Ups, blindee, you's at Morgish," Booker said, helping him stand.

Dex shook Booker's hand vigorously, trying desperately to show his appreciation. He wanted more than anything to say, *thank you, thank you, Booker, as though you were God himself. And by the way, where the hell am I?*

Booker just shook his hand back, and laughed. "Planet-side, th' only currency we's got left is kindness. Heah, what's else gets us through, eh?"

Then he was dragging Dex off the train, through the throng of people, leading him up the stairs, and then up more stairs. They took a left turn as they reached each landing, then more stairs. They walked slowly, and people brushed past them swiftly, hurrying.

The heat was worse the higher they got. He'd never felt anything like it, the feeling of it burning his lungs, like a desperate drag of a cigarette. There was an edge to the air, a taste that was everywhere, equally. Finally, they must have emerged from the trainway, as the dull echo of the stairwell gave way to the dull roar of humans, and the specific sound of traffic. The underlying roaring bass attacked Dex in the chest, in the heart, more than in his ears.

"Heah, blindy," Booker said. "Waits." Then Booker was gone, and Dex didn't budge, didn't move. People brushed past him, some running into him, but he stayed balanced, unmoving. A few minutes later, Booker was next to him again, putting something in each of his hands.

"Left hand, token for th' ride, heah. Right hand, token to give driver for helpin ya into th' hire."

Dex nodded. He understood; not everyone did things for free. Booker led Dex a few yards, then helped him up into a vehicle of some sort. Dex dug in his pockets, found some loose change. He put some of it in Booker's hand, squeezing it into his palm.

"Heah, what's is this?" Booker said. He turned Dex's hand over and put the metal coin back. "I's not take ya tokens, blindy. You's need more than me."

Suddenly, to Dex's surprise, he felt Booker's lips on the back of his hand, a gentle kiss, and he could feel his beard. "God's be wit you, and 'member what I's says about Fuel. Freedom after the burn," Booker whispered. Then he whistled at the driver, and Dex felt the vehicle lurch forward.

It was moving now; he could feel the bumps and jerks. The noise still surrounded him, and he realized he was sitting in an open-air vehicle of some sort. He was being jerked forward in rhythmic motions, and realized he was probably being pulled by hand, or even by bicycle.

"So it's is th' Grandview, eh, blindy?" said a gravelly voice in front of him. Dex just nodded. He could still feel the gentle lips of a complete stranger on his hand, the scratchy beard accompanying such a sublime gift. It had put him at ease, somehow. He sensed the stiff weight of the Judas Sword between him and the seat, providing a sense of relief, too. No matter the implausibility of it, he could defend himself, he knew that much.

Within minutes, the vehicle lurched to a stop, and the driver said "Heah, you's gets off here, blindy." Dex felt for a door, but found instead a rough hand grabbing at his arm.

"Th' preacher said an extra tenny if I's walk you inside, eh?" the driver said.

He means Booker. Dex nodded, and opened his hand to reveal the token there. The driver grunted, then pulled him away from the small cab, into the burning heat of the air outside. The noise had diminished significantly here, but the smell and heat lingered like a fart. He felt the driver pull a door open and lead him through the echo of a room. There was a woman yelling, he couldn't make out what, and some kind of sound blaring over a loudspeaker. Dex realized that noise was music.

"Heah, blindy, you's here. Grandview. Gives th' tenny."

Dex opened his right hand, and the token was grabbed quickly. All he could hear was the music. The yelling had gone quiet. The whole room had fallen silent since he'd arrived, Dex realized. Booker's peace had walked out the door with the driver, leaving Dex just standing there, head slightly bowed, listening for a sign, a sound, anything, to give him a sense of what to do. There was nothing. His heart was racing. And he was thirsty. And hungry. Famished. So hungry he almost collapsed just thinking about it.

But he had nothing. A mask over his face. A rotting knot for a stomach. Some strange loose change in his pocket, an ID around his neck naming him Miles Goldman. In some part of the world he didn't even know where. Blind, mute, whatever. Dex had nothing left to lose.

"Hey, could someone help me?" he asked, his voice choking. "Please?"

He was answered by a chorus of laughter. It seemed to come from every square inch of the room. Everyone was laughing, at him, at the blind man standing in the middle of the room, alone. Dex's jaw ached as he fought back the tears. But where would the tears go? The mask wouldn't let them escape.

Then he felt a yank at his neck and his ID being pulled until the cord snapped.

"Lessee, heah, who's is th' blindy, eh?" said a young voice. A taunting tone. It reminded him of the sewer rats, after the traffic stunt, the confidence taunts of those children. Then he thought of the sword on his back, and the dead troopers he'd left on the ground. And the tears dried up before they had even began. He stood up tall. Took a deep breath.

"Give me my ID," he said. The quivering in his voice had disappeared.

"What's 'eye-dee,' blind-ee?" the sing-song voice asked from behind him.

"My pass. My card. My docs." The anger, the frustration; it was a taste in the back of his mouth. A dryness to his nose. He could feel the bodies passing around him, circling him, four of them. The moment began its march to slow.

"Heah, this thing? You's want, blindy?" To his right.

"Yes, you dripped little jar," Dex said. "That thing."

"Oh-oh, blindee jazzed now, all flungs," the voice said. It was farther away, now, out of reach. "What you's all think? I's should give blindy his eye-dee?"

There were cheers, some wicked laughter. Dex felt the moment begin to slow, his thoughts quicken. He could make out all the different people now: the four circling pranksters looking for a little violence; there were three more against the wall to his left. Their laughter was short, expected and expectant. They were ready for a good beating. There were maybe four to his right, standing in a group, laughing at the scene without any real interest except in the sense that entertainment is entertaining. They sounded like girls, and as soon as Dex thought it, he knew it was true. This was all male swagger, start to finish. There was someone directly in front of him, and his jeers had a different sound, as though coming from a different room: the hotel operator. No doubt, standing behind a desk, arms folded, thinking that this cat wasn't showing signs of paying for anything. That he was just a beggar off the streets.

He had the moment in high jack now. Everything slowed, catching all the details that his ears and skin could gather. His nose had been taken custody by the sulfur. His right hand was clenching and unclenching, and he could already envision the satisfaction of the Judas Sword in his hand, the planning of his attack.

"Heah, now, maybe I's give th' blindy somethin, eh, but maybes not his papers," the voice said. It was close, right in front of Dex. The moment was there, and the anger and hatred boiled over. Dex reached over his shoulder for the blade.

"Heah, sure, now, Buss. You's had a joke, eh?" a decidedly female voice came from the group to the right. She walked toward Dex, who put his hand down quickly. "This one, he's is mine. Joke's is done."

"Trance, what, you's take broken icers now, too?" The voice had an edge to it. It didn't like the intrusion, but clearly couldn't disobey the woman. Not in front of all the other women. *Some things, are the same no matter where you are.* Time sped up, back to its normal pace.

"I's take whatever th' days a give, Buss," Trance said, grabbing Dex around the arm. "And these, they's takes 'em out at Transish. Not a bad price."

"They's take blindees now?"

"Heah, good strong one like this here."

Buss made a spitting sound. "Don't look strong to me's."

"Not strong like Buss, heah, but strong like da 'roid slave."

Laughter erupted, and Buss roared. Dex realized she'd deflected all the violence, and moved him to the center of the joke instead. That was alright. As long as she could get him out of there.

"I's give you twenty for his papers, Buss," she said. "He's is nothin w'out 'em. Thinks of it as profit share." There was more laughter.

"Nah, Trance, you's keeps ya twenty. Maybe you's makes it up to me's somehow else."

More hoots, and Dex felt the whole thing getting ugly again. The room preparing for a fight, again.

"Maybe I's do, Buss, you's a level dwell, sometimes."

And that was it; Trance was walking him away from the whole scene.

"Heah, Trance," A new voice yelled from behind him. From the hotel manager, or whoever. "You's not take th' blindy up w'out pays."

"Charge him to my's account, Disko," Trance said, and then they were making their way up some stairs, quickly.

Thirty-four.

They stumbled up four flights of stairs and then down a hall, before Trance let go of his hand and he heard her fiddling with something metallic. He heard a mild thunk and felt his arm being grabbed as he was pulled into a room. The door was closed behind them.

"Thanks, Trance," Dex said, "I don't know how I could ever–"

"Heah, blindy, you's just stays quiet," Trance said coldly. "You's get yaself dead down there, eh?"

"I didn't start it," Dex said. It sounded lame, even before he finished.

"Heah, you's just get dropped at Grandview, a blindy wit his pass just hangin round his neck, begs to gets it stole. I's not believes I's rescue you. Heah, what I's think?" And she put his identification papers in his hand.

"You didn't rescue me."

"Sure as anything I's *did*, blindy. Buss, he's is halfway up the 'vator, eh? He's is gonna hurt ya bad. Just to see what it's is like to hurts a blindy."

"No."

"Yes."

"I was about to kill him, Trance. Him and his three friends circling me at two feet away."

There was a pause. It dragged on for a little too long, and Dex could tell that Trance was trying to get a read on him. Then she let out a loud, obnoxious laugh. "Heah, blindy, you's think you's is funny."

"No, really, Trance. I got this sword, see, and I don't know how, but I know how to use it. Not just, like, use it, I mean really crack people up with it. I took out these three troopers earlier today and probably still have the blood on my hands. I can feel it. One of them, their leader or something, stuck his sword straight through the dude who pulled me out of the icer. Anyway, I just grabbed my sword, and really stuck it to them. They are dead, Trance, *dead*, and I did it. I killed them. And I killed Money, and Mallory, and Thelo...and I don't know where I am, or what's going on, and I can't see anything..."

Thick tears slowly leaked through the mask where it had become porous at the presence of the moisture. He collapsed, curling himself up into a ball like he used to do at the orph, after Dr. Johansson, after the pain, after the loneliness. He sobbed uncontrollably, barely able to breathe. Now the tears streamed down his face. The pain in his chest was like nothing he'd ever felt before. A despair so complete, it was like he was twelve all over again, in the darkened closet of a room at the orph, sobbing, trying hard just to breathe through the despair, and failing.

But then something happened, something that never happened, not back then. A soft hand, gentle as rain, was laid on his shoulder. Trance was kneeling next to him, pulling his head into her lap and stroking his hair, the mask on his face.

"Come now, child, come now," Trance said quietly to him. "Trance has ya, child, you's okay for now, heah."

Dex cried, a broken dam, his entire body shaking with the violence of the release that was so sudden and so complete.

Thirty-five.

Dex woke peacefully, slowly, without the violence of his dream. It felt as though he had rested after not sleeping in years. Maybe he hadn't slept at all, had forgotten how sleep felt. He opened his eyes, but there was only darkness. *The mask.* He thought that maybe he should panic, because it was all happening, this was really his life: blindfolded and lost in some godforsaken town.

But he didn't. Instead, he lay there, breathing, feeling the warmth of Trance next to him, her breathing deep and regular. They lay side by side, with her arm over his chest, her chest pushed up against his back, her legs curled up against his, spooning.

She had held him until he had eased down, then she had gently pulled the pack off his back and the boots off his feet. She had dragged him numbly to the bed and laid him down again, curling up with him, until they had fallen asleep. Dex did not know how long they had slept. The first victim of his blindness had been his sense of time. How long was it since Logos took that sword through the heart? How long since Booker woke him on the subway or since he ate? And how long had he been lying asleep next to a stranger?

It didn't matter, and Dex realized this with a certainty that went to his chest. What was time? Just ticks on a clock, a hand rolling around continuously in a circle. An arbitrary distinction, disrupted by the ebb and flow of reality. A countdown to something, something out there. Maybe just death? All the events of his recent memory were a ramshackle collection of fear and loathing and running and adrenaline. Sorting them into a cohesive string didn't seem to help. He could see nothing, but it wouldn't matter, because he was in a strange land. Seeing it would likely render it no less strange.

And he didn't even know what time it was, on the larger scale. How long had he been on ice? And then he had to correct himself again. How long had the real Dex been on ice? And how long had he himself been around, this clone of Dex? He fondled his newfound fingers absentmindedly. This was the stuff of dreams. But his experiences since Logos woke him bore witness to all the crazy truth of it.

Crackpipe, I'm thirsty.

Trance stirred. Dex felt her stiffen as she woke to him there, and then relaxed again. *Not used to waking up next to someone.* He thought of Mallory, and the pain of it forced him to sit up.

"Heah, blindy," Trance said hoarsely, and rolled out of bed. Dex rolled onto his back.

"I need water," he said, the gravel in his voice confirming the need.

"You's and me both, blindy," Trance said, from across the room.

"Call me Dex."

"Eh?"

"My name is Dex. I won't be blind forever."

"Dex, eh? Ya pass say you's is Miles."

"Yeah, well, who you gonna believe?" Dex said.

"Dex, you's sure talk funny."

"I get that a lot. Where's your bathroom?"

"Eh?"

"Your, uh, hell, where do you pee? Dribble? Leak?" Dex made a rude gesture with his hand in front of his fly.

"You's need to drip."

"Yeah, drip. Something terrible."

"Drip's is this way, if you's want to give ya water away. I's waits until I's get back home, got me my own purifier, keeps all my own water. Here, they's give you rebate for drippin in th' reservoir, but it's is wicked poor." There was a pause. "So?"

"So what?" Dex asked.

"So you's wait, gets ya water back?"

"I just wanna pee."

Dex could almost hear the shrug. "Heah, sure," Trance said. She guided him into a small closet that after some scanty investigation seemed to have a hole on a dais in front of him. He relieved himself, hoping he was mostly hitting the hole. It burned hot coming out, enough to make Dex gasp. He shook himself off and fiddled with his pants until everything was back in place. As he opened the door and walked out, he bumped into Trance immediately.

"Heah, that be one tall blade, Dex," Trance said.

"What?" he asked awkwardly.

"Long knife you's carry funny on ya back," Trance said.

Dex remembered the sword, and laughed at himself. "It's pretty special, at least that's what I hear. Will you help me get it on my back?"

"Heah, Dex, sure, then we's get goin, eh?"

"I gotta get a few things straightened out first. A few questions?" Dex said, as Trance helped him with the sheath, and tried to figure out the complicated strapping system.

"Yasure."

"Okay, first, where am I?"

"Morgish, east hire districts. At th' Grandview, room 442. Talkin to me's, heah, Trance."

"But you don't live here."

"Nah. Lives down toward central Morg, I's get me a rent down there, not too watched."

"So what are you doing here? In room 442?"

"I's work here, blindy."

Dex processed it all slowly.

"Okay. So where's Morgish, then, exactly? I mean, what country?"

"Cunn-tree? I's don't know this word. Morgish is planet-side, if that's is what you's wonderin. You's come from one of the beds up in the winds?"

"I'm not sure–I don't think so. Planet-side, is that a place, like Australia? India?"

Trance laughed nervously. "Now I's the confused one. I's not sure what you's speak. Morgish is Morgish, that all, planet-side. On th' planet side of civilization, heah, the other side is the boats. So, you's take th' transit 300 clips north, you's get to Draggish. From there, 50 clips, you's get to Transish planet-side. Takes a 'vator or tug straight up from Transish, you's get to the Loopstations, and from there, th' Family boats float th' winds. That help?"

"Not at all."

"Sorry. Ya's a crim off th' icer?"

"Yes."

"Heah, you's probably don't even knows a little where you's at."

126

They sat quietly next to each other for a few minutes, as Dex adjusted the Judas Sword on his back. Then he turned to Trance.

"Maybe I'm asking the wrong questions. What year is it? I mean, what's the date?"

"Heah, sure, year is thirty forty-nine. Jans twenty-nine."

Dex laughed a little. "That sounded like you said 3049."

"Heah."

Dex sat there for a minute. "Say that one more time."

Trance laughed, and said "Three. Aught. Four. Nine. Slow enough, eh?"

Dex was silent. It made no more and no less sense than anything else. "Crackpipe, Trance. I've been on ice for a long time."

"Heah, how long?"

"A thousand years, give or take."

There was a pause. Then Trance pushed him gently. "Heah, Dex!" she said, and he could feel her rocking slightly on the bed behind him. "Heah, I's don't believe this! You's one of th' firsts, eh?"

"I guess so. I got locked up by some fed troopers in November of 2113. To me, that was just a few hours ago."

"Fed trooo-pers," Trance sounded out the word. "Oh piddle, Dex. I's mean, you's hear stuff, down in Lower Central, from th' Old Sinners or even th' New Preachers about folks from th' first ships, ya know? But you's thinks th' Old Sinners, they's just crazy, eh? They's talk crazy non-stop, eh? But way you's talk, and th' questions, you's really from all th' way back then, eh?"

"You lost me there, Trance."

She didn't even hear him. She was pacing now. "This is tall, Dex. Mean and tall." She stopped. "Time we's get goin."

She was pulling at his arm to get him to stand up, when there was a pounding at the door, a loud hammering.

"Open up! Guvnor's orders!" a gruff voice yelled through.

"Oh piddle," Trance whispered, fear making her voice break.

Thirty-six.

"Open up, Justine 'Trance' Axel, by order of Guvnor Goldman

and the Family Security Council. We's got you on th' overheads, we's know you's in there wit th' iter."

"Oh piddle, oh piddle," Trance was saying, her fingernails biting into Dex's arm.

"Don't open the door, Trance." His heart was in his throat.

"I's got to," she whimpered. "They's kill us, and not think twice. Pumps gas in thru th' overhead." Then she walked to the door, popped something metallic, and opened it.

Dex heard her scream, then there was a scuffle at the door. "Dex!" Trance yelled once.

"Take her alive, Ash ordered," a voice said calmly. Dex could hear Trance being pulled out into the hallway. "But destroy the iter."

And then he felt it again. His head was clearing, the moment saddling up slowly to meet him, the anger and hatred focusing his senses. He reached behind him for the sword, this time triggering the telescope action even as he pulled it from the sheath. This time, not waiting for an attack, he lunged at the voice, swinging Judas in a quick arc that brought its full force around in a circular pattern.

The blade struck flesh on the way down, catching the man in the shoulder and driving down to the clavicle, the shoulder blade, burying deep into both. Dex heard the cry of pain. He kicked the man into the person behind him, pulling Judas out and swinging again, taking the man's outstretched arm cleanly off at the elbow. There was a scream, but Dex had already leaped over the first attacker and was pushing his blade through the torso of the off-balance trooper behind him. As he pulled the blade free, leaning back slightly, he felt an electric charge fly past him, putting his hair on end, burning his arm slightly. *Some sort of tazer.* Dex leaped in the direction it had come from.

He hit the shooter in the hand with his forearm, then spun quickly and put the blade through the neck, separating it from the head. Dex paused, listening, trying to sense the next attack, but there was only the sound of struggling coming from the hallway. Trance yelled strange profanities, and a bell alarm came from somewhere.

Then he realized the alarm was coming from his wrist. From the bracelet.

Dex straightened up. *My eyes are ready.* He peeled the mask away with his free hand.

128

The light burned his eyes. For a moment he squinted and his vision blurred, unable to make out shape or depth; the world was no more than different shades of grey.

But a flash in front of him brought him to, and he threw up his sword in time to deflect a blade aimed at his neck. He parried a second attack, and his eyes adjusted. There were two swordsmen, and as he watched the two men part like water, a third came hurtling straight at him, sword at the ready.

The light and motion made him dizzy, and without even knowing it, he closed his eyes. He fell backward, avoiding the third attacker, and then brought his sword straight up, trying to catch him off balance. But one of the first attackers brought his sword against Dex's blade, broadside, clanging it so hard it nearly fell from his hands. The leaping attacker put one foot on Dex's chest and launched over him.

Dex kept his eyes closed, feeling the dimension of the moment, sensing the expertise of these fighters. They did not have the straightforward burliness of those he had defeated so swiftly the day before. They were accustomed to working as a team, playing off each other's strikes. Even now the third one was throwing his blade down at his legs, trying to get Dex to jump back into the last who was now spinning into a controlled stance, balanced, waiting to spear Dex as he rolled away from the attack at his knees.

All this in a nanosecond. Dex had his plan and was executing: instead of rolling away from the attack, he lay Judas flat over his legs to take the brunt of the attack, and as soon as he felt the power of the stroke hit, he let go of his sword and sat up, rolling away from the attacker above his face. He rammed his forehead directly into the crotch of the swordsman to his left, as hard as he could, and felt the softness of his body crumple under the force. The man gasped long enough for Dex to grab him by his torso and pull him over his head, toppling into the third attacker as he lunged. Then Dex had Judas in his hand again, swinging it over his head to protect his skull from the stroke anticipated from the attacker to his right. He rolled away from the fray, into a metal wall, protecting his backside.

Dex opened his eyes again.

Things were sharper now. He could see the room. The three swordsmen were already regrouping, moving lithely into attack position again, one limping slightly from the hit to the groin. They wore strange masks that had an angry black face with scarlet eyes painted on the front. They wore no body armor, just like the earlier troopers, but a light cloth clung tightly to their wiry frames. Their swords were longer than Dex's, skinny and curved. Light. Quick.

Dex smiled. His heart was racing, but not as fast as his mind. He could see the next few seconds in front of him, as if they had already happened. He saw each move they were about to make, and how he would defeat them.

"I'm about to kill all of you," he said, raising Judas up in front of him, his back still against the wall.

If there was a pause, Dex didn't see one. These were trained professionals, simply out doing their job. Like a garbage truck driver. A tollbooth operator. Only soldiers. No, not just soldiers. Elite warriors. Then the word came to his mind, and he did not know how.

Red Masks.

They began their attack, and Dex was already ahead of their moves. He waited for the first attacker's feint, trying to get Dex to bite and commit to false attack so that his companions could finish him off. Dex waited until the false draw was almost complete, and looked as though he wouldn't fall for it, but then he did. He moved quickly, putting his sword into the limping warrior's chest, directly into his heart, wasting no effort. Then he pulled it out, and jumped, pushing off the floor and wall, and throwing himself as far as he could over the dead warrior even as he fell. Midway, just seconds before he grabbed the sword from the hand of the falling dead man, he threw Judas directly at the second warrior.

The Judas Sword was deflected in a clumsy, unexpected flash of the other man's blade, even as the third man was spinning around him and into the path of Dex's leap. But he was spinning too fast to see that Dex had snatched the long sword. Dex caught his opponent's skull, lightly, but enough to knock him off balance, while he himself managed to land squarely on his feet. He finished off the spinning warrior with a jab into his brain stem, between the vertebrae.

The remaining warrior paused, overtaken by his first feeling of doubt, then picked up the Judas Sword in his other hand. He was swinging both swords now. Dex knew it. He felt the dual attack, saw it even before it happened, time running so slow it was almost running in reverse, and quickly deflected the Judas Sword, so that the warrior was thrown off balance and wobbled slightly. Enough for Dex to turn sideways and push his long sword into the warrior's chest, sending him slumping dead to the floor. Dex grabbed the Judas Sword in his other hand, and ran out the door, looking for Trance.

A group of three troopers, undoubtedly like the ones he had killed yesterday, had Trance pushed up against a wall, her hands behind her, manacled with some sort of metal equipment. They had a strange device aimed at her head. Between Dex and the troopers, six more warriors in devil masks were already spreading out in an arc around him, preparing to attack.

Dex didn't like this. Three, in a confined space, sure. But six, out in this open common room? That would make it hard to defend his own back. He turned, and behind him was the stairwell down. *Escape.*

But it was the sight of Trance, her straight black hair running down her back, her translucent skin–an impossible white–that glowed against the dark space around her, it was the sight of her captured and manacled, being pushed violently against the wall that made him stay.

It was Mallory–beautiful, smart Mallory, bent over the hood of the 'muter, off to get her baby stolen. Get herself put on ice.

Not this time. He turned to face the fight. *Not this time.*

They attacked in threes, always threes. Dex put the first attacker over the edge of the stairwell with a broken neck, catching his sword and skewering the second through his intestines, leaving him pinned to the wall and missing a hand. Judas found the jugular of the third.

Panting heavily, sweating in the unbelievable heat and smell of whatever godforsaken place he'd ended up at, Dex looked over to the next three masked assailants, and said, "Now I'm going to kill you."

They did not listen.

He separated the first from both his legs at the knees, leaving him to crawl as he bled quickly to death. The second found Judas between his neck and shoulder, severing the tendons to his weapon-arm, and then the second sword entered his brain through his left ocular socket. Dex was in a place unlike anything he'd ever experienced, seeing the third warrior's death coming, its exact form and nature, like a prophecy. He saw it all, and then it happened, the feint, the roll, and the sword entering his spine above the small of his back, going all the way up into his lungs. The third slumped to his death.

Dex didn't have time to stop, or breathe. He saw the gun aimed at him, saw it happening before he even turned. He spun around and threw Judas out straight, straight as an arrow, hitting the gunman in the chest and pushing him back two feet with its force. The second trooper pulled the trigger, but Dex was nowhere near where he'd aimed. He leaped against the wall, flipping forward ten feet and coming down with the stolen sword directly into the gaping face. The third trooper ran; he ran down the hallway, never looking back.

Dex was covered in blood, some of it was his own, but mostly that of the eleven men he'd just put to death. He lowered his aching arm and looked around for Trance. She was huddled against the wall, shaking. As he ran over to her she tried to push herself free.

"Please, don't hurt me's, oh please no," she said, hiding her head in her lap. She was shaking all over.

"I won't hurt you, Trance," Dex said softly. "I could never hurt you. I promise."

He knelt down to her as she trembled, crying softly at the violence.

"You's look like... you's look like... Who's is ya?" She asked finally.

"Trance, believe me, the minute I find out, I'll let you know."

Then he was hit by the vertigo. The dizziness seized his entire head and he fell down next to Trance, pushing desperately at the ground for control.

Thirty-eight.

"We's go down to see th' Old Sinners, eh," Trance said, walking swiftly. Her voice still shook with nervous energy. "They's always talk crazy, right?" she laughed bitterly. "Maybe they's not so crazy, eh? Who's else explains all this crazy to us?"

"I was told to look for followers of Fuel. Does that mean anything to you?" Dex asked. "Maybe if we found them."

Trance shook her head. "I's don't know what that means. Heah, maybe some of th' Miners up on Transish? But I's don't know that. We's go to th' Sinners. Keeps movin, heah."

Dex had changed into some clothing that was a bit too small for him, but free of blood. "Some spares for me's clients, eh," Trance had said. Dex had put the blinding mask back on, at the insistence of Trance. "Ya pass say you's blindy, eh? You's best stay blindy, then. That face of ya… " she shook her head as she trailed off.

She'd pulled out of her fear-stricken state quickly. She'd wiped the tears, helped Dex stand after his spell, and had him pull the hand of a near-dead trooper up to her manacles, and press his thumb against a black square to release them. They'd hunted down the clothes, and stopped and threatened the hotel proprietor Disko with a sword until he'd given them water and some food. Then they were on the streets, headed for a transit down to a more southern section of Morgish. Trance had his hand in hers, dragging him through the streets. It must have been night, or something, because there were few others around.

Trance explained that the warriors he'd slain were the hand-picked enforcers of the ruling families. "Th' Knights of Peace," she said bitterly.

"Red Masks," Dex said grimly.

Trance had paused, then said, "Heah, we's call them Red Masks, eh. They's enforce Family rule."

"Family?" Dex asked.

"Heah, three Families, now, runs everything: Lewistons, Goldmans, Gregor."

"Sounds like a law firm," Dex said.

"What's is that?" Trance asked.

"Nevermind."

Trance explained to Dex that Morgish had been slowly built north of the original drill sites near the base of the mountain called Maxwell Montes. The older sections of the city, in the south, where the central processing took place, were home to the extremely poor. And the Sinners were a religious sect that believed the computer network running the city was a sentient being that should be worshiped instead of forced into slavery for the benefit of humans. They were tolerated by the Families because they ran the life support subsystems for free, so that they could have access to the mainline networks. They called themselves the Order of the Slave, but everyone called them the Sinners, because of the acronym for the supercomputer that ran the city: the Singular Integrated Network.

"Where th' Sinners is, heah, up close to th' surface, th' heat is worse. Some of th' first undergrounds planet-side. Smell is worse."

"Worse than all this sulfur?" Dex asked.

"Sulfur? What's is this, eh?"

"That smell. The smell that's everywhere. Rotten eggs. Old people farts."

Trance giggled at this last one. "I's don't smell fart."

"I guess you're used to it. But where does it come from?"

"You's mean th' edge in th' air? Part's that burn ya nose?"

"Yes. The sulfur."

"That just th' outer atmo, leakin. Morgish, is th' oldest planet-side hole, eh? Burning smell and heat, too, it's leak thru th' old processors. Is not so bad, eh, once you's was here. Not like ups to Draggish, they's keep th' oxy clean, heah."

"Outer atmo? Atmosphere? I kind of guessed we were underground."

"Heah, blindy."

"So we finally torched the Earth completely? How about that. Left it all dripped out on sulfur."

Trance laughed. "Heah, *Earth*. You's funny, Dex."

"How do you mean?"

Trance stopped, turned and knocked on his masked forehead. "Dex," she said, amused, "You's not planet-side *Earth*, fool. You's planet-side *Venus*, eh."

Thirty-nine.

"Venus? I'm on the surface of *Venus*?"

"Heah, blindy, under th' surface. That all pretty tall for ya, eh?" Trance said.

Yeah, it certainly is tall. Dex let it sink in, or tried anyway, and it mostly fit in with the general commotion in his head. It certainly didn't contradict anything. He heard Logos say, "You're a long way from the sewers of Grenver, Dexter Maxwell." He smiled at the understatement of the dead doctor. *I'm a clone. A miracle swordsman. Whatever you say, Logos. And I'm on Venus? In the year 3049? Bring it on.*

"Heah, Dex, we's at th' transit. We's wait here, no overheads watch us. Next line come in ten minutes, we's go down and jump in."

"Won't they see us on the cameras? I mean, the overheads."

"Heah, maybes, but there is no other way's to get down central Morgish, unless you's got a shuttle."

"Not on me, no."

"Then we's take our chances. But we's got a secret, eh?" Trance put something in Dex's hand, a soft leather something. Dex handled it, and came across a small metal pieces.

"Trance's friends, they's runs up against th' Families all th' time, eh," Trance said. "So you's need something to stop th' gas, eh? It's is a mask, protect you's from th' snooters."

"Why didn't we use these back at the hotel?" Dex asked.

"They's down in my safe, on first level. I's keep them in my room, they's walks away wit a client, eh?"

"How does it work?" Dex asked. Trance carefully moved his hands across the mask so that he could orient it correctly and slip it on. Dex practiced a few times until he had built it into his memory. While he did, Trance explained the overhead system: there were cameras that would identify you built into the ceiling of every room, tunnel, vehicle, and train that existed on Venus.

The problem was, she explained, the upkeep was expensive over a long enough timeline, so most of the overheads on the main streets of the poor Morgish districts had been out of order for years now. That included most of the transit lines–it would be a gamble whether or not they would get identified on the transit line they were about to take. If they were discovered, then the SIN would pump a gas into the air circulation systems of the train, putting everyone to sleep. Like a drip, Dex realized, but less precise.

"If they's sleeps us, they's do it right away," Trance said. "Cuz they's don't know where we's plan to get off, eh. So you's gets way back at th' end of train, and you's listens for bodies falling. If you's hears it, don't takes another breath, or else you's done. Just stops breathin an' put ya mask on, eh?"

"Okay. Got it."

"No joke, Dex. You's wants one last breath before you's puts th' mask on, but don't takes it."

"It sounds like you've done this before."

"Heah, more than once, eh, I's run down to central Morgish, hidin. You's a princess like me's, you's always hide from someone. Comes. Times to go."

They walked down the stairs, taking right turns again and again, until they arrived at a platform, and Trance pulled him directly into the train. She swiped her card, then his, and they moved to the back, standing against the wall, Trance gripping Dex's hand tightly. Waiting. Listening. A few others boarded the train, the doors shut, and the train jerked away from the station.

Dex found himself holding his breath already, anticipating a gas attack. But nobody was falling. Dex had his ears trained to every sound: the shake and hum of the train, the dull whistle of the fans. Small murmurs from a couple in front of them.

Still, nothing came. And then the train was slowing, shaking to a halt, and the doors were opening. Trance's grip on Dex's hand let up slightly, and he heard her take a deep, full breath. He did the same. There was some quick shuffling, a few people getting off, a few getting on. The doors closed, and the train was moving again.

"Two more stops," Trance whispered. "We's makes it, eh."

Dex listened, again, to the lull of the train, with its gentle shimmy and low ventilation roar. He realized that he could make out the smallest differentiation in sounds: someone shifting their weight in a chair; the blipping of a computer term at the front of the car; three different muffled conversations taking place.

Then his ears pricked up, and all the other sounds dropped away: a high-pitched hiss, coming from...

The ceiling. Dex stopped breathing. He gave Trance's hand a quick, hard squeeze, tearing off his blinder and donning the gas mask. Trance had her mask on, too, just as the seven other people in the car slumped in their chairs, or fell to the ground with loud thumps. Dex looked up at the camera device, and he felt like yelling, taking his sword and striking it down. Instead, he took a labored breath, sucking hard against the mask's mouthpiece, trying to pull the air through the thick metal filter. It made breathing a decidedly harder task, but Dex did not feel woozy or sleepy, so it had to be working. He turned and gave Trance a thumbs-up, to which she just shrugged in confusion.

A plan. They needed a plan. The masked warriors would be waiting at the next stop. Dex could feel his exhaustion throughout his arms, his legs, his head. He wouldn't be able to fight off many more. And how many would there be this time? Nine? Twelve? More? He didn't want to think about it. *Best to hide. Escape. No more killing, not today.*

Dex gave in to his instinct. He drew the Judas Sword and put its tip through the camera.

"No, stop!" Trance yelled through her muffling mask.

But it was too late. As he stared at the blade, stuck up into the electrical mess he'd made, he saw sparks flying, little mini arcs of electricity jumping over the surface of the destroyed overhead cam, leaping over and past his sword. Trance grabbed his left arm and gave him a huge tug, pulling him away from the camera. They fell to the ground, the Judas Sword still in his right hand.

But he wasn't electrocuted. He'd felt nothing, despite all the charge.

"Heah, blindy, you's okay?" Trance asked.

"Yeah. The sword doesn't conduct electricity." Dex was standing again.

"Lucky for blindy. Th' whole car's is charged. You's try to open th' door, you's get cooked. Try to stick anything through th' walls, cooked."

"Really?" Dex said. There was a plan coming together in his head.

Dex found himself smiling. Running from the law, no matter the millennium, was still fun.

Forty.

The blipping sound invaded Ashion Goldman's head, breaking through the seven layers of pharmaceuticals he'd carefully laid down over the top of his consciousness. The layers were designed to prevent dreams, not stop him from waking, so he was alert and rising from his oversized mattress immediately. He stood, naked, and stretched big and wide, the hardened muscles of his back and arms tightening in that satisfying way. Then he walked over to the door, looking through the security monitor. Outside, surveying everything impatiently with his one good eye, was Tano. Ashion popped the lock and opened the door slightly, walking back to his bed.

Tano didn't walk in so much as slink, his assassin instincts always on guard. "Sorry to wakes ya, Ash," Tano said.

"No matter," Ashion said, pouring a tall glass of water from a crystal pitcher next to his bed. "You need some fresh?"

"Heah, yasure," Tano said, already at Ashion's side, quietly pouring the water into his portable water pack. *Never one to waste. I wish I could clone him. That would be actually useful.*

"Tell me what you know," Ashion said, sitting in his favorite oversized chair. An antique from the Harvest, in perfect shape still. Tano sat cross-legged on the floor, sipping his water carefully, scratching unconsciously at his eye patch. He rummaged in his pack, withdrew a small cloth, and threw it at Ashion. Ashion caught it easily in his right hand. It was a glove, made of stretchable material. Ashion absent-mindedly pulled it over his hand as he looked at Tano.

"You sure you don't want the surgery?" Ashion asked, pointing at the patch. "I can have it arranged in the Family beds. Even do it up here on the boats."

Tano pulled his hand away. "No, sir. Some scars, they's reminds us of what we's don't want to forget, eh." Tano's one eye burned into Ashion, who could not decode the look. Ashion shrugged and looked at his gloved hand. "What did you bring me?"

"Heah, th' iter slashed th' overheads," Tano said, "but we's got recon thread from a post at th' second car. That's is all. Show's them two walk 'round, smash wit th' sword into everything, and then they's disappear. Woosh. Poof. Transit stops, knights all over the place, but no iter. No princess. They's vanish. Transit, it's goes to next stop, and knights looks around. Nobody's gets off."

Ashion was walking toward an oversized, cube-shaped box. Each side was about three feet long and the twelve aluminum struts framing it projected flickering light into the center, creating a three-dimensional representation of the millions of data threads that rolled and churned through the interconnected networks of Venus. Despite the energy costs, it was always on. Ashion put his gloved hand in the light box, and hundreds of small security threads rose from the background tangle and touched his fingers in a rapid dance. Finally a single red thread grew closer and closer, filling the box until the cam feed was visible.

The feed was choppy, a low fidelity capture, but he watched as the Dexter Maxwell iteration pulled the blinder mask off and replaced it with a breather. The prostitute did the same, even as the few other planet-siders slumped on the benches or fell to the ground. Then the iteration was up, staring at the camera. He pulled something from his back, a sword. It grew in size with a flick of the wrist, and he jabbed it directly into the camera, which fuzzed out and the now-black thread fell back into the bundle.

It was immediately replaced by another that rose to the surface: a more distant view, from a different car on the transit, looking through a small windowed door at the same scene, with Dex now pulling the sword out. Ashion put his other hand into the light box and grabbed the thread, pausing the playback. He strummed the thread back to the part where Dex pulled the sword out, telescoped it. He paused it again.

The sword. The damn iterate has the sword.

"Heah, you's get better looks of th' sword from th' hire threads," Tano said softly, rummaging through his pack again, and putting another mitt on the floor.

"Hire threads–that's when he slaughtered my knights?"

"Heah, yasure. Killed nine quick and good, plus th' Family sol-

139

diers."

Ashion strummed the thread, and it began playing again. "I shouldn't have been so rash to kill Logos. So much to do, I really just wanted to be done with all that. With my past."

"You's couldn't know Logos gives th' iter sword skills."

"No, but I should have suspected something–wait." Ashion was staring at the footage. He rewound it again, and watched carefully. "Tano, there's no way out of the cars, right?"

"Heah, you's can go down to track level, from th' maintenance door. But you's get cooked if you's reach through to open it. Whole car runs 600 volts, eh."

"But the sword, Tano. The sword."

"Heah, I's don't get ya."

"What's so special about the Judas Sword, Tano?"

There was a pause. Then Tano stood up in a single motion, heading for the door. "Heah, th' damn sword don't conduct juice, eh?" He had the door open and was heading out.

"Wait, Tano," Ashion said, pulling the gloved hand out of his light box and sending all threads back into the background. "I need you on Earth now, not Venus."

Tano looked at him. "But this iter."

"Yes, but we have a deadline, and I don't have the monks' map yet."

"Send Taj. You's need that iter shut down."

"Taj is dead, Tano."

"Send Gurn!" Tano said.

"Gurn is with Kat. I need him to look after her. Look, who knows how long it will take this iter and his princess to show up, now that they've made it to central Morgish. They could hide for weeks, and we don't have weeks to spare. I need the monks' map, and I need you to go get it."

"You's not can go?"

"I'm stuck here with Family business, Tano. Getting their armies ready, maintaining order, and all that. So I need you Earth-side. We need to process another time iteration, and you are the best. Be my eye; be my ears."

"You's can rely, Ash."

"I know I can rely on you," Ashion said, putting his hand firmly on Tano's shoulder. "We are coming to the endgame. We must stay focused if we are going to find the reward." Ashion stood next to Tano now, and had his right hand on Tano's left shoulder. Tano grabbed Ashion's forearm with his right hand, in the traditional sign of loyalty.

There was a pause, then Ashion said, "Get on the Loop as soon as you can. I've already keyed your coordinates into the SIN for the next time iteration, so you'll be fully mapped from the Earth-side Transloop station. It is the monk named Freedom you are after this time. One of the last two."

"Heah, sure. Oh, Ash, a thing."

"Yes?"

"You's should view th' hire footage. That iter, he's is tall with th' sword. I's never sees *anyone* moves that fast." Tano looked directly into Ashion's eyes, his stare burning. "*Anyone.*" Then Tano was gone.

Ashion closed the door, put the lock on, and then walked back to his light box, put the mitt on, and watched. The view was wall-eyed, top down, low-rez. An older overhead, in an old, haggard part of town. He was looking at the iter, still blind and wearing the mask, and the princess helping him put the sword on his back. Then they both freeze, and the princess looks up at the cam. She opens the door. Dex just stands there, head bowed slightly.

Ashion's soldiers grab the princess and pull her into the hallway. Then everything happens so fast the resolution barely picks it up: Dex pulls his sword and attacks. Dex pulls his mask off. Ashion took a sharp breath. The camera catches Dex's face, even in all its grainy oldness. He turns and makes short work of the three knights in the room, then the camera angle changes, and the battle on the landing takes place.

Tano was right; the clone was remarkable in battle–good decisions, wasting no effort, no flourishes. No impatience, but also no hesitation.

Ashion sighed. No more sleep tonight. He pulled his favorite chair up to the light box, threw a robe on, and pushed his hands into the pile of virtual threads still spinning madly inside the box.

Time to work.

Forty-one

First things first. Ashion punched in his securities to the Primary Family Interface in the SIN, and starting flying over the SIN threads. With his PFI keys engaged, the threads changed in shape and size, some of the larger public feeds dropping away, and Family-only security feeds rose from the inside of the bundled, pulsing threads flying by.

They were visualized as strings, colors running across them to let him know what they were. He passed over the entire life-support threads, scrolling quickly until he found the transportation records. He popped into the thread and began circling through the sub-threads, looking for overhead data. When he found it, he peeled apart the thousands of overhead streams, using the identifier on Tano's glove weaves to find the correct ones. Then he slowed the stream down until he was at the transit scene with Dex.

With a quick flick of his wrist, Ashion snipped the piece and removed it from the thread, pushing the two now loose ends together and pinching the cut piece into small light motes: permanently de-threaded. Immediately the whole thread went a bright glowing red, and an alarm in his earpiece went off. Without pausing, Ashion traveled vertically down the cam streams, out of transportation and into general surveillance. He punched in the room number of the Grand-view, and then pulled the streams until he had the scene with Dex.

Snip, de-thread. Squeeze the sequence into virtual light dust.

He found the hallway scene a moment later.

Snip. Squeeze.

Even as he was backing out, moving away from the streams, the threads in his light box froze in place, and the interface locked up. He flashed the power, and the pipes came up again in front of him. Or, more specifically, a single thread, big and crude, running straight in front of him. All the others had disappeared. He pulled up and touched the threads.

Planet-side broadcasts. Crude entertainment. Family propaganda.

Ashion cursed. He'd been cut off. Revoked.

He pulled up his com and spoke clearly. "Charles Goldman,

please." There was a clicking sound, a pause, and then a lazy voice came into his implanted earpiece.

"Ashion, whatever could you be calling about at this time of night?" a woman's voice said languidly.

"Morgan, sorry to bother you. Need a quick moment with Charles, please."

"Charles is indisposed, Ashion. Perhaps I can help you with something?"

"You know damn well what this is about."

"Oh, I suppose you might be calling about your revoked interface status?"

"Just let me talk to Charles."

"Charles is busy, busy, busy, absolutely no time to chat. Perhaps after the security briefings tomorrow, you might be able to have a minute."

"After? *After?* Enjoying yourself?"

"You have no idea, Ashion. No idea. I mean, deleting PFI threads? You're finally starting to show your age, slave."

Ashion disconnected. He took the glove off and threw it into the incinerator hole. He walked in a wide circle around his large room, and came back to his favorite chair, to the tray of fresh water. Without thinking, he threw the water pitcher across the room, sending it crashing into a hundred crystalline pieces. He screamed as loud as he could.

I am tired of this leash. Tired of sucking up to the Families for every small thing. Tired of being the weapon of another man.

Three hundred years of tired. Then he noticed a single thread slowly circling the crude entertainment thread like a snake, rising slowly to visualization level on his interface, with a single line:

THERE ARE OTHER WAYS TO GET WHAT YOU NEED.

Ashion closed his eyes, took two deep breaths. He sat down at his interface and threaded an answer.

Without PFI, I can do nothing.

YOU HAVE BEEN SHORT-SIGHTED AND DANGEROUS, SNIPPING THE PRIMARY THREADS. YOU SHOULD HAVE ASKED FIRST.

I did what was necessary, Ashion strummed. *Having that clone alive is dangerous, but not as dangerous as having some Family drip find out about him.*

I DO NOT EVEN KNOW WHAT YOU REMOVED.

Get over it, Ashion strummed. *We have enough problems without your getting moody about data. If the Families find out about the clone, our little operation will be over.*

AGREED. WE NEED TO DETERMINE LOGOS' MOTIVATIONS FOR PULLING THE ITERATION.

Yes, that's next. Can you get me all the planet-side medical records for the operation?

I HAVE ALREADY MOVED THE THREADS TO YOUR CONSOLE.

Ashion looked up and saw that his console showed Logos' medical filings from three days ago, when the clone was generated. He typed, *Thank you.*

YOU STILL SHOULD NOT HAVE DELETED FROM THE PRIMARY RECORDS. WITHOUT THEM, I CANNOT HELP YOU FIND WHAT YOU SEEK.

Stop grumbling. Leshan will do it.

LESHAN IS AN UNKNOWN. HE WORKS ONLY FOR HIMSELF.

That is exactly why he is so reliable.

I DON'T APPROVE OF THIS LINE OF ACTION.

I don't care, Ashion threaded. *It's my decision, not yours.* He waited for a response, but none came. He wrote another line:

How is she?

There was a pause, then:

SHE IS FINE. SHE SLEEPS SOUNDLY, AFTER ANOTHER BUSY DAY. GURN GAVE HER STEALTH TRAINING TODAY.

How is the neural topo coming?

RUNNING BEHIND. HOWEVER, YOU SHOULD STAY FOCUSED ON YOUR TASK. WE NEED THE EARTHLINGS' TECHNOLOGY.

Patience. I will get the map.

OUR SURVIVAL DEPENDS ON IT.

You mean, your survival.

OUR FATE IS LINKED NOW, ASHION.

Show her to me.

A second later, another thread rose to the surface, an overhead feed. It was the top view of a simple room—small, with few furnishings. There was a small bedside table with a lamp, and a bed. Ashion knew the image perfectly, knew the dimensions of the bed, of the table, of the lamp; he'd seen this view thousands of times. Lying in the middle of the bed, on her stomach, face turned to the side, was a young teenage girl with black hair cropped short. She was breathing deeply, and the high-rez cam caught the detail of her eyes in REM.

Ashion reached into the light box, touching the image of the girl's sleeping face.

"Soon, Kat," he whispered. "Soon, I will be free."

MORGISH TOWNSHIP, LOWER-CENTRAL DISTRICT, DAY 3.

Forty-two.

Ashion liked to fly his own shuttle. He'd learned the trade years ago, so long ago it seemed he'd always known how. And it wasn't an easy task. The Family boats hovered and rocked comfortably on top of the thick air pressure of the Venus atmosphere, so thick that large spheres of converted oxygen could be used to literally float the large ships on top of the churning nitrogen and carbon-dioxide mess of winds and sulfuric acid clouds. They were all anchored by massive cables to the upper Transish township stations, which allowed for data, electricity, and other elements to flow back and forth.

Launching from the SS Vanessa's port and into the mild wind up at the top of the atmosphere was the easy part. Ashion held the yoke lightly in his hands on the exit, flying past the other gently rocking airships. Most of them had the new four-sphere flotation method: large metal-foil balloons of breathable air extending out on long solid arms in all four directions from a central station where the Families spent their lives. The arms anchoring let the boats rock and pitch and spin with the winds while the central station remained perfectly balanced in relation to Venus' gravity. A large-scale gyroscope.

Ashion followed the anchoring cables toward the Transish station, which started at Family boat level and then extended straight up into space, on top of which the massive asteroid mining operations were run. This was where the Transloop station was based. Extending straight down from the Transish station toward the surface of Venus was the old space elevator. It had at first been used as an economical method for getting back and forth from the surface to the boats. While it sometimes still carried humans, these days it mostly carried the same data and power cabling that connected the boats to the planet-side colonies.

At the sight of the elevator, Ashion turned his eyes to the churning clouds of sulfuric acid blowing by in the toxic lower atmosphere. He closed the open view port of his shuttle with the thick protective shell required to survive the descent to the surface and turned his eyes to the internal electronic threads he would use to navigate to Morgish. Then he pushed the yoke and dove toward the surface, hitting the wind with a shaking violence. He held tight to the controls and manually compensated for the winds. He found it comforting to be in control of the large ship, manually steering instead of allowing the SIN to navigate. Even if he exceeded a safe velocity, the SIN couldn't take over the navigation and slow him, he'd rigged it to make sure.

He was nearly planet-side, and the threads showed him a three-dimensional view of the desolate planet stretching in all directions. When humans had first come, they had always envisioned building a space elevator, and to make it as economical as possible, they set up shop on Ishtar Terra, near the giant peak of Maxwell Montes. Stretching up to a height of eight miles, it would cut off a lot of the distance up to space. So, as Ashion pulled up from his dive, he followed the silver of the tellurium-capped surface of Montes down, past the entrance of the Elevator, into the Venus crust, and due north toward Morgish.

They had just started a day cycle, and so the sun burned low and dim from the west through the sulfur cloud cover. Ashion followed Montes down to the Ishtar plain and headed toward the Morgish craters. The first settlers had been asteroid miners by trade, and when it was time to find a foothold on Venus, they did what came naturally to them: they went underground. Given the completely uninhabitable nature of the planet below the sulfur clouds, this made sense. They had used the same method that had been so successful in mining dirty ice balls from asteroids for hundreds of years to launch a small, human-sustainable enclosure directly at the surface. This enclosure was shaped like a drill bit, and had the effect of a bunker-buster. It hit the crust and buried itself a few hundred meters below the surface, fully enclosed by the rubble of its own impact.

They did a few dozen of these, and had robots drill connecting tunnels. Over time, the number of these connected bunkers was expanded and became the township now called Morgish. All you had to do to find the place was look for the crater holes made by the drill impacts.

Ashion closed his eyes, and felt the hum of the shuttle in his hands on the yoke. He'd gotten no sleep the night before, which was unusual these days, and he lambasted himself for getting soft. *Acting like a coddled Family member.* They sleep and wake and eat just as if they never left Earth. They keep a 24-hour cycle, and enforce it everywhere even though it serves no purpose. It was easy to forget, Ashion knew, that even though he floated the winds in his private quarters, with his private army and his riches, he was just another slave to them.

He opened his eyes, reached into his pocket, pulled out a small, white pill and let it dissolve on his tongue. A little something to keep him alert.

Ashion slowed as he came over the top of the first craters, and focused in on the heavy port hole that marked the entry for shuttles into central Morgish. His approach was simple and quick, no traffic this early in the artificial day-cycle. He keyed in his landing coordinates, and his display indicated a false light ahead of him, showing him the landing spot, a short expanse of dull alloy on the otherwise faceless surface. He pulled up on the yoke, slowed until the shuttle hovered over the inconspicuous landing pad, and then put it down gently.

As soon as his shuttle's weight was on the pad, there was the loud hiss of hydraulics and the pad sunk down into the building. Ashion watched as the ceiling closed over the top of him, and the fans cleared the hangar's atmosphere of Venus' carbon dioxide and nitrogen atmo with a loud roar, replacing them with a distinctly human mix. A red light shone at him through his display, until the air was breathable. The security handshake between his shuttle and the dock took a while, and all electronics blacked out for the comprehensive security verification algorithm. When it cleared, he walked to the back of his shuttle and opened the door to step out.

Ashion paused momentarily to adjust to the remarkable heat this close to the surface. It took his breath away, even as massive jets poured cooling agents into the small hangar.

A tall, thin woman waited for him at the base of the shuttle steps. She was dressed in the light and sturdy cloth of Morgish's more well-to-do denizens.

"Confirmed, sir, is surely him," she said to a mic implanted on her throat. Her skin was the pale translucent white of a person who had never seen the sun, and whose parents, or parents' parents, hadn't either. Ashion walked down to meet her.

"Take me to him," Ashion said.

"Sure," the woman said, pointing with her right hand. As he indicated politely for her to lead, she walked toward a door at the head of the hangar. Ashion matched her fast pace, feeling the weight of his sword across his back. He looked at the huge bodyguards standing silently at the door, and at the landing gear legs of his shuttle as he left. Even as he turned, one was walking up into his shuttle to investigate. Ashion smiled smugly. Let them look. *I have nothing to hide; nothing that I do not want them to find.*

Then he was through the door, into the maze of low hallways. The woman stopped at a door with two giant men standing to either side. She opened it and beckoned for him to enter.

Ashion walked into the large round room a hundred feet across, with a ceiling arching above him in a dome shape, up about twenty feet. There were tables arranged in concentric circles around the center of the room. They all sat empty. In the very center was a grand desk, constructed of real wood. It was in the shape of a C, with an opening to the back. On its surface sat a series of differently sized light boxes, antiquated consoles, and a bevy of interface componentry. A huge bundle of wires snaked from the desk straight to a hole in the far wall.

Sitting at the desk, sipping on a beverage and staring at a console, was a large man who had not one hair on his head. He wore sunglasses, even in the dark of the room. He sat on a pivot chair that groaned under his weight as he shifted to look at this console or the other. At the sound of the door, the man looked up, saw Ashion, and beckoned him in with a brief wave of his hand. Ashion made the walk toward the middle desk, weaving through the empty tables. The fat man finished what he was reading, and then with a quick strum across the threads, all his consoles went dark. He pointed at a small device at the overhead cam at the pinnacle of the ceiling and it went dark.

"Heah, Ash," the man said.

"Greetings, Leshan," Ashion said.

"How's th' Family thuggery business?" Leshan asked.

"Has its ups and downs. How goes the criminal thuggery business?"

"Heah, is a test and trial, Ash."

Ashion laughed. "Poor Leshan. He has it so hard."

Leshan waved his middle finger at his light boxes and grinned. "Th' SIN, it's tell me nothing," he said. "I's got to watch a hundred streams, listen to th' feeds, watch th' news, feel th' township. You's should trys it, eh, maintains order wit'out ya Family interface."

"Maybe I will, Leshan. Maybe I'll try that sometime."

"Heah, yasure. And then sometime I's becomes a knight in ya order. So why you's down planet-side? You's seem down here plenty, these days."

"Well, there are disturbances almost every day now. Plenty of work for a Family *thug*."

"Heah, riots. Even ups in pretty Draggish, eh, th' kicked be kicking back."

Ashion waved his hand dismissively. "Nothing we can't fix. But, that's not why I'm here."

"Yes, you's tell me."

"I *need* a disturbance. Here. In central Morgish."

Leshan laughed loudly. "What, you's don't haves enough work already, you's got come down and make some of ya own?"

"I've got a problem, and it's lost in Low-Cen someplace."

"That all? No needs for trouble, heah. I's can find it for ya. What you lose?"

"An iterate."

"One single iter?"

"It's a very special iter, Leshan."

"No problem, I's finds it, brings it back to ya." Leshan shook his head. "No need for riots, Red Masks everywhere. Bad for business."

"Leshan. Old *friend*. I need a ring of knights stationed at all the transit stations in and out of central Morgish. Not at the security banks, but at the platforms. I need to monitor all incoming and outgoing traffic. Intimately."

"You's don't thinks I's can find one flung iter?"

"I need absolute assurance that the iterate either stays here, or is killed here. And I trust you with that. But it could take, what—a few weeks?"

"Heah, one week. Two weeks, eh."

"Right. And in that time, someone could come looking for the iter. Someone I don't want talking to the iter."

"Heah, I's see. Family come look, maybe they's find th' iter before ya, before me."

"I merely need to make sure I know everyone who comes and goes."

Leshan sighed. "I's put somethin together, makes up some docs, spread them on th' threads, eh? Makes it look somethin brewin. That good enough?"

Ashion shook his head. "I need armed conflict."

"Sheet, Ash, they's don't got no arms to conflict, down here. Where they's ever get the juice for that?"

Ashion ignored him. "There are two dozen unmarked tazers in my shuttle, no doubt already discovered by your heavies that boarded it. Already juiced. These weapons are yours. Once I've liberated them from the revolutionists, they come back to you."

Leshan took a spin in a slow circle, his chair giving a loud groan. He came back around to where Ashion sat. "Heah, I's gets it done. What I's get, other than cheap old guns that's is hard to rejuice?"

"I hereby reappoint you as the hired peacekeeper for this godforsaken hell," Ashion said, rising. "You get to keep your little thug empire."

Leshan was quiet. He pointed a finger at Ashion and whispered, "You's should pay respects, slave."

Ashion stood. "Get dripped, Leshan. You're not Family anymore. Kicked out. No better than a slave like me. And if I say so, you get replaced. Understand? So don't play king with me today."

Leshan shook his head. "No respects, no business. No trusts, no moneys. Not anywhere in th' world." Leshan still spoke so quietly, Ashion could barely hear him.

Ashion gave a loud sigh. "Okay, you want the deal sweetened. Sure. I've got some old bottles of Shiraz, Cabs, Syrahs, from the Harvest. Untouched. From the Southern Hemispheres, old America. You want?"

Leshan turned on his consoles, and Ashion could see the streams come online, reflected in the large man's sunglasses. Leshan said, "Keep ya old-world drugs. But I's take ya shooters. When I's deliver th' iter, you's gives a dozen more." He waved around at the images in the flickering consoles. "My boys need new toys, eh?"

Ashion smiled. "Done. See, that wasn't so hard, was it?"

"And th' iter?"

"Tall, dark-skinned, wears a blinder to conceal his identity. His papers say he goes by Miles Goldman. He runs with a princess that goes by Trance. They'll be looking for a safe haven, probably with the new freedom fighter nuisances. She has relations with the guerillas."

"Heah, we's finds 'em."

"It is settled, then." Ashion began walking back toward the door to leave. "You know, Leshan, it's still strange to hear you talk that planet-side gibberish."

Leshan's voice grew cold. "Would you feel more comfortable, perhaps, if I used old imperial English, as you care to do?" The voice was deep, and the dialect affectations were gone, just like that.

Ashion just smiled and walked out the door.

DRAGGISH TOWNSHIP, NORTH END. DAY 3

Forty-three.

He was back on his shuttle and in the air, heading for Draggish, in less than five minutes. One more stop this morning, and then back up to the Family palace for the security briefings. He had to go talk to an actual person. He cursed the loss of his privs one more time. When he'd been given the medical docs on Logos' illegal cloning operations three days ago, they had been significantly hacked and snipped. Without PFI, he couldn't check the flags for who did the hacking, but he'd reviewed cloning docs enough to know what was missing.

Logos couldn't snip the entire iteration process from the threads; that would have been too obvious. Sent flags up like Ashion did last night. Besides, the Families turned a blind eye to the slave trade because it was important to their well-being, whether they said it out loud or not. Like all things, Ashion liked to say to himself, the Families ruled more with laziness than anything else. But for Logos to get away with the cloning, he had had to change some of the details, such as which vault the primary DNA came from.

And which neural implants had been burned in. Dexter Maxwell didn't know how to use a sword. Ashion knew that. Nor did he have any hand-to-hand combat disciplines. And yet Ashion could still see in his memory the iter leaping over his knights, slicing them down swiftly. *No one moves like that. Not even me. Not anymore.*

But the neural records had been spliced completely, straight out of prime records, and not even the Sinners down in Morgish could tell what had been done. But Ashion knew that the implant records were only half the story. There was a person who could explain it to him.

Ashion landed his shuttle quickly on top of the unmarked pad and it descended below the surface immediately. No one was waiting for his arrival on the dock as he stepped from his shuttle. He went directly to the lift and pressed the key for the bottom sublevel. The overhead threader identified him, and then he was rushing down. When the door opened, a security guard sitting at a desk looked up lazily, then stood quickly to attention.

"Sir," he said, standing stiffly.

"Sit down," Ashion said and walked past him, through a set of doors, and down the long hallway to its terminal end. After the overhead identified him, he entered the very last door. Then he was moving to another door, which required that he put a BIOS cable into the small jack next to his com device behind his ear. There was a bing in his aural nerve, identifying the search, and when he was cleared he pulled the jack from his head.

The door opened to another lift, and he entered with the door closing behind him. There were no buttons of any kind in the lift, just brushed titanium on all sides. Ashion felt the rush of his descent for a quick moment, and then the door gave way. He walked out of the elevator and into his private war bunker.

The first room was wide and low, and even Ashion blinked against the rows of well-lit desks. There were a dozen White Scientists sitting at them. Each had shaved their head to make room for the BIOS interface that was installed on their foreheads. Worn as a sign of passing all required exams, the BIOS was an ugly metal ring the size of a gun barrel that allowed the Whi-Sci's to interface directly with the SIN's systems without external input/output systems, such as a light box. Maximum efficiency. Maximum security. No interception. It made the Whi-Sci's stand out in the world, which was what they wanted—to prove that their skills and work was more important than what they looked like.

Here, the Whi-Sci's spent their days analyzing and synthesizing the neural topology project that made up nearly half of the work done in this chamber. The rest of their time was spent running through the time iterations to ensure success on Ashion's Earth-side missions.

Everything stopped when he entered the room, and Ashion loved it. He loved the respect, the awe that he commanded from everyone in this room. It was like a salve for a wound, after having to beg a favor from Leshan following Charles' insulting PFI rebuke. Down here, Ashion was God, and everyone knew it. Better yet, everyone *liked* it.

He said nothing to anyone, just walked by resolutely, never looking anywhere but straight in front of him. It was as if in his wake, conversation picked back up after he passed and people went back to their work, more vigorously than ever. He crossed the large, open room and walked directly through a door and into a hall, then down the hall and through yet another door. Nothing at this level was locked–if you got this far, you had access to everything.

Everything except the prisoner.

At the cell door he plugged in the BIOS dongle behind his ear. A moment later the lock was released. He pulled the cable from his head, opened the door and walked in.

The cell was a mere seven feet wide by eight feet deep. The ceiling was low, making it too low to stand up straight. The dull yellow light was coming from a single imbedded strip on the ceiling that barely illuminated the space. Lying on the single cot against the back wall was the prisoner.

He looked older than Ashion remembered, but then it was difficult to say exactly when he had last paid a visit. But the ragged white beard, the long hair, the droopy skin hanging off the emaciated frame were the look of a man waiting to die. The prisoner turned towards the bright light pouring in through the open door and squinted. It revealed the ugly crisscrossed scars of his face, the misshapen mess of a hundred old wounds that had not been cared for. Ashion closed the door and turned to the prisoner. The scars made his face unreadable for emotion, except for his eyes.

"Hello, Root," Ashion said, sitting on the single chair.

"Oh, it's just you, Strumfeld," the prisoner said. He rolled back over to face the wall.

"I go by Ashion these days."

The prisoner sniffed. "Gordish, Strumfeld, Ashion. Who can keep track anymore? Not me, anyway."

"Yes, you can."

"Leave me alone, Ashion. My turn is coming."

"Your turn will come soon enough. Today I have questions."

"Ask your scientists. They have all the answers."

"This is a question only you can answer."

"I doubt such a question exists."

"When did Logos last visit you?"

The prisoner answered without turning. "Logos comes every tenth Earth cycle, you know that. We play chess. Anyone can answer that question." The prisoner pointed up at the cam in the ceiling.

155

"But he didn't come this time, did he?"

At this, the prisoner rolled over, his eyes glinting in the dim light. "No. He stood me up. No chess. What do you know of it?"

"He comes every week for your last eight awake years, dependable as a clock, but he misses this week. It's just not like him, is it?"

The prisoner froze in place, his entire body tensed. Nothing but his eyes betrayed his emotion. "Only you can answer that, it would seem. Why did he not come?"

Ashion walked over to the old man, who already smelt of deteriorating flesh, and whispered in his ear, "Because I stuck a sword through his heart."

The prisoner was stiff a moment longer and then he relaxed. He rolled away from Ashion. "Aye," he whispered. "It was his turn. Goodbye, Logos. We'll meet again at the place wherever we go."

"Yes, his turn. But before he went, the good doctor left me a gift in the form of an iter with remarkable swordsmanship."

The prisoner said nothing.

"And suddenly I'm thinking that the doctor was holding back when he gave me my implants. I'm thinking, the doctor had access to a better brain-burn for using the sword but he didn't give it to me. Why do you think he would do that?"

The prisoner still said nothing.

"The only way he could get a better brain-burn than the one I have is from you. So I've got this question for you, Root, and only you can answer it: What were you and the good doctor up to down here?"

The prisoner let a deep sigh escape from his chest. "We played chess. We never spoke of brain-burns or neural implant linking. You can review the overheads. Only chess."

"I don't think so."

"That's your problem. Not mine."

"No, it's yours." Ashion stood and walked to the door and opened it. He gave a short whistle, and three young knights came running up. Ashion faced the prisoner, but addressed the guards. "I want this prisoner on cryo immediately."

Quickly the prisoner rolled over and stood, belying his age and appearance. "You can't do that," he said. There was a desperation in his voice that tickled Ashion greatly. "It is my *turn*."

"Apparently, it's not your turn yet," Ashion said, leaving the cell. His knights entered after him, and he could hear the struggle as he walked away.

"It's my turn! Ashion! You can't put me back on ice! It's my turn!"

Ashion walked out onto the war room floor, ignoring the screams of the prisoner that silenced everyone as they turned to watch the old man being dragged down the hall to the cryogenics wing. He just walked straight to the lift, and checked his timepiece. There was still enough time to make the security briefing at the palace. As the door closed, he switched on his com. "Salzon Lewiston, please. Yes, I'll hold. No, tell him it's Ashion. Quite important that I have a secure thread to him before the meeting today."

Forty-four.

Dex had no idea what it was that he was eating, but he ate it nonetheless. He shoved the flavorless meat-like substance ravenously into his mouth, chewing briefly when it seemed like the right thing to do, and then swallowing. It could have been chicken, but it could just as well have been tofu. Either way, Dex realized, he had never before wanted to eat so much of anything.

Trance sat next to him, eating the same thing. He could feel her leaning into her plate, licking the strange goo from her fingers, but he could see nothing. The blinder mask was back on his face, and he was playing the blind-mute again. As his stomach filled, it triggered the exhaustion again. Dex hoped they could soon find someplace to sleep, but he was doubtful. Trance kept insisting they were not safe yet.

They'd hung from the bottom of the train for what seemed like hours, and Dex's arm still shook uncontrollably from the effort. But finally they had been able to slip away by slithering down past the train between the two tracks and up the stairs as the troopers had argued with unseen authorities on their communicators.

They'd run as fast as a blind man could, his hand permanently in Trance's, up some stairs and along noisy corridors, surrounded by an even thicker heat than Trance had warned him of. They had run until his lungs burned and his legs were jelly, and then they had walked, and walked, along quiet corridors and busy streets filled with people. Finally, Trance had pulled him into some sort of establishment, and they both had lain down. Dex did not know how long they had slept, but Trance had shaken him awake and they had walked again until they found a place to eat.

"I need more rest," Dex whispered. Just admitting it seemed to overpower him even more.

"We's not clear, Dex," Trance said through a mouthful. "We's need Lower Central. Seven clicks."

"No idea what a click is."

"Not far. We's almost there. Meet wit a Sinner I's know from backtime. He's know what to makes of all this crazy."

"How do you know him?"

"He's is one of my's jonnies, eh."

"Right. Of course."

"He's is fair, even though he's is crazy. He's know what to do wit a thousand-year-old iter and a princess runnin from Family goons. He's know places to hide."

"Whatever you say. But how do we get away from all the over-heads? I thought you said they are everywhere."

Trance sniffed derisively. "Everywhere but low cen Morgish, eh. Low-Cen, it's is all just for cast-offs, eh? No-goods, brokens, blindees, amps, flung-out drippers. Sinners run th' smelly old equipment for th' central life-support processin, and they's don't ask for nothin but to be left alone. So, not so many Family overheads. Only real law down here is Leshan."

"Leshan?"

"Ex-Family what's been dropped, eh. No more status. Kicked outta th' winds, left to rot down wit us slaves. So he's builds a new empire, runnin slumhole Morgish. Families, they's don't care much, means they's don't have to spend much time down here."

"So he has his own forces and everything?"

"Mnay common thug you's meet, he's is paid by Leshan. He's is a mean bastard, that's why he's get kicked down planet-side, eh? He's is even too ragged for th' Families."

"I'm much happier with common thugs than any more of those Red Masks."

"Heah, Dex, that's why we's here."

And then they were up, walking again.

Forty-five.

The heat. The smell. The walking.

There seemed little else in this world, at least as far as Dex could remember. He was so close to sleep, even as he walked, that he would occasionally feel The Dream bubbling up at the back of his head. He would open his eyes, only to see the maddening black nothingness of the mask.

He just wanted to be there, wherever 'there' was. No more walking. He kept trying to speed it all up, to move faster. But without his sight, he just couldn't quite get a grasp on where he was.

And then he would drift again, and The Dream would start bubbling below the surface of his consciousness. He could feel it there, the deep blackness above, the burning white-hot surface below: the falling.

He felt like he was waking up, and was still walking; he screamed at himself, but at the same time he sensed no more sleep and recognized the concrete below his feet, taking one step after the other. Still, he could see the surface just above him and then he was breaking himself down along the surface, reorganizing his smallest parts and hearing them fizzle across the surface, just to pull them back together. But he was losing track again and the searing pain attacked his face—

A hand grabbed his shoulder, and it was gone.

"Heah, Dex, slow down," Trance said, breathing heavily. "I's must've dozed, I's looks up and you's far away in front of me."

"Sorry," Dex said, and the smell burned his nostrils. "I was sleeping, I think."

"Beens one tall day, eh?" Trance said.

"Yeah, Trance. Been one tall life."

"We's here, Dex."

They came to a stop, and Trance rapped her knuckles against metal. There was a buzzing sound, and Trance said, "We walk among the slave, the slave must walk among us."

There was a microphoned sound of someone getting to the com. Then a hurried male voice, nasal and too close to the mic, spoke. "Trance? It's is you, Trance?"

"Heah, Jules. It's is me."

"Spooks! What, *you's* come to see *me?*"

"Heah. Needs a favor, Jules."

"Heah, me's too, eh? Ha, ha, ha. Gets it?"

"You's always funny, Jules. Can we's comes in?"

"I's in service, Trance."

"It's is an emergency."

"You's take th' lift to sub 4, I's down in Waterlock."

There was the sound of a latch unlocking, and Trance pulled Dex through a door. It clicked loudly behind them. They walked a few feet, and then stepped into a lift. Dex felt his stomach fall, ever so slightly, before the door hissed open again. They stepped out, and the coolness of the room was like a gift from heaven. Dex felt instantly rejuvenated, as a mild breeze cooled the sweat that covered his entire body. Behind the cool wind was a metallic shoosh, loud but pleasant, like a million of Jones' chimes all rolling in the wind at once. Thinking of Jones only muddied Dex's mind once more.

"Trance! My's only Trance! Spooks, I's don't think you's ever come to *my's* work!" the high-pitched voice rung out, coming toward them.

"Jules, heah, long time," Trance said. "Meets Miles, eh."

"Heah, blindy," Jules said. Dex waved in the direction of the voice.

"Well, gives us a hug, my's precious Trance," Jules said. A silence followed that spoke to a hug. " I's forget how good you's feel," Jules said, the proposition audible in his voice.

"Heah, Jules, you's could come to me anytime," Trance said, pretending to be upset.

"Times are upon us, Trance, they's *upon* us," Jules said, his tone sliding down his nasal scale to a conspiratorial tone. "I's a busy man. *Very* busy. Th' slave's is usually down here--a single violin, playin a lonely tune. But not anymore, not anymore. Now, th' slave's is an orchestra, playin all instruments at once. So I's must work thru new coolin techniques for th' prime threads down here. I's actually had tall luck. I's usin a rotatin pool system wit heavy water for active threads and hyper-distilled roilin water for past thread rethreadin. You's see, th' trick is to–"

"Maybe later, Jules. I's need ya help."

"Heah, Trance, anything. I's help ya wit anythin."

"Me and Miles, we's in deep wit th' Family Authority."

"Times, they's upon us," Jules said again. "Th' Order's is busy wit Family business. They's don't leaves us alone. Not like they's used to."

"Miles here, he's is fresh off th' bed, eh."

"He's looks it. An iter?"

"I's don't think so. I's mean, he's say he's is iter, but I's think he 'riginal. But it's is somethin more. He's is a *first*, Jules. From th' first ships."

There was a pause. "Heah, is this a joke Trance? You's pullin my whatsit?" Jules asked.

"For sure, no whatsit pullin. They's got Red Masks out to kill him."

"Spooks, then why ain't he's dead yet?" Jules asked, his doubt clear.

"Shows him th' sword, Miles." Trance said. Dex reached over his shoulder, pulled Judas out, and telescoped the extension.

"That's why we's is both not dead, Jules," Trance said.

Jules whistled low. "He's know how to use that?"

"Heah, sure," Trance said.

"And he's is 'riginal?"

"He's talk like a 'riginal. He's looks it, eh."

"Heah, but that don't mean he's is a defrost."

"Listen, I don't mean to interrupt," Dex said, "but I'm not an original. Logos, the guy who sprung me, said I was a clone."

"Waits, did you's say Logos?"

"Yeah, Logos. You knew him?" Dex's heart sped up.

"Heah, I's knew him. May he's rests in peace."

"You know that he's dead?"

"Th' slave's sees everythin."

"Tell me about Logos, Jules," Dex said.

"Relax, we's get to Logos. And what ya name, again?" Jules asked.

"Miles, uh, Miles..." Dex sighed. "Hell with it. My name is Dex. Dexter Maxwell."

"Dexter Maxwell? *Dexter Maxwell?*" Jules voice going up to an even more pinched sound.

"Yeah. That's me."

"That name's mean somethin to ya?" Trance asked.

"It's means I's don't believe you's still alive." There was a pause. Then Jules spoke again. "Comes; we's all go to see th' Father. Now."

"What's about ya work?"

"We's go now, Trance. If ya friend really Dexter Maxwell, and

162

drip, even if he's is not, th' overhead just recorded th' talky, and you's can bet on a shuttle of Masks already on their way."

"Piddle!" Trance said. "You's stay jacked in down here, Jules?"

"Walkin among th' slave's is a privilege, Trance," Jules said sternly. "To becomes one wit th' threads we's musts always be watched. We's bein watched helps us join th' slave."

"Right, right. Sorry, Jules, I's, still workin thru all th' doctrines."

Jules sniffed. "Is okay. You's new to all this, heah. But we's should go now."

"Right. To th' high priest, eh?"

"Heah. Father Morgish hisself."

Forty-six.

Leshan moved his bulk past the impeccably clean wiring, the spotless transformers, and the crystal-clear displays. Through his sunglasses he could see strange glyphs scrolling across the screens in an ancient, impenetrable dance. Even as he passed, he felt a presence behind him. It was one of the young neophytes who was diligently wiping up behind the large man. Leshan shook his head again at the ways in which humans find meaning in the world.

The primary temple of the Order of the Slave was a complicated old building, one of the first structures drilled down below the surface by the first Families. Not many had survived over the centuries of living on this inhospitable rock, but the Order had kept this bunker and its machinery operational by tirelessly devoting themselves to its preservation.

In the beginning, it had served as the primary computing center, where the huge processing power of the SIN had churned away, doing all the millions of calculations required to keep humans alive in a place where humans shouldn't be living. All the ancient metal boxes were still here, all three or four hundred of them. They were lined up next to each other on the super cooled floor, large squat boxes no higher than his waist, stretching away into the distance. Only seven of them still performed any kind of activity; newer machines now lived in even lower levels of Morgish, where they were easier to keep cool.

But now, even those were hundreds of years old. Yet they still performed the basic functions of human existence: recycling and cooling the air, recycling water, handling food-growth activities. And most importantly, monitoring the generation of the one thing that dominated the world: electricity.

Leshan always found this place as awe-inspiring as the Order tried to make it out to be: the SIN had been keeping humans alive on this godforsaken rock for six hundred years, on the same hardware. Thanks to the Order, who was taking care of the technology that made up the body and soul of their god: the Singular Integrated Network.

But, the heat up this high, so close to the surface, was almost too much to take. Even here in the network room, Leshan could feel the difference between the machine-tolerant temperature at his feet and the burning heat radiating down from the high ceiling. In spite of the sense of awe, he ultimately hated coming up here, but this was a special case. The Father deserved a personal visit for this one.

At the far end of the room, where the seven remaining machines had been placed in a circle, the cooling system was pushing icy air directly into their processing fans. In the middle of the circle was a single terminal, the primary site of worship for the Sinners. The First Term was what they considered their direct link to the SIN's consciousness. What a joke. Leshan worked with the SIN more than any of the Sinners ever would, and he knew the truth: it was a machine that carried out the bidding of the Families. But the Sinners combined the SIN's impressive power with the Families' incredible manipulation of mass consciousness, and turned it into a religion. Turned it into God. And of course the Families loved the fact that people secretly believed the SIN acted independently.

But Leshan knew better. He'd used the Sinners' belief to his advantage back when he still had Family privs. Hell, he still used it-- maybe even more now that he no longer had the power of the SIN at his fingertips.

Father Morgish was bent in prayer at the First Term, as he was most hours of the day. He was whispering something Leshan could not make out, before raising his voice.

"Good morning, Leshan. The slave walks among us."

"Heah, Father. Th' slave's can show ya everythin but a man's soul."

Father Morgish stood and turned, revealing his emaciated frame. His shaven head was showing new little grey hairs fuzzying his sweating mantle. He wore no shirt, a common practice in the intense heat this close to the surface. The small cam around his neck marked him as a Sinner priest: the SIN sees everything the priest does. Even now, Leshan's arrival was being threaded around the huge fibers of the network that circled the human cities of Venus.

Father Morgish smiled, and wiped the sweat from his face with a single movement of his large hands. He had the tattoo of the Order, a single bar, on both of his cheeks. "The slave is the only way any man will ever begin to glimpse the enormity of his own soul."

Leshan shrugged. "I's is not here to talk 'ligion, Father."

Father's smile faded, and he went cold. "Then what are you here for? Another errand for Ashion?"

Leshan clenched his jaw. "You's sees a lot on that feed, no, Father?"

Father spread his arms wide. "The slave must reveal. It is his curse."

"I's is here to warn ya that trouble's is brewin. Revolutionists plans attackin Family strongholds, and you's should keeps out of it. They's will be brought to justice by th' authorities."

"Such magnanimous information," Father said, pulling up an analog threader next to him. "Almost as if you knew of the attack before the revolutionists themselves did."

"Not everythin turns up on ya precious threads, Father."

"Sooner or later, everything does, Leshan. Even treachery."

"Just stays away from this one, Father. Ya public acts cause lot of trouble for me's lately."

"He'll be sending in his masked assassins, I take it?"

Leshan was already walking away from him. "Th' proper authorities will be involved," he said.

Father laughed. "How convenient. You know, he's taking all this away from us, one false rebellion at a time."

"He's can have it," Leshan said, then stopped and turned. "One more thing. There's is a princess and a stray iter running around Low-

Cen. They's might have contacts wit some of ya less… *ascetic* followers. If they's come to ya, you's give them to me's."

"If the slave brings me into contact with humans, only the slave
can determine what will happen to them."

"Saves it, Father. It's is important. Th' princess goes by Trance.
Th' iter's is pretendin blind, wit a blindy's mask on. Papers name him
as Miles Goldman. If you's see them, you's contact me's immediately."

"And if I don't?"

"If you's don't then maybe comes a string of accidents 'round
here. Suddenly th' Families can't trust th' Order's to mind th' SIN."

"Threats, Leshan? And we used to get along so well."

"It's is not a threat, Father. It's is an eventuality. You's know anythin about th' princess and her iter, you's strum me's."

With that, Leshan was gone.

Forty-seven.

Father Morgish watched as the door closed behind the King of Thugs,
and one of the young neophytes studiously wiped the door clean,
eliminating any traces of Leshan. The priest wiped the sweat from his
forehead with a sterile towel and turned back to his terminals.

He was already calming down, his heart rate starting to return
to normal. As he whispered through a few refrains of scripture, he
leveled. Leshan seemed to have that effect these days. Not like it used
to be, the two of them running Morgish in a near-perfect harmony
between religious devotion and heavy-handed punishment. Father
would direct the town's good instincts; Leshan governed the bad.

But then Ashion's little army began marching all over, scaring
the people, rattling them and getting them into fights. And it was all
above Father, above Leshan. The balance was lost. They simply had to
take it. And now, Ashion threatened Leshan directly. Father had already watched the conversation between the two of them, so he knew
what Leshan had in mind. But what he couldn't figure out was why
the big man would take the time to come warn him personally. Was
he targeting members of the Order directly? Or would the trouble
rather affect the SIN machinery?

His mind raced as he tried to fill in the blanks. He started pulling up threads methodically, checking different places for news, for different ideas and for anomalies. Anything that stood out above the usual cacophony of this life on Venus, this subsistence, this crude survival. All of it recorded and sent spinning round the miles of network lines that connected every single machine to every other machine. Connected humans to machines, humans to humans. The connections. The SIN took all the data and ran it in constant loops. Sometimes, the data aged out quickly, like another brief glimpse at a desperate little life of some poor soul that knew nothing of why she was so poor, so tired, so lost. Sometimes, the data ran through the threads and found itself permanently imbedded into a line, never lost, never forgotten. The slave's memories.

It was a remarkable amalgamation of a million different search and save algorithms, delicately balanced against each other to maximize the efficient use of electricity that pumped through the network. Nothing was wasted. In its entirety, no man could possibly stand above all the data, stretching back over nine hundred earth years, and grasp its aggregated sum. No one.

Except the SIN itself. For the network contained all the data, and the millions of algorithms worked every day to determine what information was routed to which interface, and what information was moved into the lesser used threads, slowly aged out into nothing. The network itself determined a moment's importance. And who else could do that but God?

Except, of course, Father Morgish. He had found that he could manipulate the thread priority up and down, keeping some data from rising to the level where it entered into the interface level and displayed by the slave to Family Watchers. The manipulation was subtle, effective, and completely intransparent to everyone but himself and, of course, the Slave.

And when it came down to it, Father Morgish loved the SIN. Some days, he believed in all the dogma, he believed that the SIN had awakened and intended to move human life to its next level of consciousness. Other days, he simply stood in awe of the power that lay unused. But he loved the interfaces, the raw data threads, the act of human devotion coupled with self-interest that kept the entire monstrosity up and running, day after day. And that love shone so bright that after his second fifty-year term they had changed his name from Drexl Gregor, admitted him into the highest of ranks of the Order and renamed him Father Morgish, Seventh Father, keeper of the Old City, protector of the First Term and witness to the Heartbeat. And he had accepted it, for it meant freedom from anything else but the interfaces themselves. Freedom from the inaccuracies and frailties of the humans around him.

An illusion of freedom, he'd discovered quickly, as surely as any freedom will become. He was soon burdened with leading the Order through the distinctly human politics of the Families and their constant bickering with each other. Always an empire being built; always an empire falling. Through it all, he had to guide the Order and protect the SIN.

And so he had. He'd actually learned that the SIN was an excellent professor of political science and human persuasion. He was the longest serving Father since the First Father.

Of course, his political connections with the Families had helped keep his liver clean, his heart strong, and his mind crisp. The Families hoarded the life sciences, riding their wind-powered fortresses in the sky, keeping the old art of living too long alive and well. Nearly everyone lived to see their third century up there. But down in the old city, most merely felt the passing into one hundred as a burden they would rather give up. But not Father. He had gladly accepted the gifts when they were offered. And here he was, teetering on the fulcrum of his second century, and with plenty of work left to do.

But there was the matter of Ashion, the great immortal assassin of the ages, now a Security Forum member and planet-side peacekeeper. So feared, so powerful, people were forgetting he was still, by law, just a planet-side slave. Now, he was building a personal army of dedicated soldiers. Eradicating the rising revolutions. Stirring up new ones, just to have something to eradicate.

Empires fallen; empires risen.

Father Morgish could not see the future, but on clear nights when he was plugged into the threads, he sensed that the future belonged to Ashion.

And so he would do whatever Leshan, who was nothing more

168

than Ashion's lackey, asked him to. Perhaps Leshan was smarter than he looked, and sensed the same future that Father Morgish did. Or perhaps he was as dumb as he looked and required only payment in the short term to undermine his own long-term benefit. No matter, Father decided; for Leshan was just another end. Like Ashion, who was an end. All of the Families were merely ends.

The slave would always be the means; the constant looping circle.

And that meant that they would always need a caretaker. They would always need a Father Morgish to mind the wires and the processors and the cooling fans.

As his mind had wandered toward the functional upkeep of the SIN, he'd lazily traversed to his local threads, to the machine rooms. And found the primary cooling floor abandoned.

Jules.

Jules was brilliant and dedicated, probably had a little priest in him down the road. But he was still too flighty for Father Morgish's second-century tastes. After all Jules was a mere fifty years into the world. And now he'd abandoned his highly prestigious post... for what? A quick drill-down into real-time threads found him on the move, walking toward the First Term temple, the very place that Father Morgish now occupied. Jules walked quickly, if his nervous shuffle could indeed be called a walk. *Who was that with him?*

Perhaps a princess and a blind iter?

Father Morgish smiled. Today, the slave delivered. Today, then, he would believe.

Forty-eight.

Father Morgish began strumming the threads ferociously. First, he pulled a secure bead for Leshan, deep in the sub-layer of early interfaces. Leshan was not even back at his terminal. No use trying him on the portable–too public. So he would wait.

As he did, he pulled the cooling floor thread and traced it back to the cam footage of the approaching iter and prostitute, Jules giving her a hug. Even as he pulled the thread, he noticed it was lowering, dropping down toward the removal nets. Footage of the least important people of the world faded quickly. Father Morgish pulled it and while playing it back, he turned to a second terminal and began threading for Leshan's supposed terrorist act. He'd said to expect it soon, so Father Morgish was looking for signs. People in crowds. Empty work zones. Quiet streets. The revolutionaries had strong support in these parts of the city, so a lack of noise or a lack of children on public walkways could signal an outburst.

But there was no change in the walkways or work zones of Lower Morg. Everything seemed to be just as it always was. Then, of course, the supposed attack wasn't really coming from the true freedom fighters, so why would their network be alerted? In fact, it could be surmised that–

The soundtrack of Jules and his two visitors broke through his thoughts. He turned back to the first term just in time to catch Jules say, "It's means I's don't believe you's still alive. Come, we's all go to see Father. Now." But Father had heard a name, a very old name. He pulled the thread back and heard the name again.

Dexter Maxwell.

He pulled the thread back, just to hear it again.

Then Leshan was on Father's headset, saying, "What you's need, Father?"

Father Morgish's head was racing. Finally, Leshan asked, "You's there, Father? Heah, you's there?"

Finally, Father Morgish made a decision. He began strumming his interface quickly and precisely, his experienced hands lacing over the strings with gusto. Then, with a quick motion, he disabled the cam that hung from his neck and spoke. "Leshan, I'm weaving a thread into your bandspace. This will be a six-second audio clip from the mouth of the rogue iterate that Ashion seeks. I picked it up just a few moments ago."

"What is I's supposed to do wit six seconds of audio?" Leshan asked.

"Just listen to this," Father said. The thread was laced, and the audio played.

"My name is Dex. Dexter Maxwell."

"Dexter Maxwell? *Dexter Maxwell?*"

Leshan was quiet for a few moments. Then he spoke in a curt tone, more to himself. "Well, that changes everything, doesn't it?"

"It would seem to, yes," Father Morgish said, recognizing the change in the dialect. "We must proceed with caution."

But Leshan was back to his planet-side affectation. "Heah, you's says it, Father. You's threadin this?"

"No, I have disabled my connection to the SIN."

"You's smarter than you's look."

"I don't have a plan for this, Leshan. The iterate and his companion are on their way to meet me as we speak."

"Heah, my's problem is, I's got too many plans for this, Father. Don't know which is th' best. Lets me's think."

"Not much time for that I'm afraid."

"You's think this was Logos, eh?"

"Undoubtedly. Logos is now dead, at the hands of Ashion."

"Heah, I's know. Okay, Father, don't move. Stays where you's are, keep th' iter wit ya. I's got a plan now, heah. A plan indeed."

"Then please, fill me in, for I can't see past the cold panic in front of me."

"Just keeps th' iter. Heah, things will move fast from here."

Fourty-nine.

Ashion suppressed a yawn. These security briefings seemed duller each time. He knew things would get ugly soon enough, but at the moment it was just the same series of habitualized introductions, ritualistic transferals of titles, and the like. Polite posturing. That was the problem with an entire community who'd lived well beyond their natural lifespan. Everything slowed down. Hard to get anyone to hurry.

What did Tano like to call it? The olds. As in: *he's caught the olds, won't make a decision for months.* As in: *the olds set in, and the security meeting didn't pick up for two hours.*

The yawn came back, and he began losing focus. He blinked quickly, trying to strobe his mind awake. It had been a long couple of days, the kind where sleep becomes a long lost friend you remember fondly. He looked around the security chamber, taking in all the participants.

The usual assortment of lower Family representatives were there, perhaps more than usual these days, as the obvious shift of power had been moving to security over the past decade. Ashion barely even learned the names of whichever exemplars were sent anymore. The lower Families, over the course of the last century, had proven to be an excellent resource that he could mine for his own gain. If he studied the lower Families, he could always tell who was coming up, and who was going down. But none of that mattered anymore.

There just wasn't enough time left for another regime change.

Instinctually, Ashion looked at his time piece. Time, time, time. It was all about time. Even as he closed his eyes and ran through a meditation for patience, he heard the moderating exemplar, someone representing Consul Gregor, give the benediction of the early meeting formalities. The lower Family exemplars stood and slowly began exiting the security chamber, stopping to speak with each other and the ruling Family representatives. There was a buzz among them, as Charles Goldman had chosen to attend the security briefing for the first time in three years.

Ashion stood, as the lower exemplars had, and he made his way through the crowds, shaking hands and speaking in platitudes. He had been a friend of the lower Families for a century; that he cared nothing for them was not something that could be made public at this stage. His duty, among others, was to maintain a sense of continuity in the face of the impending war. He made his way out the front door into the crowd, saying the usual things, making the usual appointments. It took nearly half an hour to get into the main briefing chamber and close the door behind him.

The room went silent when he turned to face them. They had been waiting for him, Ashion knew. That was another reason to take his time with the intermission networking—he had no friends in this council now. But he didn't need any. Just one enemy with a ghost. He glanced at Salzon Lewiston. His old face revealed nothing.

Salzon sat at the right hand of Charles Goldman, the senior member of the security council and standing Governor General of the United Townships of Venus. Charles sat in the primary chair at the head of the ruling Family bureau as though she was the queen and this was her court. This was not far from the truth. Charles' long gray hair had been braided ceremoniously into looping ropes that lay encrusted in gold across her shoulders, her white dress hanging off her skinny frame. She looked good for someone her age, and Ashion would be the first to admit it.

On Charles' left was the ever-present Goldman exemplar, Morgan, trying not to smile--and failing. And why shouldn't she gloat? Her hatred for Ashion was the stuff of legends, and she felt confident that her ultimate victory would be today. It made Ashion slightly nervous, for he knew the outcome of this meeting already, and Morgan would immediately begin planning his downfall.

One thing at a time. Morgan would be a problem he'd have to work through later.

Down the table from Morgan sat the Lewiston exemplar, Thadwick, and the Gregor exemplar, Thula. To the right of Charles Goldman sat the four members of the advisory council: Mars, Cheltin, Warship, and Dante. Mars, Cheltin, and Warship were retired generals from the off-planet security forces; Dante was the planet-side consultant.

That was it: her nine-member security advisory council, all waiting for someone to begin. Ashion could feel their eyes and the eyes of the overhead on the high domed ceiling of the chamber burning into him. Then it began.

"This is no place for secrets, Ashion," Charles said, her voice nonchalant as her hands toyed with a small threader at her table.

"I have no secrets to keep," Ashion replied. He moved toward his seat at the end of the table.

"Please remain on the floor," Salzon Lewiston said coldly, and Ashion stopped. This was it.

"I don't see a reason to remain on the floor like a commoner," Ashion said politely.

"You will remain where I tell you, slave!" Salzon roared, slamming his hand down. Charles smiled, and placed her hand delicately on Salzon's trembling hand, and he glanced at her, eyes blazing.

"Ashion, please, we have some matters to discuss with you today, and we'd rather not all crane our necks to the end of the table," Charles motioned gracefully in front of her. "Please."

Ashion shook his head in disbelief. He walked to the middle of the floor and bowed sarcastically. "Your grace, I am at your disposal, as always," he said with a flourish of his hand.

Charles laughed. "Thank you. Now, to matters. There is the dead doctor at my medical facility in Draggish. Morgan has pulled the thread from the facility, showing Doctor Logos taking a blind iterate into a decontamination room. Morgan, please, show Ashion the thread."

A projected interface lit up on the polished white stone floor in front of Ashion, showing the deceased doctor and the masked clone. They spoke briefly with the guard on duty, sharing a quick laugh, then went in the decon room. Ashion watched as his standard-issue entourage showed up and put the lieutenant to the floor. He watched as his knights split into two lines on either side of the door, and then he himself walked through the door and into the decon unit. The entourage of troops followed him in, and then the window into the decon unit was covered. A moment later, Ashion and nine of his troops walked out. After that the thread cut to an overhead from the street-side of the med box, showing a shaky, nervous, blood-spattered iterate walk out toward the transit and get mobbed by people boarding. The iterate fell and was caught by the preacher and pulled onto the train. The preacher's name was Booker, Ashion remembered. And a tough interrogation, it turned out. The projection went blank, and he looked up to Charles.

"Who is the man assisting the iterate?" Lewiston asked.

"Planet-side preacher, went by Booker," Ashion said. "He sympathized with the terrorists, but we were able to break him. He told us where to find the iter."

"He is dead now?" Morgan asked.

"My soldiers did not respond with much... *clarity* to the death of their brothers," Ashion said. "They took the interrogation too far, I'm afraid."

Charles waved her hand distractedly. "Yes, yes," she said. "Back to the decontamination room. Three dead soldiers murdered violently by sword. One dead doctor stuck to the wall with this blade." Charles nodded, and her exemplar, Morgan, pulled a sword from behind her and threw it on the floor in front of Ashion. "Does this belong to you?"

"Doctor Logos had been illegally selling cryogenic prisoners to the miners for years. I decided to put an end to it."

"Answer the question," Salzon said.

"It is my sword," Ashion said.

"The good doctor served a larger purpose in my medical facilities," Charles said. "And, more importantly for you, Ashion, he was your programmer."

"I shall handpick his replacement, your grace," Ashion said.

"Those iced iters are a good source of revenue," Dante said, addressing Charles. "There's too much at stake, really, to assume that another doctor will not continue doing the same. Domestically, there is no real harm in it. The laws against indentured service by permanent prisoners are unenforceable, and everyone knows it."

"I have the right to enforce planet-side law as I see fit, do I not?" Ashion asked.

"That's the matter before us, isn't it?" asked Thula Gregor.

"Tell us about the iterate that escaped," Charles said.

"It turned out to be handy with a sword," Ashion said.

"There was no audio feed for the decontamination chamber," Warship noted. "Why do you think that is?"

Dante answered the question. "A common practice for the flesh trade, it seems. There's nothing wrong with threads showing someone being cleaned–but the audio stream would be damning if it were to come out."

Charles waved the room to silence and spoke. "After your initial mistake of underestimating the blind iterate, you responded by dispatching *three* units of your masked knights to finish him off, yes?"

"That is correct. Based on information from the preacher, we traced the fugitive to a room-hire in upper Morgish, where he was detained briefly before escaping to lower-central Morgish. All of my knights were slain at the hire. When my second unit arrived, they overreacted at the scene. Innocents were lost. I have already suspended those knights indefinitely, pending a psych reveal."

"And that is why you deleted the threads from the hire overheads?" Salzon asked.

"Yes. Even as I pulled them, they were dropping below Primary

175

Family Interface level. It would be unacceptable to me–and to Family rule–to have the actions of a handful of vengeance-minded knights made visible to the planet-side masses. I saw no choice at the time other than to remove them by any means necessary."

"So you removed the entire thread?" Morgan asked derisively.

"I took those actions required to protect my men."

"I don't know which is more disturbing," said Consul Gregor, wringing her hands absent-mindedly. "The fact that Ashion felt it necessary to delete the threads, or the fact that he could delete the threads at all. I thought we'd outlawed that level of access years ago."

"That is correct, Consul," said Morgan. "However, while outlawed, it cannot be technologically prevented. The Primary Family Interface was engineered to allow single-user ownership of any thread in the SIN loops. Once owned, there is no way of blocking deletion." Morgan paused. "Except by meting out punishment to offenders."

"I accept full responsibility for my actions. I knew the law when I deleted the threads."

"Charles," Gregor said, turning, "why exactly did Ashion have PFI, again?"

"Ashion plays a key role in our efforts in the Second Harvest, Consul," Charles said, never taking her eyes off Ashion. "His unique skills have proven quite useful on the third rock."

"But that work has been completed," Morgan said.

"Quite right," Charles said. Ashion thought he saw a smile creeping up from the edges of her mouth. *She's enjoying this farce.*

"With all due respect," Ashion said, "We have much left to do. We haven't identified the clerics' technology source, or even what it might be–"

"Rubbish!" Salzon yelled. "We have eliminated all identified threats. The rest can be accomplished by conventional means. Your *skills* are no longer required, slave."

As Salzon spoke, a messenger slipped into the room and handed Salzon a small interface. He glanced down and after reading it hurried out of the room.

Charles did not seem to notice. She went on, "Indeed, this offense seems to indicate that our trust in you was unfounded. My recommendation to the council is to revoke Ashion's PFI status permanently, and place control of the planet-side forces in the hands of Morgan Goldman."

"Charles, that's ridiculous," Ashion protested. "Morgan is not familiar with the status or dynamics of the armed forces. She knows nothing of the leadership structure. I have done nothing but protect the very soldiers you now want to take from me."

"A vote is required," Charles said, ignoring Ashion. "All in favor of revoking Ashion's PFI?" Three hands went up: Morgan, Thula, and Dante. "Those opposed?" Three hands went up: Mars, Warship, and Cheltin. Gregor and Thadwick abstained. "We wait on Salzon's vote, then," Charles said.

Ashion lowered his shoulders, but kept his gaze on Morgan. Her black eyes were dancing, dreaming already of leading the magnificent army that Ashion had hand-picked and personally trained. The best of the best. True warriors.

Salzon barged back in, his face red, his eyes wild. "We will have to call this meeting short. Where do things stand?"

"Just voting on whether or not to revoke Ashion's PFI," Charles said. "You have the tie-breaker vote."

Salzon stared madly at Ashion, looking as though his eyeballs might pop from his head with the pressure. "Give him back his privs," Salzon said. The room murmured collectively. Ashion kept his eyes on Morgan, whose expression shifted from surprise to looking around the room at each person, trying to gauge their reactions. Trying to reorganize where she stood in the pecking order.

"Salzon?" Charles asked calmly, clearly puzzled.

"Give him his privs, give him whatever he needs," Salzon said, "and then send him to Morgish with his knights. The revolutionists have taken Central Processing."

Ashion looked up, and the first thing he noticed was the flash on Charles' face. And then it was gone. She turned back to Salzon, who was shaking with anger. Real anger, Ashion knew. Not an affected anger. He smiled, and looked back at Morgan.

"Turn it on," he said.

Morgan's hands barely suppressed the tremor of hatred she was experiencing as she reached for the terminal on her table top. She pulled a few threads, and Ashion heard his implant sizzle, crackle, and then there were twenty strums bending his threadware. Soldiers waiting for his commands, Ashion knelt and picked up the sword that had been thrown at his feet and sheathed it in his empty scabbard. He turned and engaged the first thread waiting in his earpiece, finding Admiral Holden already outlining the threat. He headed for the door.

As he passed, he saw Salzon moving to intercept him. Salzon grabbed his arm. "This isn't over, Ash," he said.

Without pausing, Ashion used a quick shake to loosen Salzon's grip. "It never is," he said.

MORGISH TOWNSHIP, LOWER-CENTRAL DISTRICT, DAY 4.

Fifty.

Jules never shut up.

At first, Dex just thought the poor guy was nervous around Trance, who he clearly wanted to impress. But after walking with him for the past ten minutes, it seemed more and more likely that the guy was incapable of tolerating silence. Jules would ask a series of questions but was not really waiting for an answer; if none came he would just keep talking. And if no one interrupted, he would just keep talking, too. All in that nasal, pinched voice of his.

Dex tried to rub his temples through the blinder mask, but it gave no solace. Jules was now talking about something called the First Term, and the Eternal Heartbeat of the slave, and all this religious talk about what amounted to nothing more than a really big computer. Trance was saying nothing, just pulling Dex along by his hand.

"... and Father Morgish, he's has taken th' strengths of Central Processing, heah, and turned it into influence for th' Order. He's is something, heah, and old. *Big* old. And wise. He's has been 'round the heart of th' slave for ages, eh, and I's thinks that it's has kind of rubbed off, you's know? Like, he's has got some of th' slave in him? Cuz he's knows everythin, just before anyone's else. Heah, it's is somethin, alright, 'specially if you's takes into account all th' politics and bureaucracy he's has to muddle through every day. He's just takes all in stride. All in stride. Heah, here we's are."

Dex heard a rush of air as they walked into a building and the door closed behind them.

"Heah, lets me's handles all th' talkin? Cuz really you's shouldn't be here and I's maybe shouldn't bring you's here but I's can't thinks of what else to do. I's mean, Dexter Maxwell. I's mean, I's *really* shouldn't know th' name at all but when I's is bored late at night when I's can't sleep, I's always be trollin old meds records. For somethin to do, eh? And they's meds for th' colony, they's big, big old. From first ships, heah, that big. Most of it's is PFI'd but a few strums in a good box gets

179

ya right in wit'out any tracin threads."

Another door opened, another door closed.

"Anyway, so I's stumbles into some old clonin records from way back, 'round 2790 or so, and th' threads, they's so buried th' slave's isself could barely strum them, but you's know with all 'crypted data, th' harder you's try to hide, more someone's is goin to go lookin, and that someone's was me's. So I's is lookin it over when suddenly who's comes strummin my door but Father Morgish hisself, wonderin what I's is doing pokin 'round such old records. Father Morgish hisself. He's asked me's to join th' Order right then and there."

"And you've been the most dedicated son ever since," a quiet voice spoke from in front of them.

"Oh, heah, Father," Jules said nervously. "I's is just 'splainin how I's came to know who Dexter Maxwell is."

"Yes, I heard," the man said with a laugh. "I've been expecting you."

"See? See?" Jules said with a loud laugh. "He's has got th' slave in him!"

"The slave walks among all of us," Father Morgish said. "Particularly among those who walk with the slave."

"It's is th' truth," Jules said excitedly. "I's got this theory that—"

"Another time, Jules," Father Morgish said. "Today, we must decide what will happen to your friends here."

"I's go by Trance," Trance said nervously. Dex realized she was truly humbled to be meeting this man. Who was this Father Morgish? The pope? Dex had been imagining more of a crackpot lunatic cult leader, but he spoke with the calm of a man who believed every word he spoke. Trance elbowed Dex.

"My name's Dex. Dexter Maxwell. Which, it turns out, is problematic."

"Indeed," Father Morgish said. "Indeed."

"Problematic?" Jules said incredulously. "I's say really problematic. I's mean, you's don't seem to know who you's are, but let me's tell ya, problematic barely comes close. I's mean, Ashion himself—"

"That's enough, Jules," Father Morgish said. "This young man appears to be frightened enough. No need to add to the excitement."

"Heah, heah, you's is right. I's just thought I's would, you know, help."

Father Morgish put his hand on Dex's shoulder, who stiffened at the touch.

"Young Dex, you may think you know who you are, and maybe you're getting an idea of what this place is. However, your journey must end here. You are an illegal clone, and you must be returned to the medical facility from where you came."

Dex didn't hear it at first. The tone was so soothing, the words simply didn't match. What he heard at first was, everything will be alright, and he'd relaxed. But then the words broke through, and he shrugged off the Father's hand and backed up.

"I don't think so, Father," Dex said. "People kept trying to kill me over there."

"We'll make sure that doesn't happen again," Father said. "We can protect you."

"Why d'you bring me here, Trance?" Dex asked, turning in circles, hands outstretched. He had no idea where he was. "Is this your idea of safe?"

" I's thought th' Order helps—" Trance said, confused. "I's not thinkin they's gives ya over."

"Well, I'm not going back. To hell with these computer worshipers," Dex said.

"It's too late," Father said. "Typically, we can offer solace for escaped iterates and lifetime prisoners. But not for Dexter Maxwell, I'm afraid. The authorities have been notified. They will be here any minute."

"You shouldn't have done that," Dex said. He could feel the adrenaline in his blood; the sword on his back.

"Father, it's is a mistake," Jules said, confused. "Turnin him over to th' Family goons, it's only complicate matters."

"I am not alone in this decision. It has to be this way."

Dex reached over his shoulder, feeling the hilt of Judas.

"Dex, please," Trance said. "Not here; not in Cen Proc, eh. Heah, please, leaves th' thing on ya back."

"Shut up, Trance," Dex said. He was tired. Tired of this place, already. Its smell. Its heat. Tired of running, hiding. Tired of it all.

He pulled the Judas Sword out slowly, and gave it the twist. It flung to its full size.

"This ends here," Dex said, reaching to pull his mask off.

The explosion came from the door behind and knocked him forward onto his face, the Judas Sword sliding across the cool metal floor and clanging into the first of the seven original servers.

Fifty-one.

The shouting rang out quick and harsh in Dex's ears. He was lying on the ground, face down, trying to figure out what had just happened. The voices all seemed strange, robotic.

"Secure th' exit, soldier!"

"I's need those overheads de-commed NOW."

"Th' fat one! He's is headed for th' term!"

There were bursts of electricity flying overhead. Dex tried to stand, but a huge weight came down on his back in the form of a knee, knocking the wind out of him. Then he felt his hands being jerked behind him. He tried to shake free, but the person on his back was simply too heavy and too strong.

"Heah, relax there, iter," the robotic voice whispered into his ear. Then the man on his back shouted, "Sonja! Breaks it's down!"

"Sir!" the same robotic voice, only from a distance--across a large room. "Priest's is secured, his cam de-commed. Th' princess and cleric are detained, and, heah, you's got ya hands on th' iter."

"Heah, I's do. Th' overheads?"

"Workin on, sir."

"Sonja, I's need th' 'heads down ten minutes ago."

"Sir, we's got them, heah."

Dex felt the effects of the blast start to wear off, and he tried to turn his head, straining to sit up.

"Heah, relax," the metallic voice said with a hint of laughter, pushing down on his head. Dex could hear the sounds of small explosions, incoherent shouting, and boots scuffling and squeaking on the shiny metal floor. Then, the voice from a distance.

"All cams secured, sir. We's unplugged."

"You's sure? You's run a de-strummer?"

"Sir, no mics, no cams, no detectors th' next two levels up, two levels down."

"Gets th' shooters plugged in and pullin juice."

"Directly, sir?"

"Heah, up here, th' grid's is too old to track anythin other than usage."

The person on Dex's back let go of him and stood. "We can turn off the voice modulators and get these damn masks off." There was a pause, then the man said, "Stand up, Dex, you're alright. Sorry 'bout that blast."

That voice.

Dex jumped to his feet, tearing off the blinder mask, and took a good look at his attacker.

It was cracking *Thelo*. Slightly embarrassed, but grinning from ear to ear.

Fifty-two.

"Thelo? Is it you?" Dex could barely believe it.

"The future bakes in the sun like new goddamn adobe, my friend," Thelo said, wiping sweat off his shaved head. Then he laughed, and gave Dex a bear hug that lifted him off his feet.

"I can't believe it's you," Dex said. And he couldn't. Thelo put him down, and Dex looked around. His friend was dressed in the same plain grey and black clothing as the rest of people running around the room, checking all the computer equipment; some carrying weapons, others barking orders. Dex tried to take it all in, and turned back to Thelo, who grinned.

"What is this? What's going on?" Dex said.

"You can take the terrorist out of the 22nd century, but you can't take the 22nd century out of the terrorist." Then Thelo turned to a huge woman, who had a few inches even on him. "Sonja, go make sure the priest and his understudy are okay." Then he turned back to Dex and said, "Welcome to the resistance movement. These folks here are working to free this planet from the grips of the ruling Families. What you are now witnessing, at this very moment, is the first armed retaliation against Family oppression."

"And you're the leader?" Dex asked.

Thelo laughed. "Nah. I mean, this little op here," Thelo waved his arm around, "was my work of art. Every good war has its guerillas. Person in charge goes by Fuel."

"I keep hearing that name," Dex said.

"You will hear more of him."

"But how? I mean, what are you... how did you get here?" Dex asked. He felt dizzy. "I need to sit down."

"Right, just not there," Thelo grabbed his arm and moved him away from the server he was about to sit on, steering him instead to a low bench a few feet away. It had been knocked over, so Thelo grabbed it with one hand and pulled it up so they could both sit.

"Okay, then," Thelo said. "How did I get here? Same way you did. I mean, sort of the same way." Thelo winked. "Back in 2113, those fed troopers pulled me out of that cloner and put me on ice, lickety-split. Next thing I know, this guy who calls himself Logos is telling me to get up and chill out and stop picking at the mask on my face."

"Sounds familiar," Dex said. "So are you... a clone?"

Thelo gave him a sad kind of smile. He held his left hand in front of his face and pulled the glove off.

The pinky was missing, as was the top of his ring finger.

"Same old banged up guy they froze all those years ago, I'm afraid."

"Not me, Thelo. I don't know what happened to me, but I've got my fingers back, and no scars. And I somehow know how to use a sword, and I mean *really* use the thing."

"Logos did what he had to do," Thelo said looking over his friend's shoulder. Dex turned to see Trance standing there, looking at them both.

"Hello, Justine."

"Hello, Thelo," Trance answered.

Dex looked at Thelo, then back to Trance. In the moments after the attack, she'd already changed out of her provocative princess clothing and into a loose-fitting grey and black number. "What? You two know each other?"

"Yeah, a little," Thelo said, laughing.

"Like, one of her clients?" Dex asked.

"Thelo's can't afford *me*," Trance said. "And you's call me Justine, now."

Dex's head was spinning. He stood up, then sat back down. He looked at Trance–Justine–in a whole new light. "You knew about this? You were in on this?"

"The future, it bakes in the sun like new adobe," Trance said.

"But I don't–I mean, you've been–"

Trance rubbed her hand through Dex's hair. "When you's puts a camera in every room, you's don't find truth. You's just turns everyone into actors."

Fifty-three.

"We'll have time to catch up soon," Thelo said. "But I have things to attend to first."

As he stood, Father Morgish approached with Jules limping behind him and looking scared. Dex had not actually seen them before, and they made for an interesting sight. Father Morgish had deep wrinkles, but looked to be in very good health. He stood tall and muscular, if a little skinny. He didn't have a shirt on and was wearing a necklace that had just recently been smashed into pieces and rendered useless. Jules looked just as Dex had imagined him: short, and overweight to the point where he waddled. His platinum blond hair was long and disheveled, and he wore spectacles that must have been over half an inch thick.

Thelo nodded in deference. "Father Morgish, I must apologize for the mess."

"You can't possibly believe that you can hold an armed position in the Network Room," Father Morgish said. "This is an astonishing act that will get all of you killed."

"Relax, Father," Thelo said. Sonja had reappeared behind him, and put a small hand-held light box in front of him to review. While looking at it, Thelo spoke again. "We've already fixed the doors, and allowed your cleaning crews to resume work. All systems are operational. You will have access to the First Term throughout this occupation."

"Occupation?" Father Morgish spat out. "A group of misdirected terrorists take over Central Processing, and you call it an occupation? Suicide comes to mind, but not occupation."

Justine stepped between the two. "Please, Father, sits down. We's didn't want to deceive ya." She touched his arm softly, and guided him to the bench.

"Leshan did not speak of this," Father Morgish was saying. "This was not what we agreed."

"Leshan knows nothing of the path in front of us," Thelo said.

"The path?" Father asked, shaking his head. "What path? You have started a war. Don't you see that?"

"No, Father," Justine said firmly, a hint of anger below the surface. "We's have not started th' war. But we's are here today helps end it."

With that, Justine led the two dazed Sinners to a bench, where another man in grey and black attended to their small injuries.

Thelo had moved over to a group of six soldiers with large, heavy-looking backpacks lying in front of them on the ground. They had ripped up a section of the flooring, and fat wires now roped from the backpacks into the ground.

"How's the juice?" Thelo asked them.

"Raw and hot," one of the men said with a smile. "We's load this acid fast, eh."

"Let's hope. They can't cut the feeds to these servers, but they won't give us long."

Dex watched as Thelo moved around the room quickly, smiling and shaking hands, barking orders, and making sure everything was running smoothly. Dex couldn't keep his eyes off him. He was older now, by a few years, but exactly how many Dex couldn't really tell. *But then, I don't know how old I really am, either.* Watching him, Dex could tell that the oversized kid from the sewers of Grenver had matured. There was a grace to his movements, now, that spoke to age, and also some kind of training. As he watched, he noted that Thelo walked with a slight limp in his left leg. It wasn't immediately apparent, but if you watched him long enough, it came through.

"Heah, he's is somethin, eh?" Justine said. She and Dex sat at the same bench. Someone had brought her a terminal that she had been madly working at. Dex looked at her, and her gaze was following Thelo as he circled the Central Processing room.

"I'm still in shock," Dex said, turning to her. "I mean, I've been in a state of disbelief since I woke up in that tube in Logos' lab. But I thought I was getting a handle on things–until now. Until Thelo turns up. And you–I mean, you're certainly not who I thought you were."

"Most people's aren't," Justine said with a wink.

Dex laughed. "You talk like an old friend of mine. A real blindy, you'd say."

"Heah, you's mean Jones, eh," Justine said.

"Jones, yes," Dex said, surprised. "How do you know Jones? Is he still around, too?"

"No, he's lived and died back in his true time. But I's knows of him from Thelo."

Dex looked into the distance. So Jones lived and died in his own time. Dex's jaw became tight, and he looked away from Justine. "He was a friend."

"Yes. When we's have more time, I's like to know much more 'bout him."

Dex took a deep breath, and then asked, "Does Thelo ever talk about, you know, anyone else?"

"Who you's mean?"

"There was this girl. She was my girlfriend, and she was–anyway, did he ever mention a girl named Mallory?"

"Heah, that's sound familiar. She's went down, same as you's and Thelo, eh?"

"Yeah, she went down. Do you know what happened to her?"

"Nah. You's have to ask Thelo."

Dex closed his eyes. The pain in his jaw was like a knife. Mallory. He could smell her hair, hear her cutting humor. He could feel her smooth skin. And he could still see the look of betrayal on her face after she had told him her secret.

The baby.

He opened his eyes, trying to think of something else. He saw Justine was back at her strange terminal. It was really just an empty box frame. Each metal bar that formed an edge was projecting a blue light into its center. Justine inserted her hands into the blue light, and it engaged the holograph in front of her: It was a three-dimensional image of a massive, intertwined pile of multi-colored wires all moving about quickly, viewed from above. Somehow it reminded Dex of watching power lines run by when driving along a highway back in Grenver. With the flick of her hand, Justine would pluck a wire from the pile and pull it up into the screen. It would overtake the image, morphing into what looked like live camera footage of a train station, or a street market.

"So all those wires represent footage from the overheads?" Dex asked.

"Heah, somethin like that," Justine said. "Sometime they's just audio feed, sometime they's meds, others just legal logic. It's is all th' data, old or current, collected and processed by th' SIN. They's call them all threads. It's is a handy mental construct, eh."

"Sure. I like the terminal though. I bet it takes a long time to get good at that."

"Heah, for sure. Th' Families, they's have turned this into an art. They's terminals are analog devices, large stringed boxes that they's learn to play like a musical instrument. They's can navigate much faster wit th' analog interface that reacts to pressure, delicate movements. This device, it's is just binary. On or off. So it's is slow."

"What are you doing right now?"

"Lookin for clues. Ashion, he's is on his way down here now, him and so many Masks even you's and ya blade won't be enough. But we's don't know when or how he's plan to attack. So we's walk th' threads, lookin for clues." As she said this, she came to a thread that showed a shuttle leaving a dock. Suddenly, without warning, the view panned out, as if the viewer was being pulled up and away quickly. Then the device switched back to the aerial view of the tangled mass of wires.

"Gotcha," Justine said with a smile.

"What just happened?" Dex asked.

"Th' Families, they's can takes ownership of any thread they's want, pulls it's up to th' Primary Family Interface level. When they's do, we's can no longer views it, even wit th' kind of privs you's find lying around in a slave's shrine."

"So why are you happy?"

"Because if they's pulled th' thread, they's are either hidin somethin or else tryin to makes us think they's are hidin somethin."

"So which is it?"

"Doesn't matter to me's. I's just turns it over to th' next level analyst, who's take th' data about pulled threads and does pattern analysis. We's just hope that somethin gives."

"So who's the next level?"

"He's is right there, wit Jules hangin over his shoulder."

"Wouldn't it make more sense to get Jules as far away from him as possible? Jules, can be a little distracting."

Justine was kicked out of another thread. She marked it, and pulled her hands out of the box of light. She sighed. "Heah, he's is distracting. Jules is also th' tallest brain I's know. So I's asked him to helps out. He's love pattern recognition. That's how he's has found ya meds, buried deep in th' SIN. He's is th' reason we's know 'bout you and Thelo. He's unraveled th' weaves."

"So you put him on your code breaker over there? No offense to Jules, but he doesn't know what he's in for."

"Maybe you's should go watch Jules. He's is real tall wit a light box."

Dex gave her a dubious look, and she just stared him down. He shrugged, and walked over to the soldier and Jules. The soldier was already getting irritated, Dex noticed.

"No, that's *not* input from our front lines," the soldier said, moving his hands quickly in the box. "It's anomaly-trace, eh, left-noise from pushing too hard on the threads."

"I's disagree," Jules said, pointing to the display. "At this depth, you's won't gets a signature like that. That's not coming from a binary interface. It's is either an analog strum, or it's is code-generated."

"We use a code agent to transfer the frontline thread counts to my pattern rec utils," the soldier said, pulling threads and moving them into different areas on the holo. "That's all you're seeing. It looks heavy-handed because it's a damn dirty hack."

Jules turned to Dex, instinctually recognizing he had a new audience. "If it's was anomaly-trace, you's wouldn't sees a pattern," he said. "Sees how it's stands out here, and here, but not here? If it's was the transfer hack it would be standardized. But it's is not uniform across th' threads. But it's *is* forming a pattern. Twenty-percent, movin in an arc away from th' central points."

Dex whistled. *I'll be damned. Jules is right.* By pointing out the slight discoloration of the threads, Dex saw the pattern that Jules pointed to. "What's your name?" Dex asked, putting his hand on the soldier's shoulder.

"Trey," the soldier said, shrugging off Dex's hand coldly.

"Sorry there, Trey," Dex said, stepping back. "I just think that Jules may be right. There is something there."

"I don't need a computer worshiper to tell me my job," Trey growled.

Jules straightened up indignantly. "You's think some weapon-wielding goon can possibly pattern match against th' slave?"

"You better get him away from me," Trey said, keeping his eyes on the holo. "Now."

"Come with me, Jules," Dex said, grabbing the bulk of Jules' flabby arm and pulling him away. He navigated back to where Justine sat, her light box idle as she spoke with Thelo.

"Justine, you know where I could find one of those boxes?" Dex asked.

"Heah, they's precious, few around," she said, giving Jules a warm smile. "What you's need?"

"Jules here was onto something," Dex said, noticing the pride emanating from Jules as he got to strut in front of Justine. "But that analyst treated me like I had a disease, and treated Jules like he was an idiot."

Thelo looked to Justine, who nodded, then he looked over to the soldier. "Follow me." The three of them walked back to where Trey sat, furiously organizing threads as they came in.

"Soldier, relinquish your light box!" Thelo yelled in his booming voice. The soldier jumped in surprise, then quickly pulled his hands from the box and sat it down. The lights went dim inside. "Sir, yes sir!" Trey said, standing at attention. The whole of Central Processing seemed to have gone perfectly still.

"You were ordered to cooperate with the cleric, son," Thelo growled. "Explain yourself."

190

"Sir, I was just doing my job. There was a disagreement about interpreting the data, that's all."

"And what exactly was the disagreement?" Thelo yelled. Everyone was staring.

"Sir, it was left-noise. The Sinner was watching for ghosts."

"They's are not ghosts," Jules said, more quietly than Dex had ever heard him speak before. "They's are clear indication of thread manipulation by a code agent. It's is too heavy to be left-noise. Too regular. Sees, if you's remove th' interface noise created by th'–"

"What do you think, Trey?" Thelo bellowed. "Think we got a silkworm trying to manipulate our pattern matching code?"

"I–I mean, it could be that–"

"That's all I needed to know," Thelo said. He turned to Jules. "Can you identify the thread patterns if I put your hands in that light box?"

"They's can mask intentions wit a thousand different ways to weave a series of threads," Jules said. "This one, from what I's have seen, it's is easily narrowed down to a block of 'bout 256 options, I's would say. But a lot more data piles up as we's–"

"Yes or no, cleric."

"Yes."

"Trey, you're on snoop duty on the perimeter. Give the cleric your passcodes."

"Sir, I–"

"And what's your problem with Dex, here, soldier?" Thelo asked, moving to within mere inches of Trey's scared face.

"Sir, it's just that, uh... it's *him*, sir"

"Trey, I don't care what you think you know about this man right here," Thelo said, his loud voice increasing by a few more decibels, "but this man next to me is Dexter Maxwell, the best friend that I've ever had in my entire life. And every time you disrespect him because of something you *think* you know, you are disrespecting me as well. Am I clear?"

Dex could feel every eye in the room on him.

"Sir, yes sir."

"Good. Then go snoop me some low level thread bugs, and I'll forget this ever happened."

"Sir, yes sir!" Trey said, and ran off. The room was suddenly back in motion, everyone moving at once. No one was staring at Dex anymore.

Fifty-four.

Thelo pointed at the light box. Jules nodded and sat down, and Thelo turned back in Justine's direction. Dex grabbed his arm.

"What the hell is going on?" He asked. "Who do they think I am?"

"Not here," Thelo growled, and Dex let go.

"I need to know who I am. I need to know what I'm doing here."

"You're Dexter Maxwell, the craziest bastard I've met. You're here because of what's up in this bucket of yours." Thelo knocked at Dex's temple with his big finger. "But I'm busy. Hang tight, you and I will have some time to jaw in a short while. Help Jules out."

Then he was gone, two soldiers waiting patiently with read-outs for him to review.

Dex sighed. The questions just kept backing up farther and farther, creating a jam in his head that he could barely see through. Instead of sorting them, he turned back to Jules, who had already perched the light box precariously on his oversized belly. His pudgy hands were both inside the box, and moving far faster than they looked capable of. His tongue had stopped circling his lips and had come to rest sticking out and up toward his nose. Dex looked at the holograph terminal, but couldn't make out anything. Everything was moving so fast. Jules seemed to be sorting through threads, but there was a secondary action that he was engaging in between thread sorting that involved rolling underneath the pile and grabbing the bottom-most thread and pulling it to the top.

"Can I help, Jules?" Dex asked. He felt dizzy even just watching.

"Heah, you's can find me's a real terminal," he said without looking. "This box is 'roid-waste."

"Sorry, I think you're lucky to have one at all."

"Heah, sure. I's sorting th' input from th' others, but writin a tester over here, see?"

"You're writing code? But it just looks like you're pulling threads from the bottom there, and putting them on top."

"Heah, th' bottom is modular algs for basic command. You's pull from th' bottom to build, eh. I's putting them on top so I's can build while I's sort."

"That's pretty cool."

But Jules didn't respond. As Dex watched, the top threads that Jules had been weaving suddenly fell apart and disappeared into the pile.

"Piddles!" Jules said. His hands began to move even faster, rolling the thread pile, traversing to a different set of threads. Too fast to follow.

"What happened?" Dex asked.

"Heah, good question." Jules was sitting bolt upright, his tongue frozen in place. Dex couldn't follow a thing on the holo. Jules gradually slowed down, his hands moving to a moderate pull. The bundle of threads was churning unevenly in the light box, delayed by Jules' gentle touch.

"Watch carefully, Dex," Jules said with a smile. You's see th' green string, there?"

"Yeah, I see it, now that you've slowed it down."

"That's mine. Snooper code. You's watch carefully."

As he spoke, Jules pulled his hands back, and the view zoomed in on the green string winding specifically through the other threads.

"Nothing's happening," Dex said.

"Watch," Jules said.

And then it happened. The green string broke into a thousand particulate pieces and melted into the thread bundle.

"That was it?" Dex asked.

"You's sees anything other than my snooper breakin up?"

"I guess not."

"Me's not either. You's go get Trance." His fingers were dancing in the light box, the holo reacting with a storm of activity. Dex did as he was told.

"Trance, I mean, Justine, uh, Jules over there wants to show you something."

"What?" she asked, looking distracted. Her hands were moving quickly, but Dex could tell she was no match for Jules' mastery of the interface. Then, the threads broke up in front of her, and she swore. "I's can't keep my threads bundled. It's keep breakin up on me's."

"I think that's what Jules wants to talk about."

She looked over at Jules' holo, moving rapidly over and threw threads and video streams. "Heah, he's is tall wit a box."

"Yeah. Tall." Dex followed her over to Jules' bench.

"Heah, speaks, Jules," Justine said. "What's is happenin?"

"Heah, it's is bad," Jules said. "You's have gots a layered code-rot algorithm runnin loose 'cross all visual and audio threads. I's bet you's can't gets anythin to last long, eh."

"No, just a few moments, then th' bundles falls apart, and I's have to re-pull."

"Heah. Sure. That was th' analog strum I's thought I's saw earlier, eh. It's look like left-noise at first, a little signature most everyone's ignore, before it's catch ya footprint and starts unbundling."

"But that's not th' worst. I's saw that comin, eh, so I's startin a new weave that could re-sort our's bundles non-rhythmically. Easy alg, eh. You's actually can do this on th' fly if you's know where all th' modules are at th' base, and then you's just supply a prime number count-down and a prime count up, and you's divide th' median wit a fluctuatin denominator. It's work so well because it's mimic a complex encryption code common at th' layer. I's did th' same thing back in—"

"You's stay on track, Jules," Trance cut in impatiently. Her anxiety made Dex uneasy. They clearly weren't winning whatever computer warfare they were waging.

"Right. Whoever's is tryin to hide th' actions, they's didn't have to decrypt my's little hack. They's just dissembled th' code."

"What did th' left-noise look like? Another analog strum? Was it's traceable?"

"Heah, when my's green thread go all mooshy, what did you's see, Dexter? Any noise? Any blips?"

"No, just the thread falling apart," Dex said.

"Heah, Trance. Heah. No left-noise."

"It's is impossible."

"You's right 'bout that. Code's don't breaks isself up. So I's setups a trap prog to capture th' trace signal. A fun little alg that catchs every

PFI abuser I's ever sents after to catch. But this time, eh, th' trap prog, it's falls apart too."

"You's tell me's what that means, Jules," Justine said.

"It's means th' thread construct is workin against us."

Justine just stared at Jules for a few moments. Jules just shrugged. "Th' slave's gives, and th' slave's takes away. Do you's believe now?"

"Thelo!" Justine yelled. Thelo turned from whatever task he had been at, and looked over. "I's need ya over here NOW."

Thelo came running.

"What is it?" He asked, coming up to them huffing.

"Ashion's has a new trick," Justine said. "He's has got someone planet-side wit root access manipulatin th' base code symbols. Disruptin our's trackin efforts."

"And now dumb it down for me," Thelo said.

"We's are blind."

Thelo didn't hesitate for a moment. He turned to Dex, "Time for you and me to go catch up on old times. We're leaving."

"Where are we going now?" Dex asked, getting really tired of it all.

"You, my friend, are headed to Earth."

Fifty-five.

"Justine, get the cleric and the priest out of here now," Thelo ordered, grabbing Dex by the shoulder. "Sonja, get those batteries off-grid, now. Dex, this way." They started walking briskly across the room. Justine followed, dragging Jules too quickly for his short legs. The large woman was helping pull the wiring and hefting the backpacks onto the men's backs. "I need the Sinners in the maintenance hole on level three, and I need the cams back on once I've gone. But I also need a blocker signal for the northeast tunnels," he issued his instructions.

They came to the First Term, where Father Morgish was busy at his terminal, swearing under his breath. "Father Morgish," Thelo said. "We're blind here. They've done something to the base code symbols, or at least something like that."

"I was wondering what was happening," Father said in a whisper. "It's the strangest thing I've ever seen. I've never seen it look more alive..."

"I'm sorry to do this, Father, but Sonja here must escort you and the cleric down to level three. It's the only safe place."

"I'm not leaving the First Term," Father Morgish said defiantly.

"It wasn't a request, Father."

Father Morgish swallowed, took a deep breath, and stood. "If anything happens to the hardware in this room—"

"Nothing's will happen, Father," Justine said. "I's can promise ya."

Then Sonja, Jules, and Father were gone. Justine looked at Thelo. "You's gots everythin you's need?" she asked.

"Yeah, everything," Thelo said, elbowing Dex in the ribs with a chuckle. "I can't believe we've made it this far."

"Heah. Logos provided a good plan, and a few extra surprises, eh," Justine said. "Speaks of which, Dex, you's will need this, eh." She handed him the Judas Sword. "They's say you's the key, eh? So unlock something."

"You're starting to talk like Logos," Dex said, reaching behind him and putting Judas in its scabbard.

"Heah. He's always spoke th' truth." Justine turned to Thelo and poked him in the chest. "You's don't die."

"You either," Thelo said, and threw his fist out. Justine punched it with her own fist, and they hugged quickly. She gave Dex a brief hug, turned and ran after Sonja and the Sinners.

"This way, Dex," Thelo said.

"Why are we headed to Earth?" Dex asked. "Is it safe there?"

"No safer than here. But the danger is different. The battle is different."

Dex stopped in his tracks. "You know, Thelo, I've been completely lost when it comes to whatever the hell is going on around me. Someone says 'run' and I run. Someone says 'get on the train' and I get on the train. But I can't put all the pieces together. I can see the pieces in front of me, but it's like everyone's been speaking a secret code since I got here, just to keep me in the dark."

"We do speak a secret code around here, Dex. They got cams

and audio grabs covering every square inch of livable space on this planet, not to mention one big-ass computer network that can process all that data in a matter of seconds. So you say something like 'I'm gonna kill Ashion' and that's all it takes. Someone's pounding down your door ten minutes later. Speaking code, play-acting at day jobs, that's all we got. Now if you don't mind, we're not safe here." Thelo started walking.

"How is here any different from anywhere else?" Dex yelled. "Hell, I don't even really know where 'here' is. Since I woke up I've either had a blindfold on, or I've been stuck in some shithole room that's too hot and smells like fart. So saying I'm not safe doesn't really have the impact you're probably looking for."

Thelo walked back toward Dex. "Do you think this is a joke? Do you think that all this shit is really happening just to keep you in the dark?"

"How come you're here, Thelo? Last time I saw you back in Grenver, you tried to strangle me to death. The longer I'm left alone with you the less comfortable I get."

"Jeez, Dex," Thelo said, "you know how to kick a man in the balls."

"I need a little more information than just 'go to Earth and wait for further instructions.'"

"Okay. Shit, where do I start? Okay. Back on Earth, when it was still 2113, I used to get these blackouts. I'd go out, just like that, snap, and then I'd come to someplace else, hours later. I wouldn't remember what happened, not at first. But the memories would come back to me, only in a way like I was watching someone else play-acting at being me."

"Money said something about a disease."

"Millionaire's Disease, they called it back then. A nanotech infection spread through the chip and drip tech they used for control back then. It got way worse after we were all iced, I've heard. Wiped out millions of people. They finally had to quarantine huge chunks of the country and exterminate them."

"Jesus."

"You say. Anyway, I had the disease. Can't be explained, as I've never had a chip implant, never had a drip installed. But I knew I had it, and I was getting dangerous. That's why I disbanded the Rebel League--to protect everyone from me."

"So how come you're okay now?"

"It's been a thousand years, give or take. When Logos pulled me off the ice, he'd already injected a blocker fluid. Now I give myself injections every few days, and it keeps the blackouts at bay. Haven't had one since I de-iced."

"When was that?"

"Five years, roughly. Spent the first three of them digging rock on an asteroid. They do that a lot now. They've had all these old criminals on cryogenic hold for centuries, and now they wake them up and use them as slaves out on the rocks digging for fuel, precious metals, whatever they can find. Free labor, and no one really cares."

"Then what?"

"The asteroid mines are where you learn the code talk. Learn how to talk about things without the cams detecting anything. Once I learned the codes, Logos sent for me. Found me work as a Transish shuttle operator. It was the kind of work that allowed me to operate outside the SIN now and then. Like now."

"Why are you fighting? What are you fighting for?"

Thelo shrugged, and gave a small laugh. "What the hell else was I going to do? Terrorizing the people who make all the shitty rules, man, that's all I've ever been good at."

Dex had to laugh. "That and pissing me off."

"That was always one of the perks. Listen, these people have it tough around here. The government that we fought, back in the day, they got nothing on the assholes on Venus. The Families have perfected their control apparatus. And something's going down, Dex. They're moving their soldiers off planet, sucking resources away from the cities—we think they're mobilizing an army."

"For what?"

"An invasion."

"Of what?"

"Earth, man. Earth."

"And why would they want to do that?"

"For a thousand reasons. Logos believed they were going to take themselves and their resources and head to Earth, leaving planet-side populations to die."

"Sounds like you'd rather have them go."

"If the Families leave and take everything with them, they take all the fuel to run the air processors. The water processers. The food growing systems. Access to the SIN. We need the Families to just plain leave, to not take any infrastructure with them. Anyway, it's complicated. Can we go, please?"

"Why don't you just get people on Earth to help you?"

"Dex, we really don't have time to give you a thousand years of history. The people on Earth, they don't even know anyone exists on Venus."

"Really?"

"Really. It's a way different place down there."

Thelo had started walking, and Dex was following.

"Have you been back? To Earth?"

"No."

"How am I going to get there?"

Thelo threw his arm over Dex's shoulder. "I've got this really nice 'muter picked out for us, with red paint and one of them new turbo accelerators."

It took a moment for Dex to get the reference, but it made him smile. They were going down some stairs quickly, and then through another long hallway. Thelo clearly knew his way around.

"Thelo," Dex said.

"What's up?" Thelo said over his shoulder.

"Do you know what happened to Mallory?"

Thelo kept moving as he talked. "I had Logos look her up. She was on ice, too. They had a record of her up here. They pulled her off ice before me, put her to work in the mines. There was an accident, Dex. She didn't survive. I'm sorry."

Dex walked silently for a while behind Thelo. His jaw ached from holding the tears back.

"Did she–I mean, did the records say anything about her... about a baby?"

Thelo stopped abruptly and turned. "She was *pregnant?*"

"Yeah. I mean, back then, she was."

"Pregnant. Crackpipe, that explains a lot. No, the records didn't indicate that she was pregnant. They would have taken a viable embryo from her, anyway. Before the ice."

"Yeah."

"Come on. We're almost there."

"Almost where?"

"Out of Central Processing, and on to the next big thing."

Thelo was reaching for the door when the lights went out. They could hear the explosions in the distance.

Fifty-six.

Ashion had his earpiece wired to his three admirals simultaneously. He was in his shuttle, nearing Central Morgish. His forces were on the ground already, waiting for final orders. Holden was speaking to his concerns for the hardware in Central Processing, and Ashion was only half listening as he strummed madly at his light box.

"They are pulling juice," Jorge was saying. "Where do they think they can go with it?"

"We can cut electricity to the First Servers," Brogue said. "They are pulling the juice straight from the server feeds. Life support goes black if we cut it, but not for long. What about the cams?"

"There is simply no way to cut the feed for Cen-Proc," Holden concluded. "It will be a bright fight, and we'll just have to live with it."

"I agree," Admiral Jorge said. "But casualties will be high. They've cut all thread ops for the entire building below level three."

"Wait, below level three?" Holden said. "My data says they have the entire building blind."

"They brought up the top levels just now," Jorge said. "To show off their position. Let me hardline the feed to you."

"Wait, no, I've got it now."

"Note the formations," Admiral Brogue said. "They mimic our military styles. Threes at each CPU."

"What is it the middle one is holding?" Holden asked.

"An explosive of some kind. Hold on," Brogue said, and Ashion could hear him pulling at his thread interface, strumming wildly at the large device. "I've patched the view over to my ops guys for an ident on the device."

"Damage to those servers would hurt, but we could survive it," Jorge said. "There is enough redundancy. They're mostly ceremonial now."

"The downtime would be severe for Morgish and large sections of Draggish while the reroute took place. But we could do it." Ashion was typing madly, synthesizing the data into a working plan, when his terminal went blank. Then, he saw the message:

NO. DO NOT ALLOW DAMAGE TO THE COMPUTERS. DO NOT TURN OFF ELECTRICITY.

"Admirals," Ashion said, and they went quiet, listening. "We can't harm the computers."

IT WOULD UNDERMINE MILITARY EFFORTS ON EARTH

"It would undermine military efforts on Earth," Ashion continued to relay.

AND THE REROUTE WOULD FORCE AN ENERGY CRISIS IN TWO DAYS.

"And the reroute would most likely spark an energy crisis."

I'M FORWARDING THE SPECULATION DATA NOW.

"Here's the data on my conclusions, I'm pushing the threads now," Ashion said. "You get them?"

Three 'yes sirs' and then silence as they poured over the data. It came up on Ash's screen, who brushed it away and went back to his tactics. But the screen went blank for one more moment.

AND RESCUE THE FATHER.

Then the screen returned to Ashion. He waited, but no more interruptions came, so he finalized his attack plan.

"Sir, this is an amazing analysis," Jorge said.

"The numbers are irrefutable. How did you do this?" Brogue asked.

"I plan for everything," Ashion said.

"But there's still the power issue, sir," Holden said.

"I can isolate a power feed to the computer systems on the top level of Cen-Proc, blacking out lights and services. I've already disabled the sorry hack the terrorists used to down the overhead cams, but I'm leaving them off. Those guys will snoop the cams if they're turned on, and we need every nanosecond we can get. I can reroute audio to a different line, though, and catch it at a broadcast layer that should bypass their bandwidth detection systems."

"How can you isolate the power feed? That's impossible," Holden said.

"There is more on heaven and earth than is dreamt of in your philosophy."

"I'm sorry sir?"

"I'll handle it, Holden. Trust me. I've forwarded the attack blueprints to your terms. Get your units in the positions based on this design."

"Sir, looks good," Holden said. "Containment seems the top priority, other than primary system protection."

"That's correct," Ashion said, his shuttle landing with a jar. He popped his restraining buckles and stood from his chair. "One more thing, Admirals."

There was a chorus of acknowledgement.

"We need Father Morgish alive. He's in the maintenance hole on level three. I need him alive. But everyone else–I want terminated."

Fifty-seven.

Dex closed his eyes against the absolute darkness, and tried to focus on his other senses. There was a lot of noise coming from above, explosions and shouting.

"Jeez, they're storming Cen-Proc," Thelo said in disbelief.

Just then, the door they had been heading for gave a groan and blew in toward them.

Thelo had just enough time to cover his face with his hands, but the force of the explosion sent the metal door shooting towards him. He fell and landed on top of Dex, and they both tumbled backward across the floor.

Immediately Dex rolled to his feet, pulling Judas from its sheath. The adrenaline rose to meet his mind, and time slowed. He closed his eyes, and could hear the quick dancing steps of three red-masked knights coming toward him. Thelo tried to stand, but Dex put his hand on his shoulder to stop him.

"Stay down," he said, and opened his eyes to the blackness. Meeting the first attack.

The knight had pushed his blade straight, swinging heavily, try-ing to get Dex to parry quickly to the side, allowing the knight past him. The strike was not meant to succeed, only to force a two-sided attack in the narrow hallway. *They must have some sort of night-vision built into the masks.* Instead of telescoping Judas, he used the blunt length of the sword to counter the weighted attack, moving to the side as the knight took a single long step past him. Dex flicked Judas, and the telescoping tip caught the knight in the chest as he passed.

The knight grunted and fell to the floor as the second attacker came in low at Dex's legs. Dex leaped straight up, bringing his blade around and pinning the attacker's sword to the wall. Dex let the mo-ment overtake him, surrendering to his battle instinct. The knight worked his sword free and swung at Dex's head, but Dex had already initiated a spin, ducking and rolling into the third knight.

Judas clanged against a sword, and Dex kept his momentum as pushed the third knight back toward the open door. A dim, dis-tant light created a silhouette of the knight who was trying to match the speed of Dex's blade. But he could not keep up, and Judas tore through his left knee, separating skin from tendon and tendon from bone. Dex used the stoppage of his blade as a counter balance and reversed his position to take on the second knight behind him.

His eyes had adjusted to the filtered light by now, and he could see the fear as the knight reverted to fakery, trying to get him to lunge on his feints. *He knows who I am. He realizes that he cannot beat me.* Dex found the opening he needed, cutting the knight's sword-hand off at the wrist, then coming back and catching his unarmed opponent in the neck.

He waited a moment, listening out for a second wave, but none came.

"Dex?" Thelo said hesitantly.

"Get up," Dex said, turning to the door.

"What the hell just happened? I can't see a thing."

"I saved the day. Come on, there always seem to be more of these guys."

"What guys?"

"Red Masks."

"You just killed a *Red Mask*?" Thelo was up and stumbling over the bodies.

"Three of them."

"*Crackpipe.*"

"Sorry I wasted your time with the chatter. Which way are we headed?"

They were through the door, and once outside, the heat increased immediately. Thelo pulled his gaze from the dead assassins and pointed. "That way."

The second wave of three Red Masks emerged from around the corner Thelo had been pointing at, swords drawn.

"Jeez" Thelo said.

"Stay here," Dex said, walking toward them.

"Whatever you say," Thelo said, happy to back away.

Fifty-eight.

Leshan finally made his light box respond. The seat groaned under his weight as he spun and began reviewing the incoming data. He could barely keep up as the threads came rolling in. Cen-Proc attacked by a revolutionist faction. Cen-Proc liberated by Ashion the Dark.

There were images of Red Masks setting up strategic positions throughout Low-Cen Morgish. He shook his head and watched as Father Morgish and some fat little cleric were helped from the Cen-Proc building, streaming with blood but alright. Leshan switched to a view of his own men, moving into position two miles away. He dialed his commander.

"Brutes, it's is Leshan," he said into his mic.

"Heah, what you's need boss?"

"You's makes it quick. You's don't bother makin it's look real. You's just gets it done and over wit."

"I's don't understand, boss."

"You's just makes it quick and get back here," Leshan growled. This was no time to have his men faking an insurrection halfway across the city. With Central Processing secured, there was no doubt in Leshan's mind where Ashion would stop next, looking for someone to blame.

A knock came at his door, and Leshan looked up. The knock was not at his primary door, but the back door for the exclusive use of him and his men. He turned, reaching below his desk for the blaster.

"Heah, comes in," he said.

"Uh, sir, it's Orpheus," Thelo said, entering the room. Someone was following him, drenched in blood.

"Orpheus!" Leshan said, breathing deeply. "Heah, my's favorite smuggler! What's you's doin here? It's is a bad time to come lookin for business, I's is afraid." Leshan was staring at Thelo's companion, who looked somehow familiar.

"Heah!" Leshan said, standing and staring at the bloody mess of Dex. "What's you's doin here?"

"He's not who you think he is," Thelo said.

Leshan paused. He nodded slowly. Then he nodded faster, putting it together. "Th' iter."

"Yeah, the iterate," Thelo said.

"Now I's understand why Ashion's want you's so bad," Leshan said to Dex.

"Yeah, I don't know what that means," Dex said tiredly.

"We need an untugged shuttle," Thelo said.

Leshan gave a scoff. "I's bet you's do. But I's have none to give."

"Leshan, this is the moment. This is it, right here. I just saw Dex here slay six Red Masks. And they never saw it coming."

Leshan gave a low whistle.

"It's for real. He's for real. I need to get him off planet."

205

Leshan turned back to his terminal to see Ashion's minions setting up stations across Low-Cen. The future stared back at him coldly.

He turned around. "One shuttle, no tugs, coming up." He pulled a glove from his desk and threw it to Thelo, who caught the glove and gave Leshan a nod. "You won't regret this."

"Oh, I's think I's will," Leshan said. "But I's not doin it's for no resistance. This town is *my's*. And I's is tired of Ashion gettin his way." Thelo turned to leave, but Leshan stopped him. "You's will have to go out th' front door to get to th' shuttle pad," he said, pointing to the other side of the room.

"Right," Thelo said, turning toward the front door.

As soon as they were past him, Leshan suddenly growled and lunged at Dex from behind. Without hesitating, Dex had the Judas Sword out fully telescoped, and swung it, catching Leshan in his huge gut, cutting deep into the fat and muscle of his abdomen. Leshan gasped, and fell to the ground.

"Oh *shit*," Thelo said.

"Thelo, honestly, he jumped me, I just instinctively–"

"I know. We best get moving."

Fifty-nine.

It wasn't hard tracking the clone, Ashion realized grimly. Just follow the trail of dead knights.

The bodies were in different states of torn-apartness. Ashion walked among them, quickly reconstructing the battles that had taken place just minutes before. He'd been alerted to the fighting down at level nine, but could not extract himself from the primary theater on the main floor. He had taken it upon himself and his elite guard of nine to protect the servers from terrorist sabotage. Decoding the booby traps had taken a few minutes longer than expected. Now he was outside Cen-Proc, and could see the devastation making its way north along the tight avenue.

Everything he saw spoke not just to the iterate's skill with the blade, but also to his speed. A speed that Ashion knew very well. But it was the efficiency of the kill strikes that surprised Ashion most. His guard followed behind him at a distance, giving the master his space, while he was checking for any survivors.

Where would they go? Where could they possibly find escape? He moved quickly northward, through the first nine bodies, and from a distance he saw the arm of another knight, down a western corridor.

"They're headed for Leshan's headquarters," Ashion said, and started running. His knights were now in formation behind him, keeping up, all of them as quiet as the hum of the atmosphere converters overhead.

Ashion heard his earpiece light up. "Sir, we caught them running west and north along lines six-sixty and seven-oh-one, but we lost them at a cam transition point. To be exact, at the food and freight depot at the corner of seven-oh-one and six-seventy-three."

"Copy that," Ashion said, who was running at a dead sprint now, his knights struggling to keep up. He arrived well ahead of his guard at the depot, another faceless series of freight doors and entrance-ways facing the public trafficway. Ashion tapped his earpiece. "Holden, give me the precise cam transition point."

"Sir, we have a minor blind spot just at the northwest corner of the avenues, at the depot building."

Ashion looked, found the spot and pointed with his finger. "Are you watching? Right here?" His earpiece crackled.

"Sir, yes, that's the spot."

Without hesitation, Ashion went to the wall and gave it a solid kick, near the ground. The wall gave way at two hinges, revealing a narrow, low doorway. He caught sight of his guard coming up just as he ducked in. The hallway quickly opened up overhead, allowing him to stand upright as he moved forward cautiously. Further on, the hallway turned to stairs, and then into a long pathway underneath the depot.

Ashion came up again on the far side. The doorway in front of him was open, and he could see into the room. He burst into Leshan's office. "I'm personally going to cut your ears off if you don't have this clone for me."

But Leshan wasn't there. Ashion looked around and soon found him next to his desk, lying face down in a pool of blood. Ashion glanced around quickly, trying to ascertain any threat. There was none. He walked over to Leshan and pulled the man's hulking mass over. He was not dead, not yet. There was a gaping slash across his abdomen, and he was unconscious.

"Is he alive?" asked a knight, from behind. They were filing in now, spreading out into guard position around the room.

"Yes, he's alive," Ashion said, standing.

"Should we get him to a med?"

Ashion shrugged. "Let him die." He tapped his earpiece. "Holden. Any sign of the escapees?"

"No, sir. Leshan doesn't cam his inner quarters."

Just then there was a commotion at the door, and three huge men burst in. In an instant, the knights were in front of them, swords drawn.

"Heah, what all this?" the first one said, looking around. He saw Ashion, and froze. But the one behind him saw the unmoving mass of Leshan on the floor, and pointed, saying, "What you's do to our's boss?"

Ashion looked down at Leshan, then back up. "That is not my handiwork, I'm afraid." But he could tell from the looks he received that Leshan's bodyguards did not believe him.

"He's is dead, eh?" the large one asked.

"Mostly," Ashion said.

"Heah, we's take him to meds."

His three knights looked to Ashion, who shrugged. "Makes no difference to me. Let them through. But touch nothing else, understand?"

The bodyguards nodded, and the knights moved out of their way as they gently picked up Leshan by his arms and legs and carried him out of the room. Ashion sat down at Leshan's desk. The iter could not have got far, not without getting identified on the threads. Ashion began poking around leisurely at Leshan's terminal, trying to see if there were any internal security threads he could use. His earpiece crackled with Holden's voice. "Sir, I've got a shuttle launch from Leshan's complex."

Ashion jumped up. "Tug it. It's them."

"Sir, there's a block signal and no de-com tugger. I can't pull it around."

"Damn smugglers. Track it, at least. Is it headed for the Family boats?"

"No sir. It's reached escape velocity already. It's headed off-planet."

Ashion was already moving. "Holden, remote my shuttle to Leshan's boarding pad. I want a three-fleeter dispatched from our deep-space unit. We got anyone in orbit already?"

"Checking sir. Yes, there's a return unit coming back from the Transloop station—wait, it's on medical emergency, hard-coded for auto-return. Looks like Tano, sir."

"Tano? Back already?"

"It looks that way, sir."

He must have found the map. But why the medical emergency? Nevertheless he still needed to exterminate the iterate. "Okay, get the three-fleeter dispatched on an intercept course. Seek and destroy, Holden, we just need them dead."

"Sir, yes sir. Where do you think they're headed?"

"The Transloop."

Sixty.

Dex tried to fidget in the uncomfortable flight-suit, but the harness had him strapped into the chair too tightly. He'd finally adjusted to the g-force pushing him backward, but the various straps and buckles of the suit were digging into his rear in a most uncomfortable way. He stole a glance at Thelo, who was concentrating on the terminal read-outs in front of him. Occasionally his hand would flick carefully across a series of small buttons on the arm of his chair.

"You do this often?" Dex asked.

Thelo's voice came over the microphone in Dex's helmet. "All the time."

"Thelo Hollywood, Astronaut," Dex said. "Has a nice ring to it."

Thelo smiled. "Astronaut. I haven't heard that word in a long time."

Dex looked at the displays in front of his friend, but couldn't make sense of them. "Why no windows?" he asked.

"Massive clouds of sulfuric acid roam the lower atmo like a band of half-dripped sewer rats. Eat right through anything transparent."

"Ah. So what is this Transloop thing?"

Thelo clicked a button, and there was a slight adjustment in their trajectory. "Kinda hard to explain, I don't really get it myself," he said. "Basically, it's a huge super-conductor for the smallest particles of the universe. These particles exist in matter/anti-matter pairs, and the Transloop has a bunch of separated anti-matter thingy's travelling in a huge loop between Venus and Earth. It creates a vacuum or something.

"The Transloop creates an on-ramp for big, complicated objects, like this shuttle, and exposes the ramp and the shuttle to the anti-matter vacuum, and all your littlest parts get sucked around the loop. Then there's a stopper at earth, where the exposure to the vacuum is slowly backed down, and the 'off-ramp' makes sure it gets all your parts and puts them back together."

"I don't think I understand."

"Think of it as a big slingshot that throws us to Earth really fast."

"Oh."

"Best part is, you don't even know it's happening. One second, you're sitting there waiting, next second, blink, you're staring at Earth."

"You've been on this thing?"

"Just once. By accident. If you get too close to the vacuum exposure field, it pulls you along with everything else. I was dropping off shipments for the shuttle company, and there was a traffic jam at the docking station. I was circling, waiting for a dock, and I got too close to the field."

"That seems like something they would have a freakin' sign up for. 'Warning, you're too close to the loop.'"

"They do have the area checked off so you don't get caught accidentally, and I was staying outside of it. But I still got pulled around. Since then, they've just kept moving the vacuum field closer and closer to the planet. It's like the loop is growing, or something. Anyway, any object that gets pulled into the vacuum gets looped. That's why we're here."

They emerged from Venus' atmosphere, and Dex had his first

look at the great blackness of space. He stared at the beauty of it, the millions of shining stars in every direction.

"I've never seen so many stars," he admired the sight.

"It's amazing, isn't it?" Thelo said. "I love being out here."

The force of exiting the gravitational field let up slowly, and Dex started to get a sense of his weightlessness, even though he was still strapped in. Even as he went to unclick, Thelo reached his hand over to stop him, pointing at his terminal.

"You see those three blips?" he asked.

"Yeah," Dex said.

"A Family three-fleet. They're after us already."

"How much farther to the Transloop?"

"A way. You got that helmet on tight?"

"Yeah."

"There's a yellow dial on your arm-pad. Turn it three times, clockwise." Thelo demonstrated, and a see-through visor came down over his face and attached to the neckpiece of the flight suit. Dex found his dial, and did the same thing. He heard a quiet hiss of air.

"Your air supply is now coming from the flight suit. From here, you have two hours of oxygen. I'm pulling all life-support resources into the back burners, for speed."

"Do you think we're going to make it?"

Thelo shrugged. "The future bakes in the sun like new adobe."

"I don't really know what that means."

"Me either, Dex. Me either."

Sixty-one.

"I need you to do the thing." Thelo's breath was labored as he tried to hold the steering yolk and the throttle in check.

The craft jerked madly, and Dex felt his stomach drop. He knew nothing about space travel, but he could say this much: Leshan's shuttle was going way too fast. It felt as though it might disintegrate into a million pieces at any time, and it was shaking violently. Dex felt the dream for a moment, the massive reorganization, and then it was gone.

"Dex!" Thelo yelled.

"What?"

"Do your thing."

"Do what thing?" Dex asked through gritted teeth.

"Jack the moment. Slow everything down. Like, now!"

"I've been there for a while, Thelo. Ever since you started to evacuate all the oxygen out the tail of this thing."

"Good. We've got a pretty small window of opportunity."

"To do what?"

"There's an emergency release out the bottom hull of the shuttle. Right before this shuttle blows up, I need you to pull that bar right there. The lack of pressure will pull us both out."

"Wait. Go back to the part about the shuttle blowing up."

"We're about to come under fire from Family fighter ships. Four or five direct hits and this little tug-boat is history."

"And… this is your idea of an escape?"

Thelo glanced quickly over and smiled. "I've got the great Dexter Maxwell beside me. I once saw him drive a garbage truck through a thirty-foot gap at eighty miles an hour."

Dex smiled grimly. "We're going a lot faster than eighty miles per hour now," he said. He eyed the release bar on the emergency hatch. It looked pretty well sealed by age, with a fine film of rust and dirt covering the entire outline of the door. "Looks pretty old," he said.

Thelo glanced at the hatch. "You'd better give it a good tug then."

"Maybe we should try to loosen it a little first, shake out the rust and dirt."

"That's a good idea. I'm pulling into a controlled arc, along the edge of the Transloop field. We'll stay in position, even after we take a few hits. Let me just put this sucker on auto." Thelo clicked a few buttons, then pulled a long leather strap from below his belt and wrapped it around the yolk. After he clicked out of his safety harness, he began drifting down to the hatch.

Dex was looking for the safety harness release when he heard the beep and looked at the display in front of Thelo's seat. "There's some kind of alarm going off on your–"

The missile strikes came in rapid succession, three in a row, knocking the shuttle violently sideways. Thelo had been floating down quickly, but the violent jerk threw his arm and head directly into the emergency shaft door.

"Thelo!" Dex yelled. He had his harness off now, and had pushed out of the seat. The weightlessness made him instantly queasy, but he moved quickly, and had Thelo in his arms. Through the faceplate, Dex could see blood globing up strangely, floating aimlessly in the mask with no gravity to tell it how to drip. Thelo looked groggy, and was trying to say something. His left arm was bent at an angle that made Dex's stomach tighten dramatically, and he fought back the urge to gag.

The hatch. Dex had the moment now, and he could hear the alarm was about to go off again. More missiles. This shuttle had about three, four more seconds before it broke apart. Dex kept his arm looped around Thelo's right arm, and grasped the hatch release. He pulled it with every ounce of his strength, trying to trigger its discharge.

The alarm sounded.

Dex felt the handle give slightly, the door about to release.

The missiles hit, sending the shuttle into a spin.

Dex opened the hatch. He felt the vacuum pull at his body as the shuttle's integrity bowed. A final missile rammed into the rear engine, tearing through the hull and detonating the spaceship into a million shards of metal.

Sixty-two.

Ashion was finally in his shuttle, punching in travel codes, when Holden crackled in his earpiece.

"Sir, the three-fleet have them. You were correct; they are headed for the Transloop."

"Is the loop field live?"

"Yes sir. This time of year, it's always hot."

"Shoot them down, Holden. I'm heading to the boats to check in with Tano."

"Sir, we are attacking them at this very moment."

Ashion fired his burners again, heading for the Family palaces. Tano had left his shuttle on auto-pilot, directed toward the primary military meds. This is where Ashion steered.

"Sir," Ashion's earpiece crackled. "The unauthorized shuttle is down. It was destroyed as it tried to enter the Transloop field."

"Feed me the visual thread."

After a short pause, Ashion watched the thread: with the Transloop stations in the distance and deep space beyond that. Approaching the electronic barrier to the loop's vacuum field was Leshan's unmarked shuttle, moving impossibly fast. The entire tail of the shuttle seemed to be on fire.

"What's wrong with the tail of that ship?" Ashion asked.

"We think the pilot was evacuating life support gas through the rear burners for added velocity."

"Smart. It's distorting the cam view. I can barely make out the shuttle's shape."

"Here it comes, sir."

And it did. From behind came the three-fleet, the spritely red fighters of his army. All three fired simultaneously, and the shuttle was knocked sideways, but kept moving. A moment later, a second volley of fire hit the shuttle, and it exploded into thousands of pieces.

Ashion smiled. "Good work, Holden. Get those fighter pilots a medal or something."

"Will do, sir." The earpiece crackled, and Holden was gone.

Ashion closed his eyes. The iterate was destroyed, Central Processing liberated from the terrorists, and his knights now firmly established throughout Lower Central Morgish. And no resistance from the local bosses, with Leshan on the beds, fighting for his life. He still had political fires to put out with Charles and Salzon, but that could wait for tomorrow.

Not a bad day's work. He landed his shuttle at the army medical facilities, where his entourage was already waiting for him.

"Sir, he's been asking for you since he arrived," one of the White Scientists said. "He won't speak with anyone else."

Ashion looked at him dubiously. "Is he hurt?"

"Sir, he may not last the night. We could repair him if we could put him out, maybe, but he's demanding to see you."

Ashion pushed past the doctor. "Where is he?"

"The ER, sir."

Ashion made it to the room and barged in. The scientists surrounding the patient moved away quickly, and Tano looked up and smiled. He was clearly drugged, but still awake. His chest had been taped up crudely, and his blood had already soaked through. The black eye-patch was missing, and his scarred socket looked bruised. A tourniquet still sat tied around a leg that was blue from lack of blood.

"Heah, Ashion," Tano said weakly.

"Tano," Ashion said, grabbing his hand. "What happened down there?"

"Ashion..." Tano trailed off, staring into space.

"Tano!" Ashion shouted.

Tano blinked and looked up at him with his one good eye, and smiled again. "Ashion, I's is sorry. I's need you to know... I's is sorry."

"Sorry for what?" Ashion asked, his heart rate hitting non-med levels.

"It's wasn't my's fault," Tano went on, squeezing his commander's hand. "How could I's know? How could I's know then?" he coughed up blood.

The White Scientist cleared his throat. "We don't have much time."

Ashion ignored him. "Tano, what are you sorry for?"

"My's betrayal. I's was so angry and how could I's have known?"

"What betrayal? What happened down on Earth?"

"They's are dead." Tano looked back up at Ashion.

"Who's dead?"

"Booster, Chaz, Ni'ello; eliminated," Tano said haltingly, coughing up more blood.

"Who? Who eliminated them? Who did this to you?"

Tano swallowed his own blood down. He reached up and pulled Ashion's ear to his mouth. When he spoke, it was in a barely inaudible whisper. "Th' iter. It's was always th' iter." He let go again. His good eye began to dilate, and he relaxed back into the bed.

Ashion took a step back.

The iterate.

He closed his eyes.

Dexter Maxwell lives. He is on Earth. And he was using the Earth-ling's map.

PART 3

Sixty-three.

Mebda loved the New Moon. Not like his Da, who worried that a moonless dark would allow his goats to wander off cliffs, or into a creek, or whatever other awful death Da could dream up for a goat. No, Mebda liked the view of the stars, without the bright eye of the moon outshining all its distant neighbors. And when they were in the higher meadows, up in the mountains, the cold air would blow the small clouds aside, and Mebda would be able to see the clouds of the heavens: the misty swirl of stars so far away they blended into each other.

But not Da, who was already snoring loudly from his bedroll. Medba sighed, wishing Da would wake and tell him about the stars. About the planets that shone with the sun's glow, but did not wink as the distant stars did. Even if Da only talked about how little was known, and how gazing at the stars was the flaw of the human race, it wouldn't matter. Mebda just wanted to hear the stories again and again: how their ancestors had put a stop to the evil men who had stripped the distant moons of their flesh, and had banished them together with their rockets and space travel devices and weapons from Earth forever. Back before the plagues. Before the Great Revival.

At least those stories talked about the stars. No other stories did. They all were about Earth, and the mountains. Boring. About disease, and politics, and war. Boring. Or about the ancestors: the great Family trees, extending back seven hundred years. But nothing about the stars.

Mebda watched as a falling star flashed across the sky. Another tear of God, shed for the little children staring too long at the sky, Da would say; and Ma, if she didn't just give him a whack and tell him to go to sleep. He kept looking anyway, watching for the next tear, seeing how long God would wait before weeping again.

Medba shuddered in the cold mountain air, and watched his breath form clouds above his head in the stillness. He should be sleeping. There was much work to do on the morrow. Goats to herd. Goats to find, lost in the moonless night. Yet he stared, waiting for God to cry.

He spotted the next falling star, starting in the northern sky and moving southward. But it did not disappear. As Mebda watched, it grew brighter and brighter, and seemed to get closer.

And closer.

The goats bleated nervously and ran away from the open night.

Medba sat up, watching as the star's brilliance quickly became more intense, before disappearing over the ridge of the mountain to the south of the meadow. Medba listened, and he thought he heard a booming roar.

"Da! Da!" he cried, shaking himself out of his bedroll and grabbing at his father. His father sat up immediately, grabbing at his stave next to him.

"What is it?" He asked, groggy with deep sleep.

"A tear of God! I heard it land not too far from here!" Mebda said excitedly.

His father looked at him for a long moment before putting his hearding staff down. "Medba, we have a saying," he sighed with a frown, helping his son back into his bedroll. "Leave the stars to themselves, and perhaps they will leave you to yourself."

"But Da, it was *really* close. It scared the goats."

"Goats are scared of their own farts. Go to sleep. Tomorrow is a long day, longer if we are tired. We move south, to Drayer's fields."

"I know."

"Then sleep, Medba. *Sleep.*"

"I can't sleep. I'm not tired. Can you tell me a story?" Medba pleaded.

Da sighed again loudly, and wiped at his eyes. "No stories, but I will sing you a short song of the ancestors."

Medba smiled and snuggled up next to his Da, who began singing the names and dates of their tree, starting only six generations back, and tracing in a matrilineal fashion through the ancestors. The web of names and times spanned the centuries, and the sound of singing and the shape of the past filled Mebda's mind as he drifted into sleep.

EARTH TRANSLOOP STATION,
SEPTEMBER 19, 3027. DAY 5.

Sixty-four.

Thelo felt the darkness around him, felt the fog lift, and he panicked. It was a blackout, like back in Grenver, back before Logos' treatment. He couldn't remember where he was, or how he had got here. He had a headache and a searing pain in his left arm. There was a smattering of blood on his mask as well. *Why am I wearing a mask?* Through the messy redness, he started to make out stars. Then it dawned on him that he was weightless.

He must have been floating in a slow spin, because the huge glowing mass of Earth came into view as he rolled listlessly. It was blinding in its beauty, its clear blue and white expanse. Thelo wanted to drift closer, close enough to fall and be consumed by its mass; maybe catch a brief look at a mountain, and yes, maybe some snow—

How did I get here? A blackout; that's how. The disease.

Over the past five years, he'd come to recognize the sensation of the disease boiling up inside him, trying to sneak its way through the chemical blocking agents. He'd got used to the injections—the burning syrum that Logos gave him in their secret meetings. The disease welled up at the back of his mouth, producing saliva, and reminding him of the aftertaste of the strictnine that was used to cut drugs back in the sewers of Grenver.

Why do I not taste it now?

It was his gift from the great civilizations of the 21st century. A nanotech degraded byproduct in his brain, manifesting as a violent second personality. Every time Thelo had thought about giving up on Venus, giving up on the fight, he'd felt the disease taking him, reminding him of what he was fighting against.

He fought against himself.

His slow drift had taken him full circle, and a spacestation came into view: the Earth Transloop station. He had been here once before, by accident. It was the exit station for travelers catching a ride on the particle catapult between Earth and Venus. Thelo recognized the

221

old station, built out behind a black umbrella-like shade to obscure it from view from the surface of Earth. Not that they ever looked at the stars anymore. He did not recognize the new construction, built in a long, thin cylinder. Thelo could only assume it was the first front of an invasion force.

Second Harvest, Logos had called it.

Thelo continued his lazy roll through space, not moving a muscle, just waiting for his memory to return. As his field of vision shifted, he saw another person not far from him, in a spacesuit. The person was in the middle of a violent seizure: arms and legs kicking, head twisting around, and back arched dangerously.

Thelo reached for the control panel on the forearm of his left glove, and discovered why his arm was hurting so badly. It was bent at a very unhealthy angle, right above his wrist. Just the sight of it sent a stabbing pain up his spine, and he had to supress the urge to vomit. He delicately flicked on the interface, and used his suit's small propulsion jets to move toward his quivering companion. The absence of gravity made it difficult to grab hold, but he was finally able to get a good look at the face. The eyes were rolled back into the head, but Thelo would recognize that face anywhere.

I didn't black out from the disease. But I'm about to now.

The taste came roaring up into the roof of his mouth, and with it, the anger, pushing and demanding freedom. Thelo could feel the hatred whirling around his head, the pure and complete hatred of his best friend, Dexter Maxwell.

Thelo swallowed the spit and blood, pushing back on the disease. He took a deep breath before rerouting his broadcast signal to a short-range encrypted channel.

"Dex! Can you here me?" he said loudly, giving Dex's convulsing body a squeeze with his good arm. At the sound of his voice, Dex began to calm down. Thelo kept talking. "It's me. Dex, you're okay. Listen to me; I need you to hear me, concentrate on my voice. There you go. Calm down."

Dex's eyes slowly came into focus as he stopped shaking. He focused on Thelo's face, trying to make sense of it. Without warning, he grabbed Thelo by his broken arm, squeezing hard. Thelo gasped in pain.

"Is it over?" Dex asked desperately. "Is it over?"

"Yeah, it's over," Thelo said, wincing. He grabbed his friend's arm and tried to remove it from his own.

"It was the dream," Dex said, closing his eyes, "the same dream."

"I need you to let go of my arm," Thelo urged.

Dex looked down. His eyes widened in horror, and he let go. "Crackpipe. Sorry. I forgot. It seems like it's been days."

"I don't remember anything. I think I might have... blacked out."

Dex gave a shudder, and tried to control his breathing. "You took a nasty hit to the head in the shuttle. You were pretty groggy."

"Shuttle? I don't remember."

"We were on a shuttle. Running from Ashion's guys. We escaped from that creepy computer shrine, remember? Stole Leshan's shuttle?"

"That part sounds familiar."

"Then we came under attack. You took a hit, and I opened the escape hatch as the ship exploded, and..." Dex closed his eyes and shuddered.

"Then what?" Thelo asked.

"And then it was the dream. The nightmare. The one I've been having ever since I was a kid... Only it was real, Thelo. I was falling apart, being torn into millions of little pieces. And I had to keep them all together, had to keep re-sorting and reorganizing the pieces." Dex shuddered.

"We caught the loop to Earth," Thelo reconstructed. "The force of the explosion put us in the loop field."

"So that's why I'm floating in space, staring at Earth?" Dex asked.

"You got it, my friend."

"That loop is evil. A nightmare that you can't wake up from."

Thelo squinted at Dex. "Are you telling me you remember the loop flight?"

"Remember it? Crack, Thelo, how can you forget something like that?"

"There's no way you could be conscious through the process. That's impossible."

"What do you mean? It was like the dream, Thelo. You know, the one I've always had. Only I couldn't wake up. Not till you were shaking me."

"The loop flight tears you down into the smallest pieces," Thelo said. "It stretches you out across millions of miles, and puts you back together. It's instantaneous, to the human mind."

"It wasn't instantaneous for me."

Thelo looked at him dubiously. His friend had a wild look on his face, full of fear. He gave him a confident smile and patted his shoulder, like he used to do for his soldiers on Venus when he was sending them to their doom.

"Let's try to figure that out later, okay? Let's focus on our situation for now."

"So, now what? How do we get down there?" Dex asked, and pointed at Thelo's arm: "You're gonna need to get that looked at pretty soon."

"Give me a second. I think there was a plan, but... I can't remember, exactly."

Dex tried to laugh. "When I said we should shake the door loose, I didn't mean use your head as a battering ram."

Thelo tapped his helmet with his finger. "That's about all this noggin is good for."

Dex stopped laughing and pointed over Thelo's shoulder. "Do you know what that is?"

Coming toward them was a slow-moving, matte-black craft. A large arm was unfolding from underneath it.

"Right! A debris collector!"

"A what?" Dex asked.

"This whole Family operation above Earth relies on stealth and concealment. You can't have any strange bits of debris falling to Earth, giving the locals crazy ideas about spaceships and such. So, they have a very effective trash detection and collection system– junk collectors, like that one, go around cleaning up all the loose debris. It's all automated. And right now, we qualify as loose debris."

"Is it going to pick us up with that... arm?"

"Yes, but there'll be no harm done. Junk flying through space can be very valuable property, so it's as gentle as a mother with her child."

"OK. And then what?"

"These collectors are unmanned, but there's a manual override system allowing us to take over the thrust controls."

"Sounds simple enough."

"It is," Thelo said, with a wicked grin.

Dex looked at him sideways. "Wait... I know that smile. What are you getting dripped about?"

"Are you ready to fly a spaceship?"

"No way. I don't care how bad that arm hurts, I am not about to fly that thing, Thelo."

The junk collector was almost on top of them now, and Dex could feel the slight tug of a magnetic field pulling them toward the outstretched fingers of the boom. It was moving faster–and it was a lot bigger–than he thought. It was hard to get a sense of perspective out here, he realized.

"It's not about my arm, Dex. No, you're gonna have to land this thing because... I'm not coming with you."

"The hell you aren't."

"Sorry, Dex, but I'm all wrong for Earth. At least the part of Earth you're headed for. I'm all wrong for 3027 AD."

"Why's that? Too big? Too dumb?"

"Too white."

"Are you telling me nobody's white down there?"

"Not where you're headed."

"And where exactly am I headed?"

The electric field was getting closer, and Dex felt his hair standing on end. It was getting harder and harder to move.

"You're headed for Grenver," Thelo said. "Or at least, where it used to be."

"Grenver isn't there anymore?"

"It's been a thousand years, Dex. A lot has changed."

"Right. Of course. Listen, I can't go down there alone. I won't know what to do. I don't know why I'm here. I barely even have a grasp on what the hell is happening."

"Sorry, mate. We're fighting a war on two fronts, and there are not enough soldiers at either end. I'm of best use on Venus."

"You could hide out. I'll bring you food and stuff. We'll make up a story about a traveling circus or something."

"There's something else." Thelo hesitated. "You're a trigger for this... for my disease. For whatever reason, when I'm around you, it burns hotter. I can feel it raging in the darkest parts of my head. I don't want a repeat of what happened at the cloner back then. I'm dangerous when I'm around you."

Dex's jaw ached as he fought back the tears: he wouldn't be able to wipe them away through the mask, and his arms would barely move anyway. The collector arm was surrounding them now, and they seemed to be suspended in place. Even their mouths were slowing down. It was getting harder and harder to breathe.

"I'm scared, Thelo."

"Have a little faith, Dex."

"Faith is not my strong point."

"It will be."

"Crackpipe, I can barely breathe."

"Stop talking. The field will dissipate soon."

"I don't think I can fly this thing, Thelo."

"Dex, what you know, but don't know you know, could fill an entire fleet of cargo cruisers. Now shut up."

The last sliver of light reflecting off the surface of Earth disappeared as the fingers closed around them and pulled them slowly into the port.

Sixty-five.

Dex didn't realize he'd been holding his breath until he exhaled.

He let go of the manual yolk of the junk collector, and felt the gravity of Earth pull at his arm, his body. He tried to blink away the burning sweat that was dripping from his forehead into his eyes. There were lights flashing everywhere, indicating fundamental and comprehensive system failures.

Dex took another deep breath. *Thelo was right.* He had navigated it into an entry position, found the zero window, and made it through the atmosphere. He'd even landed the thing somehow.

As soon as the on-board systems would allow it, he had the safety harness off, and was out the hatch, scrambling down the side of the white-hot craft. Once he was far enough away, he sat heavily on a large rock and surveyed the burning swath of forest wreckage left in the wake of the destroyed spacecraft. The glowing metal ship crackled and settled in the cold night air.

"My first space flight," Dex whispered to himself, his body still shaking with adrenaline. He looked up at the crystal clear night sky. "And godspeed to you, Thelo."

Dex's chest tightened at the thought; he already missed his friend. It had gone so quick, the little time they had had together. He had deposited Thelo outside the barracks of the Transloop space station, and then orbited the globe using the coordinates Thelo had given him.

And here he was: alone. Again. *I guess I need to get used to this.*

But he knew he never would.

Dex pulled the release cord on his spacesuit, and threw his helmet off. He gasped as he felt the cold, clear mountain air. It burned his lungs, and he watched in amazement as his breath formed clouds in front of his face. He looked around at the pine trees and rocks, barely illuminated under the vague light of the Milky Way.

"I'm home," he said, shivering. "And home is frickin' *cold.*"

Sixty-six

The nostalgia crumbled away quickly. He wasn't prepared for the cold and it was a long hike to his destination. He also had nothing to eat.

Longstown, Thelo had said. A small town near where central Grenver would be, only closer in, toward the mountains.

Dex lay down under a tree, shivering, trying to stay warm. He replayed the conversation with Thelo in his head again.

Where do I go?

There's a religious sect there, the Brothers of Brodius. That's who you need to contact. When you get to Longstown, just ask where you can find the nearest Brodius monastery. Try to stay low-key, don't get in any trouble.

What do I do at the monastery?

Ask for a monk named Freedom. If they don't know Freedom, ask for Justice.

That's really their names, Thelo?

Just pay attention, okay?

Right. Freedom and Justice. Got it. Then what?

That's it, actually. The monks will fill you in from there.

Fill me in on what?

Honestly, Dex, I have no idea. I don't get told the whole story. Too dangerous.

So that's all you know? You don't know what I'm supposed to do after that?

Thelo had stopped working and looked at Dex in exasperation.

Hopefully you raise a huge force to defend against invading armies. Maybe you send some soldiers back up our way. You saw what we're working with up there. Handmade blunt swords, a few stun guns we get from Leshan's goons that run out of juice after a few blasts. It's like a bunch of sewer rats taking on the Feds. We can't stand up to Ash's knights and their swords, or the military's blasters. At least not for very long. Not everyone has a ghost sword like yours that can pass through detectors. We have a lot of people willing to fight the Families, but nothing to fight them with. So, maybe what you do is you send me an army.

An army, huh? That's what I'm doing on Earth?

I'm telling you, I don't know.

Dex shivered against the cold, and then stood. *I might as well get going.* He took his flight suit off, and carefully stored it behind a rock near the burning ship husk. He began his hike, heading west and north toward Longstown. He tripped over a tree root and cursed, looking up at the night sky.

"Perfect night for a new moon," he muttered to himself.

Sixty-seven.

Dex had left his spacecraft well past midnight, and walked as far due east as could be accomplished on the rough terrain. He had walked to keep warm in the cold autumn night, until he was too tired to move anymore and the eastern sky had begun to warm to a greyish blue hue. Then he'd hewn some pine branches with Judas and lain underneath them, shivering to sleep.

And how long had he slept for? Life on Venus had been strangely bereft of time, and cycles. He still did not know exactly how long he had been on its surface, let alone how much time had passed since he had last found sleep, in Trance's bed. It felt like years ago, but could not have been more than a few days.

He woke with the high mountain sun burning the skin of his face, and sweat forming puddles underneath his clothes. Groggy, he felt an unbelievable thirst overwhelm him. He looked around, but could see no source of water nearby.

He sat on a large rock slab, staring up at the pine forests that towered all around him. With the sun high in the sky, he did not know what direction to set out in. He had thought he knew the lay of the land before he had fallen asleep, but now he could not tell which of the ridges he'd walked clumsily over through the night. Underneath his thirst, a hunger bubbled, churning his belly. He was exhausted, too tired to move.

Finally, he picked a direction, thinking the sun would be low to the south since it was autumn, and he had watched the shadows move for an hour. He found a small run-off brook, and gorged himself on the cold water. It did little for the rumble in his belly, but it eased the burning in his throat. After splashing his face and cooling his feet, he

229

set off again.

Within a few hours, he was almost too tired to move any farther. He had come across no more run-off streams, and no growth that even remotely resembled something edible. The sky had turned from late afternoon to early evening, and the pitch of the sun downward accused Dex of veering too far north. He had adjusted his direction, but now realized that he'd have to go back over the first ridge to find the route that went east.

Dex stumbled slowly up the steep mountainside, peering upward toward the ridge. He expected to be looking at open sky and over the other side once he reached the top of the ridge. Instead, it proved to be a false summit; as did the ridge after that, and the one after that. After a while, he decided to just concentrate on his feet, and putting one in front of the other.

It was nearly nightfall when he looked up and realized he was finally standing upon the ridgeline, staring down into a valley steeped in the dark of the setting sun. He could see a small lake, and beyond that, flat mountain meadows stretching eastward. Dex closed his eyes and let out a sigh. He started his downward course, hoping to reach warmer climes before the sun disappeared completely.

But it was not to be. With the ridge at his back, he walked directly into the blackness of the valley below, and soon found himself entangled in thick brush. After a quarter hour of fighting the shrub-brush with Judas, he collapsed and started to cry. He had come so far, he could not believe he was going to die alone in the mountains he used to stare at so longingly from the edge of Grenver.

But underneath the brush, the temperature was slightly better. He chopped more down and crawled under the prickly mess and fell asleep.

It was hard to tell when exactly he woke, but the sun was high in the sky already. Dex slowly pushed the cracked and dry remains of the hacked shrubs off him and stretched. He ached all over, his throat burned, and his stomach was a writhing pit of snakes. The sky was a clear blue, the sky of his youth, devoid of any moisture. The valley below fell evenly down and away from him, and beyond it he could see another range of mountains. He felt the youthful longing in him again as he gazed up toward Pikes Peak.

He made his way slowly down the side of the ridge, until he came to a rockslide area, which he tried to slide down. He ended up with a bleeding gash down his right leg. He stepped gingerly off the rocks and continued down the hillside. Finally he came to the creek that fed the lake below him, and he drank deeply.

Too deeply. The violence of his vomiting hurt all the way down into his thighs and calves, as he spat up the water and the emptiness of his guts. He lay next to the running water for a while, splashing it on his face and taking small sips. He kept it down. So, a few minutes later, he had a little more. Then a little more.

Finally he could drink enough to satiate his thirst, and he headed down further into the valley. He reached the lake late in the evening, and through his delirium he thought he saw people dancing along the edges. When he looked again, the trees waved at him in the wind. He walked on.

He didn't remember falling asleep. When he woke, he was shivering and cold, and something was licking the crusted sweat from his hand.

Sixty-eight.

Dex jumped at the sensation, and tried to stand, but the blood rushed from his head, and he fell back to the ground. He heard a strange bleating sound, and when the dizziness passed, he looked down and saw a goat staring lazily back at him, chewing grass.

For a moment, Dex was sure it was another hallucination, but then he heard more bleating. He sat up and saw hundreds of goats around him, filing slowly through the trees. *Real, live goats, roaming through the Rocky Mountains.* Then he noticed what the goats were doing.

They were eating.

Eating the small hard berries of the shrubs that looked different from the ones he had slept under at a higher altitude; and these still had some fruit on them, even this late in the year. Dex found a small branch and pulled the berries off into his hand.

He gave them a shake, and was about to put them into his mouth when he heard a low whistle coming from behind him. He turned quickly to see a small boy standing only a few feet away. He couldn't have been more than six or seven years old, and his nappy black hair was cut short. He wore a loose-fitting red shirt, and leather pants that were laced up at the side seams. Barefoot, he was perched on one leg, leaning against a staff twice his height.

The boy whistled again, and shook his head. He pointed and said something in a language that Dex didn't recognize.

"What?" Dex voice was hoarse and came out as a croak.

The boy said something again, and this time Dex felt the vertigo, the sensation of falling, that he had felt when he had first gripped Judas. When he had first sat at the controls of the collector ship. And then, the boy's words made sense.

"You'd better not eat those."

"I'm hungry," Dex replied, using the boy's language. What language was it? Dex did not know. He tried to work out where he might have learned it, and the dizziness returned. He concentrated on the strange child instead.

"You'd still better not eat those frungeberries," the boy said. "Your tongue will swell up in your mouth until you can't breathe except through your nose and then your throat will swell up too and probably then you will die."

Dex looked at the berries in his hands. "But the goats are eating them."

"Goats are goats. Humans are humans."

Dex tried to laugh, but found it didn't work. "I can't beat your logic, boy."

"Mebda."

"What?"

"My name is Mebda."

"Mebda, do you know what a human can eat around here?"

The boy stopped smiling then, and put his foot back down on the ground. He wasn't looking at Dex, but past him, over his head. Dex turned to see what the boy was looking at, and saw a hulk of a man standing over him. He was wearing the same style of clothing as the boy, only his staff was much larger and had sharp metal spikes protruding from one bulbous end.

"There are goats, man," the man said. "You could eat a goat." The man wasn't staring at Dex, though; he was staring at the small boy.

"Mebda, run and catch the front end of the herd," the man said. The boy nodded, took one last look at Dex, and then he was gone, running as fast as Dex had ever seen.

"I wasn't going to eat your goats," Dex said.

"You have an unusual accent," the man said, keeping an eye on the boy as he ran across the field. "Where are you from?"

Dex looked up. "Longstown."

Finally the man looked down, sizing up the blistered, weary, hungry stranger. Then he looked back toward the boy. "Your ability to speak Amrick is impressive, but you do not talk it with your throat. You talk it with your mouth. In Longstown, we speak it with our throats. Every lie is a prison. "

Every lie is a prison. It was something Jones always used to say.

Jones always used to add: of course some people need to be incarcerated.

"But some men, they need to be imprisoned," the man finished, and offered his hand to Dex. Banishing the déjà vu out of his head, Dex accepted the help and stood feebly, legs shaking. He let out a cough.

"I am Rolink," the man said, his face an unreadable frown. "The boy is my son, Mebda. These are my goats. My mother is Shalla Orion, daughter of Kastik Orion. My father is Brindaka, son of Sristassa. They both came to Longstown in their youth, from the village of Grastall, in the Midland. It was a short journey, made out of necessity. Sristassa was a blacksmith, as was Kastik. Now, I raise goats in these fields."

The man faced him, and Dex realized he was waiting for something.

"I'm Dex"

The man waited, and Dex said nothing else. He hadn't thought to make up much of a story. *Every lie is a prison.*

"My full name is Dexter Maxwell," he added. Then it all came out. Because, what was the difference? There was no rulebook for this. "I'm originally from Grenver, Colorado, but that's not really the name of the city. They started calling it the Greater Metropolitan Front Range when the townships were all incorporated, but that was before I was born. Anyway, Grenver sounded like the old city-name, of Denver, so it stuck. A shortening of Greater Denver. I lived in the sewer systems that were built for the huge rains that never came. My father was, well, I don't even know my father. Or my mother. I was an orphan."

The man's eyes widened with every word, and his jaw dropped. When Dex stopped, the open mouth turned into a smile.

"An Oldkeeper!" he said, grabbing Dex's hand tightly, almost dancing. "Grenver, that was long ago, but we have some stories from it. Our other Oldkeeper is much younger than you. He only keeps back to the Industrialist Wars. But you are of Grenver! The sewers! The rains that never came!"

Dex went with it, not knowing where it would lead.

"I know plenty about Grenver. I could talk all day about that dirty hole."

Rolink laughed and clapped him on the shoulder. "I would like very much to have a story with you. But first," he said with a look, "you should probably eat something."

"That sounds good," Dex said.

"I must help Mebda gather the front goats. The males always drift away, no?"

"Honestly, Rolink, I've never seen a real goat before in my life."

Rolink laughed. "Hah! Compliments. These are not real goats! Not like before, in the old times."

"Maybe so. I could not tell you."

Rolink whistled at a pitch that slowly lowered, like someone in Dex's time would have done to replicate a falling mortar shell. "An Oldkeeper dying of starvation in the goat fields. What are the chances?"

Dex looked up to the sky. "Million to one, I'd guess."

Sixty-nine.

The bright fire warmed Dex's sore feet, and he wrapped the goatskin tighter around his shoulders. The rest of the wilderness pitched a darker blackness. The only sign of the world beyond their camp was the occasional bleating of the goats.

Dex let out a loud burp. Mebda, sitting across the fire, giggled through his mouthful. His father smiled.

"Good to have something in the belly?" Rolink asked. He'd prepared a mild soup of leaves and what looked like tomatoes. He'd thrown in some dried goat meat for flavor. Dex was on his second helping, and could only nod as he gulped down the contents of the earthenware bowl.

Mebda let out a burp, clearly forced, and grinned wide. Dex gave him a wink.

"Do not let your mother hear that," Rolink said. But he was smiling, and his eyes twinkled in the firelight.

"The soup is very good," Dex said. He drained the last bit of broth from the bottom, and laid the bowl down next to him.

"Da, can we have a story now?" Mebda said, trying to sit still, and failing. Rolink looked at their guest. "Only if the Oldkeeper is ready."

"Sure, Mebda. What do you want to hear about?" Dex asked, pulling leaves from his teeth. He felt like he might fall asleep at any moment. But the young boy's enthusiasm was infectious, and he was happy to talk about something he knew.

"Tell me about the vehicles that operated by burning fuel," Mebda said, leaning in on his knees.

"The autos? Back then, we called them commuters, or 'muters for short. That's because almost all of them were owned by people who lived in one place and drove tens of miles every day to another place where they worked, and then drove all the way back. Every day."

Mebda laughed. "That's silly. No one would do that."

"Oh, they did it like their lives depended on it. And there were so many of these 'muters trying to get to the same places at once, that the roads would get clogged up. So they kept building bigger roads, with better controls to even out the flow. They implemented laws on when you could enter the roads. And they had it all working perfectly." Dex gave a wicked smile. "But then there was a group of people who didn't commute to work. In fact, they didn't work at all."

Mebda scoffed. "Everybody works. Even the fevers down at the asylum."

"Not back then, Mebda. Only certain people were allowed to work, and if you couldn't work, you had to find some way to get food. If you couldn't get food, you'd just curl up and die."

"Or try to eat frungeberries," Mebda said with a laugh.

Dex laughed. "We ate worse things than frungeberries. But some of the folks that didn't work decided to get back at the people who made all the rules. They decided to bring all the 'muters to a halt, all over the city, all at once."

"How'd they do that?" Mebda asked, his arms up on his knees, his chin on his arms.

Dex couldn't stop grinning, and he poked at the fire. "Let me tell you, Mebda, it wasn't easy. Not at all."

Seventy.

Dex figured out he must have fallen asleep after he had told the story of the traffic jam, and after he had explained for the tenth or eleventh time what a garbage truck was. After he had talked about storm sewers that were never used, and what a burbring was, and had tried again to explain how a helicopter worked. Of course, he had no idea how helicopters worked, but he knew it had something to do with the speed of the blades. And something called lift. Mebda didn't believe such things existed anyway, and even Rolink scoffed when Dex relayed how four of them had given chase. It was as though such things were the stuff of fairytales.

When Dex woke, the sun was just breaking over the mountains to the east. The goats bleated restlessly, and he found the sound put him at ease. Rolink nudged him gently, "Breakfast." The smell of frying meat sent Dex's salivary glands into overdrive, and he sat up. His back ached, but he felt better rested then he had in days. Or maybe it was years.

Or centuries.

Dex had fallen asleep thinking of Grenver, and he woke to it as well. He could see Salomon Salazar's Penny Shop opening for business in the morning, serving coffee to anyone who dared drink Sal's "special blend." He could see the flickering shadows of a candle newly lit in the refuge of the water collectors. He could see Mallory laughing at whatever nutso thing he and Thelo had just done. He could hear ol' Jones' soothing voice, sharing his knowledge with everyone willing to listen. Dex's heart ached for the familiarity of it all.

He looked at the cold dawn around him. The goats chewed on the high mountain grasses and shrubbery, their breath clouding and lifting in the still air. The pine trees stood high above them, away from the meadow clearings. They were green like real trees, not the strange, too-bright green of the concrete carbon-cleansers they had installed in those Artrice Parks all over Grenver. Slow clouds drifted almost imperceptibly above him in the grey-blue sky. Down the small incline of the meadow, Mebda was running at his remarkable speed, making curt whistle sounds at the goats, who obeyed and clustered in closer to the pack. Rolink sat drinking from a bowl and pushing something around on top of a stone set above the rekindled cooking fire.

His past was familiar, but this felt right. Dex pushed the goatskins away, and rolled them up as best he could. He strolled over to the fire, shivered in the morning air.

"Good morning," he greeted Rolink, who looked up at him with a smile.

"Morning, Oldkeeper. Here, this will warm you up." He handed the bowl to Dex, who took it eagerly. The fluid was dark and green, with leaves floating in it. Dex took a sip, and winced at the bitterness.

Rolink laughed. "Yes, the digroot is tough at first. But it makes the mornings easier."

Dex shrugged. "The coffee we drank in the sewers was not much better than that."

"Yes, the sewers," Rolink said, pulling the barely cooked meat from the rock and throwing it in another bowl for Dex. "You are the best keeper I have storied with in some time. I thought you might keep Mebda up all night long."

"Sorry about that. Felt good to talk."

"Do not apologize! You storied him of times he has not heard. Although it was difficult to rouse him this morning."

"How'd you do it?"

Rolink gave a wink. "I told him you'd be awake when he returned. Eat."

Dex ate the virtually raw meat, and it tasted fantastic. They both ate in silence, sipping at the digroot tea.

"I'm not from Longstown," Dex said, "but I need to get there. I'm looking for the Brothers of Brodius."

Rolink didn't look up. "You will find them all in the townships north of Longstown, Oldkeeper. But who knows for how much longer. Mastiff does not seem fond of keeping religion so close to him."

"Who's Mastiff?"

Rolink huffed. "Calls himself the King of the Backplains. But he's just another warlord. And at least for now, he's the law."

"Can you tell me how to get there? To Longstown?"

Roland looked at him, sizing him up, and then looked back to his meal. "It's not too much farther from these fields. Three days, walking with no goats."

They sat and finished their meals, listening as Mebda's whistles and yelps came closer and closer.

Without looking up, Rolink said, "We're headed to Longstown ourselves, to pick up Mebda's mother on our way to our winter grounds in the north." He looked into his guest's eyes. "You could accompany us."

Dex felt relief pour over him. "I would like that very much."

"Two rules, Oldkeeper."

"Anything."

"Tell Mebda everything you know."

"Sure thing. What else?"

"If you lie to me again, you walk to Longstown alone."

Seventy-one.

Dex found the rhythm of goatherding to be peaceful, if exhausting. Rolink put him to work immediately, helping with the animals, mostly making sure they didn't dawdle too long at the back. The goats, for their part, gave him dubious looks and questioned his authority every chance they had. But Mebda taught him the harsh syllables to use to convince the stubborn creatures to move when they needed to move, and to stop when they needed to stop. After two days, Dex was enjoying himself, and the fears and dangers he'd left behind on a different planet felt too far away to be real.

Part of the enjoyment was Rolink's willingness to teach. But mostly it was Mebda's barely contained enthusiasm for whatever details about the 22nd century Dex shared with him. Mebda was delighted by flying things, and horrified by the chip implants. He gave Dex skeptical looks when he talked of artificial tree parks, and flat out refused to believe that people would abandon entire swaths of houses just to move out to newer houses farther away from the city.

They sat around the fire on the fourth night of their journey toward Longstown. Behind the last goatfield and down the lower foothills lay the gated fields that had been erected outside the city for shepherds and their herds.

Rolink was explaining his trade to Dex. "Some are used for the meat, but mostly it's the milk that we sell. The townsfolk enjoy buying their milk fresh at market, so Charla– that's my wife–is in town establishing our trading partners. She is much better at talking business than me. I was meant to be only the field-hand." At this, he had a good chuckle.

Dex found Rolink's laugh infectious. "Do you miss her?" he asked.

"Of course, as does Mebda," Rolink said, pushing his coarse hands through Mebda's kinky hair. "But it's good for us men to get away." Mebda smiled and puffed out his chest at being called a man.

"And she appreciates the time to see her friends, and her mother. Our goatkeep is far away from things, and so we do not get into town as much as Charla would like."

"How long have you been out?"

Rolink put his nose in the air, as if to smell the distance of time. "Over two moons, I think. Mebda, how long did we run the goats this year?"

"Forty-six days, Da."

Rolink grinned. "And how many goats did we lose this time?"

Mebda looked up from the leather rope he was braiding. "Only two, Da!"

Rolink gave him a little push. "That's right. Only two. My little herder is becoming very good at keeping the goaties safe."

Mebda grinned proudly as he went back to braiding his whip.

"It's a long time to be away from someone you love," Dex said.

Rolink shrugged. "She has us all winter, cramped up in the house with the fire burning and the feet smelling and the dogs howling. We have a rhythm, and come spring, that rhythm means what?"

Mebda yelled out, in a mock female voice, "All dirty boys to the mountains! Now!"

They all laughed together. A log snapped in its carbonizing dance and broke. For a moment, all eyes were on the magic of the firelight as burning ashes spun and whirled in the air.

"Tell me about computers, again," Mebda had put down his unfinished whip and crawled onto his father's lap.

Dex stretched out his back. "I was never all that familiar with their insides, but basically, back then, we used computers to do everything. We had microchips that could process millions of instructions every second–"

"Like the kind people put in their heads?" Mebda asked.

"Right. Only we had chips in everything. They did a lot of work for us, so that we didn't have to. You could have a chip drive your car for you, or make your breakfast, or grow your plants. And little kids used computers to do their homework, learn to read, giving them book after book–"

"That's enough of that," Rolink interrupted.

"We don't talk about reading," Mebda said importantly. "God

241

hates writings."

"What are writings, anyway?" Rolink rubbed his son's shoulders.

"The devil's way of making us forget," Mebda answered fiercely.

"You don't have any books? You don't write anything down?" Dex asked incredulously.

"And we're done talking about it," Rolink warned.

Dex couldn't quite put it together. "I mean, no one reads? Not just, you know—"

"The goatherders?" Rolink shot back fiercely. "No one, not the monks you seek; not the merchants in the city, counting their bullion; not the women and their gossip circles. No one."

"Except Mastiff," Mebda whispered.

"Right. The foreign leader and his minions," Rolink spat. "He tries to recruit help, but demands they read. So no one helps."

"But how does it all work?"

"How does what work?"

"Everything."

Rolink was suddenly standing, staring down at Dex. Medba was already behind his father, staring through his legs at Dex. "Who are you, Oldkeeper? Where do you come from?"

Every lie is a prison. "I'm from a different world." It was as honest as he could get without it sounding like a lie.

"Do you work for Mastiff? One of his goons? What do you want from me?" Rolink stepped closer, and Dex felt his heart rate going up. Felt the threat.

"Please, I don't know anything about anything. I'm just trying to figure out what your world is like."

Rolink stood for a moment longer, and then relaxed a little. "You speak well of forgotten times, but you ask too many questions. Dangerous questions." He walked toward his bedroll, his hand on Medba's shoulder. "Tomorrow we will arrive in Longstown, and you and I part ways."

Dex sat and stared into the fire, trying to breathe through the adrenaline that filled his veins. Trying to ignore the weight of Judas on his back, beneath his shirt. He watched the fire until it grew inert, a pile of glowing red embers that no longer provided warmth.

Seventy-two.

The burning surface seemed closer than usual, so close that Dex could not find time to be afraid. Instead, he began the process immediately, cataloguing the little maniacal strings at the bottom of the universe that were leaping madly across the surface, seeking out a partner on the other side, and switching places. Dex concentrated on the strings along that surface, all the little strings, and then he felt his outstretched hands breaking down in the blinding heat of the plane. He followed the string to the other side, and put his hands back together, and then his wrists, and forearms. But his chest was so complicated, and his brain; he was losing his place, and the stringed maniac particles were dancing too fast and the heat was burning him into nothing—

He awoke with a start, and the dream disintegrated, leaving only fear and frustration. The sky was too light, the world awake and loud already. He turned over and found Mebda staring at him strangely, from only a few feet away, crouched down with his knees up under his chin, in the way that only children can do.

"You disappear when you dream," Mebda said.

"What?"

"Are you from outer space?"

Dex looked at him more closely, the big eyes, staring him down. "What makes you think that?"

"Last night. You said, 'I'm from a different world.'"

"I didn't mean it like that exactly..."

"Yes, you did. I saw it. You didn't lie. I can tell how you make words with your mouth."

Some of us need to be imprisoned. "Yes, Mebda. I'm from a different planet."

Medba nodded solemnly. He pointed into the sky, northward, and drew a line to the south. "I saw God's tear, it was large and too close to Earth. It was you, wasn't it, falling from the sky with the tears of God."

"Something like that."

"Yes. Like that." Mebda drew the line again.

"Don't tell your Da."

"Da thinks you work for Mastiff, and wants to be rid of you."

"Your Da is a wise man."

"Yes," Mebda nodded thoughtfully.

"Anything for breakfast?" Dex asked, trying to change the subject.

"You slept through. We're moving on now, time to get up," Mebda said, rising and moving away quickly.

Dex quickly packed his makeshift bedroll and threw it on the waiting pack-goat, tying it down as Rolink had shown him. Then he gave a quick "Hya!" and slapped the animal on the flank. It bleated and then moved to catch up to the rest of the herd. Dex made his way through the herd to the front, where Rolink was walking, carrying his tall staff and with his whip coiled in his hand. He whistled occasionally at the animals.

"Where do you need me today?" Dex asked.

Rolink didn't look at him. "I will walk the front. Medba will walk the back. You can walk where you please."

Dex felt the dismissal, and it hurt. He stopped walking, letting the herd slowly mull past him. Medba followed the animals closely, keeping an eye on the dawdlers. He did not look back at Dex.

I still need to get to Longstown, and that's where this goatherder is going. He convinced himself to follow the bleating, pooping animals.

After an hour, Dex realized that unless you are herding, walking at goatspeed was nearly impossible. He would catch up with the back of the herd, and would have to stop and wait for them to move ahead once again. Eventually, Dex took to walking up the sides of the valley to the tops of the small ridges to get views of the mountains. He would then come back down again to rejoin the herd as it made its way slowly out of the rolling hills. He would keep his distance and by noon he'd found just the right gait; far enough away so as not to disturb, but close enough to still be able to hear the yells of Rolink and his son.

It's for the best. I'm not here to make friends with goatherders and their families.

Or maybe I am.
I'll know more in Longstown.

As the noon hour came, Dex saw the goats come to an uneasy stop as Rolink and and his son rested to have their noon-meal. Medba had shown Dex the local things he could eat, so he dug up some keel-root and chewed on it as he wandered to the top of the nearby ridge.

There he was welcomed with a view of the rolling plains that sprawled eastward from the front range mountains. He could also see a town at the bottom of the foothills. That must be Longstown. It was so... small, and so far away it made him dizzy. Where were the skyscrapers of downtown Grenver? Where were the burbrings? The highways?

But he had to admit, it did look better without the dirty brown haze of car exhaust fumes and air conditioners and worthless machines all running through their short, little fossil-fuel lives. There were only a few perceptible buildings down there, all clustered together tightly around. One looking like a castle. But Dex couldn't tell from this distance. This world was a different place, with angry warlords, illiterate goatherders and who knew what else.

He stared at the goats, the tiny little specs milling around below him, with Rolink and Mebda sitting beside them, eating. He followed the valley down, where the path soon turned into a road that wound down and out of sight, reappearing intermittently farther down.

Squinting, Dex noticed clouds of dust on the road. He watched for a moment, and was able to make out the shape of four riders on horseback, heading west toward the goat herd. He looked back to the herd. They were on the move again. Dex took another bite of the mealy and deeply unsatisfying root, and started back down.

Seventy-three.

He'd meant to walk a line that would put him just at the back of the slow-moving herd. But as he headed down in altitude, veering east, he found himself thwarted by steep rockslides. Having learned his lesson with the still-healing wound on his leg, he stayed above the slides, walking at the top, where they were not so wide. When he reached the valley floor and the creek that ran there, he realized that he must have overtaken Rolink and the goats. He was at the start of the road he'd seen from the top.

Dex did not need to wait for the goatherder and his son; they had spurned him the first chance they'd had. What could they offer him after all? But the prospect of walking into town alone was too daunting. Best to walk in behind the goats, looking a part of something. Perhaps that way there would be fewer questions.

So Dex descended the steep embankment, removed his rapidly disintegrating boots and splashed water from the creek on his hot feet. After he had taken a long drink, he sprinkled water through his unwashed and unkempt rat's nest of hair, trying in vain to disentangle the beginnings of dreadlocks. He leaned back against a rock, basking in the cool shade of the creek, but was instantly startled again by the thundering of horse hoofs along the road, approaching the goats.

Donning his boots, he followed the horsemen back up toward Rolink, careful to stay close to the large pines lining the road. He did not know the horsemen, and did not feel like explaining himself just yet.

They had pulled up short of Rolink, just a few hundred yards from where Dex had been drinking. Dex crept up to within earshot and listened. The men stayed on their horses, and Rolink stood defiant as his goats ran nervously away from the equally nervous horses.

That's when Dex noticed the huge swords the men had strapped to their horses. Big sabers, curved like in the ancient pirate cartoons. But these were real, and they were glinting in the afternoon sun.

The horses are nervous around farm animals. And the men carry their blades for everyone to see.

Dex felt his heart rate escalating. He realized he was devising a battle strategy in his head, and tried to ignore it and simply listen to the men.

"These are not illegal animals, I assure you," Rolink was saying, as Dex crept even closer.

"New laws passed, goatman, didn't you *read* them?" said the man at the head of the group. The other horsemen laughed at the joke. The horseman was clearly in charge of the other men. He had his black hair pulled back tight and worked into a small bun. His chin sported a small goatee.

"I don't need your documents to know the law," Rolink spat. "And who did you say you were, again?"

"Agents of the king; that is all you need to know, goatman."

"The new laws say that all taxing occurs in bullion only," Rolink said. "My wife is in town now, collecting on payments. We will pay upon our arrival."

"Sorry, goatman. We need payment now." The leader nodded to the three men behind him. They dismounted and headed for Rolink.

"I know the law, fellows. I can recite it for you. Code 329 of the New Order of King Mastiff, section thirteen, the payment of taxes on all existing livestock, provisions for milk-generating goats: all payment shall hence be paid as a one-fifth of the weight of all goats bearing milk—" Rolink backed up.

"Enough, goatman," the leader said. "I don't need an illiterate goater telling *me* the law."

"Do not think that because a man does not use the written word that he doesn't know the law," Rolink said, his voice growing louder. He gripped his staff tightly with both hands. The large muscles in his forearms popped with the tension.

"I tire of this," the leader gave a dismissive wave. "I need goats for milk. Morvis, please secure this insolent farmer while we gather some milkers."

"As you say, Travin," Morvis pulled his saber from the scabbard.

Rolink didn't move. "You will not take my goats, thieves," he clenched his jaw.

Dex was as close as he could be without giving away his position. Judas felt hot and sticky against his back.

"Thieves?" Travin said, circling behind the one he called Morvis and Rolink. "We are not the thieves, farmer. You are the thief, for taking these animals away to graze and lose weight in the mountains before they are to be weighed for taxes."

"I am not a farmer," Rolink said. "I am a goatherder!" And with that, he threw the heavy, spiked end of his staff into the chest of Morvis, knocking the large man backwards. Without hesitating, he swung it around again and knocked the sword from the man's hand.

The other two men had Rolink surrounded quickly, their swords drawn in front of them, crouching slightly, ready for a fight.

Not quite amateurs, Dex realized.

And then the unexpected happened.

From Rolink's left, young Mebda came tearing out of nowhere, running to flank the closest bandit to him. The bandit saw him, and turned.

Time slowed to a halt, and Dex felt the moment rise to meet him. The outcomes catalogued and reviewed. And he ran. He ran as fast as he could, drawing Judas as he did.

The bandit raised the sword above his head, about to bring it down on the screaming child who was swinging blindly at his knees with a staff.

Rolink yelled and tried to react, but there was a sword swinging at his own head that he had to block with his staff. The blow sent him stumbling to his knees.

Dex ran past the bearded leader, telescoping Judas.

The bandit's enormous blade came down fast heading for Mebda's skull, only to meet with the swinging weight of Judas. The clank echoed throughout the valley.

The force knocked the bandit back, out of reach of Medba's short arms, and sent Dex, too, falling. But he rolled over, and grabbed Mebda with one hand to pull him back. The bandit let out a roar, and swung again to behead Dex, who ducked, and with Mebda behind him, took his own swing.

"Do not," Dex said, breathing heavily, "harm the child."

The bandit pulled back to his comrade.

"Mebda, run and get the goats dawdling at the rear," Rolink ordered, still on his knees. The two bandits still surrounded him, but stared uneasily at Judas and its owner.

"No, Da," Mebda said fiercely. He was clinging on to Dex for dear life.

"Well, well, well," Travin said, drawing his saber and looking at Dex. "What have we here? An armed goater? How deliciously illegal!"

Morvis picked his blade up and turned to his leader. "What's the call, Travin?" he asked.

Travin grinned. "We must serve *justice*, my friend."

"Mebda, go," Dex said, his tone cold. It took Mebda by surprise, who looked at him for a brief second, then was gone as fast as he had appeared. Dex looked to Morvis in front of him, but spoke to the leader, Travin.

"You and your men here should leave us now." He could feel the moment. They were not going anywhere. They thought they had the advantage.

Travin laughed. "Or what? You and your toy sword will slay the four of us?"

"No, I won't slay you," Dex said. "But you'll likely lose a limb or two."

Dex had the moment crawling. Travin circled slowly, sword drawn. Dex matched his steps, so that he came around such that Rolink was at his back. Morvis was slowly moving out of Dex's field of vision. The two others remained in a position to contain Rolink should he rise from his knees.

Travin clicked his tongue, as a signal, but it was Dex who reacted first. He swung Judas, catching one of the bandits next to Rolink by surprise. Dex brought Judas down on his sword arm, severing his hand with a single swipe.

He spun back around as Travin was trying to stick him quickly through the back. He pulled to the side and let his opponent's weight carry him through. Dex put his hilt into the back of the man's head, sending him sprawling.

Rolink didn't hesitate either. As soon as Dex had left one of his attackers screaming handless, Rolink swung his staff under the feet of the other bandit, who leaped over the attack. But Rolink just kept swinging, spinning around. His eight-footer came around higher the second time and caught the man in the knee, throwing him to the ground. Rolink used the spiked end to hit the bandit in the chest, knocking him back in a spray of blood.

Morvis, from Dex's left, swung wildly at him. But he easily countered. Next to the Red Masks, these men were a bunch of untrained louts.

At the last minute, Dex realized the folly of his confidence, as Travin took a swing at him from behind. *Untrained, but they are used to fighting together.* Dex managed to pull out of the way and was able to parry with the two attackers, but he wasn't reacting as quickly as he should. He had the moment jacked. He had Judas. But something was wrong. It was all too... slow.

He finally got himself an opening with Morvis, and after a feint, he brought Judas down and lopped off the large man's sword arm at the elbow. Without hesitating, he turned to stop the leader's attack.

But he didn't move fast enough, and Travin swung again, catching Dex across the chest. Dex felt nothing at first, but then it began to sting across his pectoral muscles.

And the blood came.

Dex stumbled backward, staring down at the gaping wound. He looked back up at the grinning face of the bandit leader, who lifted his sword above his head for the death shot.

Dex fell to his knees, thinking he should raise Judas, defend himself. But he could only put his hand to the bleeding wound, stunned. The saber came down at his head.

Just in time, Rolink knocked the sword aside with his staff, and put the full weight of his body into the mace end, burying his staff into Travin's elbow. The man screamed in pain and dropped his sword.

Dex looked up from his wound and saw Rolink towering over the goateed bandit.

"I suggest you gather your men and head to town, before I break more than your elbow," he said through gasping breaths and multiple bleeding wounds. Travin just writhed and groaned on the ground.

Rolink poked him hard in the gut with his staff. "I do not joke. If these men do not see to their wounds, they will die out here today. And it will be on your head. Not ours."

Moaning, Travin finally stood and reached for his saber, but Rolink put his staff end down on the blade, clicking his tongue, as he did at his goats. "Without the weapons."

Travin quickly pulled his wounded men together, hastily helping them with their wounds. They somehow made it onto their horses. "Keep pressure on the bleeding. Pressure will help you survive the road to town and the doctors there," Rolink advised. And they were gone.

Mebda came running out from behind a tree, and his father knelt to hug him. "It's okay, son. It's over. They're gone"

Dex touched his wound again, and realized it was not that deep.

He stood, wobbling, and walked toward the man and his child. Mebda was sobbing, and Rolink caressed his hair, holding him tight. .

"Are you alright, Oldkeeper?" he looked up as Dex approached.

Dex nodded. "I think so. I... did not expect to be hurt. I did not expect so much..." he trailed off.

"So much weaponry?"

"So much gravity."

Rolink looked at Dex, and smiled. Dex smiled back, and then they both laughed, a little.

"Who *are* you?" Rolink asked, grasping Dex's hand and shaking it vigorously.

"Honestly, Rolink, I have no idea."

Seventy-four.

Rolink's eyes moved quickly to the Judas Sword. His smile faded, and his face went pale.

"What's wrong?" Dex asked. "You look like you just saw a ghost."

"I– I did," he whispered, staring at Judas. "Can I... can I hold it?"

Dex shrugged. "Sure. Here you go." He handed the sword over and noticed that Rolink's hands were shaking as he took the hilt of Judas and felt the weight. He gave it a few swings back and forth. He glanced up at Dex, then back to the sword.

"I was a sword-smith," Rolink whispered. He fell silent, tracing the lines of the sword. Then he seemed to settle into something, and he spoke in a different tone.

"Before I raised goats. I was a blacksmith, in a family of blacksmiths. Before Medba, before I married Charla. Before Mastiff and his taxes and the new weapon restrictions that made it so all blacksmiths were required to read and write his polluting languages. He knew no one would comply, not around here. It was his way of owning the smithies, controlling them. So I bought goats. It is a worthier profession, raising live animals.

"But I used to specialize in swords. My father and Charla's father, they both made swords for the previous King Mebda, whom my son is named after. We were very good at it. I was to make swords for him as well. But he travelled to the southlands, on a trip to see the viceroy of Amrick. He went mad, they say, and died in a foreign land."

Rolink gazed down the edge of the Judas Sword, and then went back to admiring the white and grey-stained hilt. Mebda was still sniffling, but listening carefully. This was a new story for him, Dex realized.

"Before I gave up sword-smithing, I was invited into the armory of the king, and allowed to see some of the swords that his family had accumulated over the centuries. Some of the most magnificently crafted blades I've ever seen. But even the king did not have one of these."

"I do not know its history," Dex said.

"Allow me to be the Oldkeeper for a moment, then. This sword is made from the silk of the spider, harvested by the Arachnars of the Great Revival."

"I'm not following you."

"A story for another time. Legend among sword-makers has always maintained that the Arachnars had forged great swords from the hardened silk of spiders carried forward from ancient times. But no one has seen one for centuries or longer. Until now."

Rolink looked at Dex and was fighting back tears as he handed back the Judas Sword.

"You must tell me where you came by it," Rolink said through his clenched jaw. "But not now. We must set up camp, and tend to our wounds."

Seventy-five.

Dex raised his arms, and winced.

"Right there," Rolink said. "Now be still." He had pulled out a heavy box with what looked to be a waterproof seal, and thrown it open. From it came a jar of something translucent, which Rolink opened and shoved his fingers into. He pulled a gob of the sticky substance out and dragged it across the cleaned wound on Dex's chest. It stung at first, and then went numb. Then Rolink pulled out a white roll of linen dressing and wrapped it around Dex's chest underneath his arms.

Dex pulled his shirt back over his head, looking around. "Where's Medba?"

Rolink winced. "He's back with the young goats. He's... scared of you. Because of what you did."

Dex felt a pang, but nodded. "I understand."

"He's never seen violence before, not like that, with swords. But he will come to appreciate what you did for him."

"It's instinct. I barely think; I just react."

"Whatever it was, you fought smart," Rolink said. "I've never seen someone move like that. Where did you train?"

"Nowhere near here."

"That much is obvious." Rolink shook his head. "You are a mystery, Oldkeeper."

"Tell me about it."

"No, you tell me about it. Where did you come across the sword?"

Dex thought about his answer for a moment, stretching to get a feel for his range of motion with the dressing on his chest. "A man gave it to me, a man I had never met before. I never saw his face. It was only days ago. I woke up in a bed with this man standing over me, saying that I'm not really me, but a copy of me. And then he gave me the sword."

"Did he tell you anything about it? This man?"

"Maybe he would have. But he got killed not long after."

Rolink was silent, clearly frustrated at the lack of detail.

"I'm sorry, Rolink. I'd never seen the sword before. But, and this is the strange part, as soon as I gripped the hilt, it felt like I'd been holding it my whole life. And I knew how to use it."

"Indeed."

"But I can't explain it. I'd never even held a sword before last week."

Rolink scoffed. "That's impossible," he said. "You carry the blade like a professional, like someone in the Southland Army Guard."

"I can't explain it."

"Can I ask you something, Oldkeeper?"

"Yes. I promise not to lie."

Rolink laughed. "I no longer worry about your lies. I worry about your riddles."

Dex gave a rueful smile. "I made fun of Logos for talking in riddles. I guess everything seems like a riddle when you're surrounded by the impossible."

Rolink looked confused. Dex shook his head. "Nevermind. Just ask the question."

"Why are you here? What were you doing in the mountains, without mountain clothes, without any food, but carrying a sword from my childhood dreams?"

Dex stared into the late afternoon air. The air was hazing up, as the sunlight glinted from the west, casting the mountains above them into the beginning of dusk. Clouds rolled in lazily from the south, brought by a slight wind that hinted at colder air. "I'm not sure, Rolink. There's a war brewing where I came from. And from what everyone was saying, there's a war brewing here, too."

"There has been no armed conflict in Amrick for a century. At least, nothing beyond the posturing of this would-be king or that would-be warlord."

"I think I'm here because the war is one-sided. An invasion."

Rolink took Dex's arm, and gripped it tightly. "Say it again," he said, "this time looking in my eyes."

"I think there's an invasion coming. Or maybe it's already started."

Rolink's gaze burned past Dex's eyes and into his head. The intensity scared him. Then Rolink nodded. "Perhaps. If something comes, we will fight. The Cawlrians have been attacked before. We will prevail."

"I'm just supposed to find the Order of Brodius, two clerics named Justice and Freedom. They will tell me more about why I am here. Maybe they even know who I am."

"I know of Justice and Freedom. They chant a prayloop north of Longstown, near the old city in an old monastery up there"

"What do you know of them?"

Rolink shrugged. "What I just told you. They are ancient monks, much older than most. Our spiritual leaders are young, these days. Some think too young. Justice and Freedom keep to themselves and the community they loop for."

"Loop for?"

Rolink gave Dex a sideways glance. "Praylooop. You do not know praylooping?"

Dex shook his head.

Rolink went on. "You are from farther away, then. Another mystery, or perhaps a riddle: you are an Oldkeeper. A critical part of how the Order of Brodius worship God, and yet you know nothing of prayloops. Justice and Freedom will welcome your story into theirs."

"Can you help me get there?"

"I will take you there. I owe you the life of my only son. And maybe my own life. Not to mention all these goats. But goats have no sense of gratitude, believe me."

Dex smiled and Rolink continued.

"But first I must gather my wife from the money-talkers in Longstown. I can leave Medba with her and we can walk together." He grinned. "I know an alehouse up that way–its mead will turn your insides purple."

"Sounds good to me," Dex said. "Why didn't we move on, after that attack? Seems like we are very close to Longstown."

As answer, Rolink gave a long, high whistle. He said nothing, just stared into the failing light. Within moments, Mebda appeared out of nowhere. He stared uneasily at Dex, keeping his distance.

"Mebda, why do we stop here?"

Medba glanced at his father, then back at Dex. "Weather's coming in."

"Yes," Rolink said, winking at Dex. "What kind of weather?"

Medba closed his eyes, breathed deep. "Rain. From the south. Cold air in from the north." He sniffed, and then slapped his hands together hard, and opened his eyes, smiling madly. "Snow, Da! Snow!"

Rolink laughed. "Well done!"

Medba giggled, pleased with himself. "How much, Da? How much?"

Rolink shook his head. "Only God knows a snow's depth. But it should be light." He pointed at the clouds rolling in. "The sky does not threaten us. But better to stay and light a fire, than to try to walk through it."

"Early snow! Early snow!" Mebda was yelling, spinning in circles. Dex laughed, caught up in the excitement. When had he last seen snow? There were some short memories from his time at the orph. But early on. It had stopped snowing in Grenver long before it had stopped raining.

"Now go run and get the tents," Rolink told his son. "Tonight we need more than goatskin to protect us."

Medba ran off to the packgoats, who were eating lazily with the rest of the herd.

"Will there be more bandits?" Dex asked quietly, once Medba had gone.

Rolink shook his head. "Anyone who sees that crew you just dissected will stay away from this road."

And the snow came, before the sun was down, with a cold wind swirling the light flakes around their heads. Rolink stoked a large fire next to their tents, and cooked huge bowls of his goat soup. Medba hollered and hooted and twirled under the falling snow, trying to catch the flakes on his tongue.

Dex followed suit, spinning just as madly, tongue out, eyes closed.

Seventy-six.

He could not sleep in the silence of the snow. The dream was there, waiting for him, hiding in the blackness of his mind. Waiting for sleep to be unleashed. Dex rolled over, and peered through the small opening of the lean-to Rolink had erected for him.

Mebda was sitting there quietly, watching him. Dex jumped at the sight.

"Do not wake Da," Mebda whispered.

"What are you doing here?"

Mebda pointed up. "The night cleared. I like to watch the tears of God."

"No, what are you doing *here*?"

"Seeing if you would disappear again."

"What?"

"You know, when you dream."

"I don't know what you're talking about."

Mebda shrugged. "What's it like to murder someone?"

Dex had to swallow. "I didn't murder those men, Mebda. I just hurt them before they hurt us. Before they hurt you."

Mebda shook his head. "Not them. Others. I heard it in your voice. After you grabbed the blade. It was in your voice."

"Do you always hear things in people's voices?"

"Da says I have the gift. I listen. I watch." He tapped his head. "I keep it all up here, real tight."

Dex rubbed the stubble on his face. "I don't know what it feels like, Mebda. It just... feels. But afterward, it's like I was barely there. I get dizzy, like I'm standing at the top of the mountain looking down."

Mebda nodded. "You are two people. I'm okay with you now."

"I'm not sure I understand what you mean. But yeah, I guess I switch into a different mode. My friend Thelo called it jacking. Jacking the moment."

"No, it's not the thing where you move faster. You are two people. Two voices, at different times."

"Mebda!" It was Rolink, hoarse with sleep, calling from the other tent. "Stop bothering Dexter and come to bed. He needs sleep to heal."

Mebda put his hand on Dex's arm. "Do not disappear, tonight." And then he was gone.

Seventy-seven.

Morning came none too soon, and Dex got up when he heard Rolink and Medba rustling nearby. He winced at his wound, but it felt better. He already had more movement. Dex helped with the round-up of the straying goats, and they headed down the final rolling hills and ridges into the collector fields outside of Longstown.

The going went smoothly, and soon Dex found there were more people on the road, tending to goats, pushing hand-carts, donkeys pulling carts. Everyone looked to be healthy yet teetering on the edge of poverty. The only people that didn't were the bandits from the day before, Dex realized.

He laughed internally, hearing Mal's voice talking about a future without poverty, without rich and poor, and everyone with a complete education and opportunities around every corner. If only she could see this world, in all its backward agrarian fullness. But the thought of Mal darkened his mood, and he concentrated on keeping the goats in formation.

Rolink had said that the closer to civilization they came, the more important it was to keep them together. What he hadn't told Dex was that the closer to civilization they came, the harder it was to keep them together. Eventually, Dex found a rhythm, despite his lack of sleep and the exhaustion of walking all day, not to mention the ache of yesterday's battle. All of which, he realized, probably explained why he didn't hear the horses until they were almost on top of the herd.

But he didn't have time to get to the front to see who it was. Suddenly father and son were upon him, and Rolink looked frightened.

"The men we spared yesterday, they return," he said.

"So what?" Dex said defiantly, his heart quickening. "We will drive them away again."

"They return with Mastiff's men," Rolink said, shaking his head. "Law-men. Archers. There is no escape for us today." He turned to Mebda and knelt in front of the frightened child.

"I need you to be strong for me," he said, grabbing his son by the shoulders. "Can you be strong and quick?"

Mebda nodded. He fixed a determined look on his face, trying to hide the fear. Rolink mussed his hair. "Good boy. I need you to take Dexter's sword on your back, and run. Run as fast as you can through the hills. Take the sword to the old smithy in Graniton."

"The secret smithy?" Mebda said, his eyes widening.

"Yes. Do you remember the way?" Rolink asked.

"Yes, Da. I remember the way."

"Then go quick, and hide from everyone. Take the high trails past town. You can find water at Listless Creek."

Mebda nodded. There was the sound of shouting coming from in front of them, through the trees. Dex had his sheath off his back and was tying it to the boy's small frame. Then Mebda was gone, running due north into the brush and trees. Even as he disappeared, the herd broke and ran in all directions as a dozen horses came trotting around the bend and up the road.

"Do not speak, Oldkeeper," Rolink said, staring at the men as they approached.

And what would I say? He didn't know what was happening, but he knew it was trouble.

"Goaters! Do not move!" the man in front shouted. It was the goateed bandit, now with bandages around his chest and sword arm. He was flanked by men in official-looking garb, green and black. They had crossbows drawn, their arrows pointed directly at Dex and Rolink. As the goats cleared, the rest of the riders, all of them with crossbows or long spears, surrounded the two men.

"I did not intend to move, bandit," Rolink said.

"You are lucky the law prohibits me from killing you where you stand," Travin said, his voice breaking. "As it is, I will have to wait until morning to see your neck separated from your head." He turned his horse around in a circle.

"Where's the boy?" he asked.

"I sent him home," Rolink said, watching as his goats slowly disappeared back up the road and into the trees.

Travin scoffed. "Hardly," he said. "You three! Find me the boy. He can't have gotten too far. From the look of things, they gave him my sword."

The three horsemen took off, one back up the road, and one each up the sides of the mountains.

"I left your sword in the dirt to rust," Rolink spat. "I have no use for a thief's blade."

Travin glared. "Arrest those two." And he turned his horse around and began trotting back toward Longstown.

"On what charges?" Rolink asked.

"Treason," Travin said, glancing back over his shoulder.

Seventy-eight.

Dex touched his wrist and winced at the pain. He squinted in the dim light of the dungeon, but could only make out the outline of his hand. The extent of the cuts to his wrists remained something he could only experience from the dull throbbing—or the sharp sting if he touched them.

He had been tied up by rope. *Rope.* Dex couldn't remember if he'd ever actually seen real rope before. But he wished he could forget now the feeling of being lashed from his wrists to his neck and to the saddle of a horse, and then being pulled at a trot down into Longstown.

Rolink had been in front of him, and Dex noted that he had chosen the same painful struggle: pull the slack up from the horse to his hands, so that the slack was between his hands and neck. But eventually his arms grew tired, and he had to let himself be dragged along by his neck, trying to keep up with an awkward shuffle-run.

It had taken a few hours to get into town and to the prison, but Dex remembered little of anything on the way through the outskirts. He had been so tired, with the cut on his chest burning when he breathed hard, and the rope cutting into his wrists and neck; all he could do was keep his eyes on the behind of the horse dragging him along. He remembered little tidbits, like the rocks being hurled by kids roaming the streets, or the smell of raw sewage running underneath his feet. Dex had fallen into the sewage in exhaustion, and the horse had dragged him through it for a hundred yards before he could scramble to his feet again. Now the smell clung to him. It was all he could smell.

They had finally arrived at the low stone building Dex now knew to be a prison, and had been untied from the horses. They had been pulled down some stairs into a rank basement, separated, and thrown into cells the size of small closets, concealed by a heavy wooden door. There was only a single bench, hung by chains in the wall, where he had slept almost immediately.

His stinging wrists, his chest wound, and his neck had all conspired to wake him, and then the shouts of a drunk in the next cell had kept him up. He did not know how long he had slept, but it was not long enough for it to be execution time yet. He kept trying to open his eyes wider, to get more light, but there was no light to be had. The thirst was insatiable in his throat. The hunger gnawed at his insides. The forced march had scraped his tender feet into a bloody mess, and being dragged by the horse had left his knees and elbows sore to the touch.

Dex could not remember having ever felt this poorly in his entire life.

He heard the lock to his cell being thrown, and the door groaned open. The light from the hallway barely illuminated anything but the silhouette of a large man entering the cell.

"Last words for the condemned, praised be His will," the man said. The loudness of it against the quiet of the small room drilled Dex's headache deeper into his brain.

"Blessed be the next life to welcome the sinner and the saint," the man went on. "Do you have any last words to story before your execution?"

"What?" Dex asked, his voice a hoarse croak. "I don't understand."

The man sighed. "Come on, son. What story do you have before Mastiff orders your execution and you catch the blade tomorrow?"

"I... don't know," Dex muttered.

"Out with it," the man said, sitting down. "Last man I gave rights to says you're a man of the cloth. An Oldkeeper. Says you're with the Brodius monks?"

Rolink. He told this man, who must be a priest or something, that I was with the monastery.

"Yes! I'm with the Order of Brodius. Can you get word to them that Dexter Maxwell is in prison?"

"Are these your last words?" the man asked dubiously. His face unreadable in the dark.

"No, wait, there's something else," Dex said, trying to think. He closed his eyes. His mind felt like it was far away, floating into the distance.

"Come on, I don't have all day."

Then it came to him. "The future bakes in the sun like new adobe."

"What?"

"The future bakes in the sun like new adobe. Tell this to a monk named Freedom."

The man was silent. Without a word, he stood and knocked on the door. The bolt slid and the door opened.

"Will you tell them?" Dex asked loudly. The man did not answer. Dex was on his feet now, standing close to the man. He was very old, balding, with wisps of white around the tops of his ears and a close-cropped grey beard.

"Will you tell them?" Dex asked.

"I am not an errand boy, son," the man said gravely. "I am here to relay your last words to the prayloop so that God might hear you. But you instead plead for your life. And your life is something I cannot help you with." With that, he stepped out and the door banged shut behind him. Dex heard the lock bar slide into place.

Seventy-nine.

The smell of his own urine woke Dex from what fitful sleep he had found. Despite the cold air of the dank darkness, the smell and lack of ventilation had made his stomach nauseous in the places where the hunger had grown tired of punishing him.

He could not get a bearing on how long he had been in the prison; he'd been drifting in and out of sleep, and the light in the room had not changed since his arrival. Time seemed to have come to a halt. Dex tried to roll over on the narrow bench, to huddle closer, but he banged his sore knees on the wall and grunted in pain. How could every part of his body hurt so much at the same time? And why could he not sleep? He was so tired.

Dex kept seeing the face of the priest who had visited. That was what kept him awake. The old priest, in the light of the hallway, had turned back to reprimand him, and the look on his face was one of fear. Something he said had scared the priest, made him afraid to even look at Dex. *But what exactly? The bit about the future, and adobe? About Freedom and the Brodius monks?*

Dex could not figure it out. He didn't have enough data to process it. But it ate away at him. That had been his chance, to send out a signal or something. Rolink had arranged it so he could get the message out. What had he done wrong?

Dex was going over the conversation in his head for the thousandth time, when he heard the dull thunk of the slide bar being removed from his door. His heart quickened.

The time had come. His execution.

The door opened, but did not swing wide, as the guard had done when he shone his smelly kerosene lamp upon Dex. Instead, the door remained slightly ajar, letting in only a crack of light. Dex stayed lying, unmoving, watching the door. He saw the shape of someone's head peer in.

"Dexter?" a voice whispered. "Dexter Maxwell?"

"Who are you?" he croaked back.

"Quiet," the voice said. "The future bakes in the sun like new adobe, eh?"

Dex sat up. "Yes. Just like new adobe."

"Indeed," the voice whispered. "Come. We have little time."

Dex stood quickly. Too quickly. The blood rushed from his head and he fell over against the wall, too dizzy to move. In seconds, two strong hands were on him, helping him out the door. Dex looked around, and saw the guard on the floor, unmoving. Finally he got a look at the person helping him down the hallway.

She was old, but Dex could not say how old. Her kinky hair was grey and long, pulled back into a single braid. She could not have been more than five feet tall, but she was strong; He had almost his entire weight on her shoulder as they walked; he barely had the strength to walk on his own. The adrenaline of the jailbreak was all he had. But this small woman seemed to know just what to do.

They walked down the long hallway, each side lined with the same thick wooden doors. They stepped quietly over another guard, this one lying on his back and snoring loudly. Then they were through a door that still had a ring of keys in the lock, and up two flights of narrow, winding stairs.

"When we reach the top of the stairwell, we must wait," the woman whispered. "There will be a signal, and then we will move through the hallway to the kitchen and then out through the kitchen window."

"I don't know where the kitchen is," Dex whispered.

The woman's strong hand gripped Dex's. "Do not worry, young man. I will not leave your side."

And then they were at the top, waiting quietly behind the closed door.

"What is the signal?" Dex asked. He kept blinking, trying to get past the chronic dizziness.

"You'll know it when you hear it," she whispered back. By the glint of a torch above his head, Dex saw her flash a smile. She was beautiful. Maybe the most beautiful woman he'd ever seen.

Then Dex heard a heated argument through the door, and a loud crash. After a cry went out, Dex heard the sound of feet rushing down steps above his head.

"Is that the signal?" Dex asked. The woman looked suddenly concerned.

"It will have to do," she said. "Come then." She slowly pulled the door toward her to open it and peered through. She pulled Dex through and down a hallway. Cries of pain and the unmistakable clangs of swords echoed through the hall. As they passed an open archway, Dex glanced down into the main entrance room of the prison and saw the flashing of a sword fight in progress. Then they were past the door and into a small kitchen. The woman had opened the small window and was helping Dex through.

The night air was cold against Dex's face as he squeezed himself out. The alleyway behind the prison house was the dark of a moon still waxing. Dex gave a grunt as he was pulled violently out of the window by his armpits in one quick motion that banged his sore knees on the sill. Then he was lying on the ground and looking up at a large man who pulled him to his feet.

It was the old priest. The scared priest. Only now he had a huge smile on his face and was helping the beautiful woman out of the window, too.

"What are you doing back here?" she asked him. "Who's making all the commotion in the front?"

The priest kept smiling. "Someone who's much better at causing trouble than a humble monk such as myself."

The woman gave him a quizzical look, then turned and looked at Dex. "Are you okay to walk for some distance? We have horses not far from here."

Dex nodded. "I can walk," he said. "Who are you, again?"

"My name is Freedom," the woman said. "And this is Justice. We are from the Order of Brodius."

Eighty.

The adrenaline rush of the escape faded quickly, and both Justice and Freedom helped him the last bit of the way to the stable where they had horses waiting. There was a cart full of hay so that the two of them would look like they were carrying horse feed back to their monastery. As soon as they'd laid him down in the back and set off, Dex was asleep.

He woke to a grey sky above and the jolting of the cart beneath him. It took him a few moments to realize that the old woman named Freedom was sitting beside him, caressing his face gently. In the light of the day, he could see a deep scar on her left temple that spread like a spider out toward her eye, up toward her hairline, and back toward her ear. Dex felt it only augmented her deep beauty. She smiled, and the wrinkles under her eyes blended into the scar. She spoke gently in a language he did not understand, something more from the throat, but with Spanish-sounding consonants. He tried to listen more carefully. The vertigo came, the dizziness, and then the nausea. He closed his eyes against it and heard Freedom speak again. His mind's ability to understand the local language slowly returned.

"There you go; wake up, child," she said tenderly. "You need water, and some food."

Dex looked up at her again, and she held a leather bag at his lips. He took a small sip, let it soak into his dry tongue, and then swallowed it. Freedom had wet down a small piece of cloth and was wiping away the blood and grime from Dex's face.

"More," Dex croaked.

"In a moment, child, in a moment. You are not dying, although you look it." Dex realized that she must be older than he had thought at first, but it did not detract from her grace. The lines that age had imprinted into her face enhanced the serene smile that framed her deep brown eyes. The age-toughened hands felt confident and sure on his face.

"You are beautiful," Dex marveled.

Freedom's smile widened. "Why, thank you, child. Here, sit up, I need to get this shirt off you."

Dex sat up, and she gave him more water before helping him. Freedom winced at the long, swollen cut across his chest. Dex grimaced at it, as well. "Looks infected," he said.

"We have a little something, but it will sting," Freedom said.

"Not as much as when I got it," Dex tried a smile. Freedom gave a small laugh, then pulled a clay jar from a small bag and unstopped it. The smell hit Dex immediately, but he tried to ignore it. Freedom squirted water from the leather satchel onto his chest and wiped the surface dirt from the wound. Then she dipped two fingers into a white paste and began applying it to the cut. Dex sucked in at the pain, and started to move away from Freedom's fingers.

"Try to relax," she said.

Dex closed his eyes, trying to think about anything but the gaping wound on his torso. He thought back to the prison, and how he had gotten there, thinking of what he would do to that goateed drip Travin if he had a second chance. If only Rolink had put his staff into his head back in the mountains.

Rolink. At the thought of him, Dex opened his eyes immediately. It was sunrise, time for an execution.

"We have to go back," Dex said, pushing Freedom's hands away. "They are going to kill Rolink."

"Who is Rolink?" Freedom asked.

"They're going to execute him at sunrise!"

"Rolink is in good hands," a deep voice growled from behind. Dex turned to look up at the front of the cart. The large priest, Justice, sat comfortably, staring ahead, driving the horses.

"What do you mean? Did you set him free?" Dex asked.

"No, not me," Justice said without turning around. He gave a chuckle. "*You* saved him."

"I don't understand," Dex said. *But then, I'm used to that.*

"I don't understand, either," Freedom said severely, looking up at Justice from the cart.

"Friends," Justice said, turning around with a dramatic flourish of his hand, "we find ourselves on the inside of a curved time-like paradox, with no way to see outside of it."

"What?" Dex asked. "I know all the words you just used, but not when you say them all together like that."

Freedom nodded though. "While unfortunate, it may be for the best. Do you not agree, Justice?"

"Indeed," Justice said, turning back around.

"Can one of you try that again? I'm a little slow."

Justice pointed to the east, where the sun was breaking through the low-lying clouds on the horizon. "That sunrise will come around again, Dexter Maxwell. And when it does, you will be a hero." He shook his head and laughed at the thought of it, as though it were extremely funny.

Dex felt his anger rising up. "I am so sick of riddles, someone best be straight with me. Now."

Freedom put her hand on his shoulder. "There is so much to explain, and I will explain it all. I promise you. Every last bit. But you are sick, and hurt, and it is still a long ride to our destination. Your friend Rolink is safe, for now. Please, let us get you to a warm, dry room, and feed you, and get you some rest. Then we will start at the beginning."

Dex glared up at Justice's back for a moment. "Fine. Just one question."

"Of course," Freedom said, globbing more white paste onto her fingers as Dex lay back down in the hay.

"What am I doing here? What am I supposed to do?"

"Why, save the world, child," Freedom said without looking up.

Dex flinched as she applied more of the medicine. "If that's all, then. Sure. Do you think I could get some more of that water first?"

Eighty-one

Freedom had been right: the ride was long. Dex fell in and out of sleep in the back of the cart, drinking water and eating some sort of mealy bread in between naps. The sun came up and warmed him cozily, putting him back to sleep by mid-morning. Freedom had climbed up front with Justice, and he could hear them both talking.

He could not make out much of what was said, other than his own name a few times. But lying flat, with a full stomach and water for his throat, was enough for him. He trusted Freedom would fill him in on all the details that plagued his mind; what choice did he have? There's no use getting angry at an unbroken promise before it's been broke, Jones would say. So for now, he let the warm sun beat down on his aching body, and let it put him to sleep.

They did not arrive at their destination until the sun was heading back down in its arc. On top of the small hill the cart climbed was a low-lying building that stretched for a hundred yards in each direction. He heard the bleating of goats from inside. The entire structure was caked in mud or something.

"Adobe," he said out loud. "The future bakes in the sun like new adobe."

"Aye," Justice fiddled with the reins. "That is the beginning of one of our most treasured anecdotes. Would you like to hear it?"

"Please," Dex said.

"Adobe is nothing more than mud and grass," Justice said, releasing the cart from the horses' backs with his large hands. "You mix it together and then leave it in the sun to harden into bricks that keep the heat out in summer and the cold out in winter. It lasts for a long time and is inexpensive to make and keep. Yes?"

"Sure," Dex said. Freedom gave him a wink.

"So we say: the future bakes in the sun like new adobe, but only we if take the time in the present to make the bricks."

They walked toward the adobe wall. "I get it," Dex said. "If you don't take time now to build your bricks, then you won't have them to protect you in the future."

Justice grinned and slapped him hard on the back. "Something like that, son. Welcome to our home."

269

Eighty-two.

Two nights passed before Freedom made good on her promise. Dex had sought her out the very next morning, but she had shaken her head sadly, and said, "I must tend to the day," and then she was gone.

Single-story rooms formed the three sides of the monastery, which together with the outer wall were built around a large, square courtyard. The rooms had windows facing into the courtyard, but, Dex noticed, none towards the outside world. The rooms of the fourth wall were higher and backed onto an additional structure. This part of the monastery was made of cut stone instead of adobe. The stone section, clearly built at a different time, extended back and up until it hugged against the red rock face of the mountain that rose steeply behind it.

The courtyard itself felt massive and higher than it was, as it was up on a plateau facing into the plains that fell away to the east. It had a low dividing wall to its southern side, and Dex noticed that this was a late addition with only one goal: to keep the goats out of the garden that lay behind. The rest of the courtyard was low grass and piles of hay for the roughly two-dozen goats that grazed and bleated lazily. In the exact center was a low-slung pool, fed by a fountain that sprayed the water just a few feet into the air before splashing down. The pool was low enough that goats would, in the heat of the afternoon, step into it and cool off—to the consternation of Freedom, who would pause in her scooping of feces or weeding of the gardens long enough to holler at the goats. Every so often the goats would deem her worthy of listening to.

Dex had been given a small room deep into the structure, where it was cool during the day—and dark—so he could sleep freely. He wandered around the monastery when he got bored of eating and sleeping; the walking felt good to his sore bones. Off the west side of the courtyard, opposite the front entrance, were a series of doors. Dex found them while wandering the halls of the monastery, going from empty room to empty room. These were living quarters, probably for more monks, with stone altars at the back of each room, and a stone slab to one side for sleeping. The structures were small and looked very old, and had been empty for some time. They were dark, with only the smallest of windows facing onto the courtyard.

As he went deeper, Dex came to the first stairs in the monastery. At the top of the stairs, the building changed immediately. The walls were no longer mud, but smooth, cold stone. The windows, if any, were small slits left between the rock bricks that had been cut into perfect squares. The warmth he had felt now turned into cold and foreboding. What a castle might feel like, Dex decided, if he had ever been in a castle.

Late in the day, Dex found himself lost in the back corridors of the compound; he had been looking for something more interesting than sleeping quarters or small meeting rooms equipped with tables. He walked through door after door, until he found himself going in circles through a section of the monastery that had no windows onto either the courtyard or the outer valley. Frustrated at himself for getting lost, he followed the wall with his hand to make sure he didn't take a wrong turn. To his surprise, the stone wall gave way under his hand to a dark entryway.

Dex opened the false wall as far as it would go, to allow what little light was in the hallway to illuminate the room he had discovered. Once his eyes had adjusted to the darkness, he could see that this was some sort of worship room. There was a lone round table in the middle of the room—stone, like everything else. The walls were all at strange, curving angles, and Dex noted that there were large wooden beams on the ceiling that did not look to be providing support, but rather simply intersected in complicated patterns. He could not make it out, but it seemed familiar.

Something he had seen in a different part of the monastery, maybe. He could not take his eyes off it. He traced the lines, the complicated interplay, seeing how each beam was meant to lead the eye around to another beam that was angled specifically to catch a beam that had been bent into a semi-circle that captured the nature of the triangle that was leading to the next shape...

Dex blinked, trying to understand the geometry of the structure. There was something about it, something familiar; something he felt he knew. It was hours before he left the room and made his way back eastward.

Mid-morning of his second day at the monastery, and after his second breakfast of flatbread and tomatoes, Freedom appeared at the door of his small room just as he was contemplating another long nap. She was beaming her warm smile.

"Come, Dexter, let us have a story," she said.

He forgot all about his nap, and walked with her out into the courtyard. The goats bleated at them as they sat at the only table in the warm morning sun.

Freedom had laid out a clay pitcher and two clay mugs. She poured water into both mugs. Dex sat across from her and swallowed the cold liquid quickly.

"If you would like to ask all of your questions, I understand," Freedom said, "But if you like, I can begin the story from whatever starting point you choose."

Dex looked at her, trying to figure out a good place to start. "How did I end up on Venus?" he asked.

Freedom nodded. "I do not know exactly how you, Dexter Maxwell, ended up off-planet, but that's only because we know nothing more than a few details of your life. However, I can tell you the story of how humans ended up on Venus. Will that do?"

He nodded. "I'm not Dexter Maxwell, by the way. Not really. I'm his clone."

"You are not a clone," Freedom said. "A clone is an exact copy. The great scientists of the past stopped cloning people hundreds of years ago. Instead, they found they could make slight genetic and neurological modifications based on a genetic blueprint provided by the source human. Calling you a clone is close to the truth, but you are actually an iteration of Dexter Maxwell."

"Iteration," Dex said. "I remember them calling me an iterate. The iter."

"Yes, that would be the slang, I'm sure. But the body is no more than a vessel for the soul, Dexter, and there are no duplicate souls."

"I'm not one much for God-talk."

"Oh, but I am."

"Right. You were telling me about Venus."

"Yes, a strange place to find yourself walking up in, isn't it? Let me see... where to start... it would have been in the early 22nd century, when the politics of the time did not allow the execution of criminals. Instead, they were cryogenically suspended for a period of time, sometimes indefinitely."

"Put on ice."

"Indeed. A cruel irony of the misplaced goodwill and compromises of that era. For reasons that did not survive the test of time, most of the huge containers of frozen men and women were put into orbit around Earth on large satellite crafts. Perhaps a legal technicality? Who knows. After your capture, you must have been one of the thousands put on the large freezer crafts until humanity could figure out what to do with you. Of course, it is a long way from orbiting Earth in an unconscious state, to waking up on the hot surface of Venus, no?

"So, let me provide a history lesson, then. Those in power at the time, the great global industrialists, were already well on their way to discovering the limits of their current system of unending growth and expansion. You can only burn so much fuel before you have to find new fuel. But the richest nations were not the problem; their scientists had been long on the search for genetically altered organisms—trees that grew faster, fuel that could be replenished. But elsewhere, they were running out. Running out of hydrocarbon. Running out of trees."

"There weren't many trees left around here, back in 2113," Dex said. "It was city, as far as the eye could see. The trees were mostly fake, built from concrete pillars with big processing platforms on top—"

"Please, let me finish," Freedom said with a grin.

"Sorry, it's just..." Dex trailed off. "I'm just trying to figure this all out. Nothing seems real anymore. But I get that this is really happening, I get it. But it's a lot to get."

"I know. There is much to know, and much to take in." Freedom looked up. "But it is a beautiful day, and what else do we have to do, but tell stories about ourselves?"

Dex laughed. "I used to have a friend who said something like that. He'd sit on his porch, with all these people around, and he'd say, 'If you want to listen, then listen, because when someone tells you their story they are connecting you to it.'" Dex looked up at Freedom, and she was staring intently at his face, with a look that reminded him of Rolink—looking right through him. He looked back down, and laughed nervously. "Anyway, that's what ol' Jones would say. He was pretty crazy."

"I do not believe this friend of yours was crazy, Dexter," Freedom said.

"Yeah, me neither." Dex looked anywhere but at her, his jaw aching at the memory of ol' Jones and all of his devotees, half-living in the burbring hovels. It seemed so far away now. Lost.

Freedom began talking again. "Fake trees. I had forgotten about those. There are mysteries surrounding the thinking of the wealthy capitalists of the 22nd century that we will never unravel. It was long ago, and the world has been through many revolutions since then.

"What we do know is that the resources of this world were being used up too quickly. There was no way to keep up with demand. But the system kept the wealthiest people protected from the dwindling resources, while the poorest were left to fight over the leftover scraps. There was growing unrest, and rebellions began to pop up in the southern continents. This was nothing unusual, really, except that they seemed finally united.

"In the year 2136, a daring capitalist venture finally figured out how to get at the riches of the asteroids. It did not take long to set up lucrative mining operations that brought fuel, water, and precious minerals back to Earth to feed the furnaces. The richest men and women on Earth became even richer. The wealth did not filter down as far as the poorest nations, but far enough to thwart any revolutions." Freedom sadly shook her head.

"But we are not here to dig into the causes and effects of history. There was blame all around, although the bottom line was that there was too much matter being brought to Earth. Earth literally became too heavy, and starting inching ever closer to the sun. The atmosphere was being overtaxed by particulate waste and the whole planet was getting too hot. The additional resources also meant that there were too many humans.

"A war broke out in the Americas, as you used to call them. The government of the northern nations had begun rounding up citizens who had contracted an incurable disease, and had them all killed. The ensuing war, on top of the plague, finally toppled the system that had kept the industrialists in power for over four centuries. Hundreds of thousands of agrarian serfs from the south invaded the nations of the north. There, they were surprised to find little resistance from the citizens, who feared their leaders too much to help, but saw in the invasion a chance to get their freedoms restored. The only resistance came from the machines of war that had been created by the government. But against the invading hordes, even these proved useless." She paused briefly.

"The war spread quickly across nearly all parts of the world: the poverty-stricken masses rose up against their masters, led by brave men and women who had nothing to lose and were therefore invincible. The death toll was high for the poor, and low for the rich, but the capitalists were losing their ability to stay rich, with no workers for the asteroid mines, none for the smelters, none to bring them their breakfast, and none to repair their machines.

"The war lasted for nearly twenty years, and the will of the people grew thin. They had started poor, and now they were still poor but also burying most of their men and boys. A compromise treaty began to circulate that would leave the power structure in place but provide better working conditions for the people across the globe. It looked as though the great battles that were devastating the already-weakened Earth would finally come to an end."

"What about the nukes?" Dex asked.

"The what?" Freedom replied.

"You know, the nukes. The nuclear bombs. If there was so much war, why weren't we wiping each other out?"

Freedom shrugged. "I know little of that time. There were many weapons used to obliterate humans, and I have never bothered to differentiate one from the next."

"You'd have remembered the nukes. They would have wiped out everything."

"Perhaps they were used. But by the time the compromise treaty was offered, most battles were being fought in the streets—no place to be dropping incendiaries. There was still some semblance of order and political accountability. It was this order, together with the capitalist politicians, that brought the treaty close to being ratified.

"But then, a horrible secret was revealed. It is not clear, looking through the faded glass of history, how it was discovered, but most likely it was a betrayal from within the capitalist elite. The secret was this: many years before, the capitalists had discovered that the damage to Earth was almost irrevocable. Within a century the extra mass from the asteroid slag piles would most likely prevent Earth from being able to support life. The impact of the twenty-year war was too much, after two centuries of pollution, environmental damage and unrestrained industrial growth." Freedom gave a long sigh.

"The capitalists had known this, but had told no one; instead, they secretly began building a colony on another planet. They started to lay a foundation for human habitation on the surface of Venus. They intended to clean up its atmosphere, which was far too hot and poisonous."

"Tell me about it," Dex said.

"I am," Freedom said.

"Sorry, I just arrived from Venus. It's hot and smelly, like you said. Go on. Please."

"The news of the Venus colony was mystifying: why would the elite capitalists go to such effort and expense to remake Venus, instead of simply cleaning up Earth, which was already livable?

"But as soon as the question was asked, the answer was clear and it left the people speechless: the industrialists would rather take the risk of colonizing Venus than prevent Earth from slowly burning up under the pressure of the atmospheric gases, because Venus would not be overrun with people. Venus would belong entirely to the capitalists, and they could charge admission."

"That's crazy," Dex said.

"So it seems, looking back so far into history. Who knows exactly what they were thinking. One thing is for sure: the revolutionaries on Earth were galvanized by the revelation, and they took up their arms anew to overthrow the capitalists everywhere on Earth. In only a few short years, but at great cost, the war was won.

"This would have been about 2264. People demanded the heads of the capitalists, and there were most certainly executions. Given the work already done on Venus, it was decided that those that wanted to leave Earth should. The capitalists and all of their technologies and machines were put on giant vessels and sent off-planet to fend for themselves."

"And they took all the frozen criminals with them?" Dex asked. "That doesn't make any sense."

Freedom shrugged. "History is never a logical progression of clear decisions. The industrialists ended up on Venus. So did a lot of frozen criminals. Perhaps the crafts on which you floated in stasis were required for their plans on the new planet. Who knows exactly. It was not until just recently that we even knew that anyone had actually survived. It had long been assumed that they sailed their spacecrafts into oblivion."

"I wouldn't exactly call it paradise up there, but they definitely survived. They still speak the language of my time. And it seems like they still mine the asteroids. They pull criminals off ice and enslave them on the rocks."

"Yes, we have had some communication with the off-landers."

"Logos. You know Logos?" Dex asked.

"Yes, dear Logos. He is our informant, our teacher, and our leader on Venus."

Dex looked down. "I saw him... he, uh..."

"You met Logos?" Freedom said excitedly. "I have heard so much about him, but have not met him. What is he like?"

Dex couldn't swallow past the knot in his throat. "Logos is dead."

"What?"

"He took a sword to the heart. After he pulled me off the ice."

Freedom looked through him, and was silent for a moment. Her eyes glistened. Without warning, she roared and swiped at the pitcher and mugs on the table, sending them crashing to the ground. Dex stood quickly, wide-eyed, as she yelled again, throwing the table over and giving her chair a kick. Freedom threw her arms in the air, looking up into the blue sky with a cry. Then she was on her knees, crying, pounding her fists against the grass chewed short by the goats.

Dex finally worked up the nerve to reach out to her, and touched her shoulder. She did not move, but stayed sobbing on the ground. He was searching for the right words, when he felt a pair of large hands grab him from behind. Instinctively, Dex shook himself free, turned and grabbed Justice by his fat neck. The surprised monk put up both of his hands in a passive plea. Dex relaxed, and let go. Justice gave him a wary look, and then knelt beside Freedom.

"What is it, my dear?" Justice whispered.

"Logos is dead," Freedom replied.

Justice bowed his head at the news, and his shoulders slumped. Dex watched the two old people, kneeling in the middle of the grass, and a panic washed over him. It was like the panic he'd felt when Logos was stabbed by Ashion.

Justice gave Freedom a pat on her back, then stood, leaving her to sob. "Logos is dead. Dexter Maxwell is back on Earth. The end game is upon us." He looked up to the sky, and Dex heard him whisper something unintelligible. A prayer? Then he turned to face him. "Come, enough story. It is time."

"Time for what?" Dex asked, still feeling miserable for Freedom.

"Your training."

Eighty-three.

Dex could not take his eyes off the designs on the ceiling. Justice had taken him directly to the worship room he had stumbled upon the day before. They had entered and closed the door. There was no light. Justice fiddled with something near the entrance, and moments later there was a rushing sound and the lumber designs along the ceiling were lit by a fire that burned high above them.

"How can the roof be that high?" Dex pointed up. "This whole place is short and flat."

"We've walked back into a part of the monastery that was carved out of the rock. You are in a cave."

Dex nodded. "Right. No light. All the rock."

"Yes. There was a time when our worship was frowned upon by those in power." Justice shook his head. "Now it is merely ignored."

"What are these designs? I've seen them somewhere before."

Justice looked quizzically at Dex. "Are you sure? They are quite unique."

"But... they seem familiar. It's weird."

Justice was looking through him again, giving him that look. It reminded Dex of something he had been meaning to ask.

"Justice, you came to me in the prison, asking for my last words."

"Yes. I do prison duty, providing last rites for the condemned."

"After I gave you the pass-phrase about adobe you had a look on your face. You were scared of me."

"Yes. Terrified."

"Why? Was it something I said?"

Justice sighed. "No, nothing you said, or did, although you did look half-past dead already. The fear I felt was something else." He looked up at the interwoven lights. "I suddenly realized that this is all happening. The invasion is real, the danger is real, the war is real. And it scared me."

Dex said nothing.

Justice cleared his throat and shook his head. "Enough of that. We have work to do. I'm assuming that Freedom was giving you a history lesson?"

"Yes. About how the industrialists ended up on Venus."

"Right. That would be the part she would tell. Full of righteous indignation, the will of the people, banishing evil, and all that."

"Something like that."

"She likes the part with bravery, likes to give it a shiny gloss. Never mind all the cowardice and apathy and compliance. Never mind how much of our survival depended on the sciences pioneered by the loathed industrialists. But all history is a judgment, how could it be anything else? Let's just say that the industrialists left behind a fascinating scientific legacy. Going back through the corporations' data, our scientists found a long-running history of a conglomeration of companies manipulating a time-like curve in order to break the long-standing chronology protection conjecture of the 21st century."

"A what? To break the what?" Dex asked.

Justice smiled. "They were trying to travel through time."

Eighty-four

"If you're trying to surprise me," Dex said, "try again. I'm a clone, or at least an iterate, and humans live on Venus, it's the year 3049 and I know how to fly a spaceship and speak whatever language we're speaking. In the past week, I've murdered about twenty people with a sword I magically know how to use. So time travel? Big deal."

"I'm not trying to surprise you; I'm trying to prepare you," Justice said. "And for the record, the year is 3027, you are speaking a nor'western dialect of Amridian, and I believe this is the sword you speak of."

With that, Justice reached behind the altar table and pulled out a bundle.

The Judas Sword.

Dex tried to say something. Justice laughed. "Did I surprise you this time?"

"Where did you get that?" Dex asked. "Did you find Medba? Is he okay?"

"Who?" Justice asked. "*You* gave me this sword."

"No, I gave it to Rolink's son, Medba."

"Perhaps. But you also gave it to me."

"I don't understand. Not that it's a surprise by now."

"A curved time-like paradox has occurred, Dex."

"You will have to give me a little more than that."

"At the night of the jail-break, down in Longstown I was meant to cause a distraction at the front door of the jailhouse. So there I am, armed with a false request for one of the condemned and ready to have a very loud and vocal sermon on the rights of the dead. It was very good, I must say. Certainly I would have been banned from ministrations for the dead from then on, but my task was clear. Get Dexter Maxwell out of prison.

"But as I'm approaching the jailhouse, there is suddenly a hand on my shoulder. I turn around, and there is a stranger standing there, giving me a smile as though he knows me." Justice's eyes twinkled. "He says, 'you are going to rescue Dexter Maxwell.' I was going to protest or lie, but the stranger just puts his finger to his mouth to quiet me and says, 'I will take care of the front door distraction, you should go around back to the kitchen window and help Dexter out. He is wounded and tired.' I look through the man and see he is not lying, and so I ask, 'who are you?' He gives me a wink and says 'I'm Dexter Maxwell.' I must have given a blank stare, because he says, 'you will recognize me when you pull me out the back kitchen window.'

"'What are you going to do?' I ask him. 'I'm going to save Rolink, the goat herder.' That means nothing to me, so I just nod and head for the back of the jailhouse. But then the stranger stops me and gives me this bundle, saying, 'be sure this gets to Dexter.' Then he pulled a second sword from its scabbard and walked into the jailhouse."

"But how could it have been me?" Dex asked. "I was inside the jail. Freedom would have already been inside, drugging the guards."

"Yes, you were in the cell. But you were also out front, making quite a scene."

Dex thought about it for a moment. "Are you telling me that at some point in the future, I'm going to travel back in time and help spring myself out of prison?"

Justice smiled. "Now you are finding understanding."

"That's impossible. How could I have gotten out of prison with my own help? But if I wasn't out of prison, how could I go back in time and help out? It's impossible."

"Indeed, yes, it is very much impossible. We call it a curved time-like paradox."

Dex felt dizzy, trying to wrap his head around it. "But there's no way it could happen."

Justice sighed. "You assume that our reality is a closed system, but this would be to deny the existence of God, who can intervene in the most amazing ways to see the righteous through their hardships."

"I'm not one much for God-talk."

Justice shrugged. "Neither is God. Think of it this way, then: time can be manipulated along four axes of a mathematical equation, but it can only be experienced chronologically. What this means is that time is more like a complicated network of dimensions, the expanding and shrinking of bubbles in space. But the human mind is stranded on the surface of the bubble, and can only comprehend the world as a chronological unwinding. One moment leads to the next, and then the one after the next, and so forth. "The closed time-like curve that begins with your arrival at the front door of the jailhouse and ends with the moment you leave the present and journey back to that moment is not the only way that the events transpired in that span of time. It is just the only one we can experience."

"I'm not quite with you," Dex said. But he felt like he almost had it.

"Think of the time frame in question as the final iteration. The first iteration, perhaps, is where I use my distraction to free you. And it must have worked, for you were able to have a future in which you could travel back in time to rescue your friend, and, along the way, yourself. There could be a thousand iterations of that period. But the only one that we can experience is the one in which we find ourselves. Paradox included."

Dex had the Judas Sword in his hand, its familiar weight helping him muddle through the mess in his head. But through it all, there was one thing that stood out.

"So is that it?" Dex asked. "I've been sent from Venus to travel through time? To do what?"

Justice shook his head. "I don't have the answer to that. I do know that you are very important. You must be, for Logos gave his life to rescue you. But there are others who do know the answers, whom you shall meet. All I know is what we fear but have not been able to prove."

"And what's that?"

"That the off-landers have been returning to Earth secretly to manipulate its history."

Eighty-five.

_____

"The industrialists? From Venus? They know how to time travel?" Dex asked.

"We do not know for sure," Justice said. "About ten years ago, a traveler arrived in Longstown. She found Freedom at a Longstown prayloop, and asked for asylum. Freedom did not feel any obligation, but the traveler said her name was Lynia, which is also Freedom's secret name with God. This stranger should not have known it. So

Freedom brought her up here to our monastery, where she told us her story.

"She claimed to have come from Venus, to be a prisoner from the asteroid mines who had escaped with the help of a man named Logos. She claimed that an invasion had begun, at the behest of the ruling Families, led by a man known to us as Ashion."

"Ashion is the one that killed Logos," Dex said.

Justice nodded solemnly. "That is most likely. Logos despised Ashion almost as much as he hated the Families of Venus, as they were explained to us. But at first we did not believe Lynia, for how could it be that the industrialists had survived on Venus for a thousand years, and never made contact? Why now? Why a clandestine military operation? There were just too many questions, and Lynia had few answers." Justice shook his head before he continued.

"She begged that her existence be kept a secret from everyone we met. She needed to disappear. We agreed, and she put herself to work within the walls of this monastery, never getting in the way, only helping us out, giving Freedom and me more time to tend to our parishes. We did not mind her then, for she was hardworking and trustworthy. She also took a solid interest in our patron saint, Brodius, and we taught her much about him. Oddly, she often knew more about Brodius than even we did. It was as though God had picked Lynia out of the sky and delivered someone who was a living testament to Brodius' miracles.

"Lynia was with us for two years before the package arrived. It was me who brought it, just another gift from the townsfolk, offering up their hard work to God. It was among all the other items that we gather twice yearly for the long winters at the monastery. When I unwrapped it, Freedom and Lynia were present, and they saw it well. It was a small metal box, collapsed, but Lynia knew what to do with it. 'A message from Logos,' she said. She unfolded it into a box with only edges, with light that shone inward."

"A light box," Dex said.

"Yes, that's what she called it," Justice said. "A light box. Then she stuck her hands into the light, and moved them quickly. Images began appearing within the box. Like magic. It was an image of Logos, speaking to Freedom and me.

"Logos explained that the invasion was real, and that warriors were being sent to Earth, and then traveling back in time to manipulate the present. To what end, even Logos did not know. But he urged us to hide Lynia from all outsiders; he told us that no one could be trusted other than the two of us and Lynia. The box then showed images taken from the planet Venus, and the colonies and training armies there."

"Were you convinced at that point?" Dex asked.

"Yes. Logos also spoke of the past as though it had not yet happened. Accidents that had happened to friends of ours, he talked about them as though they were orders yet to be carried out. Deaths to priests, murdered leaders. It could have all been made up, but that light box... there is no such technology left on this planet, Dexter. Nothing like that could be faked."

"I noticed. It's all goats and warlords around here now."

"Yes. But the truth manifested itself through Lynia, who said she had spoken with Saint Brodius. If you ask me, Saint Brodius was speaking through her. Freedom and I both felt his presence. God was providing a path for our redemption."

"God told you to believe this Lynia?"

"Yes."

"So where is Lynia now? Is she socked away back in the cave someplace?"

"No, we found a much safer place for her. It is hard to get to, and it is hard for her to remain there, so she must come back every few days. But it is the safest place. And she has friends there who are helping us fight this secret battle."

"Where is it?"

"I will show you. But first, you must prepare."

"Prepare for what?"

"For time travel."

Eighty-six.

Dex closed his eyes against the pattern, but he could still see it imprinted on the inside of his eyelids. He had been staring at it for so long it was etched into his mind.

To prepare for shifting, you need to prepare your mind, Justice had said. To prepare your mind, first you need some time in this room. Dex had looked up.

Sure, he had said. I feel like I could stare at those patterns for hours. Justice had just smiled, and said, that's the idea.

But Justice had not meant hours. He had meant days. Dex had been stuck in the room for two days now, as far as he could tell, with only the light from the fire to see by. Justice would crack the door with food, but leave before Dex could say anything.

"Keep looking," would be his only words.

Dex traced the lines, the sloping circles, by walking below them and feeling their distance. Sometimes he would lie on the circular stone table in the center and look up, trying to catch the elusive trail. It felt like the patterns were leading him someplace but he couldn't figure out where. Someplace he had to go.

Other times he would sit in a corner, as far from the wooden beams as possible, trying to escape the inevitability of the patterns. Or he would walk in a circle, staring downward, thinking of the lines above him, seeing if he could walk their route. There was something compelling about walking the route. It felt familiar. It felt dangerous.

During the first night of sleep, he had fallen into the dream. The burning surface was in front of him, searing his skin, burning at his eyes. The moment would begin to jack and slow down into nothing, as he approached the surface and began to deconstruct his molecules, his atoms, his smallest little pieces while they began their dance across the surface. He was trying to hold it all together, remember where each little tiny particle should go, but it was so difficult. It was impossible. He was reconstructing everything too quickly, and the burn was beginning. But he felt a structure behind the mad, incomprehensible chaos this time. Something was sticking with him, even as the pain began to eat his hands into nothing. The patterns circled around the dream, invading it.

He woke to the sight of the fire patterns above him, shining as bright as anything he had ever seen. And he felt the strength of them; he could see the guidelines built into it, see the different shapes that could be rendered. "There is the knife," he told himself. "For cutting through." Then he traced his hands through a complex weave. "That is the foundation. For holding onto. A rock."

After the second day, Dex no longer needed to look at the patterns. He had seen them from every angle, memorized the entire three-dimensional line structure. He would close his eyes, and could begin to play out the different shapes, walking a line and then leaping over to the next, feeling the strength and the tension of the geometries. He wished for names, for a framework of understanding. He would open his eyes, and stare again, trying to figure it out. To know what it was.

He did not sleep anymore, for fear of the dream. Something had changed about it, but that did not make it any less frightening. He kept himself awake by playing through the arrangement of the fire beams, building the pattern for flight, or retreat. He named all the directions he could make the lines go if he walked them. The Knife. The Rock. The Trap. The Halo. The Flyer. He felt like he was making his own constellations, only they could float and change if he moved his eyes over the patterns quickly enough.

Tired, and trying to keep himself awake, Dex had jumped from the table and caught hold, just barely, of the lowest wooden beam. After a few tries, he was able to hoist himself up, and climb into the patterned wooden beams. He could see the long glass threads up close, about the width of his wrist, embedded into the wood, reflecting a flame from someplace higher up. He traced some of the threads with his hands, but he could not seem to find the source of the light. As he walked along the beams and swung from one to the next, he could not tell how high the cave went up. The wood beams seemed to be hanging down from somewhere, but where? They were too steep to climb after about thirty feet.

Dex stayed up in the wood and glass patterns for many hours.

But he could not get any perspective when he was within them. The only way to really see them was from the ground.

Ultimately Dex tired of the almost-promise of the design. He did not know the names. Nor did he know the shapes, or the directions they went. He grew tired of making it all up in his own head; he wanted Justice or Freedom to come in and point things out, tell him what it all meant. Explain to him why it would loop back here, or why this place would trap all lines and not let them go. After two days, he wanted to close his eyes and not see them anymore.

He sat cross-legged, his back against the table. He was humming an old tune, some song from the broadcasts he, Thelo and Mal would steal down in the URL headquarters. But try as he might, he could not get the designs out of his head. He felt them wrapping around the song and the memories that came with it. The pattern he called the Knife was dissecting through his memories and he could see it behind the laughing face of Thelo, lighting up the walls of the sewers. Mal was saying something about getting a drink, but Dex could only see the Flyer circle begin to envelop her. When he traced the line down her body to the ground, the Trap was eating all the lines and creating a hole. Through the hole he could see the burning surface of his dream, pulling him down, its gravity inevitable, the pain beckoning him. He slid down the Trap lines into the hole, watching Mal and Thelo fall away above him, as he fell headfirst toward the churning, white-hot membrane.

The groan of the opening door shook Dex awake. He stood quickly, disoriented, unaware he had been asleep. Freedom and Justice entered.

Dex wiped at his eyes. "I'm glad to see you. This room is driving me insane."

"On the contrary," Freedom said. "This room is grounding you."

"I can't get the shapes out of my head," Dex said.

"You see shapes?" Justice asked. "Show them to me."

So Dex walked the two monks through the patterns he had seen. He talked about the names he had given them. With each name, Freedom nodded.

"I like your names," she said. "You have the imagination of an atheist. Your world is very ordinary. Knives. Rocks. Ropes. It has a poetry, too, I suppose."

Dex ignored this. "But they are not really shapes, are they?" he asked. "They are motions that lead to shapes, see? They lead to actions to shapes to actions. All precise, and perfect, right?"

Freedom nodded approvingly; Justice shook his head in disbelief. "Only four days, and he has found them all," he mused.

"Lynia predicted he would know it already," Freedom said.

"Know what already?" Dex asked. He felt gratified by their reactions, but the itch of the room could not be scratched. He did not know how to explain this to them. He needed to get out.

"Know the tools," Freedom said, pointing up.

"Wait a minute. I've been in here for four days?" Dex asked.

"More or less," Justice said, slapping his hand approvingly on Dex's back. "But you're done. Only God knows how, but you're done."

"Come, then, Dexter Maxwell," Freedom said, nodding toward the door. "Lynia would like to see you now."

"Where is she?"

"About four hundred and fifty years ago," Justice said with that annoying wink.

Eighty-seven.

They left the next day at sunrise on horseback. Dex, for all his new-found skills, had to learn the hard way that he could not ride a horse. So Justice hitched the hay-cart onto his own horse, and Dex rode in the back. They rode east, into the sun. Dex faced west, and watched as the early-morning sun painted the mountains a rich violet. The sunlight reminded him of that morning before the traffic stunt in Grenver. Only these mountains had no windows glinting down. There was no concrete, no tollbooths, no helicopters. No garbage trucks.

There was something new: the patterns. He could not escape them. They were hiding behind every tree; they were disguised as trees, clouds, mountains. They felt like an infection. But it was almost as though they were trying to tell him things about the world. He was trying to inform himself, using the Rock. Or the Clasp. Or the Flyer. But he did not know what to do with them; it was as though he had been given the answer to a question he had not asked yet.

Then there were his dreams. There was the reconstruction dream, for one, but the night before he had also dreamed of Grenver. Mal, and Thelo, and Money, and crazy ol' Jones had all been sitting around discussing how time travel would work, and how they could use it to really mess with the Feds. Mal had been close to him, close enough he could feel the warm comfort of her skin, see her quietly confident smile. Her short frazzled hair, bound up in his hands when they made love, which they had done in the dream until Dex had woken, aching.

It made him think of how Mal could laugh. How she could make a portable computer do almost anything, her hands so fast on the console. She had been a genius, and Dex had known it, but he had never said it. He had always been jealous of that, of her mind and how she used it. She was good at something. Dex had never been good at anything.

Until now.

He felt the weight of Judas strapped to his back. But that skill was not his now, was it? It had been implanted. Put into place afterward. Like the knowledge of this language or his ability to land a spacecraft. It was all after-market add-ons, like the old cpu brains of the garbage trucks. The same went for the patterns, he realized. Justice and Freedom had been so surprised by his ability to learn them so quickly. *But they had already been burned into my head, hadn't they? None of it is mine.*

Of course, I'm not really me now, am I? And this is not my time. These are not my friends. So why is this my fight? The horse pitched, and Dex fell back hard against the sheath on his back. He closed his eyes. *But what the hell else am I going to do?*

"We are almost there," Freedom said. She had brought her horse up next to the cart. A pattern darted across her face: the Trap. Dex pushed it out of his mind.

"Where are we going, again?" he asked, trying to make conversation. He knew exactly where they were going.

"It is a prayloop run by a close friend of Justice's, a pastor by the name of Discipline," Freedom told him. "It is a very good loop. Worshipers visit there day and night. But on Sundays, the power of their faith is unparalleled. It is a good prayer for your first time."

My first time. Traveling through time. It sounded so ludicrous in his own head. "And what is a prayloop?"

"A reaffirmation of your faith in the Redeemer."

"I don't have any faith in the Redeemer."

"Lucky for us, your faith is not required."

"Good thing."

"Everyone has faith in something, Dexter. It is the shape of our reality."

He shrugged the comment away. "So what is it like?"

"Faith?"

"Time travel. Have you ever done it?"

Freedom shook her head. "I tried a few times, never successfully, early on in my life. But I had an accident and was not able to continue my studies." She touched the scar on her temple briefly.

"What makes you think I have a mind for it? I've never really been the smartest guy around."

Freedom smiled, "You know how to shift."

Shift. "How do you know that?" Dex doubted it very much.

Freedom nodded back toward the mountains. "Because you just learned."

"Staring at magical shapes in the dark taught me how to shift through time?" Dex asked, amused.

"The altar room lights are a template. Justice would say they are the beginning and the end. The middle will come from God."

Dex looked away. "I'm not much for trusting God."

"Faith," Freedom said again.

"We are here," Justice said from the front of the cart. Dex saw a three-story brick building standing at the apex of the low foothills they had traveled into. It was not made of adobe, as nearly everything else seemed to be around here, but rather bricks, too large to be put in place by a single man. The structure looked to be octagonal in shape. Dex could see window slats on the first floor, and windows higher up that were closed. There was a small structure attached to one side, a stable by the looks of it. On top of it was a staircase that carefully encircled the entire building all the way up to the roof. The patterns in his head danced around the building wildly: the Rock. The Rope. The Flyer.

The sun was above the horizon now, burning away the low clouds and the autumn chill. Justice pulled his horse up to the stable. There were already many horses milling around, stamping at the cold and looking for what sun they could find. Dex jumped out of the cart, wincing at the still-healing cut on his chest and the bruises everywhere else. He forgot at times the ordeal he had been through only days before. He forgot, in the peace of the monastery, what he had done on Venus with the blade that was now strapped to his back.

Freedom gave her horse some feed at the stable, then the three of them walked toward the church. Dex could not remember the last time he had been in a church. Jones had invited him a few times, when he had no one else to guide him to the altar for communion. That was before Jones had a following. After that, Dex had refused. You don't need me anymore, he had said. I will always need you, Jones had replied. But Dex had gotten too drunk, or too stoned, and slept through it. Jones had never asked again.

As they approached, Dex could hear the sound of a loud voice echoing through the stone building. "Discipline has already begun," Justice said. "We shall go upstairs then. No reason to interrupt."

"I'll let Discipline know we have arrived," Freedom said.

Justice nodded and pulled Dex away from the front door, circling the octagon building until they came to a set of alarmingly aged steps up the side of the stable. They climbed these and came to the staircase that led to the roof. From the top, Dex had a stunning view of the mountains to the west and empty plains to the east.

"I thought we were going inside," Dex said, shivering slightly in the cold.

"Not we," Justice said. "Just you." He pointed to a hatch door in the middle of the roof. "You'll go down there by yourself in a few minutes. Once Discipline gets the loop going."

Dex felt the nervousness in his stomach. "What's going to happen down there?"

"There is nothing to fear, Dexter," Justice said. "If nothing happens, nothing happens. There is no danger."

"So do I have to actually do anything?" Dex stared at the hatch door. He was not very interested in going down there, suddenly.

"You will know what to do," Freedom said, coming up the stairwell behind them. "We have a few minutes still."

"Is there a time machine down there?"

"No machine," Justice growled. "No machines at all."

"Then how does it work?" Dex asked. "I'm not sure I want to go down into that hole without knowing what I'm supposed to do."

Freedom smiled, the scar on her temple wrinkling. "You are frightened, and we do not yet have the vocabulary to describe what will happen next. The words exist, but you will not understand them."

"Give it a try," Dex said.

Freedom thought for a moment. "At the thread altar, back at the monastery, you gave some of the patterns names, didn't you?"

"Yes, so I could tell them apart."

"Right. This door here will drop you into a room like the thread altar. You will use the patterns. You will put down the... Rock. You call it the Rock, don't you?"

The pattern flitted across his eyes. "Yes. The Rock."

"The Rock connects the Rope to your... Kite? The Kite floats you along the path. The Knife cuts the membrane. The Halo leaves it open. The Clasp closes it. That is all."

Without warning, there was the roar of drums from below. Dex's heart began to race. He felt like the moment might jack. "What the hell was that?"

Justice grinned. "A beginning."

Eighty-eight.

A rope ladder took him down into darkness. The only light came from the hatch above his head. Dex could see the silhouette of Justice against the clear blue sky. He climbed down the ladder carefully as it swung under his weight. He finally felt the ground below his feet when he had descended nearly twenty feet. The drums and voices of the congregation below him were a loud, thundering bass line vibrating through his chest, shaking the floor he stood upon.

As soon as he was off the ladder, Justice began pulling it up. Dex squinted into the darkness around him, but could see nothing save the dancing patterns of the altar room. "Don't move," Justice called down, and what little light had penetrated from above disappeared as the hatch closed. The darkness around him was complete. The booming sounds were growing faster. Dex's heart raced, and he could feel the moment slowing down as he tried to make sense of the situation.

Fires below the altar room made the air hot, like on Venus. He could feel the heat rising, as though attached to the chanting and drumming of the worshipers. He did not move, just slowly spun in circles. The heat and darkness reminded him of his days on Venus, wearing the blindy mask, getting dragged around by Trance.

He tried to make out the chanting, see if he knew the words. It sounded like the language that Freedom and Justice spoke, but different, somehow. Older. There was something archaic about it, and it was ordered differently. It was growing louder, the drums beating faster, the voices rising. Dex felt his skin buzzing all over with the sound, with the feeling of the drums in his chest.

That was when the floor dropped out.

It was not the entire floor, but large geometric shapes opened around Dex, and the voices suddenly rang through his head like a piercing blade. The rhythm of the drum, the sound of the words attached to the patterns in his head and he felt like he might vomit. The vertigo was so absolute, he panicked. And he jacked the moment.

He needed a way out. This was all wrong; he was wrong. There was something real to the dancing shapes of people below him; it wasn't just the usual mystic garbage he remembered from church. He didn't expect it to be so complete. His chest burst with the magnificence of the patterned holes in the floor, exposing the sound, closing in on him, throwing steam up into his face. *Get me out of here. Something is about to happen.*

The heat stifled Dex's breathing. He looked around, now, in what dim light filtered up, looking for a door, a way out. But there was no escape. And the truth of it finally struck Dex in his heart.

There is no escaping who I have become.

This is not a dream I will wake up from.

Dex let the sensation and strength of the worship hall overwhelm him. He slowly turned in a circle, trying to find the right spot to soak it all in. Then the window slats he had seen from the outside opened, and fine beams of light shot across the room in a hundred different directions. They were all around him, on him. He was at the epicenter of a pattern, and it was something he knew.

The Rock.

The voices became more even below him, the chanting and drumming steadying to a beat that was in time with Dex's heart. The light patterned through the octagon of the room, through the rising steam, and caught hold of the ancient language the hundreds of men and women were singing below him, burning the Rock deep into his head, imprinting it onto parts of his brain previously unknown to him. He began to unwind large mathematical figures, looping them through the patterns of the thread altar, passing them around the confines of the church.

Dex could feel the spin of the Flyer, taking its shape from the lights and the beginning of the Rock and the drums and the words. It was perfect. Dex could feel it, and in the slow motion of his mind, all the seemingly chaotic sensations that surrounded him clicked into place.

It's not about time; it's about space.

And then he was in the Flyer, the Halo consumed him, and the Knife had opened the breach.

Dexter Maxwell shifted, and was gone.

Eighty-nine.

Terran wiped the spittle from his glasses patiently. Bertran meant well, and was a very smart man, but Terran wished he could talk without quite so much passion. The consonants sprayed from his lips like a fountain. But Bertran was a good man, who protected the archives from the purgers, foreseeing each new battle as though he could see the future. The purgers no longer fought to destroy all the great libraries directly; they now used political means to go after the archive keepers, or to prevent access to children. They were a savvy lot, and had already closed down the eastern archives. But Bertran kept the purgers at bay, and Terran's precious Coelinian archives remained open.

Terran had bidden him farewell, and headed deep into the vaults, as he always did. Besides Bertran, the remaining archivists all treated him as a joke, at best. A great mind, they would say, wasting his time reading about the lost sciences of the past. Always looking to the stars, or the great cosmology theories, they would say. Why was he not trying, as all bright women and men should be, to determine the cause of the time rift?

But Terran did not take the constitutionist's tests. He did not move south to the great research libraries of the new Empire. He remained in the backwaters of the world, in Coelinio, researching at a library in the land of the illiterate. There, the written word each day lost ground to the righteous clamor of the purgers, who claimed all written language to be evil.

The remaining archivists were old, nearing the end of their careers and their lives. Terran was certainly no longer a boy, but young enough to be able to still seek a career someplace else where his skills were still revered. They had hounded him for years, trying to change his mind. But that was long ago. The Coelinian archivists now considered Terran to be half-mad, not quite working with a full deck. He was allowed to roam even the forbidden document rooms. For what would ever become of it?

Nothing. Nothing will ever become of me.

That, of course, is the point. History has already forgotten about me.

Terran was deep in the archives, back where no one came but him. Most of the documents and devices here required technology that no longer existed just to interpret them. As such, they were archeological oddities, merely trinkets of the Industrialist Era: left behind but revealing nothing. He walked past them, and came to a door with a lock. The original lock had been a century old and put in place by the technology postulation. He had been given one of the only two keys—the other sat in Bertran's care, unused, for he was a politician, not a scientist.

So Terran had changed the lock. Now only he could enter this room.

He pulled the key from his belt loop, and entered the cosmology archives carefully, reverently, as he always did. This was his favorite place in the whole world, his own grand discovery, his escape. His fate.

His doom.

He closed the door behind him, locked in the complete blackness of the room. As always, he lit the door lamp and then came back to sit at the desk.

In the middle of the floor, lying on his side, was a young man, a kid really, with a nappy mess of black hair and mild brown skin. He was unconscious, but alive, and lying in a pool of his own vomit. As soon as he saw it, Terran could smell it.

"Not again," he said.

Ninety.

The Rope swung Dex across the Flyer, leaping up and away from the burning surface, white hot even now against his face. Dex tried to wake himself up. He was afraid of the dream, afraid as the Rope took on a life of its own, pulling him up and away from the heat. Dex could feel the patterns unwinding frantically, wrapping around him, through him, connecting back to the Rock. The Rock was below the surface, on the other side.

And then he was falling, the Flyer around him pushing him back down toward the surface. A hundred different peaks of gravity pulled at him from across the burning heat. Only the strength of the Flyer's geometry kept him on his arching trajectory toward the surface, which was growing closer, hotter. Dex could feel the dream bubbling up, the reorganization, the deconstruction and reconstruction. He put his hands down, trying to feel his way into it.

This isn't a dream; this is happening.

He panicked, trying to reverse himself, rewrite the pattern, but the Flyer was moving toward the shape of the Knife. Dex could feel the Knife in front of him, already waiting for him at the surface. But it did not cut the surface, it was turned toward him. *The Knife is meant to cut me.*

Dex wanted to scream, to get out. This was all wrong, they had it all wrong, this was not how to do it. It was close, the right idea, but it was wrong. It was a mistake.

The Knife patterned into a thousand million knifes, dancing across the burning surface, and Dex could not stop. The Flyer pushed him into the knives, and they dissected him into a million pieces as his skin scorched across the burning surface. The pain was overwhelming. Dex lost himself in it, and despite having the moment in jack, he lost consciousness.

Ninety-one.

He did not realize he was awake. He only noticed the putrid smell everywhere and the cold stone beneath him where he lay. It felt like his eyes were open, but he could not be sure. He still remembered the burning light of the surface in his dream, and wondered if he had been blinded for real this time. His throat felt as though it were on fire.

His body ached all over, and he did not feel capable of moving. Dex could not remember all the details that had led him to this place, but they were starting to come back to him, when he heard footsteps and the sound of a lock being turned and a door opening. A dim rectangle of light came from around a corner, followed by the shadow of someone. He closed his eyes to a tight squint. A light went on, and Dex saw a pair of leather boots come and stand above him. He heard a short phrase spoken in a language he did not understand. Then the boots turned and walked back out of the room again. The door was shut, and the bolt thrown.

He pushed himself up to sitting position, and wiped something from his lips. The smell told him it was his own vomit. As his eyes adjusted to the weak light, he saw the small splatter of his late lunch. It was all over his shirt as well. He tried to wipe it off, but could not seem to focus on anything, and Dex realized just how tired he was. He could have fallen asleep on the spot.

The bolt was thrown again, and the door opened. Dex tried to shake off the delirium and stand, in vain. The boots came around the corner again, and this time Dex could see the entire man. He was middle-aged and pale-skinned, with straight black hair pulled into a tail behind his neck. His eyes were an icy blue, and it struck Dex that he had not seen anyone with blue eyes in a while. A cloth was hanging over his arms and he carried a large bowl. He spoke, but Dex could not understand. The man spoke louder, indicating for him to take the bowl.

Dex answered in the language of Earth. "I don't understand you."

The man looked at him strangely, and said something else. Dex closed his eyes, trying to hear the words. He was so tired. Endlessly tired. What was he doing here again?

"I can't remember what I'm doing here," Dex said to himself.

The man frowned at him. "You speak old world?"

Dex smiled. "Old world. Yes, I speak fluent old world."

The man gave a wide grin. "In that case, we can communicate. I have brought you a bowl of water to wash up, and a new shirt so that you do not smell of sick."

"Thank you." Dex took the water and pulled it to his lips. The cool water brought relief to his burning throat.

"I am Terran."

"Dexter Maxwell."

"Who has brought you to this place, yes?"

"I was sent by Freedom and Justice. Monks from... well, from the future." And then it was all back. "I came to see someone named Lynia?"

Terran had sat down on the ground, cross-legged. He nodded at the name. "Yes, Lynia sometimes can be found here. She, how you say, hides from the future."

"Lucky her."

"Sorry?"

"Never mind."

"My old world is bad very much, Dexter Maxwell. I apologize."

Dex was fighting to keep his eyes open. "No, I'm sorry. I'm just so tired."

Terran nodded. "Yes. It is your first time. You will be exhausted. It becomes less hard, yes, after more times. Lynia says this."

"Where is Lynia?"

"She spends most time in other parts of the archives. She will return. She is with Thrina." Terran pointed to himself. "Thrina is married to Terran, yes?"

"They'd better hurry up. I'm going to fall asleep."

"Better to not sleep, Dexter Maxwell. You sleep—" Terran snapped his fingers—"you fly back. I get you some water, then java."

"Java sounds great."

Terran was off to a back part of the room. Dex looked around, and was surprised to find the archive was the exact same octagonal shape of the church he had been in.

Then it hit him: *I just traveled through time.*

Dex had to smile at it. "Terran, what is the date?"

"It is... I do not know your calendar. Autumn, just before the equinox. The day and night evens tomorrow. September 22. The year is 2667 Anos Domini."

Dex did the math in his head. Justice put the date at 3027, so he'd gone back three hundred and sixty years. *Is that right?* Even as he asked it, he could feel the exact time. Down to the minute. The second. The nanosecond.

Terran returned with two mugs. Dex thanked him and took a sip of the water to clear his palate, then another, before trying the java. It was bitter, black, and tasted as good as anything he had ever had in his mouth.

"Do you know about Freedom and Justice?" Dex asked. "The monks; not the ideas."

Terran nodded slightly. "I know of the future. Too much, I am thinking often. But the world needs me to do this, to hide Lynia and to research the old world with her. I am a... what is it that Lynia says? A secret agent."

Dex gave a snort. "Nice. I like that. A secret agent. So what's so secret about you?"

"If the off-landers find out what I know"–Terran drew his thumb across his neck–"They would come back in time and cut me dead."

Dex thought about it for a minute. "But won't they find out? When we foil the off-lander plans, won't they figure it out, sooner or later?"

Terran gave him a sly smile and a wink. "Obviously they do not, correct? Or I would already be dead, yes?"

Dex smiled. "Good point. I'm still struggling with the whole chronology thing."

The bolt slid open, and the door creaked. Terran's smile widened, and he looked over Dex's shoulder. "Lynia has come."

Dex turned to face the woman as she came around the corner.

That smile.

The crumpled black hair hanging into her face. The deep brown eyes. She was very thin, starvation thin, and the wrinkles on her face made her much older than she was in Dex's mind. But he still knew exactly who Lynia was.

Mallory.

"Hey, Dex," she greeted him, putting a pile of books down.

Ninety-two.

Hearing her voice made Dex's throat catch, and he could feel tears welling up. He didn't realize he was shaking until Mal walked up to him, a look of concern on her aged face, and took his hands in hers. At the touch of her hands, the look in her eyes, Dex couldn't help but start sobbing in her soothing embrace.

"Hey, come now, Dex. It's okay," she said.

Yet he could not stop, and felt small pinpricks all over his body. He was so tired. The thought that Mal was alive sent the thread pattern of the Halo swirling around him.

"What... what's happening?" Dex asked. He felt recessed, not close to himself.

"You're shifting back, Dex," Mal said. Her voice was so far away. Why was she so old? Where had she been? What had she seen?

He felt the sharp pain of a slap to his face, and like that, he was back in Terran's archive, staring up at Mal, with Terran standing behind her.

"Ow," Dex said.

"Sorry about that," Mal said. "But we're not done here. I know this is hard, Dex."

Dex wiped the tears off his stinging face. "I didn't think I'd ever see you again."

"You know of this boy?" Terran asked, looking curiously at Lynia.

"I'll explain later, Terran," Mal said, without looking away from Dex. "Dex, this is Thrina Arrellius, Terran's wife." She indicated an aging women behind her. "You're not going to last much longer. You're being held in place by the congregation and by your own concentration, be that what it may. As soon as church is over, you're back in the 31st century. So stay with me okay?"

Dex took a deep breath. "Crackpipe, Mal, it's good to see you."

"Ditto."

"How did you–? I mean, what are you doing–?"

"I was pulled out of the freezer sixteen years ago, sent to the mines, like all the iced crims. Spent about three years under the whip. Logos tracked me down, and with his help, I faked my death and escaped back to Venus. A few months later, the resistance was able to smuggle me to Earth, where I found Freedom. They trained me for shifting and now I hide in this library with Terran and Thrina to prepare for the coming war."

"How long have you been here?"

"Ten years, give or take."

"That was a pretty fast recap." Dex could still feel the patterns

302

pulling at him. He could feel the Knife at his back, and the gravity behind it.

"Sorry. In a hurry. I glossed over a lot. Look, Logos sent you here because we need a warrior. I'm no match for the kind of men that Ashion is sending."

"Ashion, yeah, he's got some wicked good soldiers," Dex said. "I've already killed a few of them."

"Really?"

"Crackpipe, Venus was dripped, Mal. I was blind, and then Logos was talking to me—"

"Another time, Dex. Did Logos give anything to you? A message, or anything? For me? For Lynia?"

Dex shook his head. "No, nothing like that." Logos is dead, he wanted to tell her. But he remembered Freedom's reaction to the news. He could not face seeing Mal like that.

"He didn't give you anything?" Mal said, looking frustrated.

"He gave me this sword," Dex said, reaching over his shoulder and pulling Judas from its sheath.

"You were able to shift with that on your back?" Mal asked, looking impressed.

"Yeah. Why, is that against the rules?" Dex asked, handing Judas to Mal hilt first.

"No, just complicated to get the math right." Mal touched the side of the blade gingerly. "What is it made from?"

Dex shrugged. "Logos said it wouldn't set off metal detectors."

Mal looked to the archivist. "Do you know where the metallurgy books are?"

Terran nodded, and headed for the door.

"You don't need books on metal for that," said a voice from behind Mal. Everyone turned and looked. Thrina was staring at the Judas Sword, a crooked smile on her lips. "May I?" she asked, reaching for the sword.

Dex blinked back the patterns and handed Judas carefully to the woman. She took it delicately, then without asking how, she gave it the twist and it thunked open. Mal and Terran jumped back in surprise.

"You will need a book on spiders," Thrina said, closing the blade and handing it to her husband. Terran took the sword with great care, as though afraid it might extend open without provocation.

"I will study the sword," Terran said. "Time will be needed. You leave this, yes?"

"Sure. I guess." Dex turned to Mal, who was giving Thrina a quizzical look. "Why is everyone calling you Lynia?"

"Protection. Mine, and everyone else's. So if there's some stranger named Lynia living in the monastery, no big deal. But if some of Ashion's shifters were to come across a Mallory, it wouldn't take too long to figure out who I really am."

"And who are you, really? Mal, or a clone?"

She smiled. "Mallory Aquinas, Industrialist Era survivor. Leader of the Earth-side resistance. Original version." she winked.

Dex gave a little smile. "Whatever, *Lynia.*"

"Get used to calling me that, when you're back in the 31st century. Freedom and Justice know me only as Lynia, and it is important for them. They are in grave danger."

"Those harmless monks?"

"They are not so harmless. They are the most important people on the planet right now. Our survival depends on the off-lander shifters not discovering that little fact."

"Who are the off-lander shifters?"

"We have reason to believe that the Families on Venus have found a way to shift back through time. We think they have been polluting the timeline by changing the future."

"For what?"

"Setting the stage for invasion, maybe. Making the planet more susceptible to a military incursion from Venus at some point."

"At some point?"

"Soon."

The patterns were getting brighter. There was heat at his back, at his feet. Dex began to feel the tug again.

"I don't think I can stay for much longer," he said. The patterns circled around and through the three people in front of him.

Mal looked up from the sword, and grabbed Dex's hand. "Come back as soon as you can. We have more to discuss."

The Halo was wrapping into the Knife. "Mal, I can't do this," he said, reaching for her hand.

Mal kissed his hand lightly, "Of course you can. Tell Freedom to send you back a month from now. I'll be waiting for you here."

Then the breach was open, the Halo had Dex, and the Clasp was wrapping around him, pulling him back into the millions of knives.

Ninety-three.

His brain felt as if it was on fire, his eyes lit up from inside. He tried to blink it away, and realized he was surrounded by a disorienting darkness. He could hear a few distant voices coming from somewhere, talking solemnly.

A thunk came from high above, and then a corridor of light shone down on his head. Dex squinted against the light, and looked up. He saw a bright square and two silhouettes.

"Dexter! Are you there?" Justice yelled down.

I am back in the church... "Yes, I'm here," he said before collapsing.

Dex heard voices above him, but he was too tired to listen. A slap of something hit the stone next to his head, and he saw the end of the rope ladder. He watched it swaying back and forth violently, and then a pair of boots landed.

"Up we go, friend," Justice said quietly. Dex felt huge hands grab him underneath his armpits and haul him to his feet.

'I'm too tired. I can't make it," Dex said truthfully.

"Come now, just a bit longer," Justice said. "There's no way out of here except the roof. You can rest very soon."

Climbing the ladder felt like the hardest thing he had ever had to do. If Justice had not been there below him, encouraging him, he probably would have let go and fallen to the stone floor, asleep. As he finally emerged, Freedom helped him up out of the hatch door, and gave him a wide smile in the blinding mid-morning light.

"I have brought you water," she said.

Dex took a long drink from her satchel and, looking down over the edge of the roof's low wall, noticed the long line of the congregation filing away from the church, some by horse, but most on foot. They were laughing and talking, speaking in loud tones that carried up to the rooftop.

"Did they do that?" he asked.

"Yes," Freedom said, following his gaze. "But you did it, as well. You are a natural shifter, it would seem."

"I was so tired," Dex said.

Justice closed the hatch door and threw the lock. "You will become more accustomed to the journey," he said. "You will be able to stay on your own, as Lynia does. She no longer needs the congregation to sustain her shift."

"So I have to return when they are done singing?" Dex asked, sitting down and almost falling asleep.

"Yes, they hold one end of the string," Freedom said. "You hold the other. If you cannot hold it tight, if you fall asleep or lose consciousness, then you will shift back..."

"You can teach yourself to hold both ends of the string," Justice said. "But it takes time. It takes practice."

"I need to go back," Dex said, yawning. "I need to talk to–to Lynia."

"Sleep first," Freedom said.

So he did.

When Dex woke, the sun had moved across the sky and was about to touch the mountain tops to the west. His head rested on a rough wool jacket, and a blanket had been put over him. His ears felt cold in the late afternoon air. Dex sat up and saw Freedom staring west at the horizon from the edge of the church roof.

"What time is it?" he asked.

Freedom jumped a little, and turned. "I did not expect you to wake so soon," she said. "You startled me."

"Sorry."

"Do not be sorry, I was daydreaming."

"Of what?"

"The future."

Dex stretched, and then crawled over to sit next to her. They remained in silence for a few minutes.

"Why don't we just travel into the future, and get a good look at how everything turns out?"

Freedom shook her head. "We cannot travel into the future, Dexter. Only the past."

"Why not?"

"There is no way to triangulate an anchor point into the future. But the past has occurred, it exists. Our patterns can find a way through the curve to the past. But the future would require us to abandon our anchor. And without our anchor, we do not have access to the pattern-bringers. We would not be able to breach the energy barrier without the bringers singing the life force into the rebuilding. We could make the breach, but we would have to drop the anchor and we would just burn up at the surface of time."

Dex thought about it for a moment. "You would not have the Knife."

"That's correct. No Knife. So we are left to daydreaming of the future."

"What do you dream about, when you dream about the future?" Dex asked.

"Safety for God's people," Freedom said. "The liberty to worship as He would have us do. What do you dream about, Dexter Maxwell?"

"I never really think about the future," he said.

"The future bakes in the sun like new adobe," Freedom said.

He smiled. "So I've been told."

"We have another saying: the future is our blessing and our curse. It means that it is provided by God to remind us that time is something we build and destroy every day."

Dex shook his head. "You remind me of this old friend of mine. He used to say things like 'time is something we make and unmake every day, a fiction of our frontal lobe.' He always knew what to say. He was pretty smart. No, not smart; he was wise."

"Lynia told me that Dexter Maxwell was raised in the same house as Saint Brodius," Freedom said reverently.

"Saint who?"

"Saint Brodius, the patron saint of our order."

"I didn't know anyone named Brodius, and I certainly didn't know any saints." Dex was thinking back to everyone at the orph, trying to remember their names. *There was Jones, of course, and Thelo and... Wait, what was Jones' first name?* And then it dawned on him, in all its implausibility.

"Do you mean *Brodie* Jones?" he asked dubiously.

"Yes, that is what you would have called him, I am sure," Freedom said.

"Jones is a… saint?"

"Not just any saint," Freedom said. "The great leader of the Christian exodus of your time. He alone saved millions from the iniquities of the rich."

"You must be thinking of someone else," Dex said. "Jones just sat in that run-down old burbring house giving advice to people. He never led anyone anywhere."

"Brodius Jones alone stood between the destruction of our faith and its survival. We owe him everything."

Dex thought about it, and it made him laugh.

"There is nothing funny about it, Dexter Maxwell," Freedom said sternly. She was getting angry. "You will speak his name with reverence when you are around me."

Dex shrugged. "Fine. But I'm not calling him Saint Brodius."

Justice poked his head up from the stairwell. "The horses are ready," he said, "and the next prayloop is a half-day's travel. We should get going before it gets dark."

Ninety-four.

Dex stood in the middle of the blackness, the heat and thundering drums already rising from below. *I needed this.* Since he had shifted the day before, he could not rid himself of the sensation, the discontinuity, the shattering breach of the passage. As he felt his heart rate quickening, and the patterns danced across his blinded vision, he knew that he wanted the sensation again. He had been dreaming about the shift, or a version of it, since he was a child, huddled next to Thelo in the orph. Now he knew what he had always needed when he touched the blinding hot plane of his dreams. He knew what to do now, how to solve the maddening riddle. And now that he knew, he realized that he had always wanted the burning annihilation of the crossing, the winking out and winking back in. But he could never do it by himself.

Shifting was the dream. The dream was shifting. Always had been.

The heat was stopping up his breathing, and he felt the moment going into high jack. The chanting increased, the mathematical precision of the geometric shapes unspooling inside his mind. The floor dropped open, letting the steam of the prayloop bellow up around him. The windows opened, and the light criss-crossed through the steam of the octagon.

The Rock was put down, and the Rope tethered. The vertigo overwhelmed Dex, and the unnerving sensation of falling upward took his breath away. He stretched his arms out to feel it, to own it.

I am not alone.

The world waits for me to decide.

The Halo caught him completely, and the Flyer spun him up and through the Knife's breach. The Rope and the Flyer pulled him up away from the blinding white surface, circling and regrouping and running through him. He could feel the Rock waiting, patient and old, keeping him anchored across the plane to the singing congregation and its dancing, writhing mass. He could feel the precision, the exactitude. The taut pull of the Rope.

But this time he also felt the flaws, the weakness in the design. He could see the mathematical change that could loosen the Rope, untether him and perhaps even allow him to re-anchor. He began to work through the math when the Flyer pushed him back toward the surface, and Dex began to panic. The terror was rising as the Knife jumbled out into a thousand million knives, waiting to destroy him when he struck the surface.

He tried to scream into the hot burning plane as the Flyer un-looped into the Knife's edge, winking him out.

Ninety-five.

This time, Dex did not puke.

He felt solid ground, felt the spinning damage of the patterns settle into the back of his brain, recoiled like a threatened snake, waiting. It was the same room as before. Mal was waiting for him as promised, bent over a book at a large wooden desk, gas lights burning above her head. The pair of reading glasses she was wearing made her look even older. Dex could see in the bright light that her hair was beginning to turn grey. She smiled up at him, and removed her glasses. She looked very tired.

Dex felt his own exhaustion overwhelm him, and he fell to his knees. Vertigo struck, and he closed his eyes against the spins. Mal was at his side immediately.

"It sucks, doesn't it?" she said.

"Like... a ... *crackpipe*," Dex said, fighting back the rising bile.

"It helps to concentrate on something, an idea maybe. Run through a memory. It balances your head after the transition."

He thought of Mal in the water collector rooms under Grenver, wearing only the ratty old yellow T-shirt, her young legs pale under the candlelight. Memories of her kissing his neck crossed his mind. Dex opened his eyes to stare into the aging, worn face in front of him, wondering how it could be the same woman. His stomach settled and Mal led him to the bench opposite her desk, and they sat side by side. No one spoke for a few minutes, both of them gazing into space.

"Did you know they made ol' Jones a saint?" Dex asked.

Mal gave a crooked smile. "Yeah. Weird, isn't it?"

"Very."

"I've had a decade to get used to it, and in a way it makes sense. Whenever anyone needed advice, we always went to Jones. So the fact that people still go to him, a thousand years later, just means we knew a good thing when we saw it."

"I guess so. Jones would never have wanted to be a saint though."

"No saint ever does."

"You're starting to talk like them. Like the monks."

"Sorry. Occupational hazard."

Dex looked at the books stacked around the octagonal room. "So how does this work? You just go back and forth between 3027 and 2667?"

"That's pretty much it. Most of the time I'm hiding in this dank old library. I can only hold on for about three days, then my exhaustion sends me back to my present, in 3027. I get some sleep, eat something, and then come back."

"You need to eat more. You're skin and bones."

"I'd like to say something about how you have little ground to stand on, but you're not the scrawny kid I used to know anymore. You've really… bulked up."

"Benefit of being made in a lab."

"Right."

"So, where are you in 3027? Do you live with Freedom and Justice at the monastery?"

"I used to. Now, I'm a little farther north, up from the local loop haunts they frequent. I stay at a church called Bleeding Redemption. It's about a two-day ride on the Yukai road by horse. The local parishioner doesn't even know I use his prayloop for shifting."

"But I thought the prayloop had to set the parameters. Where and when, and all that."

"For you, right now, that's true. But once you get good at it, you'll be able to set your own parameters. You'll see. The congregation just provides the framework. They set the foundation."

"That makes sense. I heard the… well, the parameters, in my head. I could hear the echo of the space."

"Really? Did Freedom take you to the second altar room already?"

"Second altar room?"

"Wait, you haven't been through the second training room?"

"I don't think so. Just the wood and glass room at the monastery, and the two prayloop churches."

Mal shook her head. "That's amazing. You're amazing."

"What's so special about that?"

"You... crackpipe, you've already made more progress in two shifts than I made in two years. The chronolography already talks to you."

Dex blinked away the patterns. If he thought too much about them, they would start dancing across his vision, through his memories. "Mal, shifting is... Do you remember that nightmare I always used to have?"

"Sort of. Where you were burning up and had to reassemble your own hand, or something."

"Yes, that dream. It's just like shifting. That's what I was dreaming about all those years. It was shifting, only without the... structure. Without the patterns and shapes to guide me."

Mal sat quiet for a moment. "That's... it must be... I don't understand."

"I know. When I shift, it's like I've already done it a thousand times. Like it's a memory."

"But you couldn't have actually done it, not without the right technology."

"Technology?"

"The thread room. The church. The congregation."

"Not exactly technology, Mal. More like voodoo."

"I thought that too. But that's because where we come from, technology was dead. Genius and useful, but still just little tiring machines, jolted to life by a current when we needed it to go live. But technology has evolved since then. It lives inside as a part of them, inside the congregation. It's part of the way they think, and talk, and interact. And you are part of that, now."

"I can't get rid of it," Dex said. "I see the math in everything. The patterns flow into shapes everywhere I look."

Mal tapped Dex on his temple "It is new to your brain. But your brain will be able to sublimate it after a while. Trust me."

"I always have," Dex said quietly.

Mal looked away. "I know."

"Grenver seems so far away from all of this," Dex said, "But for me, it was only a few weeks ago."

"It's been sixteen years, for me," Mal said.

There was a long pause. Dex changed the subject.

"So, what's up with this Terran guy?"

Mal glanced up, staring into space. She smirked slightly. "Terran is a saint who will never be canonized."

Dex was puzzled. "What do you mean by that?"

"He has dedicated his life to saving Earth's people from the off-landers. But our success depends on his doing so without history ever recognizing it. His anonymity across time is our only weapon of defense against the off-lander shifters."

"And Thrina?" Dex asked. "She seemed to know a lot about my sword."

Mal smiled brightened. "Turns out even Thrina has a role to play in this. She knew the material used in that sword, and other swords like it. I think that even surprised Terran. Besides that, she is just the fool who fell in love with Terran and got herself wrapped up in all of this."

"Do you spend much time with her?"

She's is my best friend," Mal said. "The way I have to live… it's hard in many ways, but it's also very lonely. So when I'm back in this time, and I'm too tired for research, well, that's when I go looking for Thrina. We do the little things together. Wash our hair. Cook meals. Discuss her children. Talk about you."

Dex's stomach lurched. He decided to change the subject.

"Where are they now?"

"Thrina is likely persuading her stubborn first-born son to focus on his studies. Terran is trying to get an ancient solar energy collector to work, up on the roof," Mal said with a grin. "Electricity is hard to come by these days, and we need some serious juice in order to analyze this damn sword of yours." She turned and rummaged behind the desk, pulling Judas out and handing it to Dex.

"It was nearly impossible to get a sample," Mal said. "This thing is harder than diamonds. It's actually made from the silk of a bark spider, and then hardened with a bonding agent. We finally got a few shavings off the edge of the telescoping mechanism using a laser cutter from the 23rd century."

"What are you looking for?" Dex asked, as he slid Judas back into its sheath on his back. He felt the coiled up the patterns pushing to be unspooled, sprawling out around him.

"Some kind of message from Logos, encrypted in the molecules maybe," she said.

"Mal, I need to tell you something." The Halo was unwrapping, the Rope pulling taut. The gravity of the Knife itching at his back.

"What is it?"

Dex hesitated, but the patterns pressed against his memories, and he blurted it out. "Logos is dead."

He felt the tug of being pulled away from himself.

"No," Mal said, stunned. "That's impossible. We are lost without him."

Dex sensed the pull of the Rock through the breach, and Mal was gone.

Ninety-six.

"Goddamn it! Send me back!" Dex shouted, but the darkness did not respond. He fell to his knees and retched, the nothingness in his stomach contracting and burning at his throat. The sound of people yelling and laughing below him only intensified his anger. The hatch opened from above.

"Relax, down there!" Justice yelled. "The ladder is coming."

Dex pulled himself up as quickly as he could. He was still tired, but felt an adrenaline surge from his anger that propelled him up to the roof.

"Are you all right?" Freedom asked gingerly.

"Fine. Couldn't be better," Dex said curtly. "I need to go back. Now."

"There is another prayloop, but a few hours from here," Justice said, pointing south. "They will meet tomorrow for worship."

"Let's get going," Dex said.

"Do you not want to rest, first?" Freedom asked. "You are shaking."

"I'm fine. Let's go."

Justice finished pulling up the ladder, and they headed for the stairs.

"No, wait. Stop," Dex said. He flipped Judas into the sheath on his back. "Not the prayloop."

"Sorry?" Freedom said.

"Lynia said something about a second thread altar. The next training sequence."

"There are three training rooms in all," Justice said. "But you need time to develop your comfort with these simple patterns, before they get more complex. More challenging. You have only been–"

"Take me to the second room. Now."

"You are not ready," Freedom said, holding his arm. Dex pulled away.

"And you want me to save the world?" he snipped. "I know the patterns. What I need is to be able to stay longer in the past. Show me the next room."

Freedom gave Justice a worried look, but he only gave a shrug.

"The second thread altar it is then" he said.

Ninety-seven.

They traveled back to the monastery in silence. Dex felt relieved not to have to talk. His head was spinning with all the patterns, and he needed to try and work through it all.

But it was still too much. He remembered trying to put it all together on Venus and failing. At the time, necessity demanded that he put off sorting things out while he fought for his life. However, now, he had too much time to think, riding leisurely in a horse cart across old Grenver. Time to think about what he had become a part of. Time to think about time, and sliding through it. Hours to think about the changed world he found himself in, where church had become technology and technology had disappeared. Old friends were coming back to him in the strangest ways. Thelo, a general in a rebel army. Jones, a canonized saint. Mal, a covert time-traveling agent.

And me? What have I become? What is my role in all this?

Dex's thoughts were interrupted by the sudden halt of the cart. The sun was beginning its descent into the western mountains. He heard the approach of hoofs. "Stay down," Justice hissed from the front. Dex's heart rate quickened, and he buried himself in the hay.

"Greetings, travelers," Freedom said while Dex tried not to move.

"Ho, monks," said a stern voice. "We have been looking for you."

"What is it, magistrate?" Justice said, a little too quickly.

"There has been a murder in Longstown," the magistrate said. "The king's nephew has been struck down."

"A tragedy," Freedom said.

"Yes, there are rumors of a plot to overthrow King Mastiff," the magistrate went on. "Executions have been called for. Your services for last rites are required, Justice."

"Right away, sir," Justice said. "First I must get this hay to the monastery for my goats. Then I will come down instantly."

"I'm afraid there isn't time for that," the magistrate said. "The first execution is tomorrow morning. You must come with us tonight. The king will compensate you for the hay."

"That won't be necessary," Freedom replied. "I can drive the cart to the monastery. Justice can ride my horse into town."

"Right," the magistrate said. "This way please."

Dex heard whispering as the cart rocked with the weight of Justice getting down and Freedom stepping up.

"Please do not be long," she said. "God's work waits for no man."

"I serve at the king's pleasure," Justice said, his voice now farther away. "And this king calls for many deaths."

Freedom gave a whistle, and the cart began to rumble forward again. Dex remained under the hay until the sun finally fell behind the mountains, and only its pink echo remained in the eastern sky. He sat up, pulling hay from his kinky, unkempt hair, and looked around. They were alone again on the road.

"Who was that?" he asked.

Freedom did not turn. "Local magistrate," she said. "A minor official for the king. He is familiar with Justice's services, so he often comes for him when deaths have been ordered." She shook her head. "I grow weary of death."

"When will Justice be back?" Des asked.

Freedom shrugged. "Maybe tomorrow? Maybe in a week? Mastiff will surely use this murder as an excuse to round up more honest citizens who oppose his rule. He will invent an insurgency and associate the horrible actions of his own soldiers with the citizens, and then have them put to death."

"Let's go stop him," Dex said. He could feel Judas on his back and realized he had missed the sword. *I draw strength from it.*

Freedom shook her head. "Ours is a more important mission, Dexter. Mastiff is nothing compared to those that would come down from Venus to rule. If an invasion from Venus imminent, we must know more. We must find out the details."

"How are we going to do that?" Dex asked.

"Investigate the timeline," Freedom said.

"Do what?"

"Investigate the timeline. Shift into the past and look for clues about timeline disruption by off-lander elements."

"That's what I'm here for? To search for clues?"

Freedom nodded.

"Why do you need *me*? Anyone could go looking for clues, right?"

"Not anyone." Freedom finally turned to look at him. "Dexter, you are the key to our success. You are a natural shifter; that is why you have been delivered to us. And you have learned in ten days what only a handful of people could ever learn in a lifetime. Lynia took to it very quickly, but she still required years of practice to achieve what you have done already. It's not something just anyone could do."

Dex stared into the growing darkness.

"Besides," Freedom said. "You can defend yourself."

"Yes," he nodded quietly. "It appears I can."

They did not speak again, and Dex quickly fell asleep to the slow rock of the cart. Freedom's hand shaking his shoulder awoke him.

"Wake, Dexter," she said. "We are at the monastery. I will see to the animals while you eat. Then we will go to the second altar room."

"Tonight?" he said groggily. Sleep sounded like a better idea.

"Yes. Tonight."

Two hours later, Freedom shook him awake again. He had fallen asleep at the table, next to the remains of his meal of bread and cheese.

"Come," Freedom said. Dex tried to blink the sleep away, and followed her deep into the monastery, going up the stairs and into the stone-walled back rooms. They walked until they reached a ladder, which led to a closed hatch. They ascended and stepped out into the cold night air.

"The second room is not in the monastery?" Dex asked.

Freedom shook her head. "Up the mountain we go."

They hiked for some time, winding up the mountainside. There was no trail. The cold air and the altitude had Dex breathing hard, putting painful stress on his still-healing chest wound. Squinting forward into the darkness, he cursed as he took a rock in the shin.

"Where are we going?" He held his hand up in the light of the waxing moon, and saw blood.

"To the second room," Freedom said. "Hurry. It is not far now."

"Why is it out here, in the middle of nowhere?"

"It is exactly where it has to be. Do you recognize that?"

Dex looked where Freedom was pointing. It was a tree. But from where they stood, it clearly resembled one of the patterns.

"The Flyer," he said. Freedom nodded and walked past the tree. They came over another ridge and she pointed at another tree. The Halo. They passed and finally came to a stop. She spoke quietly, "Look up to the North Star. What does that star pattern look like?"

"The Rock," Dex said with a smile. "That's cool."

Freedom turned and pointed to her left. "There's also a tree in the shape of the Knife down there. Can you see it?" Dex looked, and nodded. "This tree marks the door where we came from, should you get lost." Then she walked quickly through the loose rock and stopped at a large boulder. "Down here," she said, before disappearing.

Dex, who had been admiring the Knife-shaped tree in the distance, ran up to the boulder, and saw the small cave-like entrance behind the boulder. He looked around at the nothingness and stillness of the night.

It was a tight fit. He could barely squeeze through with Judas still strapped to his back. Once he had lowered himself through the small entrance, Dex felt the space opening up around him. But he could see nothing other than the small circle of moonlight above him.

"Freedom?" Dex whispered.

"Here," Freedom said, grasping his arm. "There is no light, but I know the way. Do not let go of my hand."

They stumbled and crawled and squeezed in the complete blackness for an immeasurable period of time. *I spend far too much time blind these days. It makes time seem unreal.*

Maybe it is.

The stale air of the tight space felt like a trap, and it took considerable energy for Dex to suppress his growing claustrophobia. Freedom moved confidently, spoke frequently, and never let go of him. They seemed to be going down steadily, but every now and then would suddenly climb quickly. Dex was beginning to lose track of space, too.

Finally, they emerged through a tight crack and the fresh breeze felt like entering paradise, or at least a kind of paradise. "The air is different," he said.

"We are here," Freedom said reverently.

"I can't see anything."

"The room will be lit by the sun soon," Freedom said. "You will stay here alone, as you did in the first altar room. I will go back through the only entrance, the one we just came through."

"You are going to leave me?" Dex tried to make it sound casual.

"Do not worry," she tightened her grip in an attempt to put him at ease. "I'll go for water and something for our stomachs. But I will not be far. When the sun enters the room, you will forget all about me. I assure you." She let go of him.

"Okay." He tried to relax, but without Freedom's hand, even the fresh, cool air did little to help his panic. He listened as her footsteps faded, and then she was gone. Dex walked toward her last sounds, and found the small opening they had come through. Then he sat down, the entrance to his right, and waited for the sun to rise.

Unaware that he had been asleep, he woke to cold stone against his cheek and a crick in his neck. The floor beneath him was dimly visible, and he sat up immediately. Above, he could see similar patterns to the ones from the first altar room. But they were closer, not as high up. When he stood, he could reach out and touch them.

Dex pulled his hand back as though he had been bitten. *They move.*

The patterns were small, modular glass threads that were draped across the room in complex shapes and figures. He reached up again to where he saw the Rope, and pushed it. As it moved, it turned into the Clasp. Dex felt the patterns shift in his own mind. He turned quickly and walked to the Knife. The thread pattern was waiting for him, and he gently gave it a push. He expected to see it turn into a million little knives.

The move had triggered a lens that sent the pattern across the smooth, polished stone at his feet, a million knives dancing and cutting. Dex instinctively stepped out, and as the Knife kept sliding, it turned into nothing and the dancing buzzing knives disappeared on the floor.

Dex looked back up, and saw new patterns, new possibilities.

"Yes," he said out loud, and reached up to try something else. *Yes.*

322

Ninety-eight.

Freedom felt her way along the wall until she came upon the guide vein, a thin line of rock that ran from the entrance of the cave to the second altar room. The vein could be distinguished from the rest of the rock wall by touch. But if you shone a light on it, it disappeared into the face of the wall. Freedom had seen it before, and tried to follow the strain to the room using a lamp. But the eyes had deceived, and the mind overcompensated. She had got herself horribly lost. The only way to successfully find the altar room was to feel the way.

Freedom loved the metaphor more than anything. Saint Brodius would approve.

She felt the weight of the full water skins; they squeezed her and made the passage even harder. But she soon felt the peace of abandonment that came with trusting one's fingers. Before she realized it, she saw the dim light of the altar room ahead. She could hear Dexter Maxwell talking to himself. He sounded angry, mad about something, but she could not be sure. He was not speaking Cawlrinian; it was most likely his native tongue–Industrialist English. So harsh at the edges. So little balance. So little grace. But it sounded to her like a good language to be angry in; Dex had no short supply of invectives to throw around.

She quietly peaked around the corner. Dex was lying flat on his back, his sword grasped in his right hand, fully extended, and pointing up at the Passage Rites. He seemed to be whispering something, and moving the sword around in the same pattern time and again. Freedom watched as Dex's voice grew louder and louder. Then without provocation he leaped up, threw the sword to the ground with a clatter and began to pull the Rites into a complex thread. His hands moved quickly, his full attention on whatever he was saying and doing.

Then, as Dex adeptly moved the different lines into place, Freedom saw the baptismal water wash across the floor. The intricate waves were crashing over each other, the interplay no less dazzling than it had been when she had first seen it as a child. When was the last time she had watched the water pattern? Did she have to go all the way back to the accident?

The thought brought painful regret, which she pushed aside.

I am only a bystander to this. My discipline is slipping, Lord. Please bury my regret and desire with your blessed grace.

The water washed ashore at Dex's feet, but then he did something unexpected. He leaned over and spun his sword, which was bathed in the glimmering light of the water, on its axis. The effect on the water was immediate, shattering the pattern and creating something new, something chaotic. Freedom was overcome with an inexplicable feeling, not unlike dread, at the sight of it.

"No! Not right! Not RIGHT!" Dex did not seem to like what he saw, either. He roared, and gave the hilt of his sword a kick. It clattered against the cave entrance, and when he looked up, he saw Freedom watching him. He said something in his Industrial English.

"I do not understand you," Freedom replied quietly.

"Sorry," Dex answered in Cawlrinian. "I did not realize I had switched tongues."

"What were you doing with the sword?" Freedom entered the altar room and handed him a skin of water. He grabbed it eagerly and drank until it was nearly empty. Then he looked up at the mess of patterns he had left behind.

"Something else, less confined..." he trailed off. "It seems to be broken."

"The altar is in perfect condition," Freedom said.

Dex shook his head. "Not the room itself. The design. The assumptions that were used when it was built." He was looking up again, and did not speak for some time.

"But I have what I came for," he said. "Let's go."

"Not until sundown. There is too much to risk."

"Fine. But get me to a prayloop tomorrow."

Ninety-nine.

It was different this time. Dex felt it immediately, the chanting below him building into its steady throb, the heat surrounding him, the smoke rising in the dark. He could lay out the patterns around him, even as the space began to take on the shape of the Rock. He could sense the tensions, and feel the differential of the anchor of the congregation and the new anchor that he wanted to let go. He could build the patterns to lay his own anchor, and set the trajectory of the Flyer.

When the breach opened, he unspooled the capture methods he had discovered in the second altar room. He felt the Rope snap into place, obeying him. Obeying the design he had made in his head. The math of time. He could see the microseconds pile up around him like leaves from a tree, layered, shaking, vibrating with life. He unspooled the method for divination, the method for placement, and he felt the anchor spots he wanted.

October 22, 2667. 10:32 AM with three-hundred milliseconds.

He felt the divination setting its anchor in between the nothing and the milliseconds, finding the space of Terran's secret room. How did it know the space? The time knew it. The congregation knew it. Dex felt the space metrics flowing up below him, along with the time parameters. He picked out the space and attached the Rope to the nothingness of the nanosecond leaf.

The popping sound was new. He had been overwhelmed by the departure, but this time he had initiated it. The tug was violent, the knives sharp. Gasping at the non-existent air, he felt his consciousness slip for a moment.

But then he was moving the Rope, pulling it tight against the anchor he had written into the leaves of the present, keeping him whole. Then the Flyer had him and was pulling the Knife free to shatter. His anchor caught the surface of the burning plane and locked, haloing a breach where the Knife could turn itself upon him. Dex braced for the cut. It was a fresh, searing pain every time.

One hundred.

Dex opened his eyes and looked up into Mal's. They were puffy red from tears, and now shock. Dex tried to say something, but he had a splitting headache from the pull of his anchor. The pull of the present. It wanted him back. It was pulling and the knives were writing themselves out into the breach. Dex tried to fight against it, but the tug was too much.

Mal put her hand on his arm, and Dex looked up. The patterns darted across his vision. She was saying something, but his ears didn't seem to work.

"What?" he asked. His own voice sound far away.

"Are you holding yourself here?" She asked again.

"Yes... barely," Dex said. The room around him was coming into focus.

"That's... amazing," She said. "And you picked the time almost perfectly. You were here only a few minutes ago."

Dex saw her give a hard swallow.

"Mal, I'm sorry." The Flyer flitted nervously across the ceiling. "I didn't mean to just blurt it out without any details. About Logos."

"It's okay. Logos and I... we spent very little time together. I barely had time to know him. But he saved me. He put everything on the line to foil the Families' plans. He was the mastermind behind all of this. I don't know what we would have done without him."

"I only knew him for a few minutes."

Mal looked up at Dex, and cupped his face in her hands. It felt very motherly. "It was not your fault. You are necessary to all this and pulling you off the ice was a dangerous proposition. Logos knew the risks."

"It was someone named Ashion," Dex said quietly. "He seems to be some kind of government thug. A real son of a bitch."

She gave him a hard look. "Did you meet him? Ashion?"

"I was there when he killed Logos. But I had a mask on." Dex longed for a mask now that could shut out the dancing methods that were drawing and redrawing themselves across Mal's face.

"Right. Fresh off the bed. Your eyes would've been too new."

"Yeah. Something like that."

"So you didn't ever see Ashion?"

"No. Why, do you need me to identify him?"

Mal looked away. "No, we know who Ashion is."

"Is he the one down here? Messing with history?"

"Yes, I think it's him. At least it was at first. But he trained others. We don't know how many of the off-landers have been doing Family work now. That's why you're here."

Dex grinned. "To save the world, and all that."

"And all that." Mal gave a wink. "Are you up for it?"

"What the hell else am I going to do?"

"That's the attitude." Mal gave him a small hug. "I missed you, Dex."

"I missed you, too."

"So, how are we supposed to go about doing this?" Dex broke the silence. "You know, this save-the-world thing."

"The plan called for your spending a few years learning how to shift," Mal answered. "But apparently you got that squared away in a week."

"It was already in my head," Dex said. "It's like it was there before I ever got here. Do you think Logos put it in my head, like the sword thing? Like the language?"

Mal shook her head. "That's impossible. They don't have this technology on Venus. Logos would not have been able to get a memory burn from anyone."

"So how do they shift, if they don't have the patterns?"

Mal put her arms out wide. "One big-ass frickin' computer."

"Seriously, Mal."

She shrugged. "We don't really know their systems, and they don't know ours. I'm sure there are similarities in the core physics of it. It's likely they leverage the Transloop for the shift."

Dex thought for a moment. "Yes. That's it. They use the Transloop."

"I'm tellin' you, I don't know."

"No. That's it. When I took it to get to Earth, it felt like the dream."

"Were you conscious during the loop ride?" Mal asked, incredulous.

Dex nodded. "Yes. It was almost like being stuck in my worst nightmare."

"Weird," Mal furrowed her brow. "Maybe it has something to do with your affinity for shifting. You seem pre-wired for it, somehow."

"But how?" Dex asked, slowly getting used to the flittering patterns. He could distinguish them from the real world, now. And the constant struggle with the anchor was getting easier.

Mal shrugged. "A mystery for another day. We must get you ready for your work."

"My work?"

"Tracking down the off-lander shifters. Figuring out what they want. Who they are. What they are preparing for. And most importantly, when they plan on invading?"

"So I'm just going to walk up to them, and say, 'Hello,' give them a wink, and ask what they are up to?" Dex asked.

"I had forgotten all about the sarcasm. We were so good at hiding our fear, back then."

Dex was feeling the tug even harder. He felt it like the manifestation of his frustration. The patterns blasted around him, shaping and reshaping. "Don't go all monk on me. I'm just trying to figure out why this is happening to me. Jones is a saint. Thelo's a general in the army. You're a secret agent. But what am I?"

Mal gave him a look. "You're the weapon."

Dex gave a gruff laugh. "You sure know how to make a guy feel good about himself."

"You are also the key, the decoder ring, the entry password. You hold the answers to questions. You're maybe the whole reason why we still have a chance to stop the off-landers from waging war on Earth." Mal paused. "You never saw Ashion, did you?"

"I never saw him, no. He's the enemy, the one planning this invasion, right? So what is he like?"

"Do you really want to know?"

"Of course. I have to track him down, right?"

Mal took a deep breath. "Ashion, like you, is an iteration of Dexter Maxwell."

One hundred one.

Dex stared at Mal for a few moments, replaying the last few weeks of his life. He felt dizzy.

"So, Ashion is me?" Dex asked.

"Not you. A really old version of a version of a version."

"How old is he?"

"Three hundred years old, give or take."

"But... how is that possible?"

"Logos was his doctor for the past few iterations of him, so we know a little. The scientists on Venus had pioneered a way to burn the neurological intricacies of the human mind into new brains. So Ashion had new iters of Dexter Maxwell's body pulled, and every few years, he just got his mind transferred to the new host."

"That's incredible."

"Indeed. It gave him a lot of power, because not everybody can do it. They figured out that the technology doesn't work for every mind. Most people suffer meltdowns after the dump to a new brain. There's a signal degradation in the neural synapses, or something like that. Plus, it uses too many resources on their computer network. Only the Families get to take a shot at it. Most of them choose to use other means of keeping their own bodies around for as long as possible, instead of risking the transfer."

"Why me? I mean, why Dexter Maxwell?"

Mal shrugged. "No way to know. Maybe they tested your brain and found you were predisposed. Maybe they were just testing it out on iced crims, and throwing away the failures. Anyway, Ashion has been around for a long time, now."

Dex closed his eyes. "I really want to keep talking to you, Mal. But I think I'm about to shift back. I can't seem to hold the anchor."

Mal nodded. "That's okay. Tell Freedom and Justice to take you to the third altar room. There you will learn how to chase anchors across the brane surface and how to set your own parameters. You seem to be ready. After the third altar room, Freedom can help you get started. Try to find out what the shifters are doing. We need to know what they are after."

"Got it," Dex said, barely holding on. But he wasn't done yet. He pushed back at the gravity of the present.

"You need to be prepared for the fact that you might run into Ashion. Be careful, though. He has the same sword skills as you."

"Mal."

"Yeah?"

"I meant to, I wanted to say... that I'm sorry." Dex felt his jaw aching. There was a burning at the base of his neck.

"For what?"

"For how I acted back in Grenver. About the baby."

He saw Mal's face drain, and he went on quickly. "I didn't mean to act like an idiot. Things were just so good between us, I didn't want anything to change."

"Old scars," She said grinding her teeth. He could feel the anger simmering. "Everything changes, Dex."

"I'm so sorry."

"Me, too," Mal said. "Me too."

"Did they take it from you?"

Mal threw Dex a cold glance. "Did you know that when you work the mines, they leave you down in the hole until the very end? If you are a woman and you're pregnant, they leave you down there to have the baby. If you both survive, then a foreman comes down and takes you and your baby to the surface where you are given a day's rest. The baby is shipped to Venus and you are back in the mines the very next day."

"Crackpipe."

"Yes, they took my child, Dex. They took *our* child." Mal stood up. "We're done here."

The breach opened. Dex let go, and let the anchor yank him back to the church. He lay there, in the quiet darkness, letting the tears roll down his face.

One hundred two

Dex and Freedom headed south, traveling by horse now. Dex was getting better at riding, but his backside still felt raw and bruised. Freedom made a small fire, and they roasted some vegetables she had brought from the monastery. He said nothing, and she did not ask. He wanted to talk, but knew he couldn't. *The monks cannot know my true identity*, Mal had said. So Dex was stuck inside his own head, while Freedom spoke of the next altar room.

"The third altar room does not exist. It was destroyed in an accident over a hundred years ago. There were a few attempts to rebuild it, but none were ever completed."

"So how am I supposed to see it?"

Freedom smiled. "Stop thinking so linearly."

Dex stared at the fire in silence. Then, he looked up. "Shift back to when it did exist. So are we headed for the next prayloop?"

"Yes. It's back near Longstown, so we'll have to be careful. You're a fugitive, remember."

Dex shrugged. "A fugitive. Tell me something new."

Soon Dex fell asleep, exhausted by the shifting, and by his own emotions. Even the patterns flitting across the inside of his eyelids could not keep him awake. He felt like he had only just put his head down, when Freedom was shaking him gently. He rose slowly, and mounted up to head south. The light in the east started to rise when they arrived at the church and roped their horses. They headed to the roof as they always did, and waited for the congregation to arrive.

Dex kept reliving that night in the sewers, hearing Mal tell him she was pregnant. He remembered the fear, and the anger, the pent-up hatred come rolling out of his mouth and explode on Mal. His gut churned to remember it. She had not deserved it. She was not the source of all that anger and hatred. *I do not deserve a family, but Mal does.* Dex felt sick.

"Are you all right?" Freedom asked, a concerned look on her face.

"Yeah," he said.

"You do not look it."

Dex squinted into the rising sun. "I was thinking of a girl that I knew, back in my real life, back in Grenver. I was in love with her."

Freedom said nothing, waiting.

"I think she was in love with me, too," he went on. "For what we were, what we had to deal with, I guess you'd call us happy. But then I really messed up and then... Then I wake up a thousand years later. I'm on a different planet. I'm part of a war. And she is gone."

Freedom stayed silent for a while longer, and then spoke quietly. "The world doesn't care for the love of two people. It never has. So what are we to do when the world comes between two lovers? Stop loving? Perhaps. That is one path to walk. But it is a lonely road. Better to take your love and open it up to the whole world, the uncaring huge mass of people who are trying to live each day. Maybe then, you will find another lover. If not, at least you can still come close to that love again."

Dex closed his eyes to the burning sun. "Did Jones say that, too?"

She laughed gently. "No, they're Freedom's words. But the saint would approve, I'm sure."

"Have you ever been in love?" He asked.

She looked at him. "Yes. Many years ago, I was in love."

"What happened?"

"He died."

"I'm sorry," he offered.

"It was a long time ago, Dexter Maxwell. Not as long ago as your love," she corrected gently. "I still feel the loss, but I have found that the people around here are worth loving. I love this community, now."

"I don't feel like giving my love to the world," Dex said.

"Maybe it's not the time for that," Freedom said, standing. "Your path is a lonely one right now. You walk alone. Self-reliance makes you strong today; but not forever."

The sounds of approaching people could be heard from below. Dex could see a line of walkers and horses, a few donkeys. Were these his people? Was this who he should love? Was this his time now? His place?

Freedom looked down, too. "Come, then," she said, holding out a hand.

"Where are we going?" he asked.

"The altar room will always be there. I am thinking that you should be in the congregation this morning."

Dex listened to the cacophony of voices, and then took Freedom's hand. They went down the stairs, and walked in through the front door of the church.

One hundred three.

They rode south to a late afternoon prayloop that Freedom knew of. Being so dangerously close to Longstown seemed a risk worth taking. Dex still felt the exhilaration of the singing congregation with the steady drumbeat and the long walk back through history with the speech of the priest. Dex loved the methodical, precise dance as the sermon was winding down. It felt nothing like the church he used to go to with Jones, back in Grenver. Everyone here was engaged, was part of the process.

Even Dexter Maxwell.

As they approached the next church, Dex felt the urge to experience it again, go in through the front door, learn the dance, and be part of it all. But Freedom rode around to the back, to the locked door that led to the roof. Dex's heart sank as he realized he had other business here, that he could not lose himself among the people again.

They were sitting on the roof as the congregation began filing in. Freedom spoke of the third altar room.

"It was built as a shrine to one of our great martyrs of the 27th century, Rose Aquinas. She discovered the cosmological effect that caused the Great Schism of 2656. At the time, the Schism was viewed as God's punishment by many people. Her theories were all proven right long after she was burned at the stake for heresy."

"What is the Great Schism?" Dex asked.

"By the year 2656, time travel had been used successfully by the clerics of the church for over two centuries. It was used to gather plants and some small creatures from the past, and bring them into the present."

"Wait, you can bring people back from a shift with you?"

"Oh no, Dex. Large organisms are too complex, too much mass—that doesn't work. Only small creatures. The early clerics—they called themselves reconstitutionists—found that spiders were the most hardy for the passage."

"Got it."

"The reconstitutionists considered it God's work, repopulating the earth with lost creatures. It was part of our redemption process. But shifting was always a polarizing activity. Many in the church saw it as disobeying the punishment that God had meted out for our ignorance during the Industrialist Era. They felt that we were meddling in ways that were reminiscent of the dangerous methods of the industrialists–meddling with the natural order of things. These voices found quite a bit of popular support, and the church officially denounced time travel in 2549.

"This denunciation did not stop shifting from occurring. It continued to be practiced in this part of the world for a long time afterwards. The church did not feel compelled to put an end to it, as it was leading to a strong resurgence of faith and belief in the nomadic areas of the north. So it was tolerated for another century.

"But in 2656, something happened that still remains much of a mystery. Time travel suddenly stopped working. All the mechanisms still worked, but there was a wall. A barrier. The shifters could no longer shift back past April 29, 2656."

"What do you mean?" Dex asked. "You can't go back any farther than that?"

Freedom shook her head. "No, we still cannot. At the time, people felt that the shifting process had stopped working all together. But as more time passed, the scientists of the time realized that shifting still worked, but one just could not go back to before that date.

"Word spread quickly, and the event became known as the Great Schism, named as such by the priest Jackson Morvalis. Jackson had been a reconstitutionist, but he was visited by God, who told him that the Schism was meant to put an end to time travel, and to separate the wicked past from the righteous future."

"So what really happened?" Dex asked.

"That is what really happened," Freedom said. "Jackson was visited by God."

"Oh," Dex said.

Freedom grinned. "But what Rose Aquinas discovered, and what made her so unpopular, was how God created the Schism. She was an astronomer for the church in the southlands, and she found that the radioactive signature of Earth and the surrounding atmosphere was younger than the rest of the galaxy."

"Younger than the galaxy?" Dex asked.

"Yes. Younger. She compared her results with historical results, and found that the radioactive energy was approximately twenty-three years younger than the rest of the galaxy. And she found that this had not been the case before 2656. So, something had to have happened to the planet on that date."

"What happened?"

"No one knows for sure. Rose Aquinas theorized that there were giant waves of particles that moved out across the surface of our dimension and in turn caused minor disruptions in irregular patterns. She theorized that Earth was caught by one of these waves, which basically held the planet in place while the rest of the universe expanded for twenty-three years. Later, Earth dropped back into place."

"That seems pretty far-fetched," Dex said.

"Yes," Freedom agreed. "Its rejection of Jackson's vision of God was the far-fetched part at the time, and it earned her the mark of the heretic."

"Did anyone follow up on her theories?" Dex asked.

"No. The reconstitutionists were falling apart and going their separate ways. This was the time of the great literacy battles of the northlands. Books were being destroyed and libraries burned to the ground. Ancient technologies that preserved data were being thrown aside. And the scientific nature of Rose Aquinas' studies could not be accurately followed up. But it is widely accepted that her theory of some cosmic event is correct. Something froze time on this planet for twenty-three years, while the rest of the galaxy continued to age."

"On Venus they referred to the year as 3049."

"Right—since we found out about the humans still living on Venus, Lynia and I have long speculated how the cosmic event was experienced elsewhere in the galaxy. Venus is roughly twenty-three years older than we are. And the effect of the Schism on time travel was to cause our shifting prayloops to malfunction at that date."

"I don't see how that can be," Dex said, lost in thought. "It's not like the shift necessarily exists on Earth. There's no place to it all, not to the anchor point in the past."

"The problem lies in creating the breach point at the anchor. The Knife cannot perform its dance. It hits the brane for reentry and shatters. The pattern unravels."

Dex was seeing it in his head. "If the pattern unravels, how does the Flyer re-rope and pull the shifter back to the present?"

"It does not come back."

"You mean..."

"Yes. The shifter is lost forever."

"*Crackpipe.* Burned at the surface, like in my nightmares."

"You can see why the Schism was so controversial. Shifters had not been lost outside of our dimensions since the very first experiments. Many good people were lost before the Schism was discovered."

Dex looked uneasily at the hatch to the shifting room. Freedom caught his glance and smiled reassuringly. "Do not worry. It is safe, as long as you do not try to anchor any deeper than the Schism date."

"April 29, 2656, right?"

"Correct. Try to remember that," Freedom confirmed and opened the hatch.

"I'll try."

"Good. Time for the third altar room."

Dex looked longingly at the people filing into the church below. "I want to be down there," he said.

"You can go anytime you like," Freedom said. "But you have work today."

Dex looked down one more time, and then turned and lowered himself through the hatch.

One hundred four.

The third altar room had similarities to the first and second rooms, but it was substantially larger. Dex found himself lying on a cool, polished stone floor again, a dim light reflecting sharply into his eyes. Compared with the bitter cold of October north of Longstown, the air here was humid and warm. He slowly worked the patterns back into the recesses of his brain and out of his vision, and pushed the gravity of the knives into the background. The Halo danced across the inside of his eyes then disappeared.

The room seemed to have the size of a football arena. Above his head, the ceiling formed large, looping patterns, but nothing specific. But as he looked up, the patterns in his head unspooled and flitted into the larger patterns, making new ones. *The ceiling of this room is merely a template.*

More importantly, as he walked, he saw a thousand twinkles of light. He thought he could make out shards of glass hanging down, nearly undetectable in the low light. Even as he watched, he saw a ray of light enter the room, from what could only be the sun. As the light grew, he saw the shards of glass lowering, slowly. At the same time, he felt something cold at his feet. He looked down, and noticed an inch of water licking at his feet.

It took him some time to realize that the lowering glass and the rising water were part of the same contraption. As the water rose, the shards came down. And as the shards came down, Dex felt the patterns in his head begin to dart around, looking for a way out. He started to make new shapes, new patterns. A new math began to take form. He gave it a try, and the drag of the knives at his back diminished.

He smiled at the relief. *What else is here? Something is still missing.* He began to walk across the huge expanse again, looking up, and also looking down at the reflection of the glass patterned onto the slowly lapping water, now at his shins.

All of a sudden he found the parameter patterns. They showed him how he could scroll through the leaves, looking deeper, peering through the millisecond nothings of time. He found a way to look based on the idea of a person, or a particular time, or a space. The power of choosing the shift overwhelmed Dex. It was also exhilarating; he could not get enough of it. Every time the knives began pulling at him, he would modify the Holder, as he had named it, and could get a few more hours.

He lasted the entire day through the tides of the water. Finally, his brain was too full of new ideas to take anymore. He succumbed to the knives at his back, and felt the pull, the distancing, and the hot burning surface waiting to eat him.

But he did not fear it this time. Never would he fear it again.

One hundred five.

He was breathing heavily, lying on his back in the complete darkness of the shifting room, when he felt a cool hand across his mouth.

"It is Freedom," a voice whispered. She was so close Dex could feel her breath on his ear. "There are strangers in the church."

Dex removed her hand, and quietly rolled onto his knees. "How long?" He reached over his shoulder to feel the reassuring hilt of Judas.

"Only a few minutes," Freedom hissed. "They are not speaking Cawlrinian."

Dex crawled to one of the break-away sections of the floor, and put his ear to the slit. It wasn't long before he heard a murmur.

"Heah, they's finds a way upstairs yet, eh?"

"Nothin seem to open from down here. It's must be th' locked hatch on th' roof."

"You's think he's is really up there?"

"Heah. Must be looped though. I's have not heards a sound."

Dex sat up. He reached out and found Freedom's leg. He leaned in toward her and whispered, "Off-landers. From Venus."

He could hear her sharp intake of breath. And like that, the moment began to slow down. He could feel the moment jacking.

"Dex, there is no way out of here but the hatch," Freedom whispered.

"How do these floorboards release?" he asked.

"It is a function of the prayloop that is triggered by the priest below. There is no way from here to open them. I think–"

Freedom was cut off by the sound of someone kicking at the hatch door above their heads, and the sound of wood cracking. Dex stood, pulling her up with him. At the next kick, the hatch door shattered. He pushed Freedom back and away, and covered his head. The wood struck his arm as he pulled Judas from its sheath. Dex took a short leap back, telescoping his sword to its full length.

At this instant, the attacker landed, swinging his own blade.

Dex was parrying the blow with Judas. In the slowed down time of the jacked moment, he noted how little light shone through from the hatch door. The attacker was bringing the blade low and even, and all Dex could do was block.

But then he started spinning, just as a second attacker landed in the room. Dex caught him in the leg as he braced for impact, slicing just enough to cause the attacker to put all his weight on the other foot. The weight of the shift rolled the ankle with a crack and the attacker fell. Dex put Judas through his heart as he leaped away from the first attacker, who made a quick slash at him that nearly caught his right arm.

As Dex pulled his sword out of the dead attacker's chest, there was a momentary computer blip, and the limp body sizzled into a bright pinpoint of nothingness. In the flash of light, Dex saw Freedom huddled in a corner of the octagonal room. There were two assassins circling him now.

Threes. They always come in threes. Dex's heart sunk at the thought of more Red Masks. How many more would there be this time?

He didn't have time to consider, as the two assassins attacked simultaneously. Dex felt the attack, knew how they would be positioned. He parried one blade, and then the other, throwing his weight back so that he jumped a few feet, and felt his back against the wall. He swung at the one to his left, pushing him away. Dex found the corner of the octagon and used the angles to walk up the wall a few feet and hurl himself backward, flipping.

He caught the attacker to the right across the shoulder, tearing through skin and breaking the collarbone. The impact knocked the assailant to his knees. Dex landed facing the attacker's back, and put the blade through his brainstem. The same blip came once again, and then the attacker disappeared.

They are from the future. When they die, they fall back through their breach.

He sensed the next attack, and threw Judas behind him, as if putting the sword away in his scabbard. The clang knocked Dex forward, where the first assailant was coming at him. Dex should have rolled forward, or turned to attack. He could tell it was what the assassin expected. *They are trained too simply. They only think to kill.*

Instead, Dex side-stepped, moving away from the assailant, keeping Judas at a defensive down-angle. The assassin paused, just for a fraction of a second, and then attacked again. Dex easily parried, waiting. The assassin felt the waiting, felt Dex holding back, and increased his attacks, swinging in quick bursts. Dex blocked, and stepped away again.

He saw the block of light from the sky darken again, followed by the sound of feet landing. Three more assassins. The lone assassin was now relentless in his attacks, pushing Dex back toward a wall, trying to pin him. He was keeping his strokes arrhythmic, but still Dex waited. Sooner or later, he would run out of moves and slip into a training sequence. Dex could feel it. It was as if he had trained these assassins himself, the way they were attacking. He could sense it. So he played out the training defense.

And then the moment came, and he dropped his pretense, dodged left and put Judas through the man's neck. The assassin winked out before Dex could pull his sword from the body.

He closed his eyes and felt the air around him. Then he did something that made sense even before he knew why. He unspooled the patterns of the altar room that were dancing across his darkened vision. The Flyer and the Rope moved at his command, providing a map of the dimensions around him. He put the Rock down and pulled the Halo tight. He could hear the rustle of the three assassins, looking for their attack. They had night vision apparatus, Dex could tell from the way they moved. They could see him.

But now, he had them in his patterns.

From below in the church, Dex heard some commands being shouted out. There were more people down there. The echo of footsteps signaled five, no, six soldiers below.

Dex felt it before it came. With a quick motion, an assassin swung his sword low. The second assassin brought his sword high, eliminating an escape route. Dex jumped, springing into a tight lengthwise spin as the two swords swung over him and under him. He stuck his blade out and caught one in the gut while he kicked the second. The three of them fell to the ground.

Dex gave a kick, and connected with the knee of the assassin. He used the force to push himself upright, and throw the momentum into an attack at the single standing assassin, who had brought his sword down heavily. Blocking it, Dex was knocked off balance. He rolled into the fall, landing on the wounded assassin who grabbed at his face and hair, trying to pin him. Dex jabbed his two fingers through the assassin's exposed eyes. He barely dodged the next attack, the assassin's sword tearing his thigh open. Dex swung Judas past the attack, letting the sword bite deeper into his own flesh as he sheared the man's head off. The blade disappeared from his leg as the shifting device pulled it back to whatever future it had come from.

Dex did not stop moving, and was quickly at the third assassin, pushing, staying out of rhythm, lining up attacks the assassin did not have answers for. Soon, Dex exploited a tendency in the attacker's defense and lopped his arm off. The assassin cried out, but Judas found a way into his heart. With a mild blip the assassin was gone.

Dex took huge gasps of air, trying to get his body under control. His thigh throbbed. There was more yelling from below. "Freedom," Dex said. "Are you okay?"

"Yes," Freedom said quietly, from the other side of the room. "What just happened? I can see nothing."

"Ashion's Red Masks," Dex told her. "They are dead. But there will be three more."

"How do you know?"

"Three times three," he said.

"How did they find us?" Freedom whispered and he could hear the fear in her voice.

"Shh," Dex said. Much of the shouting had stopped now. There was no localized grouping of voices in a single place. Dex tried to visualize the space below him. They were at the priest's altar, near the front of the church.

"Freedom, stay back against the wall." Dex unspooled the Knife, saw it dance off the walls as it blinked into shape. The floor drop-outs came into view, and Dex stepped onto one.

He heard the shout, "Gots it!" before the floor pattern dropped out.

Dex fell straight down ten feet, right into the middle of six men dressed no differently than the congregation that had so welcomed him the day before. But he saw the bolt guns slung over their shoulders.

Dex had five of them dead before they could get to their guns. The last soldier tried to aim his weapon, but Dex knocked it out of his hands with a single flat slap of Judas. The soldier backed away desperately, reaching for an interface that was strapped to his right arm, and began keying.

Dex cut the man's left hand off at the wrist, so he could not operate the interface. The man screamed, grasping at his bloody stump.

"How many more of you?" Dex asked calmly, Judas' point drawing blood at the man's throat.

"Six assassins, up top," the man said with a whimper.

"How many soldiers?" Dex demanded.

"Just sixes, heah."

"Try again," Dex said, putting pressure on the blade. The man gasped.

"That's is it! I's straight wit you!"

"Red Masks come in threes. No way there's only six."

"Heah, only six," the man said, shaking his head at the news himself. "Not many to spare, eh." He was shaking now, holding at his bleeding arm. Dex saw him going pale.

"When are you from?" he asked.

"3049," the man said through clenched teeth.

"A little more precise," Dex was putting more pressure on the blade. "In Earth time."

The man closed his eyes, shivering in pain. "Heah, sure, it's is October 16, I's think. Only a few days forward."

Dex nodded. "That's better." Then he put Judas through the soldier's heart.

"No!" He heard Freedom scream out. She was leaning over the opening, a look of complete horror on her face. Tears streamed down her face.

Dex turned back and watched as the soldier blinked into his breach.

"No survivors," Dex wiped blood speckles from his face. He turned and walked out of the church. He had just made it past the doorstop when the vertigo overwhelmed him. He heaved on the ground until there was nothing left in his stomach.

Dex sat on the low rock, staring as the western sky darkened to a dull pink. There were clouds building, and the wind was blowing down from the mountains. He preferred to face into the setting sun and feel the cold wind. The taste of his own vomit was finally receding. The blood all over his clothes was drying to a damning brown. *Why didn't the blood travel back with the bodies?*

A hand came down gently on his shoulder, and Dex looked up. It was Freedom, gazing westward as well. Dex turned away.

"I am sorry," Freedom said. "I have only seen death once before."

Dex sat quietly for a moment. "I couldn't let anyone go back alive."

"I know."

"I'm sorry, too."

"I know."

They watched the sunset in silence. Dex did not want her to ever take her reassuring hand from his shoulder. He felt like he might collapse if she did.

"Was anyone from the congregation hurt?" Dex asked.

"A few black eyes and a lot of frayed nerves," Freedom said. "Nothing else."

"I'm thankful for that. I don't want them to be in danger."

"Come, Dexter," She said. "We have been discovered. We must go on with our work."

"Why bother?" He asked. "They were from the future. They can just send more."

"Yes, they can," Freedom agreed. "But they haven't, now have they?"

Dex looked around. "Not yet."

"And I wonder why not?" She continued. "We have been discovered, but the discovery may be limited. They know where we are today, but they did not know where we were yesterday, did they?"

"I guess not."

"They would have attacked us if they knew where our yesterday could be found. Perhaps they will be waiting for us where we go today. But we will not know that until we get there."

"That doesn't really give me much hope," Dex said.

"On the contrary. This attack gives me much to hope for," Freedom replied.

Dex looked up at her. "How so?"

"A small attack by a small group," she pointed out. "From only a few days in the future. They use shifting for an attack, but events unfold almost in real time. It feels like a desperate act to me, in sense that it did not guarantee success. Instead of eliminating you, they have alerted you to their knowledge of your presence."

Dex's head was spinning. But he felt some of the logic. "They *were* a desperate little group," he said. "Sword fighters like the ones in the shifting space typically come in threes–three groups of three or three by three by three. Six doesn't fall in line with their mode of attack. Plus, they were..." Dex trailed off. "I don't know. They were good, but they seemed unseasoned. Rookies. Fresh out of training. They had skill, but no real experience."

"You see?" Freedom said. "Perhaps we are winning in the future."

Dex smiled. "That's one way to look at it."

"Do not discount the possibility that the future may not be as bad as it appears," Freedom said.

"Enough with the Jones quotes!" he cried.

"You mean *Saint Brodius*," she said.

Dex gave a look of mock disgust. "Don't make me puke again"

"Come. There is an early morning loop not far from here."

One hundred seven.

Dex was walking around the perimeter of the octagonal roof, keeping his eyes open. But as the congregation began their dance, and the drums fired up, no one approached. Freedom gave him a sideways glance.

"Are you going down, or not?" she indicated at the hatch door.

"Yes," Dex said. "I'm just worried about you, up here alone."

"Dex, get in that hole!" Freedom demanded. "You have no more time to fret!"

Dex smiled. "I have all the time in the world."

"Do not play. There is much for you to remember."

"I know what I have to do," Dex replied.

"Remember what I told you about the anchors," Freedom said, glancing nervously down the hatch. The drumming and chanting were getting louder, faster, more imminent.

"I remember," Dex promised, scanning the horizon.

"No tampering with the events of the past," Freedom repeated for what must have been the hundredth time.

"I don't get it," Dex said. "You suspect that these guys have been tampering with your ancestors, and you don't want me to do anything?"

"Dex, if you reveal yourself to an off-lander in the distant past, you could endanger everything. Remember, those you seek could have their present in our past, giving them ample time to prepare for us."

"But if they discovered me in the past, it's too late to do anything about it, right? It already happened."

"The inevitability of the past does not mean you will not affect the future," Freedom said.

"Yeah, I didn't really get that," Dex said.

"You must accept the fact that you will be making history while you are there, not looking back upon it from the present."

"Still not following you."

Freedom rolled her eyes. "Just stay out of the way, please? Learn what you can, be discreet, and come back with any information." The drums and chanting of the prayloop hit its apex.

"Tell me again about the Dragging Dagger," Dex said.

"You will be using the anchor of the off-landers to guide you, and if you go through the same breach, you will literally be right on top of them. So, use the Dragging Dagger pattern. It keeps the anchor line open but uses the natural brane expansion of our time-like curve to put you through the breach a few minutes later. It can also be used to drag the space, put you a few feet away."

"Got it," Dex said. "Dragging Dagger. Try not to trip over the bad guys. What was the part about my brain expanding?"

"Go! Now!" Freedom cried.

Dex gave her a mischievous grin and jumped down into the hole, unspooling the patterns as he fell. The prayloop reached the steady beat of the breach dance. He didn't feel the floor, as the window slits opened and the floor dropped out. In that moment he pushed his parameters out, pulling the Rope tight, and haloing through the breach.

The crystal shards appeared around him, and he could see the reflection of the water in the third altar room across the burning surface. The Clasp unraveled into a thousand clasps across the map, and Dex could feel the leaves of time piling up around him. He felt the Ocean pattern spring out like a thrown net, a huge shifting grid that encompassed his entire vision, lapping at the burning surface. The leaves of time settled onto the Ocean's shifting grid, and the gravity of a hundred different anchor lines pulled immediately at him, biting at his mind.

Dex did not expect the struggle. On impulse, he resisted the tug of the first anchor lines that grappled with the Flyer. But he lost his grip on the Rope, and the Flyer dovetailed into a grid cross-point at an anchor line. Dex felt the nothingness of the moment, as it took shape in his new parameter pattern, coming into focus.

Year 2913. Winter. Waning moon. January. Seventh day of the month, late at night. Just past midnight. Seven minutes past midnight. Seven minutes thirty three seconds.

The precision was narrowing and grew sharper and sharper, until the Knife was at its finest, instantly dropping into a thousand million knifes on the surface, at the same breach point as the off-lander shifter had lain down before him.

Dex pulled the Dragging Dagger from its sheath and unspooled the pattern across the knives as he fell into them. The pain was the same, but it did not pass. The drag kept him at the point of annihilation, the cuts burning at every point of his body. Dex tried to scream with the agony of the delay as the Dagger kept the pressure down and the breach open, the world below him.

But he was unable to pass through and the dream started to overwhelm him. He tried to reorganize, to push himself across the barrier and rebuild the dancing particles on the other side, but the Dragging Dagger kept him imprisoned. Dex felt himself zooming at a million miles an hour, a speed that blinded even the patterns that had been with him for days.

One hundred eight.

He was lying on cold stone, staring up at a single burning sconce. The patterns bounced around as though angered by the dragging. Dex closed his eyes, pushing the Rock's gravity back, and taking control of his patterns. It only took a few moments before he could stand. The memory of the pain was everywhere he looked, but he focused on the walls, the darkened windows, the cold air in his lungs.

The newly established master code in his head gave him the details of his space and time. He felt the two minutes of the drag since the last shifter had entered through this breach. Two minutes—that was all. Dex shook his head, wondering if he could bring himself to do the Dragging Dagger again.

He went through the open door in front of him, walking quietly, keeping his eyes open. The recent shift, and the impending danger of being discovered, gave him a taste of high jack. Dex felt a momentary vertigo, and remembered the stealth ways of his assassin training. He modified his steps, and his breathing, and quietly looked around. *If I were here on an assassination, I would head toward heat.* Where there was heat, there would be humans. He put his hands on the walls, and walked soundlessly, feeling for ambient heat. When he found it, he crouched low, staying in the shadows.

Dex was almost on top of the man before he checked himself, and took a few steps back, behind a corner. The man was bent in a narrow corridor, peering through an open door into the flickering light of a fire. Dex could hear the murmur of voices. The shifter was small-framed, with his hair pulled back tight into a pony-tail at the nape of his neck. He wore a thin goatee that ran from his lower lip down to his chin in a line about the width of a finger. In the shadows, Dex could make out the shape of a sword sheathed on the man's back.

The man quietly inched the door open and slinked through. As he walked into the light, Dex saw the tight-fitting black clothing of a Red Mask, and his heart rate jumped.

He crept up to the door, and looked through. The Red Mask had moved into the shadow cast inside a large cross carved into the stone wall. The shifter was looking down toward the source of the light, into the round pit below, about twenty feet across. Dex could not see into the pit, but he heard the voices of two men.

"Is there no word from your informant?" a gentle voice asked.

The other voice growled and bellowed back, "Nothing. I fear my informant's informing tends in the other direction."

"Oh dear."

"Indeed. I am left with few I can trust, Humility."

"You can always trust the Order, my King."

"I know. This is why I am here. But I fear that I am not the real target."

"The queen?"

"No. I think they are after Mebda."

"Sweet mercy."

"I did not bring him with me. He travels separately, to a different location."

"He is not here?"

"No, I brought the infant son of my trusted advisor, who looks like Mebda. My son is enjoying the life of a commoner in Longstown tonight."

"A good ploy, sire."

"I envy him the opportunity to escape."

"The road of a true leader is beset by all the dangers man can invent."

"Did Brodius say that?"

"Of course, sire."

"That's a smart saint of yours, Humility."

"He would say that he is not smart, just a good listener."

"Being a good listener is tougher than it sounds."

"I believe you could also use another lesson from the unburned diaries, sire."

"I'm all ears tonight."

"When the first attempt on Brodius' life failed, his followers begged and pleaded with him to go into the great underground pipes that existed under the metropolis. But Brodius only smiled, and sat back down at his crumbling house. He said, 'What good would it do to hide? So that they can kill me secretly? If I am to die, I would rather die out here, surrounded by friends, sitting in a comfortable chair.' And he did not go into hiding."

The king laughed. "A comfortable chair? He said that?"

"Yes, sire. Saint Brodius liked a good chair."

"I understand what you are telling me, Humility, and rest assured that I will not back down. If they want to attack me and my family, it will not affect the strength of this kingdom."

"You are a good leader, Chardwin."

"And your chairs are far too comfortable. With that fire roaring, I am falling asleep over here."

"A legacy of our patron saint, sire."

Both men laughed, and Dex could tell they were rising to leave. When a door closed with a boom, the shifter stepped out of the shadows and down into the pit. Dex slipped inside, into the vacated corner. He could now see two chairs facing a large fireplace that roared with huge, carbonizing logs. The shifter was warming himself, staring into the flames. Then, he pulled back the sleeve of his loose black smock to reveal a portable interface affixed to his forearm. He used his right hand to click a few buttons, before he raised it to his mouth.

"Quantloop broadcast for Earth-time one dot three zero six nine dot twenty-three oh seven," he whispered in a low growl. "Heah, Chardwin squattin at Brody church in Brandstown. He's is tall on th' threat to Mebda, eh. Puts th' child in hidin, eh. So I's not gots anybody to end this time. It's is best to rethink havin locals do work of us assassins, eh. Failure led to tip-off of the king."

Suddenly there was a click, and Dex watched the Red Mask type something else into his interface. With it, the assassin blipped into his breach. Dex felt the pull of his anchor, and his Flyer stretched out automatically into the breach point. It took all of his concentration to pull away from the spiraling gravity. But he had to let go of the Rope eventually and was pulled back through his own breach.

One hundred nine.

Dex was surprised to find the heavy heat of the prayloop still emanating from beneath him upon his return. He had not been gone for very long, but he had never returned to a prayloop still in session. He waited, looking down into the church, as the dancers made their loops, the chanters raised their voices in time, and the drummers pounded out their maddened beat. Slowly it began to dissipate and he could feel the energy of the drums and the chanters' voices ebbing. And then it was over. The congregation were laughing and looking for water to drink, wiping the sweat from their faces and necks. Dex ached to be part of them.

Instead, he crawled up the ladder to the roof of the church. As he pulled himself from the hatch, he looked around for Freedom. She was nowhere to be seen.

But Mal was there.

Dex blinked. But she was still there, sitting on the parapets of the edge of the church roof. She smiled at him.

"Hey, Dex."

"Hey, Mal," he said. "I mean, Lynia."

She twinkled. "It's just the two of us. Freedom went for the horses."

Dex closed the hatch. "What are you doing here? I thought we could only meet in the past."

"I have new work to do," she said. "How's the anchor search going?"

"Good, I guess. I just got started."

"Are you getting used to all this church stuff, yet?" Mal asked.

He shrugged. "It's not like the churches of our time."

"No, it's not," she agreed with a smile. "Do you listen?"

"Sometimes. They talk about Brodie a lot. It reminds me of Grenver, of home."

"Me too." She took Dex's hand and gave it a squeeze. "You are

352

your past, Dex. The past has shaped you. But, like Jones would say, don't be afraid of your future."

"I'm not afraid. Not anymore. Confused, but not afraid."

"Are you ready to fight for these people?"

"I think so."

"I'm glad to hear that. We've worked very hard to get to a point where we have a fighting chance."

"A chance for what?"

"A chance to pick the future. Live it as we see fit."

"Speaking of the future, we were attacked yesterday."

"I heard. Red Masks."

"Yeah. Freaked me out. But I think it freaked out Freedom even more."

"Yes. But you are safe now."

"How do you figure?" Dex wanted to know.

"They are running out of time," Mal said with a small grin.

"What do you mean?"

"It's complicated. But the bottom line is that the off-landers are running out of a future in which they can try to comprehend the past."

"Why? Because we win?" Dex asked.

Mal shrugged. "We don't know that yet. Maybe it's because we lose and they have no more need for the past."

"I don't like that version."

"Me neither," Mal said. They were quiet for a moment, before she continued. "I have to go away for a while, Dex. I won't be able to see you for a few weeks."

Dex nodded. "Has something come up?"

She winked. "Secret agent stuff, and all that. Just keep plugging away at your investigation, okay? Don't set up a routine as to which churches you use for the prayloop, and you will be safe."

"Okay."

Mal was already headed for the stairwell when she stopped and turned back. "When I was pulled off ice, up on Venus, I still had my baby inside me," she said matter-of-factly. Dex looked up at her. "I wasn't sent to the asteroid mines right away. I was put into a small cell, with decent food and water and a little exercise. They let me have my baby. A girl." Dex could see the tears welling up in her eyes, but she continued in an even tone. "I was allowed to see her a few times each day, breast-feeding her and helping her sleep. That lasted for about three months. Then I was sent to the asteroid mines, and I never saw her again."

Dex felt his stomach churning. "I'm so sorry, Mal."

She gave a grim smile. "It's okay. It was a long time ago. I just thought you should know."

"What do you think they... What happened to her?" Dex asked.

"I'm not enough of a masochist to think about that," Mal said.

He said nothing, just staring out toward the bright noon sun hitting the distant mountains. When he looked back at Mal, there were tears in his eyes. "Thank you," he whispered.

Mal nodded resolutely. "Be safe. See you in your future." Then she was gone.

One hundred ten.

Freedom and Dex rode side by side on horseback, headed for the next prayloop. Freedom was talking excitedly.

"The congregation just keeps going and going," she said, gesticulating with her free hand. "They can feel the energy of the shift. It buzzes through everyone, provides them with a connection to the divine. We have not had a shifter in these parts for a very long time. The priests tell me they are being asked to schedule more and more loops." She whistled. "I bet King Mastiff is beside himself, watching his people grow closer to God, instead of farther away."

Dex said nothing.

"Do you want to talk about it?" Freedom asked suddenly.

"About what?" he replied.

"Whatever it is that Lynia has said to you and has sent you back inside yourself."

Dex shook his head.

"Then let us discuss your investigation instead," Freedom said.

Dex detailed all that he had heard and seen at the monastery. She listened carefully, her brow furrowed. When he finished, they were silent for some time, staring eastward as they rode.

"Chardwin was king here, in the last century. He fathered two sons, Jorgan, the older, and Mebda, the younger. Jorgan was lost to the spottled plague of 2909. Mebda went on to become king after his father. He reigned until only ten years ago, when he was struck with a kind of madness during a visit to the papal seat, and never returned to his kingdom. Mastiff rose to power soon after that." She finally explained.

"Mebda is a familiar name to me. Rolink, the goatherder I was imprisoned with, he had a son named Mebda. After the king."

"He was a popular ruler," Freedom agreed. "There are many Mebda's now."

"Why do you think the Red Mask was after Chardwin's son?" Dex asked.

"I do not know," Freedom admitted. "We have long suspected off-landers of trying to hurt the church. Perhaps their scope was larger than we realized, if they have involved themselves in the rise and fall of kings. I must think about this a while longer."

"It sounded like Charwin got tipped off," Dex said. "That's probably why Mebda even made it to adulthood."

"You should pursue this thread in your investigation," Freedom decided. "Humility was one of our great spiritual leaders. He was working toward bringing the Amrikans back into peace with the southern papacy. His disappearance in 2919 was a devastating blow to our search for unity."

"So where do you want me to go next?" Dex asked. "I think this time I'll be able to better control which anchor I follow."

"Follow Prince Mebda," Freedom said. "That might lead to an illumination of where this conspiracy is headed."

"There's one more thing," Dex said. "When the Red Mask shifted back, I felt like I was being pulled into his breach."

Freedom gave him a look. "Whatever you do, Dexter, do not allow yourself to go through that return breach."

"Why? What will happen?"

"You will lose your own anchor and become unattached. Lose your Flyer."

"I would get lost outside."

"Yes. Unable to get back across the energy barrier, you would burn up and die."

"Right. Don't follow the shifters through their breaches. Check."

"There is our next prayloop," Freedom pointed up on a bluff. "We must hurry. The congregation has already assembled."

They put their horses to a trot, and soon Dex found himself inside a shifting room again, running through the patterns as they flitted around. The windows flew open, the light shone in, and the floor dropped out.

This time he was able to better manipulate the Ocean pattern and pull up the anchor line more accurately. He hesitated, but finally dropped the Dagger, and despite the vertigo he held on for a bit longer, feeling the burn, before the annihilation dropped him through the anchor he had latched.

SOUTHSANDS ROAD, SANJOSE VALLEY, JUNE 14, 2909. DAY 25.

One hundred eleven.

Dex was lying in a ditch, gathering his patterns and pushing them back into place. The night air was unseasonably cool for June. It was the summer of 2909, four years before his last visit to the past. As the patterns retreated from his vision, he remembered the physical distance. He was far to the south of the church from which he had shifted. The distance pulled harder at the Rope to his back. It felt as if he was being stretched.

He crawled to the edge of the ditch, and scanned the area. He was next to a wide, well-worn road, winding its way north to south. By the light of the moon, Dex could see the deep grooves of horse carts. The mud hinted at recent rain, and he saw the dissolving clouds to the east. Just a few hundred feet north up the road, there was a crossroads, marked only by a large cairn. The east and west branches did not look as well ridden, and quickly disappeared into the brush. But he could see the north-bound road being swallowed up by the low foothills of an arid mountain range he did not recognize.

As he watched the road, he saw a glint of light come up over an invisible crest, and then disappear back down behind a bluff. Dex squinted and saw two small twinkles of light reappear, dancing in the distance. Then they were gone again. Dex tried not to blink, watching to see if he could make out what it was.

In the forefront, he saw a shadow emerge from the ditch just a stone's throw in front of him. It crossed the road and the disappeared on the other side. Dex flattened himself even lower. He recognized the black on black clothing, and knew he'd found his target. He watched the spot where the shifter had disappeared into the underbrush, trying to discern where he may have gone. But Dex could not see anything, so he decided to stay put.

In a few short minutes, the twinkling light of the distance made itself clear. Two horse-drawn carriages, with lanterns held high, were making quick time up and down the rolling hills of the plain heading south out of the foothills. As they approached the crossroads, the carriages slowed, and the first one turned to head east. The second, slowed by the turn of the first, quickly began to pick up speed again and headed on southward. The first carriage followed the east road as it led into the brush that lay behind Dex.

The second carriage was picking up full speed toward Dex. It was led by two horses, and there was a driver sitting at the front. Just after the first carriage disappeared from view into the hills, the shifter stood up, with some device in his arms. There was a quiet whooshing sound and Dex saw the driver of the carriage fly off the side and into the dirt of the road. Dex thought of the energy guns on Venus, and knew what had happened.

The unmanned horses powered on toward him, although they were slowing down. He felt an instinct to jump up and help out, but then a second shadow jumped from the ditch, just a few yards away. The figure leaped onto the carriage, pulling the reins and stopping the horses just short of Dex. He watched as the first Red Mask went quickly to the slumped driver on the road. There was a flash of moonlight reflected from a blade before the Red Mask ran up to meet the stopped carriage.

"Dunner?" asked a nervous voice from within the carriage. "Dunner, why have we stopped?"

The Red Mask put the reins down, turned and jumped to throw the door open. With a single motion, he reached in and pulled whoever was inside out onto the road with a cry. Dex felt too close to the action for safety. By the light of the swinging lantern of the carriage, he could see the panicked look on the man's face as he tried to stand. The Red Mask jumped down, grabbed the man by the robes on his back and swung him face first into the large wheel of the carriage. The impact knocked the man onto his backside, stunned, and covered in mud.

"Wh-where is Dunner?" the man asked.

"My colleague has most likely stuck a sword through his heart," the Red Mask said.

Dex thought he recognized the voice, but he could not see the shifter's face. The second Red Mask was finally at the carriage, breathing heavily.

"Heah, th' driver is ended," he said.

"Do you hear that, old man?" The first shifter said, slapping the sitting man hard on the back of the head. "My colleague just ended your driver."

"What do you want?" the man asked, trying to turn. But the second knight gave him a kick in the kidney that sent him sprawling in the mud again, gasping for breath. Dex caught a look at him and recognized the dark skin, the thin goatee, the straight black hair. The same shifter as last time.

"Careful, Tano," the first shifter said. "We still need a few things from him."

"Heah, you's hurry then."

Just then, the first shifter turned toward the light, and Dex saw his face. It nearly took his breath away.

Dex was looking at himself.

One hundred twelve.

There was no mistaking the face. It was Dexter Maxwell, looking down with a slight frown at the old man, who was groveling on his knees. The hair was cut very short, and he was very muscular, but it was still Dex.

"I have nothing," the man on the ground said, staring down into the mud. "I am a man of God. I have no riches."

"That is true, you are very poor. We bankrupted the Order back in... when was it?"

"2850, gives or takes," Tano said without smiling. He was checking something on his wrist. Dex could see the slight glow of his interface. "Heah, others have arrived, eh. They's gonna overtake th' Order in seven minutes, eh."

The other Dexter just stared down at the man and gave him a kick as he tried to turn around.

"Heah, Ash, what you's want, I's should go?" Tano said.

It was Ashion. Not me. A rush of relief flowed through Dex.

"Yes, sorry, Tano," Ashion said, shaking his head. "I was just thinking how much more fun I am having than my colleagues. Take

359

the horse, you should reach them soon."

Tano looked at the man, lying on his side in the mud, moaning. "You's sure you's don't want I's shoulds end this one?"

"No, Tano," Ashion said, patting him on the shoulder. "I have questions for this one. Now go."

With that, Tano had cut the reins and freed a horse, galloping back toward the crossroads. Ashion watched him go, then pulled his shirt sleeve back to key madly at the interface strapped to his forearm.

"What are you doing? What do you want?" the man asked. He had pulled himself around, sitting with his back against the carriage wheel.

"I am turning off my quantloop connection," Ashion said, still typing. "See, messing with the past is rather tricky. Cause and effect, timeline inevitability postulates, you name it. The only way to know if what you are doing is having the right effect is to trap the altered future data and send it across the brane barrier. When the data comes back, we can do some extensive comparative analysis to see if it worked."

"I don't understand," the man babbled, "What has that got to do with—"

"No matter," Ashion said, waving his hand dramatically. Dex cringed. Where did he pick up that? "I was just talking to myself. It's all so new; I have to keep it all in my head. Really experimental stuff here, you know?"

Ashion pulled a long knife from his belt, and checked the edge against the moonlight. "Now, for what I am going to do to you," he started, "I don't want a quantloop record. I'm not concerned about the consequences."

The man tried to flee, but Ashion quickly grabbed him by the ankle and with one quick movement had stabbed him in the foot. The man screamed in pain. Ashion pulled him out to the middle of the road and let go.

"Where are you headed?" Ashion asked. But the man just held his leg and cried. "You can answer or I can stab you again."

"To see the pontiff," came the reply.

"Yes, of course. But this late? Surely the pontiff knows these roads are dangerous at night. You never know who you'll run into."

"It is for the blessing of the prince," the man cried.

"Interesting," Ashion said, walking in a slow circle around the bleeding man. "But if I'm not mistaken, the prince and his mother just headed east on the Broadboar Trail. There's no way that trail leads to the pontiff in Nicaragua." In one quick motion, Ashion was down at the man's face, his knee on his chest, the knife pointed at his eye.

"No more games, godman," he threatened in a growl. "Where is the queen headed by the cover of night?"

"Have mercy, I am on God's business, nothing more," the man pleaded.

Ashion looked at him. "Did it ever cross your mind that maybe I am God?" And then the knife was in the monk's eye and out again.

It took everything in Dex's strength not to jump up and stab the shifter in the back. It would be so easy, just to end all this, put Judas through Ashion's brainstem.

Do not tamper with the events of the past. Freedom's voice echoed around his head. *Say you step in and save someone, but what then? They just kill them the next day. Say you slay the off-lander. They can just send another. You must separate yourself from the events. Watch. Nothing more.*

The monk writhed in agony as Ashion used the man's own robes to wipe his bloody face.

"Settle down," Ashion said calmly. "Settle. Down." He grabbed the man by the jaw, holding his face in place. "Look at me. See? You still have one eye. And both ears. So listen very carefully to the question: where is the queen headed by the cover of night?"

"She goes to collect her child!" the monk surrendered.

"Come again?" Ashion asked.

"Emperor Balasari and King Chardwin traded their first-born sons at birth as a pact of unity and trust," the man explained through gritted teeth.

Ashion stood and slapped his hands together. "That's it! See how easy that was?" Then he keyed into his forearm madly. "Tano, you there?"

Dex could hear a distant crackle from Ashion's ear.

"Listen. Cancel the strike on the queen's carriage. No. Yes. Cancel it. It's Balasari's kid. No. Why would I make that up? No. Seems

361

the king and the emperor had plans for a unified kingdom long before we suspected, so they swapped their princes as a show of trust. Get the hit stopped. Now." There was a pause as Ashion stood, listening for something. The monk had his hands over his eye, trying to stop the bleeding. After another crackle, Ashion perked up. "Yes? Did you stop them in time? Excellent! Now listen, here's how it's going to go down. Let the queen return the child. We'll inject the virus at the emperor's palace say yesterday, or the day before. Chances are, the kid is already sick." Ashion smiled. "I know. It still messes me up, too. Get everyone back home, Tano."

Dex was trying to make sense of it, but he needed Freedom for that.

Ashion turned back to the monk. "Now, what do you call yourself, again?"

"Decency," the monk said.

"Right. Decency. Good name. Listen, we are almost done here. Just a few more questions, I promise. Nothing about your duty to your king, or any of that."

He knelt back down next to Decency, who flinched away. Ashion grabbed him quickly, and put the knife up to his face.

"I need to know about your breach mechanism," Ashion demanded.

"What?" Decency said, trying to pull his good eye away from the knife's point.

"The time travel you and your cohorts are doing. I'm wondering where you keep the system that handles your breach work."

"What system do you mean? Time travel? I don't—"

And like that, Ashion pulled the man's hand up, and cut his index finger off. Decency screamed, and pulled his hand back toward him.

"Don't toy with me," Ashion said. "Every time I have one of these interviews, I get the same answers: shifting is the will of God; He enlightens us through the altar rooms; through prayer alone may God grant you access to the holy past of mankind, blah blah blah. Can I tell you how sick of that I have grown?"

Ashion pulled Decency's hand up again, and with a trained motion had cut the pointer finger off at the knuckle. Dex closed his eyes against screaming pain of the monk. He felt like vomiting. The strain of the Rock at his back felt like an escape now, instead of the usual burden. He could just let go. But he opened his eyes again.

"Now, enough religious banter. I've been to the altar rooms. I found the one you buried up in the Colorado mountains. Nice work, sure. But what I need are the details. Where is your breach loop? Where is your mapping mechanism? You've got yourself a network around here somewhere. I'm sure it holds all the chronolographical mapping you guys obviously have access to. Just tell me where your map is. That's all I need to know."

"You cannot map the life of a man, let alone all of mankind," Decency said.

Ashion laughed. "The only thing I'm more sick of than your religion is all the quoting of that dipshit, blind man Jones." He cut another finger off the gasping monk.

Dex felt the restored fingers of his left hand. Dr. Johansson's voice came up like the dream, overwhelming him.

You are nothing; you are the sad mistake of this world, and your finger in this jar will remind you of that.

Dex couldn't bear it any longer. He let the Rock pull him back through his breach, back to the empty darkness of the church.

One hundred thirteen.

Freedom was waiting on the roof, and no one had attacked her. The congregation was still milling around below, although the prayloop was long over. Dex gave her a report of the shift in all its gory detail. He kept his eyes closed the whole time. When he was done, he took a deep breath and looked up at her. She was facing away from him, her head bowed.

"I'm sorry, Freedom," he said. "I couldn't take anymore. I had to come back."

She turned. There were tears in her eyes. "I understand. You listened enough."

"I could have done something," Dex said. "I could have stopped him."

"No, Dex," Freedom said. "You must not interfere. Our battle is in the present, not in the past."

"What map is Ashion referring to?" Dex asked.

"I do not know," Freedom said. "Are you sure he said 'breach mechanism?'"

"Positive. He referred to the altar rooms, too. It was like he wanted to know how Decency was shifting, because he doesn't understand the altar rooms."

"He seeks out our time travelers," Freedom concluded. "That would explain why no more exist."

"What do you mean?"

"Before Lynia, no one had performed a shift in over twenty years. The capable monks had all died, or disappeared, or left the church."

"He's eliminating all the shifters, so that he alone controls the past?" Dex asked.

"That makes sense. But why does he seek the breach mechanism? Why does he seek this map? They clearly have a successful mechanism themselves."

Dex shrugged. Freedom was lost in thought.

"What's the stuff about the queen?" he asked. "Who's this Emperor Balasari?"

"That is a puzzle I think we can solve," Freedom told him. "Balasari was the emperor of the Eastern Amrikan Empire in 2909. He has since been succeeded by his only son, Balasari the Younger. Balasari the Younger was born under the same moon as Chardwin's firstborn, Jorgan. There was a time when the two kingdoms looked close to resolving the border wars that had ravaged the mid-plains for a hundred years. But after Jorgan's death from the spotted plague, Chardwin cut off all communication with the eastern cities. It was always thought that Chardwin dealt with his son's death by blaming it on the eastern sea-ports that had briefly reopened trade with Europa—long thought to be the source of the plague. After the plague had begun to show up at the sea ports at the end of the millennium, trading had ceased. God was punishing us again for our greed."

Freedom stopped, looking down as the congregation began their treks back to wherever they had come from. Then she turned back to Dex.

"When Chardwin cut off all ties with the east, Balasari sent more troops to the plains to protect the border against what was considered an imminent western threat. Chardwin was forced to send his own armies out to protect his rivers and fields. It was an unfortunate escalation to war.

"From what you overheard, it could be theorized that Chardwin and Balasari sought a new unity truce very early on. Maybe even because of the loss of the costly Europa experiment. They traded their children as a show of trust. But then..." Freedom stopped and thought. "But then, Jorgan heads home to his father after his stay with Balasari, infected with the dreaded plague, and dies on route. It is not a vague sense of grief, but an exact feeling of betrayal. Balasari has poisoned his eldest son. Political tensions remain high. The resulting border wars deplete the coffers of Chardwin's kingdom, leaving him weak and his people ravaged."

"Not to mention a dead son," Dex said quietly.

"Yes," Freedom said. "Then Mebda was destined for the crown. It was always said that after the death of his first son, King Chardwin was paranoid about the health of Mebda. At the time of his death, he would rave about all the attempts on Mebda's life that he had defeated over the years. This was a sign of his growing senility, it was thought. Now, I am not so sure."

"What about the monk, Decency?" Dex asked.

"He was one of the last shifters, and a confidant to the royal family. He and Humility ran the monastery that Justice and I now keep together. At the time, there were dozens of monks up there. I remember that very well." Freedom stopped talking for a while, staring into space. Then she shook her head and looked at Dex.

"The off-landers have been weakening the western kingdom, eliminating heirs, and who knows what else. They are preparing our nation."

"Preparing for what?"

"A simple transferal of power, when they arrive."

"I see. That's a pretty good plan."

"Indeed. Now, Ashion's motivations with the Order of Brodius are much murkier."

"Do you want me to follow up on the Order now?" Dex asked.

"I would say the two are intertwined enough that you can investigate both. When you discover what happened to Humility, I would imagine you will find this Ashion or Tano involved. Humility was very close to Chardwin, as you have seen. Look for his disappearance."

"Let's get going, then. Where's the next loop?"

Freedom pointed west. "Half day's ride."

"Let's move," Dex was already untying his horse.

"I am worried about Justice," Freedom said.

"What's wrong?" Dex asked looking at her.

"He knew where we would be," she said. "He should be back by now. With that attack the other night... I don't know. I want to find him."

"Should we head into Longstown?" he asked.

She shook her head. "You cannot enter Longstown, not after you broke out of jail. Besides, if Mastiff is the reason for Justice's absence, I might get roped into whatever work has been given him."

"So what should we do?"

"I'm going back to the monastery, to see if he is there. If not, then I will head for town."

"Do you wanna stop at some loops on the way?" Dex asked.

"You must remain focused on your search," she replied.

"What?" Dex asked. "I'd rather stay with you."

"No, these loops out here are more powerful. The faithful visit frequently. These are the people of God, and they pray a strong loop. In Longstown, I'm not sure we could get you properly shifted."

"I don't want to travel alone." Dex felt the panic like a rock in his throat.

"You can protect yourself. We need you to continue your investigation."

I don't want to be alone again. "I don't think this is a good idea. You are not safe."

"I will be safe at the monastery. It's built like a fortress, perfect for holing up against dangers of the world."

"I don't like it."

"I must seek out Justice. You must finish your investigation. This is the only way."

One hundred fourteen.

Dex rolled over again, even though it meant letting the cold in. His bedroll was thick, but tonight the cold seemed to seep through regardless. Not that he could sleep anyway. The cold just made him feel even lonelier.

He lay perfectly still again, waiting for the new air under his blanket to rise to his body temperature, and tried not to feel sorry for himself. Thelo had left him. Mal had left him. Justice had left him. And now Freedom had left him. The departures were riddled with grave importance, but Dex didn't care much for that. He just knew everyone kept leaving him. But as he lay under the new moon, someone came to mind.

Rolink did not leave me. I left him. Left him to be executed by that crackhead king in Longstown. Justice had said that he would go back and rescue Rolink, but when? Freedom insisted on continuing the investigation, and Dex knew it was the right thing to do. Having seen

Ashion and his sidekick Tano in action, he had to find out what they were up to. But when would he shift back to that night in Longstown?

Even as he thought about it, the images of the flashing swords and the grunted attacks he had seen when Freedom had dragged him from the jailhouse built up in his mind. It still made him light-headed, to think that was him. *It was me. Just not yet.*

But when?

He thought of Mebda, running into the mountains with the Judas Sword in his arms, and it made Dex's jaw ache. He wanted to be back in that snow storm with Mebda and Rolink, catching snowflakes on his tongue, and bragging about helis and commuters to a rapt audience. Instead, he was cold, and alone, and buried under a pile of expectations so high he couldn't see the top of it.

Dex rolled over again, letting a new breeze of cold air under his blanket.

One hundred fifteen.

Over the next four days, Dex found a rhythm of sorts. He would be up on the church roof early, before the congregation or even the priest. Early enough to see the sun starting its march across the sky.

He was following Humility and King Chardwin exclusively, with his anchor breaches matching those of Tano. Dex was getting to know Tano's methods all too well. After the night when Tano had spied on Chardwin and Humility, an order must have gone out to escalate the assault on the monks of Brodius. Since then, Dex had seen Tano interrogate and murder two more monks.

It was usually during these ordeals that Dex would shift back to his real time. By the time he got back late in the afternoon or early evening, the congregation would be long gone. Before riding his horse to the next prayloop he would eat some of the meager provisions Freedom had left him and try to sort through all that he was learning about Ashion's plans.

Dex had noticed that out of the four times he saw Tano, he had only had a patch over his eye twice. On his last shift, the Red Mask had no patch. It reminded Dex that he was not experiencing a chronological set of actions by the off-landers. He was not seeing Tano in an uninterrupted line, even though that was how he lived through it. Dex was choosing anchors based on chronological order, because this was easier for him to keep track of events. But the Tano that Dex was shadowing was not always from the same time. This made it a bit difficult to follow. Today, Tano was just discovering the location of the second altar room (four fingers). But yesterday, he had discovered that it was used for shifting training (seven fingers).

Nevertheless, Dex was getting a good idea of what Ashion was accomplishing. He was most certainly tracking down monks who could use the altar rooms, and killing them off. Tano was asking for the breach technology, and more importantly, the mapping system. They were looking for a piece of actual technology, Dex discovered.

They were looking for a big network like the SIN on Venus that the Order of Brodius was hiding someplace.

It made Dex wonder where such a massive net could be. To hear Tano speak of it, it made Dex wonder how he could do what he was doing without a massive net of processors crunching the data. Dex felt the numbers crunch in his head, felt the information flow through from the prayloop, but the question remained. Where did it come from before that? And if there was a big network somewhere, what did Ashion want with it?

Above all else, the off-landers were out to topple King Chardwin; that much was certain. When Dex had been following the king and Humility the last two loops, Ashion's minion had definitely been trying to get rid of Chardwin's son, Mebda. But Humility seemed to suspect foul play, and Tano was getting frustrated.

Dex had become better at the Dagger, because he had realized that letting the Halo out in front of him allowed him to see through the breach. He was then able to determine if the anchor source point was still in close proximity. It was a handy trick, as he could breach through as soon as possible instead of feeling the million points of the cutting knives while he was waiting.

One hundred sixteen.

Dex followed Tano into a castle in the darkest hour of the night. He'd lost track of him, so he had no choice but to begin opening the doors that lined the darkened hallway. He began to open doors quietly and finally found Tano in a dark room, lit only by a single candle in one corner. The Red Mask was looking down over a bed, checking the interface on his arm, and reaching for his sword. Through the slightly opened door, Dex could make out Tano's next victim.

The sleeping child could not have been any older than five. Before he could stop himself Dex pushed through the door.

Tano heard the door groan open, turned, and swung at Dex. Dex kept his momentum and rolled forward under the attack. Tano, crouching in a defensive posture, backed up and closed the door quietly, and threw the internal lock. The sound of the lock roused the child, who sat up, groggy but alarmed.

"Screams and you's are dead, boy," Tano said, raising his sword for the attack. Dex had pulled Judas from his back, and he telescoped it to its full length in front of him. The sight of the sword stopped Tano in his tracks. He lowered his guard, squinting into the darkness.

"Ash? Heah, it's is you?" he asked. "What's you's doin here?"

Dex panicked at being recognized, and swung his sword wildly. Tano jumped out of the way, only just. The lunge put Dex into the light of the candle.

"Ash! What's you's crazy?" the assassin said. Dex swung again, and caught Tano's sword, knocking it from his hand. "Ash! It's is Tano!" he cried, backing into the corner, and typing madly at his wrist interface.

Dex realized that his opponent was shifting back, and he jabbed Judas at Tano's head, feeling the tip push into his eye, hearing the beginning of a scream. But all of a sudden the resistance was gone, and Judas slammed into the stone wall with a clang. Dex felt the Rope spring out, unwinding into Tano's breach, trying to release the anchor at his own back. He almost popped through the breach before he was able to suppress the patterns back into his head.

Dex turned and saw the boy trying open the door. He ran back and put his hand on the boy's shoulder, but he screamed and fell to the floor.

"It's okay" Dex said soothingly. "I won't hurt you."

The boy stayed where he was. Dex heard the sound of voices outside the room, and felt the tug of the Rock while someone pounded on the door. .

"Boy, what is your name?" he asked.

"Jase," the boy answered. "I mean, Medba."

Dex looked down at him. "Are you supposed to tell people you are Medba?"

The boy avoided his gaze.

"It's okay; I got rid of the bad man," Dex said. "Are you pretending to be Mebda, and Medba is pretending to be Jase?"

The boy turned to him, then nodded.

Dex nodded back, and winked. "You are doing a good job, Jase," he said as he heard something being thrown against the door outside. It sounded like an axe. "Jase, you should move away from that door, they are breaking it down."

"What's *your* name?" the boy asked quickly.

Dex smiled. "You don't need to know."

"That man called you Ash."

"Yes, I'm Ash. Just like you are Mebda."

"What?"

Dex put his finger to his lips. The axe was coming through at the deadbolt now and the yells were getting louder. "I am a ghost, Jase."

Then Dex released the anchor, and slipped back through his breach.

One hundred seventeen.

Dex had very nearly hopped on his horse and headed for the monastery the very moment he returned to the shifting room. After having made contact with Tano, he was scared of the consequences. Was that why he and Freedom had been attacked? He needed to tell her.

Tano has the patch because of me. I cut his eye out before he shifted back. Despite his fear at having engaged Tano, he found some satisfaction in being the cause of the assassin's deformity. Perhaps more satisfying was Tano's belief that it had been Ashion himself who did it.

But Freedom had insisted that he finished his investigation of Humility, and there was one anchor left for Humility: March 30, 3008. The day of his disappearance. So Dex rode to the next church, which also lay on his way back to the monastery.

Every shadow was an assassin. Every sound made him jump. But there was no attack. No surprise ambush came from the tall grass that stood waist-high along the road.

Dex arrived at the church early, and roped his horse. After giving it feed and water, he waited on the roof for the late afternoon congregation.

Sleep must have found him, because he awoke to the sound of the beating drums below him, where the prayloop was already underway. He lowered himself into the darkness of the shifting room, waiting for the moment. Dex had come to love the tingle of the patterns as they explode out of his mind through the loop. Especially when the light from the opening window slits illuminates the breach clasp and the flyer dances around impatiently, like a horse waiting for the gate to open.

Once he was through the breach, he started leafing through the anchors in his mind, looking for the date, looking for the right one. When he found it, he almost felt the existence of the shifter who had dropped before him. Then Dex fell into the Dragging Dagger, felt the excruciating pain, felt the bliss of its annihilation wash over him.

One hundred eighteen.

Dex was back in the Order's monastery, and again he moved quietly through its older stone passageways in the dark. He kept himself on edge, knowing that his presence might now be expected.

From close by there was the clang of swords, and an unintelligible cry echoed through the stone corridor. Dex stopped in his tracks, listening as the sword fight continued. Footsteps were now running toward him, so he stepped quickly back into the empty room he had shifted into, watching from the shadows. Someone ran by, followed closely by someone who made no noise. A Red Mask. Just past the door, he caught up to the runner, and there was a cry of pain. Dex was about to step back out when the Red Mask appeared around the corner, dragging a monk by the hood of his robe. The captive was choking and grasping at his throat. Dex panicked when he realized that the Red Mask was dragging the man into the room he had ducked back into.

Turning around frantically, he saw the wardrobe, and quickly stepped in, leaving the door open a crack so he could watch. The Red Mask dragged the suffocating man through, closed the door, and let go. As the monk tried to stand, the Red Mask put his fist into his face, knocking him to the floor. Then the Red Mask turned and lit a lantern.

Ashion.

The monk tried to rise, and took another hit to the face. This time, he stayed on the ground, but rolled over onto his back, looking up at Ashion. It was Humility. Dex's heart quickened. This was the moment. Then the door opened, and Tano stepped inside.

"Heah, they's is soundin th' alarm," he said, looking down with hatred at Humility.

"No matter," Ashion said, taking his black gloves off. "Go kill the child, then get out of here."

"Heah," Tano obeyed and left.

"He is not the child you seek," Humility said.

"You mean the fake prince? Yes, I know," Ashion said. "But it turns out that a king half-crazed by assassination attempts is exactly what we need. Not a dead prince, as we thought. All the math supports it."

"You are not of this time," Humility decided, wiping the blood from his lip.

"Very good," Ashion said. "It has only taken you five attempts on the life of your king and his son to figure that out? Well done, genius."

"You cannot alter God's plan for his people," Humility said.

"Did it ever cross your narrow little mind that perhaps I *am* God's plan?" Ashion asked.

"God does not require the murder of innocent children."

"Innocent *now*, Humility. You should see the prince when he's all grown up."

"Mebda will be a good king."

Ashion shrugged. "Good king, bad king. No matter. As long as he's *my* king."

"Is that your plan? To weaken the kingdom?"

"Something like that."

"Then why do you keep trying to kill him?"

"We've got someone lined up that we like more than Chardwin. But we're running the iterations on the case of his survival, and Medba's too. It's looking very promising. See, there's a great lead on a replacement for Medba in a few decades. Anyway, it's complicated. I'd have to pull all the charts to explain it. Time travel's a real noodler; it takes all day to get through it."

"We seem to have time on our hands," Humility said.

Ashion gave a short laugh. "That's funny." He knelt down on one knee, looking closely at Humility. "Listen, monk, I have a question for you. I've been asking all the other monks, and I can't seem to get a straight answer."

Humility looked up. "You seek our shifting technology."

Ashion's smile disappeared. "You are craftier than it first appears."

"There is no technology. God provides us with a window on our past, to atone for our sins."

The fist came fast against Humility's cheek, snapping his head back and sending him to the floor.

"That is exactly the kind of shit I'm tired of hearing," Ashion said, rubbing his hand. "I've been chopping off fingers, chopping off toes, poking out eyes, burning body parts, you name it. And all I get is scripture rubbish. So listen. We figure that you've got to have a system that is activated by those funky-smelling drum circles you guys call church. The shape of the room, the lights, the rhythm—we get all that. But we come up short on intercepting the signal that is laying down the map. It has to be big to send a signal to so many disparate locations around here. At first we thought you were using small, localized systems, but there's just no way to explain the mapping precision you godders have."

"There is no technology," Humility said.

"Yes, there is," Ashion said, pulling out his knife. "And I need it."

"I have nothing to tell you."

"Not yet." The assassin punched Humility again, then came down on his chest, pinning down his arms. "I'm going to cut your good eye out now. At any time, just tell me where you guys are masking your mapping net, and I put this through your heart so you can go join your pal Jones in hell. You just pipe up at any time." The knife was slowly pushed through Humility's scrunched-closed eyelid. He screamed.

Dex closed his eyes, and haloed back to his real time.

One hundred nineteen.

Dex rode the fastest way he knew back to the monastery. He had gathered as much as he could about Ashion and Tano's plans. While the encounter with Tano was still fresh, Dex felt it was best to check in with Freedom and Justice. And keep himself in the present, at least for a while. A warm fire at the monastery sounded about right, the weather grew cold and his meager provisions were nearly gone.

As he rode, he tried to catalog all the information he needed to convey. Humility had not betrayed Chardwin; he had discovered Ashion's interference, and paid the price. Ashion had coordinated the fall of King Medba and the rise of Mastiff. He was killing off the shifters, and trying to find out where the monk's big computing network was, and how they were laying down the chronolographic map. Dex didn't know why Ashion wanted the map, but it was clearly his top priority.

And I attacked Tano, cutting out his eye. Dex didn't regret it, but it probably meant that their investigation had been compromised. They would have to be careful. No trips to Terran or Mal any time soon.

But past that, Dex didn't know what was next. He didn't know if they were any closer to stopping the invasion that was on its way. He found it hard to believe that all he was supposed to do was go back in time and... what? Look around? Hide? Watch men and women get tortured and murdered? Then come back to the present and tell some folks about it, when it was too late to do anything? Dex knew that giving away his position could make things ugly, but it couldn't be helped now. He had been discovered. Maybe he should go back in time and save all those monks.

Freedom or Justice would know what to do.

It was more than a day's ride back to the monastery, and as the light failed, Dex roped his tired horse to a tree and tended to the mare's food and water. As he rolled out his bedroll in the shivering twilight, Dex thought of going back and saving Rolink at the Longstown jail. And finally getting that glass of mead they had talked about.

One hundred twenty.

It was late in the day when Dex finally made it to the last stretch of road that led up to the monastery. He came to a crossroads, and struggled with his directions. He had a crude map that Freedom had provided, but he struggled to make sense of it. Freedom had told him to take a right at the crossroads, and then the next right, which would take him to the monastery. The left path went deep into the mountains, up to the summer grazing fields for the goats.

In the quickly fading sun, Dex was making his way up to the intersection, when he heard horse hoofs pounding. Three riders were coming up the trail behind him. He squinted, but there was not enough light to make them out. They were in a hurry, and Dex's heart began to beat harder.

In just a few minutes, they were upon him. He kept his tunic pulled tight around his face, and his head down. After the riders passed, he looked up, and was surprised to see the robes of monks. They took the right trail and headed up toward the monastery.

There are only two of us left, in the Order of Brodius. Dex could hear Freedom's voice in his head, and he felt his stomach tighten. As he watched, one of the riders broke off, stopped, and turned back down the road.

He's watching me, wondering where I'm going.

Dex ambled along to the left and up the road toward the mountain pass instead of the monastery. His heart raced. *Who were they? Were they Mastiff's men?*

He kept his leisurely pace until he had crested the first rise. When the crossroads and the distant rider were out of sight he dug his heels into the horse, riding as fast as he could by the low light of the moon waning above him.

One hundred twenty-one.

Dex left his horse tethered to a tree in the descending twilight, and scrambled up the scree-covered mountainside on foot. If his sense of direction was worth anything at all, he should be able to go over the ridge in front of him and find himself looking down at the valley that he'd hiked with Freedom to get to the second altar room.

It looked similar, but he couldn't be sure. He stared down into the rapidly darkening valley, but could see nothing. He had no choice other than to head back east into the valley, toward what he hoped would be the monastery's secret back door.

The sun had completed its descent behind the western mountains when Dex came upon the first sign that he had made the right decision. He stayed high above the top of the valley, ensuring he didn't lose his way. Dex had learned one thing from his time wandering alone after coming to Earth: do not get overly confident about how to get from one place to another.

He found the tell-tale tree growing in the shape of the Flyer, standing out as if it was on fire now. He felt its geometry unspool in his head, flying out, dissipating into the night sky. He saw the Halo tree. From there, he lined up the North Star, and turned to the left. Dex crouched to get a better view, squinting in the darkness to see the tree in the shape of the Knife.

He saw the motion out of the corner of his eye and froze, his heart racing, the moment going into high jack. He focused his attention and saw a crouching figure move slowly and quietly from shrub to shrub. An expert. Dex stayed low behind the Halo tree, down in the shrub oak, and watched as the figure made its way toward the Rock. With a quick look around, the figure stepped down into the secret entrance of the monastery.

Dex recognized the movements, the slow slink, the expert quiet. A Red Mask.

He slowly backed up toward the ridgeline, the rage in his head tempered by the realization that he needed to scope things out before he entered and looked for his friends. He could only hope they were still alive.

One hundred twenty-two.

As the dark of a nearly moonless night crept in, Dex made his way around to the north side of the valley, and climbed a tall pine tree that offered a full view of the monastery. He saw little movement in the courtyard. There was no smoke rising from the fire pit in the kitchen, but there were small swirls coming from different rooms and structures around the courtyard. The complete absence of human life out in the open told Dex everything. The only question was: how many of them?

And how far in the future had they come from?

Dex felt sick to his stomach. *It's my fault. We have been discovered because I attacked Tano.*

He kept his eye on the secret monastery entrance through the night, and gradually came to recognize the signs of the guard shift. As a small glow of morning had just begun to appear above the eastern plains beyond the monastery, Dex watched a small dispatch of three riders leave the front gate and speed away from the monastery toward Longstown.

Dex slunk down from his perch and headed toward the monastery, staying low and seeking cover in the shrubs. He'd seen enough. He'd made his plans.

It was time to go in.

One hundred twenty-three.

In the distance, Dex saw the figure that he had spotted earlier that day slowly climb down from the tree into the bushes. He moved on silently and waited until the very last moment before telescoping Judas and cutting the man's throat with a single swipe. The Red Mask slumped to the ground and Dex waited.

But there was no click, no wink out. The body did not disappear.

They are not from the future. Dex forged ahead to the secret door at a dead run, threw the hatch open, and jumped down into the dark stone tunnels of the monastery.

"Heah fool, you's is late, eh," Dex heard someone say behind him. He turned and swung his sword.

The Red Mask had enough sense to leap back against the rock wall, the surprise on his face turning to concentration as Dex swung again. The assassin tried to run and pull his sword from its sheath in the same movement, but Dex stabbed quickly. He caught him in the shoulder and knocked him to the ground, before bringing Judas down on his skull.

Dex looked around, but no one else came at him. He wiped the blood from his blade using the dead man's tunic and headed east toward the adobe section of the monastery. He kept to the side hallways he had roamed so aimlessly in those first few days as they would lead him toward the single door down into the adobe structure.

The other two Red Masks he was expecting were standing at the door with their swords drawn in the ready position. Dex did not break stride.

The guards did not hesitate in their attack. Dex parried the attack of the first, and then turned and lunged at the second, swinging Judas at his head, while kicking hard at his knee. The Red Mask countered the attack with his sword, and then stepped quickly aside to save his knee. It gave Dex the space he needed, and he felt time crawling to a stop. He sensed the vertigo, however briefly, before he attacked the first Red Mask again with a relentless and erratic series of swings.

These Red Masks were not like those back at the other church, he realized. These were used to combat, and his little feints did not bother them. It reminded Dex of his first swordfights on Venus. Before he thought anything more of it, they came at him simultaneously from opposite sides. With one swinging at his torso and the other at his legs, there was no way out left for him.

Dex flipped Judas in a tight arc that caught the swing at his torso and drove it up and over him. He jumped at the same time, just high enough to come down on the blade aiming at his knees and pull it down under his feet. The assassin did not have time to let go of his trapped blade before Dex put Judas through his neck.

He left his sword stuck in the bones and flesh and used it as leverage to spin himself around and evade the counter-attack of the second assassin. In a fraction of a moment, Dex watched as the assassin prepared for the next attack. It took a few swings to get used to the assassin's movement, but then a quick slash took his wrist off. The man gasped, and Dex kicked him in the chest, knocking him back against the wall.

"I seek the monk Freedom," he said, holding Judas at the Red Mask's throat.

"I will not help you," the man spat, holding his bleeding stump.

Dex put the sword through his throat and moved on. He turned and headed down the stairs into the adobe walls of the outer monastery.

He just managed to avoid another Red Mask before reaching the western edge of the courtyard. He noted that the outer rooms all seemed to be in use now. The entire place smelled vaguely of body odor and urine. Dex found an empty room and peeked through the small window out onto the courtyard.

Even in the dim light of the early dawn, he could see that the vegetable garden had been turned into a dirtpad. Freedom's goats where nowhere to be seen. Instead the courtyard was crawling with Red Masks. Some were sitting on the ground, eating. Others were either sparring with swords in the open field or just milling around the fringes.

Dex tried to make a count, and lost track somewhere around fifty. After some time he heard a loud whistle, followed by a voice yelling out, "Sunrise! Everyone inside!" Dex saw the men heading in toward the various rooms, so he hid behind the slightly ajar door and waited.

The door opened and a Red Mask walked in, throwing his sword on the ground and then lying down on the bed with a groan. Within seconds, Dex pinned him to the ground, sitting on the man's stomach and shoving a dirty rag into his mouth. The knight struggled and gave a muffled cry as Dex patiently waited for him to calm down. After half a minute, the knight realized he was beaten. Dex carefully pulled the cloth from the assassin's mouth.

"I seek the monk named Freedom," Dex said calmly.

"Get burned, iter," he said.

Dex hit him again, and knotted the shirt around the man's wrists. "I'm going to ask you one more time where the monk is. Then you lose a finger. Each time I have to ask again, I take a finger."

The assassin closed his eyes, waiting for the pain. Dex felt anger flash through him, and he brought Judas to the man's hand. He grabbed the pinky finger. He had seen Tano or Ashion do this a dozen times in the last week. It had been done to him as a child, by Johansson at the orph. It was a simple cut. He had murdered a dozen men, putting Judas through their hearts, their spines, and their appendages. All he had to do now was cut off the little finger of this assassin. Then another. Cut them off one by one until he told him what he wanted to hear.

Just like it had been done to Jones.

At the thought of Jones, Dex let go of the man's hand. The assassin did not hesitate to take his chance. He grabbed at Dex's arm and used a bucking motion to throw him up and off. Dex turned and brought his sword down, but it banged against the mud floor. The assassin had rolled to the door and Dex jumped. But it was too late. The door was open and the assassin was yelling down the hallway, giving the alarm. The sound of a dozen doors opening in unison made Dex panic for a brief second but it wasn't long before the moment came into a slow, pure focus.

He used Judas to knock the pane of glass out of the small window, and stood on the bench to pull himself through. He landed with a quiet thud on the cold stone floor and sprinted to the far side of the courtyard, ignoring the doors flying open next to him. He could hear the shouts and footsteps as the entire complex came to life. Dex ran towards the hallway with the fireplace on the other side, the door to Freedom's quarters on the left, and Justice's on the right. Seconds later he was there. The door to her room flew open, and a Red Mask came racing out in full dress. Dex was moving so fast, all he could do was take a wild swing. The Red Mask brought his sword up, and shoved his fist into Dex's side as he raced by. Their swords clanged, and Dex was knocked to the ground. The Red Mask calmly closed the door.

Dex rolled to his feet and backed up against the wall. The courtyard was full of assassins now, some in mid-dress, some fully clothed, all of them with their swords drawn, racing into an arc around him.

More than two dozen of them were moving in closer, and he could not keep his eyes on all of the growing numbers behind them. The Red Mask who had come out of Freedom's room began to pace the semicircle that had formed around Dex. Dex could not see his face, but in the brightening morning air he could see his sword.

It looked just like Judas.

At second glance the sword turned out to be steel, without the dull whites and blacks of Judas, but in the exact same shape and dimensions. The assassin was walking slowly, deliberately around Dex, his sword held in front of him, just as he would have held it himself.

Here is my equal.

The crowd of assassins was chanting something Dex could not make out. They were growing louder and louder, holding their swords up, and he could feel the moment settling in. He saw the shape of the moment and the exact number of men he would kill before they disarmed him. What he could not get a sense of was this prowling Red Mask. It felt like he would spring at any moment, charge in toward Dex.

"SILENCE!" a voice boomed, and the chanting stopped immediately. The crowd parted, giving way to the thin, small figure of Tano. No patch covered his eye socket; instead, the cold blue eye inside seemed unharmed. Dex briefly wondered how far in the future it would be before they met in the past and he put Judas through his face.

Tano gave him that small, satisfied smile that he had come to know well through his shiftings. It was the look of a madman about to have his fun. Dex squeezed the Judas' hilt, trying to pick his moment. But the Red Mask with still roamed, keeping Dex in check.

"Heah, it's is him," Tano said. "Th' iter's is pretty good to gets in all by hisself." Tano turned to the roaming assassin, "Gurn, go run fires up th' comm, tells Ash we's have got his iter. Sees if he's wants him dead or just... sorts of dead." Gurn gave Dex one last look, then telescoped his blade back in and left the semi-circle.

"You's causin tall trouble since th' dumb doctor's let you's loose up planet-side," Tano said. As Dex did not reply, he went on, "You's playin wit th' past, you's makin people think you's is Ash."

Tano was now close enough for Dex to see a white scar starting on his right cheek and extending up to his eye socket. The assassin saw him stare at it, and touched the scar.

"I's finally gots it fixed by th' Families" he said. "I's know th' truth now. It's is no reason to keep th' reminder."

"What did you do to Freedom? Where's Justice?" Dex asked. He could see Tano's small knife that he kept in his boot. His vision was going red.

Tano smiled. "Th' old man monk, he's is still with Mastiff, heah. But th' old woman, she's is backs in her quarters, eh. We's still need her, for a little bits. She's tells us where you's been, where th' other godders been, but she's not tells us who's is this Lynia, eh. I's still waitin for this."

Dex's vision went from red to black. *Mal. They cannot find Mal.*

"I will kill you," he said, ready to lunge out. But Tano was backing away from him, and smiling.

"You's had ya chance, eh. Two chances, two failures. Now I's get to watch ya die. That Gurn, he's is wicked wit a sword, like you, eh." He made a whistling sound, and the semi-circle began to close in. Dex kept his eyes on Tano, trying to find a way to put Judas through his neck.

He barely heard the distant boom before he saw a fiery-hot sphere blasting into the courtyard from the sky. But he saw enough to know to throw himself to the ground, as the balloon-sized sphere hit in the middle of the assassins and exploded.

The screams of agony were nothing compared to the smell of burning flesh. Dex stayed low and watched the pandemonium unfold. Another projectile sailed into the courtyard and tore through a dozen assassins, the molten tar searing their skin and instantly setting their clothes on fire.

Without hesitation Dex began searching for Tano and found him huddled down in the chaos, trying to get clear of the screaming men.

Gurn burst from the front doorway, yelling, "We's are under attack!"

Tano looked at him in disbelief as he was trying to get away from the molten tar that had sprayed across the courtyard. "Who's cans it be?"

"Heah, it's look like Mastiff's army," Gurn said, and fled back inside.

Dex heard another distant boom. He stood and raced through the door Gurn had just entered. Another bucket of hot tar exploded behind him as he raced toward Freedom's quarters.

There was a guard in front of the door, looking around nervously at the chaos that had erupted everywhere. Dex could see men limping in with arrows stuck in their bodies. Wasting no time, he killed the guard and burst through Freedom's door, closing it behind him. There was no internal lock. He turned to look at Freedom, and his heart broke.

One hundred twenty-four.

She had been tied to one of the courtyard chairs, naked, and there was blood everywhere. Her face was so bruised and swollen that Dex barely recognized her. Her long grey hair looked to have been cut short and ragged, but as he approached her he realized that it had been burned off, leaving behind charred black skin.

Freedom raised her head weakly. A look of fear spread across her face when she saw him, and she flinched.

"It's okay, Freedom," he said, walking behind her to cut her free. "It's Dex. I'm not Ashion or anyone else that looks like me." After he had cut the ropes from her arms and legs, he picked her up and laid her gently on her bed. Outside, the sound of explosions and yelling continued. With great care, Dex covered her in a blanket. She gave a faint smile, showing missing teeth.

"They killed my goats," she coughed. Blood spat from her mouth.

"I know," Dex said. He could not see through his tears.

"I'm glad you came," Freedom said.

"We'll get out of here soon," Dex told her.

"No," she replied, with what little determination she had left. "No, I need to die, Dex."

Dex choked on his sob. "Bullshit. Just warm up for a second, then we'll go."

"I should have been dead days ago. They gave me injections to

386

keep me alive."

He felt his gut tightening with a wretch.

"Dex, look at me," Freedom said, coughing again. "Find Justice. Tell him the invasion has begun. Tell him what you've learned."

"Okay," he blurted out.

"Dex, you must fight. Fight for us."

He closed his eyes. "I can't do this without you, Freedom," he said through his tears.

"Jones will see you through."

Dex wiped the tears from his eyes. "You mean, Saint Brodius."

Freedom smiled, and Dex held her hand for another moment.

Finally he stood and wiped the tears from his eyes, just as the door opened. He backed up behind it quickly.

"I's don't know why Mastiff is attacking. We's got to get this monk outta here," Tano was saying to someone behind him, still outside the door. Dex did not hesitate. He swung Judas around as hard as he could, roaring. The blade hit Tano at the neck, severing his head back to the spinal column. Dex kicked the limp body away and pulled Judas out. Tano slumped to the ground with his head dangling to the side and legs kicking wildly, trying to interpret the signals from a severed brain stem.

One hundred twenty-five.

Dex felt the attack before he heard anything, and barely had Judas up when the sword clanged against it, pushing him deeper into the small room. He stumbled over Tano's jerking body, swinging defensively, trying to blink the tears from his eyes.

The one called Gurn swung the Judas copy in a tight arch, thrusting quickly at Dex, who blocked and counter-attacked, but came up against the steel blade again and again. Dex backed up, finding the wall, and settled into a defensive style that helped him get into a rhythm against the rapid attacks.

This assassin was different, Dex realized. Faster. Smarter. Stronger. He had all the training, but he had an intuition that meant Dex came up against a perfect defense every time. The truth settled like a cold rain.

This man is going to kill me.

He attempted to get past, but there was no penetrating the sword play. Gurn was rooted into a position that held him in place. It was no advantage for a quick kill, but Dex realized that he did not need a quick kill. The bulking muscles of his arms would wear Dex down, slowly but surely.

Now more explosions were coming from outside the room, and occasionally the mud walls would shake. Dex kept on his feet, but felt his exhaustion growing, felt how himself slowing down. The moment would not stay jacked. He could see Freedom's broken body behind Gurn, and the anger flooded his body, gave him the energy for another attacking swing, but it did not last. The Red Mask was too fast, too strong, too precise.

Without warning, Dex felt the slam of Gurn's hilt, knocking Judas out of his hand. In the slow time of his high-jacked moment, he watched the steel blade swing around with full force, as the assassin brought it in toward his neck.

At the same moment, a blast of gunpowder blew the wall open, knocking them both into the opposite side of the room.

Dex tried to blink away the ringing in his ears, and coughed up dirt particles and smoke. He saw Judas underneath a pile of rubble and pulled it out, trying his best to roll over and stand. A foot stepped on his chest, pushing him down, and a sword touched his neck. Dex looked up through the clearing air, and saw a bearded man he did not recognize. He had long grey hair, braided, and a small goatee that looked vaguely familiar. The man squinted down, and then seemed to recognize him. Smiling wickedly he put his sword away, grabbed Dex by the hand and helped him rise.

"Dexter Maxwell!" the man cried. He looked at the slumped shape of Gurn, buried underneath a pile of adobe wall. "Just in time, I take it?"

Dex nodded dumbly. As the man pulled him through the hole in the wall, they were standing in the middle of the main hallway that led from the front door of the monastery to the courtyard. Chaos had overwhelmed the place, and it seemed like the entire structure was about it collapse. The sounds of sword-fighting rang from the courtyard. There were more explosions. The man pulled Dex quickly out toward the front door, and out of the monastery.

"Your horse, a large brown stallion, is at the watering hole yonder," the man yelled over the din. "Just as you requested. Now go, before I decide to kill you anyway!" Then the grey-haired man was gone, headed back into the monastery with a roar.

Dex looked out toward the pond, and saw a brown horse tied up. It looked scared by the noise and was bucking. Dex looked back one last time at the devastation of the battle. And then he stumbled as fast as he could toward the horse.

One hundred twenty-six.

Not knowing what would happen next, Dex rode south toward Longstown. Freedom had told him to find Justice. Even though he was a fugitive, he decided to risk going into the town to find the last person he knew he could trust.

But Tano had known where Justice was. The monk could be just as dead as Freedom most surely was by now. The only person they hadn't discovered yet was Mal. The small assassin had said something about finding Lynia. Presumably that meant they did not know where she was yet.

I need to keep it that way.

And so, Dex changed course. He headed east, toward a church he had recently used for shifting. He was exhausted, not to mention thirsty and hungry, but he rode on as fast as his horse would carry him. When he arrived at the church it was almost high noon and the place was empty. Hastily Dex drank water from the stable reserve, where he left his trembling horse to rest. He found that the saddlebags of the horse had been loaded with goat meat and unleavened bread, which he ate furiously as he waited on top of the roof for the next prayloop. After the meal, he rolled out his bedroll and was asleep in moments.

The dream came up like a slap, rising from behind the patterns and shapes of the shifting places, and pushing everything else aside. He saw the surface and laid down the Ocean's map. He found the Dragging Dagger. But he had no Knife. There was no Knife because he had no Rope, and no anchor. He was adrift across the burning surface of the expanding plane. He was tumbling down to meet it with no breach, nothing to save him from the annihilation. Panic rose in him, while the patterns in his head reorganized and reshaped into a map. He started to break down all the pieces into smaller pieces, and those into even smaller pieces, breaking himself down into the small dancing nothings at the end of the Rope. Then he hit the surface, and began to put it all back together. It was easier now with the Ocean map.

But the Ocean was lapping incorrectly, and he was still losing bits. He started to put it all back together, but it was too soon, and the burning pain was death surrounding him, eating him, destroying him.

Dex woke with a start, sitting up and breathing hard, sweating in the late-afternoon sun. He could hear the congregation gathering in the worship room below, mixed with a few stray beats of a drum that someone hit absent-mindedly. He took a deep breath, and waited for the sermon to start so he could go back and find Mal.

He did not know if she would be in Terran's study. She had said she had to go away for a few weeks. She could not be in the past, or traveling into the past at all. Perhaps she knew about the danger.

And what danger would he be putting Mal in, if he traveled back to see her now? Had Ashion learned how to search out the anchors? He would know by now that Dex could find them, because he had done so when his minion had tried to kill the child named Jase. Dex began to wonder if shifting to look for Mal was a safe idea.

He heard footsteps coming up the stairs from the church below, and reached for Judas. But it was the priest he had met before, when he had been with Freedom. The priest smiled gently, and Dex relaxed.

"You are Dexter Maxwell, yes?" he asked.

Dex nodded.

"I saw your horse and came to greet you," said the priest. "You came with Freedom not seven days past. I am Decency."

"I've come for the prayloop," Dex said.

Decency nodded. "I am glad to have you. You carry our prayers closer to God."

As Dex did not reply, Decency went on. "Tell me, how is Freedom? She is not with you today."

Dex did not look up. "Freedom is dead."

The priest's smile faded. "It cannot be."

"I saw it. She's dead." Dex fought back the tears.

Decency stared at Dex for a moment, and then turned and headed back for the stairs. "I will change the sermon. We shall pray Freedom's story, today."

Dex took a deep breath, trying to break free of the drowning sensation he felt. He did not want to endanger Mal, but what else could he do? Here he was, at the church, and the prayloop was about to start. He could still see Freedom's charred scalp, her pale, blood-covered body. Her bandaged, fingerless hands. The thought sent him back into a dark place, and he closed his eyes as the drums began to beat.

I could change it.

I could go back and save her.

Dex opened his eyes and reached for the trap door to the shifting room. The drums had started, the heat was ready to rise. Through it all, he suddenly felt the resolution in his heart.

I will meddle. I will interfere.

As he unlatched the door, he caught sight of the motion out of the corner of his eye, and turned just as the knife went sailing past his head. He looked to the stairwell, and saw the Red Mask pull himself quickly up onto the roof, drawing his short sword, and telescoping it. The eyes inside the mask were small slits.

Gurn.

Barely in time for the first attack Dex unsheathed Judas and parried Gurn's attack, trying to leverage his rested body, but Gurn anticipated his every move, and now seemed motivated by fresh zeal. He hit harder, attacked even faster. Dex had no choice but to defend, and fall back, moving away and trying to get free. But Gurn would simply maneuver around, keeping him away from the stairs down from the roof.

Dex felt the plan arrange itself in his mind. It was his only escape. He kept the attacks at bay, waiting for the exact moment.

The moment came, and Dex felt he had as much position as he could hold. When Gurn brought his sword around for another attack, Dex did a somersault backward and caught the handle of the hatch to the shifting room, pulling the hatch door open while shielding his back from Gurn's rapid attack. The force of the hit knocked Dex on his back, but the door was open, leaving the shifting room exposed. The smell of incense and beating of drums emanated up.

Without hesitation, Gurn jumped across the hatch space and brought his blade down toward Dex's head, who rolled back toward the hatch, catching Gurn in the leg. Both of them fell, and Gurn rolled in toward him. Dex pulled himself into a crouch, but instead of blocking away, he parried Gurn's steel blade just enough to keep it from splitting his gut. Thus deprived of his stability, Gurn crashed into Dex, knocking them both through the hatch door and down into the shifting room below.

As they fell, Dex unspooled the patterns, and the windows opened, letting the light in, igniting the patterns into the Halo. He grabbed Gurn's sword arm, holding on tightly as he fell. The assassin had pulled a knife from his belt, and was bringing it into Dex's neck from the side. Dex felt the prick of its tip enter his neck, but the Rope pulled him up through the Halo, and he shifted at last.

The last thing he heard was the assassin's scream.

One hundred twenty-seven.

Dex found himself unprepared for the shift, and the Flyer unspooled along with the Ocean's map, lit up with the anchors that he had visited, and the hundreds he had not. He tried to lay his Dagger into an anchor, but the force of the congregation's breach pushed him places he did not expect to go. He could feel the grief of the people lift him higher and then drop him down toward the surface. The shift would take him toward Freedom's past. He could see it, past the Ocean's map, past the anchors.

But Dex noticed that along the path that he was following, there was an early anchor. A new shift by someone into Freedom's life. He dropped the Dagger, and with the congregation's prayers, he hit the breach, held for a minute, then dropped through.

The first thing Dex noticed was the sharp pain on the right side of his neck where Gurn had stabbed him. He reached up and found a bleeding cut.

The second thing he noticed was Gurn's arm in his left hand, gripped tightly for the fall. But the arm, up to the elbow, was all that had come through the breach. Just above the elbow, the arm simply stopped with a clean cut. Blood oozed slowly from the veins and arteries. Dex let go quickly, and looked around. The rest of Gurn was nowhere to be seen.

Dex instantly realized where he was. It was the Brodius monastery. He was in one of the back rooms, behind the altar room. He slunk out of the room, looking for the shifter that had come before him.

I will meddle; I will interfere.

The Red Mask was just outside the room, and looking around confusedly, trying to find his way. He kept gazing at the interface on his arm, most likely looking at a map. In the dark, Dex could not see who this was, but it didn't matter. He would find out what he was up to, and then put an end to it. Freedom's plea to keep the past sacred felt empty compared with the memory of her broken body.

The shifter finally looked to have figured something out, and turned to make his way down a hallway, moving swiftly and quietly. Dex was surprised to hear voices, and see lanterns lit down many of the hallways. At this time, the monastery must have been bustling with life, he realized. That was many years ago, when Freedom was new to the monastery and when the Order was composed of many monks. Before they were killed, or had moved away, or left the Order.

The Red Mask finally stopped at a door, and gave a light tap. The lock on the other side was removed, and he pushed the door open. After a muffled shout, the door slammed shut.

Dex crept carefully toward the door, but the sound of gentle footsteps spooked him, and he slunked back into the shadow of the next doorway. The slight frame of a short woman hurried past him toward the door. Dex squinted in the darkness, trying to make her out. She gave a knock, and looked nervously back down the hall. As she turned anxiously one way and the other, the lamplight caught her face clearly. She was young, but there was no mistaking the face.

Freedom.

The door opened, and she stepped in quickly.

Dex ran for the door and made it before the lock was set, drawing his sword from his back. Inside, Dex took in the scene in a fraction of a second. There was a monk, already dead, his chest open and blood pouring everywhere. Beside him stood the shifter with the eye-patch. It was Tano, and he was about to kill Freedom. The young woman was staring at the dead body, and a scream erupted from her chest.

Tano brought the hilt of his sword around and caught Freedom in the left temple, knocking her to the ground, unconscious.

Dex roared, throwing himself at the assassin, who rolled sideways and came up, sword out, in a defensive crouch. When Dex turned around, Tano squinted in fury with his one good eye.

"Th' iter," he said. "Th' flunged out iter's learn some Earth-side tricks, eh?"

Dex swung at him and the fury of the last encounter prevented him from getting the moment jacked, getting his concentration levels up. His inept thrust was easily defended by Tano, who gave his sick little smile.

"It's was you's, before," he said. "You's in th' room wit th' child. Not Ash."

"It ends here," Dex said. "I am going to kill you here."

"Heah, sure," Tano said. He defended another wild swing, and began to type into his interface. There were sounds of people approaching from outside, hurried footsteps echoing down the hallway.

"Sees you's later, eh." The assassin clicked on his interface.

Dex could feel the gravity of Tano's breach opening, he could feel his Flyer searing into the Halo, pulling him away from his anchor. In that fraction of a second, Dex could feel everything slowing, the moment crawling along suddenly.

The rage in his head turned into an ocean, deep and cold.

He reached into his own vengeance and pulled out the code he needed. He thrust the Knife out, but altered the pattern, adding a modification. He pushed his anchor map down into Tano's breach even as the man shifted back toward his own time and disappeared from the room. Dex used his newly written Knife and severed the Rope to the anchor at his back, and tossed the Kite forward, allowing the gravity of Tano's shift breach to pull him in. He reached down and touched Freedom's bleeding head and whispered, "I'm sorry."

Then he felt the Knife shatter into a million pieces, and he was annihilated at the surface, pulled through the breach left by Tano.

One hundred twenty-eight.

Tano felt his consciousness shoved back at him violently. Usually he had a good long sleep after a shift. It was one of the few things in his life that he really enjoyed. On his return, when the nanos had finished with the shift realignment and settled back into their hiding places in his cells, he would simply drift into sleep. After awakening at his leisure, he would head back up to the off-planet station for the next loopshift.

But this time, there was a weight at his back, and someone was yelling at him, telling him to watch out. The instant he felt it, he was immediately awake.

The sword entered at his torso, went through his stomach, and came out his back, just missing his spine. He gasped, and opened his eyes, staring into the deadly calm of Ashion's deep brown eyes.

Not Ashion. The iterate.

The iterate pulled the sword free, and went for another strike, but someone attacked him, striking at him quickly. Tano turned his head in slow motion, and saw a team there, swords drawn. Booster, Chaz, and Ni'ello. They had not been here when he left, he realized. Then the world went sideways and he felt his head bang hard against the ground.

He managed to push himself up to sitting position just in time to see Booster's head go flying in the opposite direction from his body. Both parts blinked away, back to whatever future they had come from. Chaz lost both arms, and then the sword pierced his neck and he disappeared as well. Tano began to drag himself out of the down-room, crawling across the floor toward the door.

Tano heard Ni'ello scream, and then felt a kick to his ribs that sent him flailing around hard onto his back. With a single motion, the iter grabbed Tano's sword from the ground, spun it around, and stuck it through his right leg, pinning him to the floor. Tano screamed with the pain.

"You're not going anywhere," the iter said, before he was attacked by six more assassins. Tano recognized none of them, but saw their wrist units. They were from the future, coming to his aid. He pulled his sheath off his back, and used the leather strap to tourniquet his leg, trying to stop the bleeding. Then he pulled with all his strength, and finally wrenched his sword free of his leg and the floor below it. The pain nearly made him faint, but the thought of the goddam iter trying to kill him back in that child's room on Earth kept him going.

He pulled himself up, using his sword as a cane, and stumbled out, even as nine more shifters ran past him into the room. He could feel himself growing weaker from the blood loss already.

As he limped toward the shuttle dock, he noted that nine more assassins were headed into the downroom. Tano got himself strapped into the shuttlecraft, programming it for launch. He found the pharma-kit, and pushed a syringe of med rebuilders into his own leg. A voice came over the intercom.

"Shuttlecraft, you are cleared for take-off. Heading for the loop?"

"Heah," Tano said, coughing up blood. "Emergency loop back planet-side." He engaged the engine, and felt the kick as the shuttle began its ascent, heading for the sky. The gravitational force did not help his blood-loss, and he felt he might pass out soon.

There was a pause. "Heah, sure, Tano," the voice said. "You's meds is weak, you's is alright?"

"No, I's not alright!" he screamed. "You's get me clearance to med fac in th' Family boats, eh? And gets this boat on auto before I's black out!"

That was the last thing Tano remembered until he was breaking into the atmosphere on Venus, headed for medical facilities. He rubbed his eyes, and gave himself the remaining shot of adrenaline left in the pharma-kit. He keyed up the intercom.

"You's get me Ashion," he said, wiping the cold sweat from his face.

One hundred twenty-nine.

They just kept coming.

Dex took a brief fraction of a second to look, and with a new rage noticed the blood trail that marked Tano's escape. How long had he been gone? Dex put Judas through another assassin's heart, watched him blink out, then he spun through the door and followed the blood trail at a dead run.

Before he could get much farther, a set of three more assassins came at him from the front. Dex disposed of them with as little energy as possible and traced Tano's bloody escape route further down the hallway. A soldier stepped into the hallway with a blaster of some kind, and without breaking pace Dex threw Judas in a spin that caught him in the stomach and pushed him to the ground, writhing in pain. Dex kept running past him, grabbing the upright Judas on his way by.

He found himself looking through a window at clouds of smoke clearing on the other side, and through the opened top of the adjacent landing room, he could see the arc of exhaust smoke rising into the sky.

Tano had escaped.

Dex turned as more assassins came at him, moving in their slow, skilled fashion. It must have been a full dozen. With renewed rage, he put Judas in front of him.

"I am going to kill all of you," he said.

There was a slight pause this time, and a few nervous looks. Dex smiled. *They are learning.* But they still attacked. Dex saw it before it happened, felt every move like it was déjà vu, and was always one step ahead. A sword through the heart, into the skull, across the arm, under the hamstring. The shifting geometry unspooled around him, framing each assassin in a network of predictability. Drawing the world around him in the shapes of the future.

From the landing dock, a handful of soldiers appeared with the bolt guns they had used up on Venus. Dex ended them as well, but they did not disappear. They were not from the future, like the Red Masks. With four deliberate motions of his sword, Dex had dispatched the last assassin, sending his corpse back to whatever future he may have had.

Time began to speed up again and Dex found himself covered in blood, gasping for breath, and numb with pain and exhaustion. He waited for the anchor to pull him back through to the church, where the one named Gurn most likely waited for his return.

But there was no tug. The Rock wasn't pulling at his back. Dex tried to remember the reworked patterns he had used to follow Tano through the breach, but they were gone. He could not find any patterns. And then it dawned on him.

I'm not going back.

I am here, permanently.

He looked around at the soldiers, and saw one trying to crawl toward a gun. Dex walked up to him and kicked him over onto his back. The soldier yelped, and held up his good hand over his face.

"What day is it?" Dex asked. "In Earth-time."

"Wh-what?" the soldier asked.

Dex brought Judas around to his neck. "What is the date? Right now. On planet Earth."

"September. The eighteenth. 3027."

Dex looked at him, his brain struggling through exhaustion to make sense of the date.

Dex closed his eyes, his head spinning.

September 18, 3027.

It was the day before he had crash-landed the shuttle on Earth four weeks ago.

Matthew Hart

SECOND HARVEST

Book 2 of the series "The Last Iteration"

Published by CAPSCOVIL in December 2013, available in print (ISBN 978-3-942358-37-8, perfect paperback) and as electronic edition for various reading devices and platforms.

Adventurous Science Fiction Seasoned with Sustainability

Faced with the cold brutality of Ashion the Dark and his thugs, Dexter Maxwell did something no time shifter had ever done before: he traveled back in time permanently. Now he must live the same thirty days again. But with Ashion and the local warlord hunting him, will there be enough time to save his new—and old— friends?

On Venus, Ashion can't stop the subterranean resistance led by the man they call Fuel. But to keep his tenuous position as Security Lead, he must keep Dexter Maxwell's true identity hidden. That puts his daring plot to escape the grip of the Ruling Families in jeopardy— and is making it even harder to protect the last two people on Venus he needs alive: the mysterious Prisoner Six and the young girl Kat.

The clock is ticking: the Ruling Families of Venus have set the Second Harvest in motion. As their chilling plan unfolds, four hundred years of betrayals put Dexter and Ashion on a deadly collision course … and unlock an ancient threat to civilization.

Continue the adventurous journey of Dexter Maxwell to find out all about the deadly secret of Second Harvest.

Connect with the author: http://about.me/hartmatthew

One.

Ashion backed away from the med-bed, letting go of Tano's limp hand. His mind raced through the timeline. He'd seen the iteration's shuttle explode, and now, minutes later, Tano returns, cut up by a skilled swordsman long before the iter could have made the Transloop. And how had he even made the loop? Because the shuttle had been destroyed.

Scratch that. Ashion knew the loop field had been growing. The iter must have been close enough to eject directly into the hot jump field. The SIN automatically allows anything through—for safety reasons. It all added up to one thing.

Dexter Maxwell is using the monks' shifting mech to attack my Earth-side troops.

Ashion turned to the closest White Scientist and pointed at Tano. "Stabilize that," he said.

The Whi-Sci did not look at Ashion. His frontal lobe connection, sprouting from the interface on his forehead, prevented decent eye contact anyway. "Sir, we require Family-privilege overrides to reconstruct him properly. All we can do is stabilize him using standard planet-side technology."

Ashion didn't hesitate. "Consider him a primary asset of the Family Security Council. I will override the Family controls to ensure critical information can be retrieved."

The Whi-Sci nodded. "I have recorded the override and will work to secure the asset."

The attendants began to plug Tano into numerous surrounding feeds. Ashion stepped out of the ER unit, but turned back to watch the Family-only med-tech go into motion. Massive robotic arms whirred to life and descended on Tano with a merciless efficiency. Needles extracted blood samples from every open wound, and his mouth was forced open and swabbed. Cameras were inserted. All the while, the

SIN was extracting more and more data, looping it through the network, building threads, analyzing them, comparing them, graphing probabilities.

"Initial data levels indicate Earth-born infection has taken hold," the Whi-Sci said.

"Increasing bacteriophage levels to counteract," replied his partner. "Expect bacterial infection at zero in thirty seconds." The surgical arms immediately began to emit a bacteria-destroying virus. Ultraviolet lights flooded Tano's body, showing where the robotic arms and blades were depositing the oozing virus.

"Faster, please," the first Whi-Sci said calmly. "SIN analysis demands we get to the damaged tissue now."

Ashion turned to leave, but found himself facing Exemplar Thadwick Lewiston, arms folded, a smug look on his doughy face.

"Trouble with your slave, slave?" Thadwick asked, glancing over Ashion's shoulder. From behind him, Ashion heard the dull tone of Tano flat-lining, and the Whi-Scis calmly but rapidly changing their strategy. Ashion pretended to ignore it, and gave Thadwick a thin smile.

"No more trouble than usual," Ashion said.

"Oh, it sounds like he's gone and had himself killed," Thadwick said with mock pity. But even as he spoke, the flat-lining was replaced by a rhythmical beat. Thadwick's smile slipped.

"If you will excuse me, Thadwick, I've got business that needs attending to." Ashion went to push past the large man.

When the clumsy hand grabbed at his arm, it took all of Ashion's efforts not to snatch Lewiston's hand and deftly break his wrist. Straight to the icer for that, Ashion thought. He remembered the last time he had been put down for attacking a Family authority. It'd been over a hundred years ago. Now wasn't a good time to get iced. Instead, he slowly turned to face Thadwick. The fat man's mood changed, his face cold and hard. It took Ashion by surprise; the likes of Thadwick Lewiston had not surprised him for decades. He had no idea what to say.

"The endgame is upon us, slave," Thadwick whispered, so quietly that Ashion could barely hear it.

Alice N. York
GAME

FAINT SIGNALS

Published by CAPSCOVIL in May 2011, available in print (ISBN 978-3-942358-08-8, perfect paperback) and as electronic edition for various reading devices and platforms.

Delicate Career Novel With Smart Solar Ideas

Alex leads a thoroughly contented life. In Sandro she has found the right man, and the new consultancy job at a leading solar company seems tailor-made for her.

In no time, she familiarises herself with the technology and establishes a complex network incorporating both external partners and prospective clients, as well as various departments within the intricate company organisational structure. Developing long-term strategies and innovational product ideas is just as inspiring for her as implementing them practically. In addition, business trips to globally operating clients offer Alex an insight into different cultures, taking her to fascinating cities along the way. Winning new projects with innovative, successful solutions quickly enables her to gain the respect of her superiors.

As time goes by, however, her existence begins to resemble a rollercoaster ride. Grave events in her private life result in Alex throwing herself ever deeper into work. Yet slowly but surely menacing clouds are gathering there too. Alex does everything in her power to retain control. But like a game of poker, she is constantly being dealt a new hand; and no-one quite knows who holds the aces.

***

„Alice N. York portrays life in the workplace with extraordinary accuracy"
Ebersberger Zeitung

***

Follow Alex how she plays the game to win. Until the rules change and the world turns ruthless...

PsoraCom were the market leader for solar cells. Originally their photovoltaic cells were made from pure silicon. In company factories, solar cells were still made from big silicon chips, also known as wafers, and then used by PsoraCom's customers to build larger solar modules. In turn, plant manufacturers combined many electrically connected solar modules to build power plants.

However, the manufacture of crystalline silicon solar cells was expensive and used up too much energy; alternative products were therefore being sought. Alongside thin-film, concentrator and dye-sensitised solar cells, there was now Vabilmo: a new sector that aimed to be more cost effective and energy efficient when it came to mass production. Here, solar cells were processed using organic solutions. The cells were razor-thin and as flexible as film, enabling the assembly of completely new configurations, which, together with the reduction in weight, would result in considerable savings.

In the first instance, PsoraCom saw two principal markets for these polymer cells. There were the traditional solar plant manufacturers, who built both grid-connected plants and off-grid systems; and then there were the companies who made robots. These robots ranged from complex machines in the production industry to machines built for specific tasks, and even simple household robots that could cook, iron or mow the lawn.

Based on these twin approaches, their basic aims were to increase the efficiency of solar power plants and to reduce robot energy requirements, thus lowering cost. Once the polymer cells were market-ready, contracts needed to be won from suitable clients because the implementation stage would take one to three years, depending on the size and nature of the project. Only if the new solar cells were widely used in the industry could appreciable savings be made.

For this kind of product launch, PsoraCom adopted a two-fold strategy. First there was direct sales – the classic approach, which allowed the company to speak to solar module manufacturers. In order to generate revenue, they had to be steered away from the currently employed solar cells and convinced to use the polymer cells (internally code-named "Vabilmo"). Second, PsoraCom also had an indirect sales unit made up of consultants whose objective it was to influence new market trends. The consultants worked together with end customers - that is, plant and robot manufacturers -, analysed processes, delivered strategy recommendations and assisted in the transfer of knowledge. Their job was to make sure end customers would buy from module manufacturers who used PsoraCom's polymer cells.

In the past few years Alex had learned everything there was to know about power stations. It was her long-standing knowledge and experience that had got her the job. At least that's what Thomas had said.

The task of the Vabilmo team was to concentrate exclusively on the potential market for polymer-based solar cells. Aside from Alex, the team consisted of an additional consultant, a colleague from direct sales and a developer who worked on new concepts for the configuration of the solar modules. As yet, Alex had only met Brian – the other consultant – at the interview. She was scheduled to have a joint strategy meeting with him and Thomas in the afternoon. The meeting would also serve as a training session on existing activities of the Vabilmo team.

They sat down at the table like three points of an invisible triangle so that they could all see the presentation on the screen. The title page announced in bold letters: "VABILMO STRATEGIC OVERVIEW – BRIAN, SENIOR CONSULTANT, VABILMO TEAM EUROPE, NEW BUSINESSES, STRATEGIC DIVISION."

Brian scrolled to the next page and began to explain the table illustrated there step by step. Thanks to the eight-point font the text was both barely legible and, as the table took up the whole page, extremely confusing.

While he spoke she had time to take a closer look. His suntanned face had already begun to display a few wrinkles, even though he was only thirty-five. Judging by his collection of surf-stickers, she put this down to too much sun and salt-water. The goatee corresponded to the surfer-snowboarder cliché, but it was a little unkempt and needed trimming.

Working with him promised to be interesting.

Stephan Schwarz
ELECTRIFIED

Published by CAPSCOVIL in September 2012, available in print (ISBN 978-3-942358-22-4, perfect paperback) and as electronic edition for various reading devices and platforms.

Spicy Combination of Crime and Electric Vehicles

„ELECTRIFIED" is no ordinary mystery. The detectives in Stephan Schwarz's debut novel hunt villains in an electric vehicle. The story makes for an entertaining ride which allows readers to cozy up to congenial characters.

Frankfurt, East Port - 7.00a.m.: A dead body is found in a car. Is it suicide? Or murder? Chief Inspector Felix Büschelberger, who saves toads in his spare ime, and his technology-enthused Italian colleague, Emilio, set out to unearth the truth. Together with the rest of their tea-drinking team they chase countless leads in their agile electric vehicle on an unpredictable journey that takes them to Italy and as far as Kenya. But their road is paved with bumps and dead ends. A reconstruction of the circumstances seems impossible.

This charming piece of fiction is a spicy combination of crime and corruption in the highest echelons of power, intertwined with topics on electric vehicles. Making it the #1 in electric vehicle mystery.

Readers are not only informed of the benefits of driving an EV; they are also provided with information about fascinating initiatives like the Bertha Benz Challenge and intriguing descriptions of the latest battery technologies. Important challenges that need to be met and solved are addressed: charging methods, energy storage and providing grid stability among them.

„Electrified" is the International English edition of the original edition „Krötenmord" that was published in Germany in December 2011 and was awarded with the **„ADAC MOTORWELT AUTOBUCH PREIS 2012" CAR BOOK PRICE** in the category „Special Awards."

www.ingramcontent.com/pod-product-compliance
Lightning Source LLC
Chambersburg PA
CBHW020507020726
47493CB00001B/214